Sheila sensed the world was waiting for something.

She had the curious impression that someone else was guiding her. It was as if another woman were inside of her. This woman inside was strong, was energizing her, was making her feel as alive as she had felt during the séance.

She *was* that interior woman now; and in their melding she felt transformed—become a matrix of energies of earth, sky, and self. Goddesslike. That was it; she had the sensual, frightening, liberating impression that she had become one with Ishtar, Astarte, Isis, Kali, and the thousand other named and nameless incarnations of the power that was all around her, pouring through her, roiling within her.

THE POWER WAS HERS.

EMERGENCE

ROBERT D. SAN SOUCI

AVON
PUBLISHERS OF BARD, CAMELOT AND DISCUS BOOKS

EMERGENCE is an original publication of Avon Books. This work has never before appeared in book form.

El Centro, the Sierra Morenas, the Rio Sonoliento, the Tawa Tribe, the Casserite Padres, and the area of New Mexico in which the action takes place are wholly fictional.

AVON BOOKS
A division of
The Hearst Corporation
959 Eighth Avenue
New York, New York 10019

First Avon Printing, July, 1981

AVON TRADEMARK REG. U. S. PAT. OFF. AND IN OTHER COUNTRIES, MARCA REGISTRADA, HECHO EN U. S. A.

Printed in the U. S. A.

10 9 8 7 6 5 4 3 2 1

For Elizabeth

Four days will quickly steep themselves in night;
Four nights will quickly dream away the time;
And then the moon . . . shall behold the night
Of our solemnities.

A Midsummer Night's Dream: I, i.

PROLOGUE:
March 4, 1632 (Midnight)

Padre Alonso Perez was at prayer, kneeling on the rudely fashioned prie-dieu beside his pallet. A small prayer book lay on the shelf in front of him. In the corner opposite the priest was a single uncomfortable-looking chair.

The beeswax candles in their several sconces gave the little room a smoky, uncertain light, which played fitfully over the whitewashed adobe walls. The only ornaments in the room were a small painted icon of St. Bernard, a crucifix, and a statue of the Saragossa Madonna set in a single niche above his bed. This wondrous and terrifying vision of the Queen of Heaven, as she had appeared to the founder of the Casserite Order of Priests years before, held a bloodied skull in one hand and a chalice encircled by a serpent in the other. It was said that St. Bernard, the Order's founder, had fainted upon first seeing this vision.

The eyes of the man at prayer sought out the tiny painted skull in the Virgin's hand as he prayed, *"Memento mori—"*

There was a knock at the door of his chamber. Annoyed that his prayers were being interrupted, he ignored the summons. He dropped his eyes to the open prayer book, letting his fingers trace out the Latin phrases he loved so well, as he continued, *"Horas non numero nisi serenas—"*

The knocking came again, more insistently this time.

With a sigh he arose and opened the door.

The blow from a heavy candlestick struck him just above the right eye, crushing that portion of his skull . . .

EMERGENCE

PART ONE

. . . madmen have such seething brains,
Such shaping fantasies, that apprehend
More than cool reason ever comprehends.

A Midsummer Night's Dream: V, i.

Ay me, for pity! what a dream was here!

A Midsummer Night's Dream: II, ii.

1 The Mission

They left the little New Mexico town (neither of them had bothered to learn its name) right after breakfast. Paul had not touched the runny eggs and greasy bacon, settling instead for the cold toast and lukewarm coffee which completed the "Ranch-Style Breakfast" at the motel coffee shop.

Sheila had offered to drive for a while; Paul, still not feeling fully awake, had quickly agreed.

Now he sat staring out the dust-streaked window of the Volkswagen as the shops, houses, and service stations of the desert town dwindled into thin lines of weathered rail fences on either side of the road. Even these faltered and fell away, and they were alone on the empty highway slicing across a mind-dulling expanse of saltbush, rabbit brush, greasewood, and the omnipresent sagebrush.

Far ahead, the desert rose in gentle gray-green swells toward the blue-hazed foothills of the Sierra Morenas. Soon, Paul knew, the road would veer north, away from the blue-appearing mountains toward Sante Fe, their next destination.

They had driven several miles through the warming silence of the desert before Paul asked, "What's the name of that mission you want to see?"

"Mission Nuestra Señora de Agastan," his wife answered. "Also called Our Lady of Whitenesses."

"Ummm . . . would it upset you terribly if I said I was getting a bit tired of these missionary historical landmarks?"

She smiled slightly. "This is the last one for a while. I've got enough information already." Sheila—Dr. Sheila Barrett, Ph.D., cultural anthropologist and head of the special Task

3

Force on Women and Religion at Oliente College, was on sabbatical while she researched a paper tentatively entitled, "The Role of Female Saints in Spanish Colonial America with Special Reference to the Casserite Missions of Arizona and New Mexico."

That was the official reason for her taking a leave of absence. Paul, who had been on medical leave following a nervous breakdown, also taught at the college, but in the English Department. He was working on a novel, officially; it was also understood that he would help Sheila prepare her paper for publication.

Those were their *official* reasons for being in New Mexico.

In actuality, they were attempting to salvage their marriage. Paul's illness, Sheila's increasing preoccupation with her classes, the separate pressures both of them felt equally —this had all brought their marriage to the straining point.

The administration of the college was sympathetic. Paul was a self-confessedly indifferent teacher; they would have let him go without much real regret. Sheila, on the other hand, was a first-rate academician; the conferences she had organized over the years on the Past, Present, and Future Role of Women in Religion had put Oliente solidly on the map of academe. They agreed to her request because they did not want to risk a decline in the quality of her work or the possibility of losing her altogether if her marriage fell apart.

So Sheila and Paul visited historical monuments, local libraries and historical societies, took endless photographs, debated obscure historical possibilities.

And all the time they were really exhuming the foundations of their marriage to see if they were built on anything solid enough for them to go on any longer together. They were retracing, roughly, their honeymoon journey. Then they had driven west from Florida after a wedding at Indian Harbor Beach, Sheila's home town. Paul, who had taught briefly at University of South Florida, had taken an assistant professorship at Oliente College in California. Sheila planned to finish work on her Ph.D. at Berkeley, which was just a short distance from the San Francisco suburb of Point Oliente, with its private college—originally a Catholic college but now nondenominational.

It was during their first leisurely trip across the Southwest that Sheila had decided that the statuary, sculptures, and frescoes of the ancient Spanish missions were more interesting to her as a dissertation topic than the Byzantine artifacts of Ravenna.

Her interest had become a passion; the passion she and Paul had felt for each other, however, had cooled considerably in the ten years since that very different trip in the battered old Chrysler.

Paul chewed on a fingernail and reflected; the fact that Sheila had proposed this trip, that she really seemed to be making an effort to bring them back to what they had once had, convinced him that she knew nothing—in spite of his fears—about Taya. Except what she may have read in the papers.

Memories—unbidden, unwanted—crowded into his mind. Taya. Enotea Cole, a student of Paul's, had, according to the newspaper reports, died hallucinating on a bad acid trip.

Had, according to all accounts, died alone.

Died horribly: smashing in a terrified frenzy through a plate-glass sliding door onto the balcony of her student complex apartment and, blinded, her skin in bloodied streamers, had pitched over the ornamental railing and into the midst of a poolside party three stories below.

But Paul had been there, had seen everything, had been a party to what had happened, had never been able to forget her last screamed words before she had fled what she thought she saw and escaped into oblivion.

And he had managed to keep his cool enough to run away, flee down the fire escape before anyone thought to leave the horror beside the pool and investigate her apartment.

Poor Enotea. Their affair had been mostly a diversion for both of them. Paul, who had never fooled around before, had been seeking some excitement in a marriage and career gone inexplicably stale.

And Taya . . .

Taya's first love was the psychic world, a world she felt she reached through what she called her "acid trances." She would explain, her thin arms and graceful hands moving in amazing patterns, that she would "do acid only to reach the other side. But I *control* it, Paul! That's the key, dig? It's like lucid dreaming, you know? . . . Hell"—she'd laugh suddenly —"you don't know shit! Not about what counts. There's a whole *world* outside of this one: lots of worlds, like onion skins one up against another . . . oh, *shit*! you've only got one thing on your mind." And she would fold her arms around him quickly in a sudden, vigorous embrace and the two of them—the thirtyish, overweight professor and this passionate mulatto full-time student, his part-time lover— would tussle delightedly on the ancient mattress on the floor of Enotea's tiny studio.

He had often asked her to stay away from the acid; he dutifully recited all the horror stories he had heard about bad trips. She would look at him, casually light up another cigarette in the chain she was smoking, and tell him, "If you're uptight about it, then it's not for you. Don't do anything you're not up for," and she'd leer at him suggestively.

Then, that last night, she took the acid; she was going to read his aura, or something.

It had all happened so fast . . .

He put the memories out of his mind; concentrated, instead, on the scenery they were passing through.

Overhead he could see the single white speck of a private plane against the vacant metallic sky. Paul wished he were in it, headed back to California. He wanted nothing more than to get off this seemingly endless round of early risings, indifferent breakfasts, miles of driving, wretched dinners at the end of an exhausting day of sightseeing and note-taking, followed by sleepless nights in uncomfortable motel beds, tossing and turning into the morning, when the whole roundelay began again.

He had decided days ago that he preferred research to field work. In spite of his appreciation for what Sheila hoped to achieve, he was growing impatient with the trip, with his own inability to feel better, with Sheila. He had also decided that there were, simply, not enough pieces left of what they had been to put them together again. He was feeling disinterested and frustrated; the effort of hiding his impatience was wearing on him.

Sheila, her eyes on the road, was lost in her own thoughts. He wondered just how much she was aware of what he was feeling. So far she seemed satisfied that things were going as well between them as could be expected. She had never commented on the fact that they had not slept together in over a week—and that the last time had been a failure, though Paul had managed to satisfy her manually.

And he had begrudged her her pleasure, wanting desperately to share in it, cut off from it by something locked in his mind since Taya's death and the breakdown he had suffered almost immediately afterward.

He followed the flight of the plane until it disappeared into the cloudless expanse.

The day was already warm. Miles away, sunlight glanced off an aluminum roof out in the desert; it washed hotly over the hood of the car, causing him to fumble in the glove compartment until he found his sunglasses behind several paperback books and clumsily refolded maps of Texas, New Mexico, and Arizona.

He thought of the distance yet to cover between where they were in New Mexico and their apartment in Berkeley. California suddenly seemed light-years away.

He slammed the glove compartment shut, asking, "How far is it to this mission?"

"About forty-five minutes, I guess. It doesn't really matter, does it? We have all the time in the world." She turned to him; her mouth, under the orbs of her sunglasses, was set in a worried smile that seemed to him almost *pleading* . . .

"Fine, great," he said, as convincingly as he could.

Given a reprieve, she turned back to watch the road; he felt a faintly perceptible increase in acceleration as she pushed a little harder on the gas pedal. With a sigh, he settled back into the seat, annoyed with the sweat that was collecting at the small of his back and under his buttocks.

The two-lane highway rose and fell as it followed the gently undulating sweeps of dry grass, brush, and weeds. Only an occasional outcropping of shale broke the gray-green monotony.

He knew she hadn't been sleeping well herself: he had sensed her moving restlessly in her bed the night before. But when, over breakfast, he had suggested cutting the trip short, she had only looked annoyed, and said, "*I* feel fine. You'd feel better yourself if you'd just relax and enjoy things a little more."

Now, looking at her out of the corner of his eye, he could see that his wife's eyes were red and slightly puffy behind her sunglasses. And tiny lines at the corners of her eyes matched those at the corners of her mouth, now set in a tight line.

She had used an old red-and-black scarf to tie her straw-colored hair into a careless ponytail. Against the bright bit of chiffon, her hair looked faded and the youthful hairstyle seemed inappropriate. She hadn't bothered with makeup—rarely did so on a trip. But her clear skin and the high, almost Indian, cheekbones (she claimed some trace of Blackfeet blood in her) reminded Paul what a handsome woman she still was.

He had loved her very much, once; what was it in him that made him unable to muster more than an indifferent fondness now?

His thoughts were interrupted as they both saw, simultaneously, a black spot in the road ahead.

"Rock?" Paul asked, straining to see the object more clearly through the windshield.

"Probably," she answered. She maintained an even rate of speed.

"That may be a boulder," he cautioned. "Better slow down."

Sheila ignored him, accelerating slightly.

"*Slow down*," he insisted.

She didn't seem to hear him. She kept her face rigidly fixed on the road ahead. He noticed that she was breathing rapidly; a bead of sweat ran down the side of her face.

He could see that the spot was a vulture that was tearing at the remains of some animal killed on the highway. When it spotted the oncoming car, it began moving its wings sluggishly, struggling to pull its ungainly body up and out of the way of approaching danger. But the immense black wings seemed incapable of the task. Paul wondered if the creature had overgorged itself or if the heat of the day was causing it to move with such excruciating slowness.

He grabbed the upper part of her right arm and squeezed, but was afraid to make any violent move for fear she would lose control of the car and swerve into the shale walls through which the road had been cut. He yelled, "Jesus Christ! Sheila, *slow down*! You're going to kill both of us."

But she made no response, as though she were in a trance or asleep with her eyes open. He remembered once falling asleep himself for an instant while driving, to wake up to a blare of horns as his car veered into the oncoming lane.

They were at the top of the last incline in the road; at the bottom, dead-ahead, the fully panicked bird was straining for the sky and shrieking a warning all the time.

Sheila accelerated again.

"Goddammit! What's the matter with you?" He thought for a second of grabbing the wheel, but he was equally afraid of losing control of the car at this speed.

Sheila maintained her expressionless air of calm. He could see, however, that she was chewing on her lip: a single drop of blood beaded there. Then her mouth moved and she said, "What—?" then, "Oh my Jesus, no!"

She pulled her foot off the gas pedal and slammed on the brakes. But it was too late: the car swayed violently from side to side, just inches from the rock walls on either edge. The air was filled with the stink of burning rubber and a nerve-shattering screech . . .

The car lurched forward. The bird was in the air now—but just barely so: not enough, Paul was sure, to clear the car.

He saw clearly the patch of dried blood and fur the thing had been feeding on.

Then they were at a collision point. He bellowed as an immense mass of black feathers blotted out the sky on his side of the car and swept by inches above the door frame. He had the impression of a huge, pale beak gaping in protest and a tiny red hate-filled eye glaring into his own.

The shadow was gone; the bird was behind them, gaining altitude; the road ahead was unobstructed as far as they could see.

Sheila continued pumping the brake, finally coasting to a stop on the shoulder of the road some hundred yards beyond the point of near-impact.

"What the hell was that all about?" Paul shouted, "Something that size would have *pulverized* us at this speed."

His wife slumped forward, resting her forehead on the backs of her hands, which were gripping the top of the steering wheel. She closed her eyes and took several deep breaths before she answered, "I don't know. I just blanked out for a minute—daydreaming or something. *I don't know what happened.*"

"Do you feel all right now? Are you going to faint?"

She rocked her head back and forth across her hands. "No, no, no. I guess I'm just more tired than I realized; I should have had more than coffee this morning."

He put his hand gently on her shoulder; he could feel her sobbing silently. He felt sorry for her, realized how much she had been pushing herself. Her face seemed drained of blood.

The sudden thought came to him that she might have realized subconsciously that things were not working; maybe she had wanted to kill them both. Or had she, in momentary confusion, had some idea that she would kill only *him*?

He rejected the crazy thoughts.

Sheila sat back and took several more breaths. Then she pushed her glasses up, wiped her eyes with her hands, and replaced the glasses squarely across the bridge of her nose. When she spoke, her voice had a business-as-usual quality. "I think you'd better drive for a while."

She climbed out of the car and walked around to the passenger side while he slid over and claimed the driver's seat.

After a short while he began to feel the tension draining out of himself. Sheila, seemingly fully recovered from her "spell," opened the guidebook and said, "We should hit the Old Mission Road turn-off pretty soon. The mission is just inside the Tawa Indian Reservation."

"What do you know about the Tawas?"

"They're Pueblo Indians, like the Hopis or Zunis. The Casserite padres who built this mission originally came here to convert the Tawas. The Indians still perform rain dances and fertility dances, so I guess the good fathers didn't *quite* wipe out the old religion. . . . Careful, Paul, here's the cut-off now."

The Old Mission Road, a single-lane, poorly maintained strip of asphalt running north into the sage- and cactus-choked flats, seemed to waver in the heat. A lone sun-bleached wooden sign informed them that this was the road to Mission Nuestra Señora de Agastan.

He drove carefully; they both watched for rough spots; but even so, the car frequently jounced in and out of an unanticipated pothole.

They had all the windows open, but the air blowing into the car was hot. Paul's jeans and shirt were soaked with sweat, and he was now sticking to the vinyl-covered seat. Sheila's blouse clung damply to her breasts; she kept rubbing her hand across the back of her neck.

Beer cans and broken bottles littered the side of the road; wads of paper were caught in the dusty gray sage bushes alongside the road.

They bounced around an unexpected curve in the road and the way suddenly forked. One branch continued in a northerly direction; the other branch ran east.

There were no signs indicating which way led to the mission.

Where the road forked, a single building of whitewashed adobe lay in the wedge between the roads. The walls were as painfully bright in the sunlight as the sweep of white sand on which it was built. The legend "Trading Post" was painted in peeling letters across the front.

A handful of cottonwood trees grew behind the structure, but cast little shade. Two or three old, dusty trucks were parked on a graveled area in front.

Paul pulled onto the side of the road, asking, "Which way?"

She shrugged. "I *think* we want to keep going north; but since there aren't any signs and the guidebook only shows one road, not two, we'd better ask some directions."

"Fine. Maybe we can buy a cold beer inside." He swung the car across the road and parked in front of the Trading Post.

Several old Indian men and women sat on wooden benches on either side of the building's entrance, in the shadow of the overhanging roof. Their faces—earth-colored, the features blunted, the skin thickened and textured by wind and exposure to the sun—were expressionless. But their eyes were alert as they silently watched Sheila and Paul.

A windchime of terracotta clappers hung on leather thongs was suspended from a porch beam; it made a tinkling bell-like sound in the ghost breeze blowing in from the desert. The only other sound was made by the couple's shoes crunching on the gravel.

Sheila nodded and smiled and Paul called out a greeting to the watching old ones, but they got no response. They quickly mounted the three wooden steps and crossed the porch.

The inside of the shop was dark. Weak sunlight filtered in through small windows filmed with dust and grease; several low-watt bulbs were set haphazardly among the darkish ceiling beams, but even two of these were burned out.

The counters were arranged in an L-shaped pattern. The longest side of the L was a collection of white-painted metal and glass units holding meats, dairy products, and frozen goods. The shorter side was a mismatched series of wooden cabinets with glass fronts, the grimy glass shelves inside laden with a hodge-podge of pottery, baskets, and kachina dolls.

One waist-high case, opening only from the back, was filled with jewelry. They both moved toward this. As they looked over the display of silver, turquoise, shell, glass bead, and coral finery, Sheila pointed out which of the pieces were distinctly Hopi or Zuni or Navajo in concept. She was also able to recognize designs as stylized sun-figures, road runners, thunderclouds, squash blossoms, thunderbirds.

All of the pieces had the look of age about them: a darkening of the silver, a design partly worn away, a missing piece of shell or coral. Most had pawn tickets attached to them.

One massive silver necklace caught both their eyes at the same time. The chain was composed of alternating silver beads and flared, trumpetlike squash blossoms, climaxing in a smooth disk of blood-red coral set within a thick circular silver frame. At the center of the coral, etched in lines of eye-straining fineness, was the design:

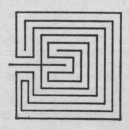

"Do you recognize the design?" Paul asked.

"I think the pattern has some religious meaning, but I've never seen a piece quite like this. It's magnificent!" She looked around for a clerk. She signaled a short, thickset Indian man, who detached himself from a conversation with a young Indian couple shopping for groceries at the far end of the counter. The woman, in jeans and buckskin jacket, moved toward a display of canned goods; the man with her, in tee shirt and overalls, folded his arms and stared at the other couple with undisguised hostility.

"You want something?" the clerk asked; there was something slightly threatening about his tone and stance. Paul decided to skip buying the beer; he would only hang around long enough to let Sheila check out the necklace.

Sheila, who apparently did not notice—or was ignoring—the man's surly attitude, said, "May we take a look at that necklace," and pointed through the fingerprint-smudged glass.

"The blood-moon? Sure," he said, unlocking the case and sliding open the wooden panel at the back. He pulled out the silver chain and dropped it with elaborate casualness onto the countertop. It clattered into a silver heap. He made no effort to offer it to Sheila. A pawn ticket, its ink faded, was tied near the clasp.

She picked up the necklace, turning it over and over in her hands in an almost hypnotic fashion. She didn't take her eyes away from it when she asked, "Why do you call this 'blood-moon'?"

The man shrugged and said, "It's a design, lady. A round piece of red coral inside silver that way, with that carving on it, is always called blood-moon in these parts. It's an old Tawa design. It goes back before the Spanish governors. Back before the Franciscan and Casserite padres, even."

Sheila handed him back the necklace, asking, "How much?"

He glanced at some crayon markings on the back of the disk. He was interrupted by a slight cough. All three turned to see an ancient Indian woman in black skirt and blouse. She had pulled aside the faded rug that acted as a door at the entrance to the area behind the counters. She blended into the shadows as if she were some part of them. Her white hair was drawn into a single bun at the back of her head;

her face was a mass of wrinkles like spider webs. A milky whiteness indicated that she was blind in one eye. Her good eye watched the Barretts, but Paul noticed her attention was mostly fixed on Sheila.

The crone beckoned to the man; he walked over to her, still carrying the necklace.

They discussed something in hurried whispers. Though the man's back was to them, the old woman's eye never ceased flicking back and forth between Paul and Sheila. Paul was uncomfortably aware that the eye, rheumy and bloodshot, was like the eye of the vulture that had shot past the car window hours earlier.

She gave some final argument; the man shrugged his shoulders and turned away; the woman dropped the curtain back into place and disappeared from view.

When the man dropped the necklace back onto the counter, it almost seemed to Paul that the Indian was unwilling to handle the piece for very long. He stood with both hands pressed flat against the top of the display case, on either side of the coiled necklace, his fingers not touching, yet looking protective of, the necklace . . . like the guardian of some sacred relic at a primitive shrine. He quoted them a price far lower than they had expected.

"We'll take it," said Sheila, gathering it into her hand.

While she signed over the necessary travelers' checks, Paul asked the Indian, "How do we get to the mission from here?"

"Our Lady of Agastan?"

Paul nodded.

"Take the right-hand road—the one running east. A couple of miles, you're there."

"You should put up more signs," Paul said. "The road's not well marked at all."

"The signs was tore down two—three days ago by some goddamn drunk punks. . . . You want anything else?" he asked, having copied down Sheila's driver's-license number on the backs of the blue-green checks.

"No," said Sheila, tucking the necklace into one of the inside pockets of her shoulder bag.

"Wait a minute," Paul said. "How far is it to Carlsbad?"

"You trying to get there today? It's too far, more than two hundred miles." The man shook his head. "You should think about staying in El Centro—just down the road. Give yourselves time to see the mission."

Paul was surprised at the man's sudden talkativeness after his surly attitude. He said, "We plan to see the mission—but we want to hit Santa Fe tonight."

"You'd be late. Real late. There might not be nothin' open. You'd do better to spend the night in El Centro. They got a good motel there, the Four-Star. Lots of people in town could tell you about the mission. Tomorrow you could go on to Sante Fe."

"Thanks for the advice," Paul said. "We'll think about it. Now, if you'll bring us our change . . ."

When the man had deposited the checks in the register and counted out their change, he walked off to wait on an old man who had just come into the store, remarking over his shoulder, "You think about staying in El Centro. Folks are real friendly there."

"We practically *stole* that," Sheila said as they left the store. She seemed almost dazed by their good fortune.

"It's a bargain, all right," he agreed. "But he seemed to know what he was doing. It may look like more than it really is."

"You'll never convince *me* of that," she said happily as they made their way to the car through the discomfiting stares of the still-seated oldsters.

A little way beyond the trading post the sagebrush suddenly thinned, yielding to cacti and sandy barren patches.

Ahead they made out a spot of white that could only be the mission. This rapidly resolved itself into a tiny cluster of buildings in front of a single hill which rose unexpectedly from the vast, pale smoothness of the desert.

A half mile or so from the mission gates, the road ran past a little cemetery. The gravestones were decorated with clusters of bright-colored artificial flowers and flamboyant crosses made of foil or sequins that flashed pink/silver/blue in the afternoon sun.

In the center a group of figures dressed completely in white—the women in long white dresses, the men in loose Mexican-style pants and tunics—stood around an open grave. The men were bareheaded, though they all held broad, flat straw hats in front of them, dangling from their clasped hands. The women had covered their heads with black scarves—the only departure from the overwhelming whiteness.

Sudden, inexplicable panic engulfed Paul. There was something about the open grave, the sun, the dark-skinned mourners that terrified him . . . as if the burial concerned him, threatened him. The thought made no sense; it was crazy. But he felt suddenly light-headed, could feel his heart pounding. His palms, sweat-drenched, slipped on the steering wheel, causing the car to swerve slightly, so that Sheila murmured, "Careful, Paul, you hit a pothole. . . ."

He tried to tell her what he was feeling, but fear—sourceless and absolute—had frozen his throat; he couldn't make a sound.

It was the same mindless, groundless fear that had engulfed him just before Taya had flung herself through the glass.

He had forgotten the mind-wrenching taste of it until now.

And, recognizing it, he dealt with it the way he had done that other time, when he had forced himself to walk out of Taya's apartment, locking the door behind him, and not allowing himself to come apart until days later. . . .

He gripped the steering wheel as tightly as he could; he refused to let his foot slam down on the brake.

Sheila, intent on the mission, was unaware of his struggle.

If he could just keep functioning, the terror would subside; everything would right itself.

His fear dissolved as quickly as it had appeared. By the time he pulled the Volks into the parking area in front of the mission and brought it to a complete stop on the hard-packed earth separated from the desert by a row of white-painted boulders, he felt fine. God! he would have killed for a drink, but he wasn't ready to dig out the half-filled bottle of bourbon from the trunk and swig it lukewarm. He promised himself a triple when they stopped for lunch.

Four or five other cars were parked in the little lot.

Mission Nuestra Señora de Agastan herself stood harshly white in the sunlight, her adobe walls whitewashed to painful brilliance.

Before they climbed out, Sheila retrieved her camera case

from the back seat. While Paul made sure t̲...
curely locked, she took several shots of the mi̲...

The air around them was still and hot—broodi̲...
yet oppressive. The brightness of the mission and̲...
buildings seemed to slice even through his sunglasses. ...ere
was a silence all around, like heavy layers of fabric—Paul
felt smothered in the warming silence.

They paused momentarily to examine the carvings around
the massive, unadorned wooden doors, which stood slightly
ajar. A faint stream of cool, incense-fragrant air issued
through the opening.

Sheila reached out to touch a carved leaf, then stood back
a moment, finally deciding to photograph the decorations
before going inside. Paul, holding the camera case, stood
staring out across the desert briefly, then turned his attention
to the carvings also, noting how the somewhat abstract
flower-and-leaf design was transmuted into twin angels
(vine thickening to torso, leaves broadening into wings)
reclining on the arch above the doors.

Higher up on the impressive facade were three tall, narrow identical windows. Deeply set in the thick wall, the
black rectangles were a welcome break in the achingly
white expanse.

Two towers were upthrust from the corners of the roof of
pale red tiles. Originally twins, the towers were now mismatched: the left-hand one had burned at some time and
had never been repaired. It was roofless, the window arches
were blackened and cracked, and much of the whitewash
was scorched.

How in the world, Paul wondered to himself, did a fire
begin up there? Lightning seemed the only logical explanation.

Sheila interrupted his musings by asking, "Shall we go
inside?"

She pushed the doors open a fraction wider, and they entered the cool semidarkness within.

The air inside smelled thickly of centuries of burned
candles and incense. Rows of high-backed, uncomfortable-
looking wooden pews marched up either side of a wide aisle
toward the main altar, draped in plain white linen em-

broidered with red crucifixes. It seemed to sag under the weight of brass candlesticks and gaudy paper flowers.

Floating in the shadowed space above the altar was a massive representation of the crucified Christ, nearly life-size. The pale face was twisted in agony; the feet, wrists, and forehead were slathered in gore.

An elderly couple was standing looking up at the crucifix, conversing in high-pitched whispers. After a moment, they went out by a half-concealed side door, leaving the Barretts alone in the church.

Sheila wandered off by herself while Paul hovered near the back door, unwilling to step further into the gloomy interior.

His eyes roved over the baroque decorations. Every bit of wall space was encrusted with painted angels, saints, flowers, birds, cupids, and madonnas. Row upon row of shallow niches, each about a foot high, lined the walls all the way to the main altar; in each was the image of a saint. Paul recognized a few of the more obvious: St. Francis . . . St. Peter . . . one that was probably St. Teresa.

One female saint (or was it a manifestation of the Virgin?) caught his eye because of the especially startling border of red roses on a wide band of gold paint that outlined her niche. The blue-and-white robed youthful figure held a gory skull in one hand and a serpent-entwined goblet in the other. He was unfamiliar with the likeness.

The passage of time, aided by layers of incense and candle smoke, had reduced the brilliant colors to mere resonances of their original garishness.

His eyes wandered to the roof vault. Higher overhead, above the slanting bars of hot white sunlight, the clay ceiling was covered with a fresco representing the Battle in Heaven. Familiar with traditional Christian mythology, he recognized the Archangel Michael, in gold-trimmed white robes, leading the heavenly host as they cast down the rebellious angels. Paul could make out Lucifer himself, tumbling back and down in a swirl of dark robes toward the gaping fires of hell.

But in the shadows, and under the veiling of soot and grime, the picture seemed to waver. To Paul it seemed for a moment that the figure in white and gold was falling, while the Dark Angel raised his sword in victory. And on the edges of the celestial battlefield, the demons and angels of lesser rank that had been locked in life-or-death combat were now linked in obscene couplings. . . .

The painting returned to its original form. Then it seemed to change again. . . .

The longer he stared at it, the more the scene stubbornly refused to resolve itself—like a familiar word repeated until the sound of it becomes nonsense.

He looked away, blinking his eyes, no longer sure he was focusing properly. The plaster saints in their peeling niches looked at him demurely and ignored the confusion overhead.

He remembered Taya screaming about the crazy, horrifying things she had seen on the walls of the apartment, reaching out for her, things in the shadows that burst out of the walls, out of the ceiling, *out of him.* "You're splitting open like a rotten fruit and something—!" Then there had been the smashing glass, the screaming wail, the blood . . .

From somewhere in the real world, Sheila called, "Come here a minute, Paul: I want you to see this."

Startled by her voice, he risked one more look at the ceiling. The painting was the familiar study of goodness triumphant . . . faded, smoke dulled, nonthreatening.

He rubbed his hand across his forehead, confused, wondering if he was overtired or overwrought. Sheila's spell while driving, his unease at the trading post—and the raw fear he had felt driving past the cemetery . . . now *this*: it was as if, when they had driven into New Mexico, they had entered another place altogether. Each mile farther seemed to be bringing them deeper into puzzles and terrors which made no sense to the rational mind.

Whoa! he advised himself; *follow this train of thought and you* will *lose it. Too much coffee, too much sun, lack of sleep: those are the answers. Forget the nonsense about an undiscovered country.*

Coffee, sun, lack of sleep: he made a mantra of it to protect himself. Then he went into the alcove where Sheila stood before a small side altar.

In a cavity beneath the altar . . .

"Good Christ!" he whispered, drawing back in revulsion.

A body in a burial robe reposed in the rectangular space. Nothing—not even a sheet of glass—separated the corpse from the two people who stood behind the knee-high railing. Either of them could have reached out and touched the thin hands folded across the chest or the gaunt cheeks or the open, glazed eyes. The pinched and anxious face suggested there was no peace even in death.

The burial garment was a blue satin cerement, spilling off the body and out of the niche, extending halfway to the floor.

Sheila hadn't expected his reaction; she quickly assured him, "It's not real; it's a statue—probably a likeness of the founder of this mission, San Alonso Perez. I think this type of thing is fairly common in Spain and Italy."

Overcoming his initial reaction, Paul leaned a bit closer. "It looks so real—the face and hands even look *decayed*." But something bothered him beyond the mere grotesqueness of the statue. It was as if the plaster face held some special meaning for him—that if he could see behind the painted eyes he would discover . . . he had no idea. The shrine disturbed him deeply but the reason was unguessable, and so he quickly dismissed the troublesome thoughts.

"Just a mixture of age and beeswax-candle smoke. Look at the offerings and reminders there."

The sweep of blue cloth was spangled with little silver medals depicting parts of the body (eye, foot, hand), holy medals, scapulars, bits of ribbon, and even an occasional plastic flower or lock of hair. Someone at some time had pinned on a tiny fading photograph of an olive-skinned infant.

Sheila reached over and touched the picture of the baby with a fingertip. "This brings back all the funny/sad/foolish things I grew up with before I retired from Catholicism." She shook her head slightly, half with regret, half with some other emotion. "We'd get memorial cards when someone in the family died, with a picture of a saint on the front and a prayer for the soul of the departed on the back. Children's throats were blessed so they wouldn't choke to death. And" —she laughed—"don't forget the St. Christopher's medals. All the failed magics of childhood; the beliefs you put aside . . . though not entirely, I suppose, since I'm still interested in the anthropology of religion."

She stood back suddenly. "Let's get out of here before I regress entirely."

They left the church and strolled across the little patio between the church building and the *convento,* or priests' house.

They passed through a small garden. Lizards flickered among the cacti and desiccated bushes.

An elderly Indian man was sitting on the coping of a low wall. His close-cropped hair was silver-white. He wore faded jeans and a heavily patched workshirt. He smiled and called out something to them as he fanned himself with a large straw hat. They couldn't understand him, but they smiled and wished him good day as they continued on their way.

At the back of the garden with a little gate and, beyond, a path leading toward the hill behind the mission.

"This is called The Hill of the Vision, or, more simply, Vision Hill," Sheila reported, reading the highlights of a pamphlet on the history of Mission Agastan, which she had picked up from a rack as they left the church. "According to legend, the Virgin Mary appeared to Father Perez and told him to build a mission here and convert the Tawa Indians."

"Orders straight from heaven, huh? I hope he liked the territory."

"That's something else I was raised with: you *never* disobey that kind of direct intervention. Unless you want trouble."

The footpath climbed some two-thirds of the way up the hill, then broadened into a ledge which completely encircled the hilltop.

They wandered around the rock-strewn shelf, pausing frequently to look out over the desolation of sage and yucca and cactus surrounding the mission like a still, green-gray ocean.

The sun was directly overhead, but an unexpectedly cool breeze blew across the hilltop, for which they were both thankful.

They had made an almost complete circuit when they discovered a grotto in the hillside. The shrine was lined with cement and separated from the path by a high metal fence topped with spikes. Through the grating they could see the following tableau:

A statue of the Virgin, high up in a niche above an undecorated altar table, appeared to a kneeling replica of Fray

Perez. In the simulacrum of the priest, Paul recognized a younger version of the coffin-effigy inside the church—though this had none of the gruesome flavor of the latter. The Virgin, her eyes fixed on heaven, was all in white; the statue of the saint was angled in such a way that, though the painted eyes were fixed on the white-robed figure, the two observers outside the fence could see the look of ecstatic joy on Father Perez's face as he contemplated the Queen of Heaven.

The fence itself was decorated with knotted scarves and fading bouquets of real and artificial flowers, which had been tied or wired to the metal bars. Along the base of the fence was a scattering of half-burned vigil lights, extinguished by the winds which moved so restlessly across the hilltop.

He heard his name called and turned to Sheila, asking, "What is it?"

"What's what? I didn't say anything."

"But I heard you, just now."

"You must have heard something else. Or imagined it." She shivered a bit. "Let's get off this hill; that wind is really *cold.*"

He was glad to leave. The little hilltop under the shining sun had become as oppressive and disturbing as the inside of the mission.

Sheila took several more photographs, then complained about the chill she felt.

How could that be? he wondered. The day was blazing hot; what breeze there was seemed to blow off a blast furnace. He could feel the rivulets of sweat running down each side of his face, soaking his stomach, groin, armpits. He leaned against the Volks, feeling suddenly dizzy. There was a roaring in his ears; the sky and desert suddenly turned red, as though he were viewing everything through a film of blood.

He felt, if he let go, if he gave up the effort for a minute, he would drown in all that red.

He willed the redness away, refusing to blink until the sky returned to blue and the desert to tawny hotness.

"I've finished with the photographs; we can go now." She

didn't notice that he kept silent, was leaning heavily against the car even while she climbed inside.

Once he was sitting down, starting the engine, getting them *away*, Paul began to feel much better.

The little cemetery was deserted; he felt no echo of his fear, passing it this time.

Sheila unfolded one of the maps and they began estimating the amount of time until their arrival in Santa Fe.

2   El Centro

Paul was feeling sleepy. The desert was an implacable expanse of pale sand with knots of olive-green creosote bushes and blue-gray sage.

It was almost three o'clock.

Air only slightly less hot than the air inside the car blew in through the rolled-down windows. Heat shimmers danced over the desert. *I wouldn't want to get stuck out here,* Paul thought, and he had the momentary vision of the two of them mummified in the shell of a Volkswagen buried to its windows in sand.

"What are you thinking about?" asked Sheila; "You've been so quiet over there."

"Nothing, not much. Woolgathering. This desert is so much the same everywhere that it hypnotizes you."

"Yes; well, cheer up: we'll be passing through bustling El Centro pretty soon. That should liven things up." And she laughed disparagingly.

Paul laughed too, but his mind continued to play with various questions.

Did he *really* want things simply to go back to what they were? Back to the round of routine classes and dull-eyed, uncaring students? Back to Dean Arnie Matthias's informal evenings, when one of the younger teachers would try to corner Sheila with another discreet proposition? And Dr. Matthias, after too much brandy, would let his hand slide up and down Paul's thigh while he passed along some inconsequential bit of gossip in "the strictest confidence" and kept Paul wondering how long before the errant fingers would finally slide into his crotch and the gossip became a proposition? Paul had no way of knowing how he would respond because the situation hadn't arisen yet. He would know his response only when he was through responding. He had no tenure, and Matthias was almighty within the small world at Oliente.

"Are you feeling all right?" Sheila asked. "You seem . . . miles away."

"I'm fine. Really. I'm just getting bored with the sagebrush and cactus. I'll even welcome downtown El Centro for a change of scene."

"I'll just be glad to get to Santa Fe . . . stop a few days . . . relax."

There was a sudden *click-click-click-click* sound from somewhere beneath and behind them. They were on a slight upgrade, and the car began to lose momentum.

"Hell's bells!" said Paul. "What's that?"

"I don't know. I think—I don't *know!*" Sheila sounded outraged that the car, which had run smoothly up to now, should choose this moment, miles from anywhere, to break the faith.

Paul's vision of being stalled out on the desert came back to him. There was not another car on the highway; they were an unknown distance from the nearest town; and the afternoon was already well along toward evening. These facts were not encouraging.

The clicking noise became a *clunk-clunk-clunk* sound, louder and more threatening. The green light indicating loss of oil pressure lit up on the dashboard and stayed lit.

Now they had almost no momentum at all. The engine sounded like it was grinding itself to shreds.

"We'd better stop—fast!" Paul said, steering the car into the shoulder of the road.

He climbed out of the car and walked to the rear, then lifted the engine cover. He could see nothing wrong immediately, but there was a strong smell of burning oil. Or was that usual? He cursed himself for not knowing more about the car than he did. Beyond seeing a fire or the engine falling out onto the road, he was an inadequate diagnostician.

He knelt down and looked under the car. Again he could spot nothing obviously amiss. He dropped back into the passenger seat. "I can't see anything wrong. Do you have any ideas?"

Sheila had pulled a copy of *How To Keep Your Volkswagen Alive* from under the driver's seat and was thumbing through it. After a moment she said, "It looks like we've either thrown a rod or we're just about to."

"Expensive?"

"Probably." She continued reading to herself.

"Can we drive it at all?"

"We shouldn't"—matter-of-factly giving him the information from the manual. "If the damage isn't already done, that would probably do it. It's going to have to be towed to a mechanic."

"Great. Now where do you suppose the nearest phone is to call a tow truck?"

"In El Centro, obviously. Which is where I hope we will also find a mechanic! . . . One who knows something about Volkswagens," she added.

"I hope someone comes along soon. I don't like the idea of being stuck out here after dark." He glanced at the westering sun.

"We might try walking. That town may be closer than we think."

"Or it may be twenty miles up the road. We really have no idea of how far we've come. We'll wait," Paul decided.

They rolled down all the windows of the car, but the thick, hot air was unmoving. Paul began recalling all the stories he had read in which characters died, or nearly died, of thirst. He tried the radio, but got only infuriating bursts of static, so he shut it off.

Sheila kept an eye on the rearview mirror, watching for approaching cars.

"Ah!" she said after a few minutes, "here comes someone."

They started to climb out of the car, but the sedan shot past them without slowing and sped into the heat-hazed distance.

"Go back and raise the hood," Sheila told Paul. "They may have thought we stopped for lunch. Or a nap."

He did what she suggested. Shortly afterward, they spotted a truck approaching. Ancient, covered with dust, it slowed down and pulled off the road just in front of them.

Paul got out of the car and spoke to the young Indian man who was climbing down from the cab of the truck. "Thanks for stopping. Do you know anything about Volkswagens? I think we've thrown a rod."

The man, who was wearing a sweat-stained headband but no hat, held up a hand to shade his eyes. He stared at Sheila, glanced back at Paul, then said, "I don' know nothin' much about Volks. I'll take a look, if you want. Give you a lift into town if you need it."

"That will be fine," Sheila said, shading her eyes. "Please don't go to any trouble."

The man shrugged. "I'll do what I can." He wandered over to the car and poked around the engine for a moment, then crawled under the car.

Paul glanced across into the truck's cab and smiled at the dark-haired woman who sat watching him somewhat uneasily; once or twice she smoothed her windblown hair self-consciously. A child was seated on her lap: the little girl's black button eyes were wide with curiosity.

"Thank you for stopping," Paul said to the woman.

She smiled and nodded, but said nothing. He returned to stand beside Sheila as the man climbed out from under the car and brushed off his overalls.

"Yeah, I'd say it's a rod for sure. You're gonna have to have this towed," he reported. "There's a truck in town can do the job. We'll take you there." He started toward his own truck, saying, "You can lock up. I think we can all squeeze inside. It's not far."

But Paul was uncomfortable about leaving their luggage behind unprotected. After some discussion—ended rather quickly when their rescuer leaned on his horn and waved them toward the truck impatiently, yelling, "I'm happy to help, but we ain't got all day!"—it was decided that Sheila would ride into town in the truck and Paul would remain with the car, awaiting her return with the tow truck from El Centro.

When the others were gone, he lowered the engine cover and hood, then climbed back into the car, keeping to the passenger's seat to avoid the sunlight falling across the driver's side and steering wheel.

The inside of the car grew stifling. Somewhere in the back

a trapped insect buzzed persistently, though Paul couldn't locate it behind the luggage.

Two cars passed by; a third started to slow down until Paul waved it along, indicating that things were under control.

After a bit, he opened the car door and sat sideways, gazing out across the waste toward the curiously isolated Hill of the Vision and the even more distant hills behind a thick veiling of heat shimmers.

He rested the side of his face against the still-cool plastic of the neckrest.

He closed his eyes a moment, lost in the warm, buzzing stillness.

Then he was awake, suddenly. He had the strangest feeling that something essential had changed. But what? There were no other cars visible. The sun had slid only a bit further west. He could have dozed only a few minutes. The insect had stopped buzzing. The silence lay thick and gelid around him. A suffocating mixture of heat and quiet and unease made it momentarily difficult to breathe.

What was wrong? What had changed?

And then he saw, out of the corner of his eye at first, someone coming across the desert toward the car. The figure, approaching on foot, was so far away that it was hardly more than a dark speck against the sun-blanched wastes.

Paul was tempted to go out and meet the stranger, but he felt listless, as though his blood had thickened in the desert air and was refusing to flow. His mouth was as dry as if he had slept for days.

The approaching figure was distorted by the heat: it wavered as though it might suddenly flicker out of existence like one of the desert lizards darting to safety. It was little more than a shadow amid the barrel cacti and greasewood. Paul wondered if he might be seeing one of the little desert whirlwinds called "sand devils," and not a man at all.

His sluggishness and drowsiness refused to leave when he tried to blink away the sight. He could not clear his head. The tiny figure, now midway between him and the Hill of the Vision, was so unsubstantial-looking that he took off his sunglasses and checked the lenses to be sure that no smudge or tiny insect was creating the impression.

But the figure was there beyond any denial. And coming closer. It was close enough now for him to see that it was a man wearing a monk's robe. The hood was drawn up so that the face was hidden in shadow.

One of the fathers from the mission, Paul decided, was lost. Or was he merely in the habit of taking a—it seemed to him—rather hazardous jaunt across the open desert?

He felt that there was something very wrong.

He had the urge to lock the door and roll up the windows, as though the friar represented some sort of a threat.

If only his head didn't feel so light; if only his thinking weren't so muddled.

The shadow figure was very close now. It seemed tall, startlingly tall—some trick of perspective, Paul decided, or perhaps the high cowl . . .

Am I dreaming? Paul wondered, forcing himself to stand at last, leaning against the side of the car for support, because his legs seemed to have fallen asleep.

My God, the man's a giant! He could see that the priest was bearded and walked with his hands rigidly at his side and drawn into fists, frequently obscured by the gray-brown folds of his robe, which billowed as though the man were fighting his way through a ferocious windstorm, though the air around Paul remained still. The upper half of the padre's face remained shadowed by the monkish hood; his eyes were hidden.

The man came several steps closer, and Paul's feeling of wrongness turned abruptly to fear. No thing human was *that* tall!

This . . . *thing,* moving toward him through the heat-ripples, could not be human.

Shout/ run/ climb back into the car! his mind ordered; his body, trapped in the viscous dreamstuff of the moment, was helpless to obey.

It was only a short distance away now. It loomed, throwing a shadow crazily all around it, as though the shadow it made sprang from itself and not from the figure's relation to the sun, which Paul could feel burning the right side of his face and neck. He could feel the sun scorching his bare arms.

The thing came to a stop, extended a hand, reaching out for him. Paul felt the immense hand could gather him up or crush the life out of him in an instant. But it paused in what seemed to be a supplicating gesture, palm out.

The shadow was all around him now; it covered him and the car and the road for a hundred yards around, though he could still feel the unseen sun burning his neck and arms.

The hand was moving toward him again. In a moment the tip of a single monstrous finger would touch him, and he was so helpless, *helpless,* that he wouldn't even be able to scream and—

There was a horn blast from somewhere behind him. Then a swirl of dust and the sound of tires crunching over gravel.

The desert in front of him was an empty expanse of sage and sand.

Nothing moved in the heat haze.

Nothing.

He turned to look at the tow truck which had come to a stop a few feet in front of the Volkswagen. Sheila was walking toward him, her boots grating on the sand and rock underfoot with a loudness that was alien in the desert stillness. She was saying, "We're in luck, Paul. This"—she waved toward the stocky, sunburned man in the cowboy hat who was coming around from the far side of the truck—"is Jimmy Shore. He's the town's only auto mechanic. But will you believe this? He used to work in a VW repair shop in Texas before moving here. He may have to send out for parts, but he's sure he can fix the car."

She had come close enough now to see Paul's face. She asked, "Are you all right? You look like you've seen a ghost." She put out a hand to steady him, he seemed so unsure of himself as he stepped away from the car.

"I'm fine," he protested, gently removing her supporting hand, "I just—I think I got too much sun. I want a cold shower, a colder drink, and a nice long snooze."

"You and me both." Reassured that he was all right, she turned to the other man. "Jimmy, this is my husband, Paul Barrett. Paul, Jimmy."

The mechanic smiled pleasantly and shook hands with Paul. His hand was dry and calloused and his face was good-looking in a weathered sort of way. Paul guessed that he was somewhere between thirty-five and forty.

Jimmy took a quick look at the engine, a quicker look under the car, then came over to Paul and Sheila, rubbing at a spot of oil in the palm of his right hand with the fingers of his left, then abruptly gave up his attempt at clean-up and wiped both hands on his jeans, which were already very oily. "Yep," he said, "you've thrown a rod, all right. Have to tow you into town to have a better look at things."

While Jimmy hitched the car for towing and Sheila watched the process, Paul stared out across the empty desert toward the Hill of the Vision. Except for the rapid jerking movements of a jackrabbit, he could see nothing else. Sheila had to call his name twice when everything was ready to go.

He climbed into the cab of the tow truck with the uncomfortable feeling that he was being watched—though by whom or for what reason, he couldn't guess.

He showed none of his feelings to Sheila; he attributed them to fatigue and nerves and did his best to ignore them.

El Centro turned out to be only a twenty-minute ride up the road. The town was a cluster of one-story adobe buildings bisected by the highway and surrounded by occasionally irrigated fields. Heat shimmered over everything. They passed several gas stations, cafes, a drug store, a dry goods store, a grocery store, a fair-size Mexican-American restaurant with lots of glass and a splashy neon sign, a Greyhound Bus terminal, and several motels. All of the buildings burned white-hot in the relentless sunlight, relieved only infrequently by pockets of shade under the tall cottonwood trees.

Just past the Four-Star Motel on the far side of town, Jimmy slowed and turned a corner to follow a pocked road, along which were a few houses; then it straggled out into the desert. At the very end, just before the road faded into the surrounding scrub, was a single house with a little wooden barn attached. Jimmy turned onto a packed-earth driveway. Where the driveway forked, he headed toward the barn; the other branch ending at the front porch of the adobe house.

The barn doors were open; several cars were parked haphazardly in front of the building. Some were obviously being worked on; most were without tires. Just inside the barn, a late-model Chevrolet was sitting on blocks, its engine suspended above the engine cavity by a block and tackle.

As the three of them climbed out of the cab of the tow

truck, Jimmy said, "I'm gonna have to strip down the engine, and send for parts over to Carlsbad. You're probably gonna be stuck here until, oh, day after tomorrow, I'd say."

Paul was feeling uncomfortably hot; he moved to the shade just inside the barn. The heat didn't bother the other two.

Sheila asked, "Where's the best place to stay in town?"

"The Four Star, just up the road." Jimmy laughed. " 'Course, I'm prejudiced; it just so happens my wife's folks own the place. We manage it for them. They're away now— visiting Louise's sister in Montana. As soon as I get your car unhitched, I'll drive you there, if you want. Don't feel any obligation . . ." He laughed again. "I'll fix your car even if you stay at the Roosevelt or the Motor Inn. . . . 'Course, your *guarantee* won't be so good on what fixing I do." He chuckled.

"The Four Star sounds fine to me," said Sheila. She glanced questioningly at Paul.

The Four Star. Paul had recognized the name immediately as the place the man at the trading post had suggested —almost *insisted*—they stop at.

He shrugged. "Sounds fine to me too. I just want a shower and a cold beer."

Jimmy Shore dropped them off in the dusty, gravel-surfaced courtyard surrounded by sagging little white cabins. The motel units were joined in pairs, with double garages between each pair. Blue asbestos shingles on the roofs looked conspicuously new and at odds with the blistered and peeling paint.

Jimmy told them, "Look around. Make yourselves at home. If Louise isn't in the office, she'll be cleaning one of the cabins. She'll take good care of you."

He waved to them as he drove off.

"Welcome to El Centro," said Paul, picking up the two suitcases while Sheila gathered up his shaving kit, her overnight case, and the cameras.

The office of the Four Star Motel was empty. They called into the semidarkness of a room visible through a half-opened door behind the desk, but no one answered.

Somewhere outside a dog barked.

They called again, louder, to no avail. Sheila found a "Ring for Service" button and pushed it; it buzzed somewhere in the rear of the building, but no one responded.

"I'll see if I can find someone," said Paul. "You can stay here and watch the luggage." She nodded, looking very tired.

One cabin had its inner door open, and a broom and dustpan rested beside the closed screen door.

As he walked toward it, he could hear someone inside singing a familiar country-and-western song very off-key. He knocked on the screen door and a woman answered in a drawl, "C'm'on in: it's not locked."

Inside was a single long room, furnished with mismatched pieces of scarred blond oak. A brown rug was worn to almost paper thinness. Every flat surface—dresser top and chair arms and window ledge—showed cigarette burns and glass rings.

A youngish woman with a wire brush was busily digging tufts of dust out of the insides of a partly dismantled air-conditioner.

"Be right with you," she said, not looking up. She was wearing tight white shorts and a thin white blouse of some shiny material with a faint pattern of embossed flowers. Her breasts, Paul could see, were very full, and she was wearing no bra, since the nipples were outlined clearly through the blouse fabric. Her sun-faded red hair was short and curly; her skin was very pale. Her worn leather sandals made little slapping noises against the soles of her feet, as she kept time to the tune she was singing.

When she was satisfied with the amount of dust she had removed, she stood up and turned to face Paul. "Now, what can I do for you?" she asked, setting the brush on top of the still-unassembled air-conditioner.

Paul guessed her age to be around thirty. There was a little-girl prettiness about her, though the face and figure were full.

"Mrs. Shore?" Paul asked.

"Um-hmm," she said, sizing him up with her eyes.

"Your husband said my wife and I would be able to rent a room here."

"We got lots of rooms. How long you staying for? And where'd you see Jimmy? I tried phoning him twenty minutes ago, and he wasn't at his shop." When she spoke, all of her sentences had a rising inflection at the end which suggested a question mark.

"Our car broke down—threw a rod—just outside of town. Your husband towed us in. He says it's going to be two days before we'll be on the road again."

She shook her head sympathetically. "Everything breaks down these days. This air-conditioner? . . ."

With this last remark, she snapped the front of the air-conditioner back into place and pushed the start button. The machine turned over lazily, noisily.

"Not the best, but it'll do." She shrugged. "Let's go see about a room for you folks." She picked up the vacuum cleaner standing near the foot of one of the twin beds and grabbed hold of the bag into which she had been dumping the dust from inside the air-conditioner. "I might as well give you folks this cabin, number twelve, since I just finished cleaning it. And the air-conditioner works now."

She pushed her way through the screen door, letting it slam almost in Paul's face. "Sorry 'bout that," she apologized. "Oh, will you pick up that broom and dustpan?" He did so.

As they walked toward the motel office, the woman turned to Paul and asked, "Did you folks visit the Mission on your way here?"

When he nodded, she went on, "It's kinda pretty in the sunlight, but I don't see how anyone can live out there. It's so lonely at night. And you can't trust the Indians. Besides, *they* don't go there after dark. There was even a story once" —she had stopped near the office porch—"that the priests out there had a haunting. They had to keep the doors shut and the windows bolted because something no one ever saw pounded on them during the night. Well"—she resumed her pace—"like I say, I wouldn't want to be alone out there when the sun sets. Just be glad you didn't have your car leave you stuck way out there after dark. After you . . ." She held the screen door of the office open for him.

3   The First Night

Paul held open the door of number twelve for his wife. Her only comment as she entered was a toneless, "Oh, well . . ."

They set the suitcases on the ends of the twin beds, which were covered with ugly overly mended green bedspreads. He took the bed nearest the door.

Sheila pulled back the covers of her bed to check the sheets; "Lots of patching," she announced, "but it seems clean enough. . . . What time is it?"

Paul glanced at his watch. "Not quite five-thirty."

"I guess we can clean up, then go to that Mexican restaurant—the chrome-and-glass monstrosity we passed on the way to Shore's Repair Shop."

Sheila opened her overnight case. "I get first crack at the shower. OK? That is, if there *is* a shower. I doubt if I'd risk a tub without scouring it myself, and I'm too tired for that."

"Go ahead. I want to lie down for a minute or two."

Sheila went to the bathroom door at the far end of the room and pushed it open. "Eureka! I see a shower stall! I'll be out in about ten minutes."

She closed the door behind her. A moment later, Paul could hear the sound of water running in the shower. He settled back onto the bed and kicked off his shoes, letting them drop to the floor with a thump. After a bit of shifting around, he found a comfortable position and relaxed with a sigh.

He shut his eyes for a moment, then opened them to stare

at the ceiling, watching a tiny spider making its way across
a large water stain.

He drifted off, then woke up suddenly. The spider overhead was gone. Water was still running in the shower. He
was tempted to call out to Sheila to hurry things up, then
he decided it didn't matter, since they were in no particular
hurry.

He closed his eyes again.

Someone was walking far ahead of him through shadowy
rooms, which seemed to flow one into another so that he
wasn't aware of any transition—only the perception that
the *there* was no longer the same *there* of a moment before.

Something was wrong with the rooms: the walls and
ceilings were damp and rough. He realized they weren't
rooms at all; they were caves, underground chambers lit
with a grayish phosphorescence from the rocky walls on
either side.

He was following someone, but he could hardly see his
dark-robed, hooded guide because the gray light of the
place was so uncertain. Something about the figure was
elusively familiar. He could not guess why he had come to
this place; he only knew that he was compelled to follow
the shadowy figure deeper and deeper yet, as the floor underneath slanted sharply downward and the gloom massed
thicker around him.

Then, unexpectedly, they stepped from a narrowing passageway into a vast open space which was, at the same time,
an immense cavern and the interior of a church of unguessable dimensions. The gray light was gone, but the church
cavern was lit by hundreds of votive candles in ruby-glass
holders, floating all around him, staining the stone walls
a moist, soft flesh color.

Staring upward to where the walls converged overhead,
he had the impression of the inside of the vault of some
medieval cathedral or of a pair of hands folded in prayer. . . .

And the skin of those immense, enfolding palms was filled
with pores the size of rat holes. He could see countless tiny
red rats' eyes, reflecting the drifting candles, watching him
from the rows of holes in the flesh-colored walls.

All around he heard voices whispering and giggling.

Terrified, he was helpless to do more than follow his guide toward an altar of glowing white stone in the center of the vast open space.

The altar was bare of linens or candlesticks; a single design, in thick black lines, was scrawled upon the side he was facing:

The monkish figure knelt before the stone and moaned loudly. He struck the symbol with his hands, smearing the thick lines, but was unable to eradicate the design completely. At last, from within the folds of his robe, he took a piece of thick, blunt chalk and scrawled a cross over the hated emblem, applying the chalk so thickly that the chalk stick was quickly worn away. He tossed the nub end aside with a satisfied grunt.

Now the thin, dry hands were fumbling eagerly with a panel set in the stony floor in front of the altar; he was trying to slide it open, but the panel resisted his efforts.

Paul came and stood over the man, noticing how sweat was runing down his forehead and cheeks, dripping from the end of the thin, elegant nose, and glistening in the massive black beard. Paul could feel the heat in the place too, could feel his armpits and the back of his neck growing damp.

"What are you trying to find?" he asked. "What is it you want to show me?"

"The truth," was the answer, and the monk began to weep with frustration because the panel refused to yield up its secret. "We have so little time: the Old Enemy will soon be here and everything will be undone."

In sudden anger he raked his fingernails across the obdurate stone. Then the man turned to Paul with such intensity that he was aware only of haunted dark eyes and ruby-red sweat-gleams in the man's beard. The monk whispered desperately, "Only the truth will set me free. Only the truth will keep away the Old Enemy."

"What enemy?" Paul asked, trying to penetrate the secrets in the ancient eyes.

But the other pressed both hands to his face and began to weep, sobbing, "Too late, too late. The power of the moon is hers to command. The power of the blood is hers to draw upon. The power of the fire is hers to wield."

He crumpled into a darkish shape upon the floor, his head hidden beneath his robe, his hands outstretched in supplication. He was no longer aware of Paul as he wailed softly to himself, "The bell is *hers* now: its unholy sound summons *her* hence. The book is *hers* now: its unholy pages display *her* secrets. The candle is *hers* now: by its unholy western light will *she* perform her evils."

Then there was no figure, no altar, no cavern . . . nothing but a gray fog which became the darkness inside his eyelids.

"Wake up, Paul, you're having a nightmare."

He opened his eyes and found himself staring at Sheila, who was wandering back and forth in front of him, toweling her hair vigorously. She was wearing only her bra and panties, and her still-damp feet left faint marks on the rug. She stopped long enough to ask, "Are you all right? It must have been some dream. You were thrashing about and yelling, so I woke you up."

Paul was sweating profusely and still shaking. He was puzzled by these dreams of monkish figures. They made no sense—except to indicate how much local history he had absorbed. When he mentioned this to Sheila jokingly, she merely shrugged and said, "The padres may have left some psychic residue. I've read enough to know that a lot of 'sensitives' claim that they can pull impressions out of an object and even see past history that way. Didn't that girl who died —Enotea—claim to have some special talent for—what was it called?"

"Psychometry," he said, the flatness of his tone belying the painful rush of memory Enotea's—*Taya's*—name conjured up.

Sheila caught something in his tone. She said quickly, "Anyhow, if a rock or a piece of clothing can store up impressions, why not a stretch of land? Especially one with as interesting a history as this area."

Screams and smashing glass and the wet sound of Enotea's bloodied body hitting concrete pavement . . . STOP! he commanded himself. He refused to let the terrifying memories in.

Sheila had turned away and was combing her hair, looking at herself in the dresser mirror opposite the beds. The mirror was a tall, oval one; and she was able to stand up while she worked impatiently at several stubborn knots and tangles. "Remind me to buy creme rinse tomorrow, before I start pulling out hanks of my hair."

"Creme rinse. Yes," murmured Paul, who had come over to stand behind her. He was still reacting to his dreams and to the memories that had come in their wake. He put his hands—shaking slightly, though she did not seem to notice —on her sides, just below her bra; he then slid them gently down her smooth skin until they came to rest on the little roll of flesh just above the thin elastic band of her panties. He started to tease her about the little mark of overweight, but stopped, remembering how sensitive she had become on the subject of her looks. He began rubbing his fingers along the elastic strip. He felt her tense, but was uncertain about whether she was becoming aroused or merely irritated. She laughed uneasily, as though she herself were unsure of her reaction, saying, "None of that, now. I want dinner. I'm *starving*."

He pressed his face into the curve of her neck and said, "Can't dinner wait a few minutes?" He wanted to forget his fears and sense of frustration in the business of sex.

He slid his fingers under the elastic, at the same time hitching himself up behind her and feeling himself stiffen. He reached down further, his fingers touching her pubic hair now, and pulled her back toward him, pressing the softness of her buttocks against his crotch. He began grinding himself gently against her as he started to slide off her panties.

But she pulled away suddenly, saying, "Paul—no! I don't want to—*that's all*."

She dropped onto the edge of the bed, combing her hair in rapid strokes, not looking at him.

He grabbed a towel and left the room without another word.

The bathroom was still steamy. Its one tiny window would only open a crack because of the security grating outside. The window panes were painted over the same shade of watery blue as the rest of the room, giving a faintly claustrophobic effect.

There were two lights: a single naked bulb screwed into a ceiling socket and a small hooded light over the basin mirror that was still filmed with steam.

For a few minutes he stood as the moisture evaporated, watching his face appear in the looking glass.

He unbuttoned his shirt and hung it over a towel rack, shucked his jeans and briefs and hung them up also.

He pressed his face close to the mirror, disapproving of his mustache (sadly in need of trimming) and his thinning hairline. His nose was sunburned and peeling (in spite of the railroad cap he wore to prevent this) and his eyes—too deep-set in his haggard face—were an even more washed-out blue than the bathroom walls.

He decided that he looked like an unhealthy twenty-eight-year-old instead of a reasonably healthy man of thirty-eight.

The paleness of his shoulders and chest, even after so many days in the Southwestern sun, came as something of a shock to him.

He ran a hand down his stomach, realizing that some of the spare tire was gone, at least. His hand stopped in the tangles around his half-erect member.

With a sigh, he stepped into the shower, massaging himself with the bar of soap Sheila had left. He stepped a little way out of the steaming water and began lathering his crotch. Gradually he began moving his hand, thick with soap, along his now rigid penis, up and back, increasing the speed of the strokes until the final tension broke and drained away.

He stayed under the running water until Sheila banged on the door and called, "Are you all right? Should I go to dinner alone?"

"Be right out," he called, shutting off the water and reaching for his towel.

It was twilight when they emerged from cabin twelve. The air around them was pleasantly warm, smelling faintly of dry grass and sand. Clean.

There were few cars in the street; no stores were open. As

they walked, they passed the Greyhound Station, where an elderly couple, a suitcase beside each one, sat staring resentfully through a plate-glass window at Paul and his wife. Two blocks further along, the neon logo of a white duck, alternating with rippling blue-green letters, announced the Pata Blanca restaurant.

The pretentious glass, steel, and brick exterior concealed a depressingly formularized small-town cafe: a yellow formica counter, a row of yellow-and-white tables, and a row of window booths with thick, splitting yellow plastic cushions. A few gaudy piñatas dangled from wires overhead, twisting gently in the breeze from overhead air-conditioning vents. Sheila glanced with brief interest at the collection of mytho-Aztec scenes crudely painted on black velvet and set in garish frames along the walls.

They took a corner booth. The tabletop was sticky and the seats had to be brushed clean before they sat down. When the waitress, a cheerless dark-skinned girl of sixteen or seventeen, came by, they ordered a pitcher of sangria, and guacamole.

A few people were dining, mostly at the counter. From the familiar way they spoke to one another and to the waitresses, Paul gathered they were locals. He had the impression he and Sheila were the only out-of-towners in the place. There was a jukebox on the far wall near the end of the counter. A middle-aged man, his stetson perched on the empty counter-stool beside his own, kept playing Tammy Wynette's "Dee-Eye-Vee-Oh-Are-Cee-Eee" over and over, until one of the waitresses said, "Bill, play that song one more time, and I'm putting a bullet through that goddamn machine. There's a hundred songs in there; for God's sake, give the other ninety-nine a chance."

The man switched to a song by Dolly Parton.

The food, when it finally did show up, was bland and greasy. Neither of them ate very much. Sheila seemed tired and preoccupied; Paul felt tense and restless, not eager to return to the motel. While the waitress was clearing away the dishes, they ordered another pitcher of sangria.

Paul had just refilled their glasses when Louise and Jimmy Shore came into the eating house. Louise spotted them immediately and dragged Jimmy toward their booth. She was wearing a denim skirt and red sandals and the same blouse with embossed flowers; Jimmy was still wearing his grimy jeans but had changed from a sweat-soaked to a fresh work-shirt.

"Mind if we join you?" Louise asked.

The Barretts shifted around to make room for the other couple.

"I haven't had a chance to do much with your car," Jimmy apologized, "but I *promise* I'll get to it first thing in the morning." He tried to catch the eye of one of the three waitresses in the place, asking Sheila over his shoulder as he looked around for someone to take his order, "How'd you get into town in the first place? I never did ask you. You just turned up at the repair shack. I didn't see who dropped you off and never thought to ask."

Sheila said, "A young Indian and his family drove me in. I tried to give him some money, but he wouldn't take it. I think he said his name was Estevan Jaramillo."

"Damn!" said Jimmy, turning back to face the others at the table. "Those girls are always busy filling the sugar jars or taking a coffee break when you want to order." He shrugged. "Well, someone'll be by pretty quick. . . . You were lucky to run into Estevan. He's a good man. He and his family live two–three miles the far side of town"—indi-cating the direction with a sweep of his hand.

"Keep to themselves pretty much," said Louise. "All the Indians around these parts do. Don't have more to do with Anglos than they have to. They've still got some funny ideas, you know what I mean?" She paused to scratch a front tooth reflectively, then ran her tongue over her teeth before she continued, "Some of their ideas weren't so far off base, though. Used to be in the old pueblos that the woman called the shots. Mama held the community property. The house and such was handed down from mother to daughter, and to hell with male chauvinists like my friend, here"—and she gave Jimmy a poke in the ribs, which he accepted with a good-natured smile; he was more concerned with trying to signal a waitress.

Louise continued, "If a woman wanted a divorce, she'd just put her man's clothes and junk out on the doorstep. When he came home from farming or hunting or fooling around, he'd just pick up his stuff and go home to Mama or an older sister." She smiled before adding, "Sounds like a pretty good system to me."

"Sounds like a lot of crap," said Jimmy without rancor.

"Better mind your manners, Mister; you may just find your toothbrush and socks outside the door when you come home after your next card game."

"Try it and see how long you have a door to put things outside of."

Paul offered to order some other glasses and share the sangria, but Louise declined, saying, "That stuff's too sweet: makes me hung over next morning. Just one glass, even. And Jimmy never drinks anything but beer."

Her husband finally had succeeded in attracting a waitress. She looked them all over with the same sullen look before asking Jimmy, "What'cha want?"

"Two beers," said Jimmy, glancing at Louise, who nodded her agreement. "Dos Equis."

The girl scribbled this information on her order pad and left.

Louise said, "Too bad about your car blowing up, or whatever. But don't worry; Jimmy will put it right as rain." She smiled at him before continuing, "I guess El Centro must seem like the end of the world to you. . . . More than the end of the world," Louise went on, following a train of thought, "a *cemetery*. Heck! there's even a story the Four Star is built on the very spot where some Spanish soldiers cut down a group of Tawa women and children during one of the uprisings. Afterward, the padres from the mission sprinkled the bodies with holy water and made the soldiers bury them in one big grave. We've never had any ghost-squaws come back, so I guess the priests did all right by them." She shrugged. "Anyhow, you *gotta* admit this is the worst boondocks you've ever seen."

"Not at all," Sheila protested, unconvincingly.

"Well, I was *born* here, for God's sake, and it seems like the end of the world to *me*, sometimes. It's sure a lot different from California, you have to admit." Paul started to make a comment but Louise forged ahead, "I'd sure like to go back to California. We were out there on a visit two years ago. Jimmy's brother and sister-in-law live in Sacramento. Gerald and Susan Shore? . . .

Sheila shook her head, "I'm afraid that name doesn't ring a bell."

"Well, I guess it *would* be a pretty big coincidence, your knowing them. I tried to talk Jimmy into moving out there. God knows, you got enough cars in California. He'd find plenty of business. But" —she patted her husband's arm— "Jimmy likes it here well enough. Come to think of it, I guess I do too. And, with Mommy and Daddy semiretired and travelin' in their trailer so much of the time, I don't know who'd take care of the Four Star. It keeps us busy, keeps us out of trouble."

There was a sudden lull in the conversation. The waitress brought Louise and Jimmy their beers; for a minute or two, everyone drank very deliberately, trying to think of something to say next.

Paul found himself staring across at Louise, who was sitting with her hand around the beer glass on the table in front of her. There was a thin line of foam across her upper lip. She was staring back.

Sheila was following some thought of her own, watching the occasional car passing in the dusk. Jimmy was trying to signal the waitress again.

The red-pink tip of Louise's tongue moved to erase the bit of foam in a gesture that was at once disarming and arousing to Paul. She was smiling at him now.

But Paul, his perceptions momentarily fuzzed from the wine, suddenly saw Taya smiling at him. Her matted red-brown hair and her silver-nailed long hands around a glass of herbal tea with a spoon in it to keep the glass from cracking . . . The impression faded; Louise was looking oddly at him.

The waitress returned and Louise and Jimmy ordered a meal for themselves.

Paul used the momentary interruption to press his fingertips, wet and cold from his still half-filled wine glass, against his feverish forehead. Only Louise, out of the corner of her eye, noticed the gesture; she said nothing. Paul felt better, but he wanted to get away from the talk, the stuffy restaurant, Louise.

Jimmy asked Paul, "What do you do for a living, Barrett?"

"I—we—teach at a private college near Berkeley. Oliente College?"

Jimmy shook his head. "Never heard of it. Sorry."

"It's small," said Sheila. "We have less than fifteen hundred students. Paul's speciality is contemporary literature and drama. I teach cultural anthropology and history of religion."

"That's nice," said Louise, clearly uninterested. Then she brightened as the waitress brought their dinners, saying, "*That* was sure quick."

The girl shrugged, pushed the check under the corner of Jimmy's plate, and left.

"Real personable, that number," Jimmy commented.

Louise said, "I forgot you get a *chile relleno* with the combination plate." She forked it off her dish onto her unused bread plate, "I can't eat them—the peppers, you know? Would either of you like it? It's a shame to let it go to waste." She pushed the item in question across the table in the general direction of Paul.

Paul shook his head, saying, "We overate earlier. Thanks anyway."

"Well, if no one else wants it," said Jimmy, "I guess it's mine." He pulled the *chile relleno* toward himself.

"I don't want to seem rude," said Paul, "but I think we'd better get back to the motel. I'm wiped out. Sheila?"

She nodded wearily.

Louise said sympathetically, "I can just imagine you *are* tired. You just run along; we're gonna have another beer, the evening being so warm, you know?"

The Barretts stood up; everyone wished everyone else good night while Paul left money to cover their dinner.

"Your car—tomorrow—first thing," Jimmy promised as they headed toward the door.

Back in the motel room they undressed quickly and went immediately to their separate beds, both too tired even to read.

Paul fell asleep to the clatter of the air-conditioner and woke up to the sound of a car with bad brakes stopping just outside the window nearest his bed. He had no idea what time it was, but it was pitch black outside and he had a middle-of-the-night feeling.

Someone gunned the engine a moment; then there was abrupt silence. The only sound was the air-conditioner churning away.

One car door slammed. Then another. There was the rattle of glass bottles and two male voices talked loudly in what they clearly thought were whispers. Paul, wide awake and straining to hear, could make out a few words in Spanish. He turned onto his side, facing the window.

Shadows slid across the drawn curtains; he heard laughter.

The door of the adjoining unit banged shut, then was opened and closed more gently, as if someone was trying to undo the initial noise. He could hear muffled voices. Then there was a moment of relative quiet, during which he could hear the air-conditioner running.

When he turned onto his back and tried to fall asleep, chairs scraped on a bare floor as they were dragged across the room beyond the wall. Glasses rattled. There was more talking, more laughter.

Paul called out tentatively, "Sheila?" but she was sleeping soundly, undisturbed by the activity next door.

A smaller, slighter shadow crossed the curtain furtively. There was a faint tapping on the door of the next unit. After a momentary silence, the door was opened. There was more talking; one of the voices—a woman's—seemed vaguely familiar to Paul.

He was fully awake now and trying to hear everything that was being said, but he could catch nothing more than sounds and laughter. Then the voices died away and there was only the occasional soft laughter of the woman.

A sudden thump against the adjoining wall. The sound of bedsprings. The woman laughed louder this time.

He sat up in bed; he could see Sheila was still sleeping, though stirring slightly.

On the opposite wall, light from the other room showed through the cracks where the paneling had warped and separated slightly.

Not disturbing his sleeping wife, Paul got up and pressed his eye to the widest slit.

What he saw was a triangular corner of a bed and a bit of the room beyond—indistinguishable from their own, except that the rug had been removed at some time and never replaced.

A woman was sitting on the bed with her back to him. She was naked—her clear, firm skin almost as pale as the sheet on the bed.

She was talking to someone outside Paul's line of vision. She spoke in Spanish and a man answered her in the same language. She reached behind her and toyed carelessly with the hair at the back of her neck. The ends of her short-clipped auburn hair stuck moistly to the nape, looking almost blood-colored against the sallowness of her skin. She let her hand slide down a bit further, absently scratching a shoulder blade with her silver-painted nails.

Then a man who had evidently been sitting beside her in the bed slid over alongside her on his knees. He was a young Chicano with a thick mustache. He was wearing a loose silky yellow shirt and chinos and was barefooted. He bent down and began nuzzling her neck.

She remained sitting, but moved her hand around to touch the back of his head, signifying something with a momentary pressure of her fingers.

Then she laughed.

The man assumed a half-crouching position behind her on the bed. His mouth and tongue began tracing the line of her shoulders.

She shifted slightly. Another man, shorter, brutish-looking, with thick, curly hair, clean-shaven, wearing a filthy tee shirt and grease-stained chinos, climbed onto the bed in front of her. She extended her breast, supporting it in her hand like a gift of fruit. Paul could glimpse its taut red nipple. The man ignored her gesture and cupped the back of her head in his hands and pulled her forward, kissing her mouth.

Paul felt like a spectator at some porno house; he had the impression that this was all being staged for his benefit—a private show for his private fantasies. He felt excited and uncomfortably like a voyeur, much the way he felt when Taya—high on some drug—would perform a striptease for him and draw him, resistant/willing, into some bizarre sexual act she had seemingly devised on the spur of the moment.

The younger man was rubbing his chin back and forth across her shoulder blades; the stubble on his chin and cheeks left soft, pinkish traces on the pale skin. After a moment he reached around to cup and massage her breasts.

She began unbuttoning the shirt of the man facing her.

The man behind her was darting the red, wet lizard-tongue into her ear as he stroked her breasts.

Paul could not see her face. As he watched, hypnotized, the three heads—two dark, one russet—seemed to move together in a kind of unity.

The younger man was working his shirt off, pushing down his chinos. The woman had removed the older man's shirt, and though Paul couldn't see her hands, he guessed that she was unzipping his pants, working them down over his hips while he continued to cover her face with wet, sloppy kisses.

When all three were free of encumbering clothes, the older man attempted to pull the woman down on top of him so that he could enter her from the front in such a way that the younger man, apparently, could enter her from the rear.

She seemed agreeable to this arangement, moving around to make the awkward positions more comfortable.

All three were soaked with perspiration; their bodies were slippery with it.

Paul could feel his own body was drenched with sweat; he felt himself caught up in the ménage in the next room. Again he had the fleeting impression that he was being treated to a private show.

Everything was moving in a slow motion toward the climactic . . .

"What on *earth* are you doing, Paul?" Sheila demanded as she snapped on the lamp on the nightstand between the beds.

Paul turned, embarrassed and confused, feeling like a child caught masturbating by his mother. He explained quickly, "I thought I heard something. Next door."

"I thought that cabin was empty."

"So did I—but listen. . . ."

There was only silence.

Sheila, sitting up in the bed, looked at him. "Paul, you've been on edge all day. For God's sake, take one of your pills and give us both a break. This edginess . . . Paul, you *know* if you get too wired, if you don't sleep—we'll be right back on the brink of another breakdown. You pushed yourself too hard before; you've got to take care of yourself now. *You owe it to both of us.*"

Taya. Did she know about Taya? He could not resolve the question. And the guilt he felt around her death was always reinforced by the guilt he felt every time the question of his nervous collapse came up.

"It's been a hell of day. I'm worked up. And there's . . . the heat and that damned air-conditioner."

"We could turn it off."

"Then we *would* roast." He started for the bathroom door. "I'm going to take that sleeping pill."

When he returned, he kissed Sheila and assured her, "I'm *fine. Really.* So turn off the light and let's get some sleep."

But she kept the lamp on a few minutes longer, watching him as he settled into bed. He closed his eyes but he could still feel her staring at him. Finally he said, "I'll *never* get any sleep with that light on."

She turned off the lamp, but he could tell from her breathing that she wasn't asleep.

There was silence next door; no light showed through the cracks in the wall opposite him.

Later, when the pattern of her breathing assured Paul that his wife was asleep, he went to the window and pulled back the curtains.

No cars were parked on their side of the courtyard; two station wagons and a sedan were parked in front of units on the other side of the gravel strip.

Nothing was moving. The moonlight was undisturbed on walls and roofs and ground.

He went over and pressed an ear to the wall, but heard no voices or laughter.

Confused, he went back to bed and yielded to the night and silence, underscored only by the relentless clatter of the air-conditioner.

The pill did its work; he fell asleep in short order.

4 Willie Kavan

They had their morning coffee at a small cafe, half a block from the motel. Neither felt very hungry, though Sheila ordered some toast for herself.

Neither mentioned the night before; in fact, they said very little to each other. Paul noticed that Sheila looked exceptionally tired.

Outside the windows, the day was clear and warming fast. There were no clouds in the sky.

The waitress who brought them their coffee asked them in an offhanded manner where they were from and how long they were staying, but she seemed uninterested in their answers.

Afterward they walked out to Shore's Garage. Jimmy came out to wish them a good morning, wiping grease off a wrench with an oily pink rag. He had obviously been working on the car for some time: the engine had been torn down and lay in pieces underfoot. Paul felt a momentary amazement that such an unimpressive assortment of metal and rubber had somehow brought them this far and had the responsibility for bringing them home.

They listened attentively to Jimmy's explanations of what he had done and had yet to do. They were encouraged by his assurances that as long as the parts arrived on the truck the following morning, he'd have them on the road before noon the next day.

When he returned to work, they walked back into town to do what sightseeing might be done in tiny El Centro.

Their first stop was a little shop promising its customers "Authentic Indian Handicrafts." After searching among shelves and racks of everything from redwood-burl salt shakers (from Santa Rosa, California, according to the manufacturer's stamp) to Monopoly sets, they found a large selection of items on shelves labeled "Indian Handicrafts & Pueblo Art." It only took a moment to discover that the "Genuine Artifacts" were products of Japan, Taiwan, and Mexico.

A few doors further along they discovered The Anderson Gallery, featuring (according to an ornate, hand-lettered sign in the window) "The exclusive paintings of Cyrus and Helen Anderson."

The gallery was closed, and the hands had fallen off the little plastic clock face under the legend "Sorry we missed you. Back at ————," so they had no idea when the place would reopen.

They stood for a time in the shade of a broad canvas awning, looking at samples of the Andersons' paintings on display in the front window.

Clearly, Cyrus's scenes of a *Cattle Drive, Snowbound Ranch House, Solitary Indian Scout* and *Empty Desert at Sunset* were derivative of the Frederic Remington/Charles M. Russell school of Western artists. Helen, on the other hand, followed the spirit of Georgia O'Keeffe in her nearly abstract desert landscapes of *Blue-Black Evening Mountains* and *Mesa Burning Redly Under a Noon Sun*, in the twisted form of a *Joshua Tree Against an Empty Cobalt Sky*, and in the intense whiteness of an *Adobe Wall With a Single Doorway Visible as a Rectangle of Absolute Black*. Though the paintings were adequate, clearly neither artist had more than an amateur's grasp of the skills possessed by the original artists.

El Centro boasted a single movie theatre. A faded poster in a glass display case announced that the main feature was a horror film called *The Lamia*. Someone had put three BB holes through the glass; one had gone through and punched out the right eye of the female vampire who leered out of the poster with blood-smeared fangs.

Sheila wanted to keep moving, but Paul delayed. He said, "Listen, don't rush off; we may end up at this film tonight."

"No way," said Sheila.

"Oh, it's probably not as bad as it looks"—and he began to read, "A demon spawned in ancient Rome reawakens with a centuries-old hunger for blood. Hell's child, beautiful and deadly, she drew men helplessly to her to satisfy her unnatural thirst for human blood."

Sheila said, "Whoever put a bullet through the poster should have plugged the producer instead. *And* whoever wrote that copy." She began walking in earnest away from the theatre.

Near the edge of town they located a little shop in the front of an adobe house set back from the sidewalk. Several barrel cacti grew in the front yard amid scattered weeds and fair-size stones. The house was surrounded by a waist-high wall of paint-daubed multicolored rocks. A sign beside the gate said "Willie's Curios"; most of the red paint of the lettering had flaked away, exposing the steel gray of the sun-baked wood underneath.

"Shall we have a look?" asked Paul.

He held open the rusty iron gate for her, then followed through, taking care to close the gate behind them.

A bell jangled loudly when they pushed open the front door of the shop.

They found themselves in a dark hallway, with rooms opening off it on either side. In front of them was a rose-wood chest topped with an immense oval mirror, much of its silver backing gone. They stared at themselves looking out from the beveled glass. Instinctively, Sheila put a hand to her hair and Paul touched a finger to his mustache, as if these gestures could correct the careless way they looked.

Then they entered the room on the left. It was small and filled entirely with rock samples: nodes, crystals, tur-quoises, hunks of obsidian, and the like. They found noth-ing of more than passing interest.

They recrossed the hall and entered the opposite room. It was jammed with display cases and tables. One wall was lined with bookshelves. A lumpy purple couch was pulled away from the bookcases; it was stacked with bundles of old magazines tied with string. The shelves and cases were filled with a haphazard selection of books, baskets, pottery, jewelry, gourds, bookends, and dishes filled with arrowheads, beads, buttons, key chains, Indian-head pennies, and fragments of pink and red coral. Dominating everything was a triangular display case filling one corner, holding an impressive selection of the tiny painted wooden figurines called kachina dolls.

A sixtyish man was seated behind a table near a doorway hung with strands of blue and red beads. He was repairing a small pottery jar. A lamp with a metal snake-neck hung over his skilled, spidery hands. He wore a green visor pulled low over his eyes. Through the transparent green crescent they could see a thin nose and lips pursed in concentration; he was totally bald, and the skin of his head was moist from the warmth of the room, since none of the three grimy windows was open and all had the look of not having been opened in some time.

He did not glance up when they entered the room; he just continued applying glue with a tiny brush to the V-shaped chip in the jar's rim. Only when he had set the missing bit of pottery firmly in place did he raise his eyes to look at the two visitors. He smiled at them and said, " 'Morning, folks. Anything special I can show you?"

They returned the greeting and made the usual "Just browsing" disclaimer.

"That's fine," he said. "Browse all you want." He returned his attention to the newly repaired item.

They wandered around the room, occasionally picking up this or that dusty artifact. As far as they could tell, the Indian handicrafts were authentic.

"I see nothing is priced," Sheila whispered.

Paul nodded. "You can bet it costs an arm and a leg," he hissed back.

As though sensing what they were discussing, the shopkeeper said without looking up, "If you have any questions about the price, just ask. If it seems too high, well, it might be we can come to an arrangement," and he chuckled to himself.

After a little more desultory looking, Sheila said to Paul, who was investigating several Indian rugs standing rolled up against the wall, "I want to go back to the motel and rinse out a few things. Maybe I can start one of those nice, juicy novels I brought along. You know—the ones I wouldn't dare be caught reading at home. You can stay here if you want."

Paul hesitated a moment, then said, "If it really is all right, I think I'll poke around a little more. I want to have a look at those books while I'm here."

"Fine. We'll have lunch when you get back. Do you have any idea how long you'll be?"

He glanced at his watch. "An hour—no more."

"See you in an hour, then," and she was gone, the bell jangling loudly on the front door as it closed behind her.

Paul crossed to the shelves of used books, relishing the familiar musty smell they gave off. He pulled out a large volume labeled *Scenes and Stories from the Life of Fray Perez.* It was a reprint of a book written by a Rev. A. A. Domingo, C.S., in the early nineteenth century.

Paul opened it at random and carefully lifted a sheet of protective tissue to study an etching of a very young Father Perez. Under the carefully shaped beard and delicate tonsure, the priest's fine features had an epicene look. His head was tilted back and his eyes were fixed on heaven; his hands were folded in an X across his breast as he knelt at his prie-dieu.

Another plate was labeled "Agastan Mission, Circa 1638." The mission proper had changed very little in all the years, though the present-day outbuildings were different from the cruder structures surrounding the mission in the etching. In the illustration, several Indians stood near the church doors, under the watchful eye of a dark-robed padre.

There was also a plate of a pueblo plaza surrounded by two- and three-story terraced buildings, the different levels connected by a maze of short and long ladders leaning against walls and roofs. The upper levels and the edge of the plaza were crowded with people watching a circle of dancers, the men wearing white kilts and the women draped in black robes. All the dancers, men and women, carried bunches of feathers or rattles. A knot of drummers stood to one side. This illustration was labeled, "Dancers, Pueblo Agastan, Circa 1638."

The proprietor's voice, coming from just over his shoulder, startled Paul. The man said, "You're interested in local history, I see."

"A bit," Paul said, closing the book carefully and replacing it on its shelf. He turned toward the man.

The other said, "Well . . . Oh, I'm Willie, by the way. Willie Kavan. Pleased to meet you . . . ?"

"Paul. Paul Barrett. My wife and I are having some repairs made on our car."

Willie nodded. "Very pleased to meet you, Paul."

The two men shook hands, then Willie continued, "I just want to warn you not to expect to get much out of that book. The plates are nice, but the text was put together by one of the Casserite padres. Alonso Perez was a Casserite priest himself. They were a group who came here from Mexico—Spanish, originally. There are no Casserites in the Americas any longer, as far as I know. I've even heard that the order itself seems to be on the way out. They only have a few churches in Spain now. Anyhow, that book pretty well follows the pious party line. It omits . . . *things*," the older man said, giving an odd emphasis to the last word. He raised his eyebrows.

"*Things*," Paul repeated; then he asked, "Such as . . . ?"

"A lot of what went on after Padre Perez died for instance." When Paul nodded, the old man smiled and peeled off his visor, clearly settling into a storytelling posture. "Story has it that one of the Indian servants did it. Nothing was ever proven, though. It's all outlined in another book I'll show you in a minute. As for what went on, the book you just had only mentions that the mission was abandoned for a time, then reopened by the Franciscans. They run it today."

"I guess any place with a long history is bound to have a lot of strange stories connected with it."

Willie nodded. "In 1646, there was a scandal when an Indian charged one of the friars with fooling around with the man's wife. Another friar was accused by the Indians of sexual crimes of a . . . less *savory* nature. Then, in 1652, Fray Jose de Guerra hanged himself. Still later, another one of the brothers apparently went mad and wandered out into the desert, where either the sun or the Indians finished him off. His body was never found."

The old man's intensity and the information he was providing intrigued Paul, who said, "So the mission had a pretty checkered past, hmm?" knowing full well that his words would encourage Willie.

"Indeed it did, indeed it did." Willie chuckled to himself at some private joke, then continued, "The last two Casserite padres were killed by the Indians during the Pueblo Uprising of 1680. The mission was empty during the rebellions of 1692 and 1696. Funny thing, though—the Indians never came near the place."

"Why was that?"

"Superstitions, I guess." He shrugged. "Any Indian who knew, kept it to himself."

"There's mention of Agastan Pueblo in this book. Is it still standing?"

Willie shook his head. "The Spanish burned the original pueblo of Agastan in 1681, when they tried to recapture these parts. It was in the hills due west of here. The Tawa folk who lived there were either killed or made slaves or scattered to other pueblos. When Vargas retook the territory from the Indians in 1692, the Franciscans came and took charge of the mission and restored it. Later, a branch of the Tawa tribe moved into the area and built another pueblo, Nuevo Agastan—but that's north of here. They wouldn't go near Old Agastan. The place is in ruins now, but some of the old stories hang on."

Paul felt a growing curiosity and something of the excitement of small boys exchanging spooky stories in the dark as he asked, "What sort of stories?"

"That the ghost of Father Perez still haunts these parts. And the ghost of El Brujo."

"Who was El Brujo?" asked Paul, now thoroughly caught up in the narrative.

"A local witch doctor/medicine man/sorcerer . . . what have you. He got a lot of the Tawas worked up by claiming to have visions of the future. He told the Indians the land would run red with the blood of the Spaniards and that divine fire would purge the land of all foreigners and their foreign ways . . . meaning the Spanish, of course. He was especially outraged by the Catholic religion. He claimed that the Spanish beliefs were the marks of madmen, and that they—the padres, especially—were making all the Indians insane by forcing them to become Christians.

"Needless to say, Father Perez and El Brujo clashed head on. Father Perez saw the medicine man as the servant of the devil; El Brujo saw all Spanish priests as crazy men who were contaminating the Indian people with their insanity. They skirmished a couple of times before Perez was murdered."

Willie paused to study the effect of his words on Paul. Surprised, the younger man said, "Someone murdered the priest?"

Willie gave a harsh chuckle. "This area has a lot of strange history. Murder's just a small part of it. We've got a couple of folks in town who claim to be able to get in touch with spirits and feel out what kids today would call the 'vibrations' of this place."

"Well?" Paul was impatient with the old man's stop-and-go storytelling. "What have they found out?"

Willie put a finger to the side of his nose, looking like an emaciated, hairless St. Nick. "The vibrations are not good. In fact, according to some, we're sitting in an atmosphere of violence, weirdness, demons. "He bugged his eyes exaggeratedly. "To hear them tell it, we're a direct line to the nine circles of hell."

He had gone too far. Paul was more interested in the factual. He asked, "Did El Brujo murder Padre Perez?"

"It's pretty certain he at least had a hand in it. He lit out on a 'holy pilgrimage' to the west right after, and was never seen in these parts again."

Willie added reflectively, "There's a legend that when the padre and the sorcerer went at each other, they dragged their respective gods into the fight. Some folks hold that things got pretty well stirred up—things which maybe haven't quite settled down, even yet. The same people point to the up-and-down history of the mission as a kind of proof."

"And you, Mr. Kavan—what do you think?"

"I think the history of this place is pretty interesting. I've made it a hobby. As for ghosts and such like, well, I'm open on the subject."

Willie went back to his desk and opened a bottom drawer, saying, "Well, now that I've about talked your ear off, let me get you the other book I was talking about." He pulled out a thick red-bound book and handed it to Paul. It was titled *A History of Mission Nuestra Señora de Agastan* and was written by someone named Bradford Loomis.

"Seems innocent enough," said Paul, "—the title, I mean." He felt a curious reluctance to touch the volume.

Willie ignored his hesitation and thrust the book into his hands. "Oh, Loomis is pretty deadpan about his information. Only, he includes *all* the facts—or, at least, what he *believes* are facts. Poke through it. Sit on the couch, why don't you? I'll be in the back if you need anything."

Willie left through the narrow doorway at the back of the room, pushing aside the strands of red and blue beads.

Paul moved two grimy stacks of *National Geographic* off the couch and sat down, as Willie had suggested. But he didn't open the book at first, letting it rest, closed, on his knees. He was aware of the smells of dust and mold; there was no sound from the back of the shop. And the room, in spite of its sunlight, was surprisingly chilly. He looked at the book and thought of a magician's grimoire—filled with magic spells and ages-old secrets. His hand shook inexplicably when he finally took a deep breath, opened the book, and began to read:

In 1621, Fray Alonso Perez, a priest of the Spanish missionary Casserite Order, led two other Brothers of the same order out of Mexico City. With a handful of native guides, the party made its way north into the Territory of New Mexico.

Early in 1622, just southwest of the Rio Sonoliento, he founded the church and *convento* (priest's house) of Nuestra Señora de Agastan (Our Lady of Agastan) when, it is reported, the Virgin appeared to him on The Hill of the Vision and told him that his duty lay here in converting the Indians from their "heathen" ways.

The mission was established near the Tawa Indian pueblo of Agastan. Fray Alonso and his assistants, Fray Tomas de Zavalaeta and Fray Diego de la Cadena, worked tirelessly to convert the Indians of the pueblo.

They were hampered in their good works when a medicine man, known only as El Brujo, The Sorcerer, appeared out of the west (perhaps from the Hopi or Zuni pueblos—though his actual origins are unknown to this day) and urged the Indians to return to their old, pantheistic religion. So strong were the personality and persuasions of El Brujo that the work of the missionaries faltered. The attendance at mass grew sparse. Father Perez's assistants began to talk of abandoning the mission and returning to Mexico City.

Father Perez remained unshaken; he was convinced that he had a mandate from heaven and that, thus supported, his efforts would prevail.

In 1632, with the outcome of the struggle still uncertain, Father Perez reportedly healed a case of blindness in a native child by spitting into his palm, rolling a little mud in it, and placing this on the eyes of the boy while speaking the words, "Be opened." This astonishing cure resulted in the immediate conversion of numerous Indians.

El Brujo, angered at his subsequent loss of power through the adherence of so many of his people to the padres, pretended to make amends and presented Father Perez with a gift of some loaves of *pan de maíz* (corn bread), which were poisoned. After sampling the bread at his noon meal, the priest immediately realized what had happened and prevented his assistants from touching the lethal bread. Then, refusing assistance, he went to the chapel alone, where, he later reported, an angel appeared to him and placed a hand upon his forehead, saying, "Thy time is not yet come."

The priest recovered and spent the night in prayer. In the morning he walked to the pueblo and confronted El Brujo, accusing him of his crime and proclaiming the power of the Spanish God. El Brujo lost face and the ranks of converts continued to swell. The mission flourished; the padres prospered. Father Perez made several missionary journeys among the more westerly Navajos and Zunis.

Then on Sunday, February 22, 1632, El Brujo managed to convince most of the Indian converts not to attend mass. Father Perez, fiery and zealous as always, set out toward the pueblo, accompanied by Brother Tomas. Meeting some baptized Indians along the way, he began to remonstrate with them. The Indians, however, responded by drawing weapons. Realizing that the Indians intended to kill them on the spot, Father Perez knelt down and raised a crucifix toward their attackers; then he and Brother Tomas said a prayer to the Virgin in Latin.

According to reports, the Indians started forward, then halted; they were terrified by something which seemed to stand behind the two Casserites. Both Father Perez and Brother Tomas reported feeling a cold wind at their backs. Neither would turn around because, they felt, "The power of the Lord was manifest, and we were unworthy to behold such majesty." The Indians fled, nor would any of them ever talk about what they had seen.

Father Perez and Brother Tomas proceeded to the plaza of the pueblo. Father Perez went into the house of the sorcerer, who was absent, and took out more than two hundred kachinas and burned them in the public square, proclaiming them the handiwork of the devil. The Indians watched in silence; no one opposed him.

The following Sunday, the church was filled to over-flowing.

Three nights later, Father Perez was murdered in his room and his head removed from his body. There were no witnesses to the crime. Brother Tomas discovered the body when he went to arouse his superior for matins the following morning.

In the resultant uproar, it was discovered that an Indian servant from the pueblo had also disappeared. The immediate conclusion was that this man was responsible for the murder. His whereabouts was never discovered.

The other Indian servants pleaded ignorance and distress about the crime. They soon fled, however, fearing the wrath of the Spanish authorities.

The mutilated body of Father Perez was interred in the mission cemetery; his head was never recovered.

When the authorities investigating the crime visited the Agastan pueblo, they found that El Brujo had disappeared. The natives talked vaguely of his having gone on a "holy journey" to the west. Inside his house, the soldiers reportedly found a strange wall painting showing a bearded priest, presumably Father Perez, being struck down by two giant kachinas. This part of the story is the most doubtful of all, since the single witness proved highly unreliable on other occasions, and the sorcerer's house was burned by the Spanish as a warning to the Indians.

Paul set aside the book and looked at his watch: it was almost one o'clock. He should have been back at the motel long ago.

He stood up and called, "Mr. Kavan?" When he got no response, he moved closer to the bead-hung doorway and called again, more loudly this time, "*Mr. Kavan?*"

"I'm sorry," explained Willie, pushing aside the bead strands; "I was having some lunch in the back."

"I've got to leave; my wife is expecting me. I enjoyed the book; is it for sale?" Paul felt a desire to reread and study the passages he had just read. He had the nagging feeling that he had missed something, that he had let some piece of information important to himself slip by.

He was thinking, too, of his dream of a giant priest the day before while he slept out on the desert. The book and his vision seemed connected, though he couldn't really grasp the thread tying them together.

But Willie said, "It's a collector's item; I couldn't sell it."

Instead, Paul bought another history called *Legends of the Tawa,* and some other books he had chosen.

As he was opening the front door, Willie said to him, "The ruins of the old pueblo are just a short drive out toward the hills. Most tourists seem to miss them, and they're worth a look-see. There are caves just behind the pueblo with interesting formations. I'd be happy to act as a guide for you and your missus. The Agastan Caves aren't really open to the public, but I could give you a quickie tour . . . if you're interested."

"We don't have a car . . ." Paul was unsure why he hesitated. Something about the idea of caves disturbed him. He had a fragmentary flash of memory—dim caverns and red, watching eyes—perhaps from a dream.

"I always use my jeep."

"I'm afraid not, but thanks anyway. Knock wood"—Paul

tapped the doorframe for reassurance—"we'll be on our way to Santa Fe tomorrow."

"Well, if you change your mind or things don't work out with the car on schedule, let me know. We could drive out tomorrow and spend the afternoon. I think you and your wife would find it worth the time."

"I'm sure we would."

"Just let me know if anything changes. There's not much to see at the ruins, but the caves are something special."

"Thank you again, Mr. Kavan," said Paul, stepping out into the sunlight.

"Willie," the other corrected with a smile.

Paul returned the smile. "Willie, then. Maybe we'll see you again before we leave town."

"I hope so. Enjoy your books." The scarred wooden door shut behind Paul.

The screen door of cabin twelve was closed, but the inside door was open. Paul could hear voices.

Sheila and Louise Shore were sitting in the room's two chairs. A bottle of bourbon and a coffee can filled with ice were perched on the edge of the dresser, within easy reach of both women, who were drinking out of styrofoam coffee cups. A copy of *Shogun* was tented open on Sheila's unmade bed.

Paul came in and sat on the edge of his own bed, not removing his sunglasses.

"I'm sorry I'm late. Hello, Louise."

Sheila said, "Are you late? I guess I lost track of the time." From her voice Paul could tell she was a little high.

Louise said, "What in God's name did you find to *do* out here at the end of the world?"

"I was talking to the old man, Willie, who runs the souvenir shop on the other side of town."

"Willie Kavan?" asked Louise. She laughed. "Did you ever hear *anyone* who could talk as much as Willie?"

Paul started to make a remark, caught a *look* from Sheila, and held his tongue.

Louise, oblivious, continued, " 'Course, old Willie knows a shitpile—pardon my French!—about the history of the neighborhood; his problem is that nobody else much cares.

He can sure talk up a storm; I'm surprised you got away the same day." Louise noticed the books he had slid carelessly onto the nightstand and asked, "You buy those from Willie? What are they?"

Paul showed the women the books.

Louise made a face and said, "Well, I'd have preferred a good story, myself."

"Actually, they're a gift. For Sheila. She's also very much interested in local history."

Sheila smiled vaguely at Paul. "Thank you for the books. That was sweet. I'll look at them later. When we don't have company."

Louise confided to Paul, "We're both just taking a little rest from our chores, what with this awful heat and all." Paul was aware of how skimpy her yellow halter-top seemed, how full her breasts were as she rubbed a hand lazily across her chest.

She was wearing lime-green short-shorts so tight they were cutting into the flesh of her thigh. She had taken off her sandals earlier and was rubbing the ball of her right foot in lazy circles on the worn carpet.

From behind his sunglasses, Paul glanced at Sheila. She was wearing a tan long-sleeved blouse and jeans and had tied back her hair with a blue scarf. She seemed tired and slightly tipsy and a good deal older than Louise—though they could be no more than five or six years apart in age.

Louise said, "Find yourself a glass and join us. Or we can share mine; I'm just about finished."

Paul shook his head. "Not in this heat, on an empty stomach..."

Louise shrugged, refilled her cup, and dropped in another ice cube. "One for the road," she explained, then asked abruptly, "Willie tell you about the ghost?"

"Which ghost?" asked Paul. "He said there might be quite a few hanging around."

"I don't know about that. I meant the ghost of Padre Perez. Without a head. He's supposed to wander around, looking for his head. They say he can't rest until he finds his head and everyone knows the truth about how he died. Which is pretty stupid, because everyone *knows* it was the Indians who killed him."

"Sounds like the old Headless Horseman stories from back East."

"Yeah, it does, doesn't it?" She shrugged again. "Still, it's a good story."

"Talk about headhunting ghosts," Sheila interjected, "ancient man was pretty fond of collecting heads himself. In the Old Stone Age, men thought that a man's vital energy was stored in the head. They would eat the brains of their enemies to increase their own supply of life energy. They would remove the head and break away the bone at the base of the skull, then—"

Louise interrupted, "Ugh! I—"

But Sheila quieted her with a queenly wave of her hand. "Oh, brain eating was pretty widespread among the Neanderthals. Sometimes—but not necessarily—cannibalism went along with it. The idea of all that life-stuff stored there made the head a pretty valuable item. Later, in more civilized times, skulls were turned into drinking cups which were supposed to increase the drinker's life-span. Even some good Christians made skull-cups in medieval times." She paused.

Louise was using one red-painted fingernail to punch holes in the top of her styrofoam cup. Paul was trying to decide whether two aspirins or a ham sandwich would help his head more.

Sheila made a face and said, "That's enough ghost stories for now. I—" She hiccoughed. "Excuse me a minute," she said, getting somewhat unsteadily to her feet, "I think I'm going to use the powder room."

Both Louise and Paul watched her shaky progress across the room and through the bathroom door, which slammed loudly.

When Paul heard the sound of running water, he turned and asked Louise, "Do you know anything about the Agastan Caves? Willie Kavan talked a lot about them." He was having a hard time not looking at the gleaming sweat filming her throat and breasts.

"Oh, sure, they're famous in these parts. Willie took Jimmy and me over there once. They aren't nearly as nice as Carlsbad Caverns, what with the gift shop and lunch room and all they have down there. And there's some other caves, over in Texas, that're *really* something to see: they've got colored lights all around and a drive-through shuttle bus." Louise considered a moment. "I don't really like poking around in caves; I'm always afraid that the lights will go out and I'll be lost in the dark forever." She shuddered and finished her bourbon in a single gulp.

The bathroom door opened and Sheila announced cheerily, "Well, I'm ready for lunch." She had her own sunglasses on. Though she sounded fairly pulled-together, she was still unsteady. Paul crossed to her and took her arm, saying, "I've been ready for ages. Let's go see what our favorite coffee shop has to offer. . . . Uh, would you like to join us, Louise?"

She buckled her sandals and stood up. "Thanks for the invitation, but I've got to get a move on and take Jimmy out some lunch." She gathered up the nearly empty bourbon bottle and the ice can and dropped the empty cups into the wastebasket beside the dresser. "See you folks later. Have a good lunch."

Paul watched the figure in the lemon-and-lime outfit cross the motel court and disappear into the office while Sheila hunted for her purse.

5 Helen Anderson

The heat in the Pata Blanca suppressed their appetites. Paul only poked at his omelet and Sheila left half her sandwich on her plate.

They sat at a table near a window; both left their sunglasses on. They sipped the strong, black, chickory-flavored coffee. Paul's headache, which had subsided momentarily, had returned and was now a steady pain behind his eyes.

He slipped his fingers up under his glasses and pressed them against his closed lids; the pressure gave some relief from the pain. After a moment, he reached to his right and picked up Sheila's purse from the empty chair between them. He rummaged for the tin of Bayer Aspirin she always kept in the side pocket of her purse. His fingers encountered the coolness of metal links; he drew out Sheila's blood-moon necklace, holding it over the center of the table while sunlight glinted off the silver circle framing the disk of blood-colored coral.

"This really is a beautiful piece. Why do you keep it in your purse?" he asked, his eyes never leaving the silver chain wrapped around his fingers.

"I'm afraid of losing it; I feel safer knowing it's with me."

"Why not put it in a safe? Even a dump like the Four Star must have a safe."

"I feel safer when it's with me," she repeated. "I *want* it with me. Besides," she added, "I don't think I'd trust a safe at the Four Star at all."

"It's your necklace." He let it slip back, snapped the purse shut, and handed it back to her.

She said, "You never got your aspirin."

"I think you're out."

"I must have left that tin somewhere. We can pick up some more when we leave here." She started to get up; he reached for his wallet to pay the waitress.

After the heavy, greasy heat inside the restaurant, the air outside, smelling slightly of gasoline and dust, was a pleasant change. The day was warm, but heating up fast. Paul and Sheila walked under awnings and overhangs to avoid direct sunlight.

As they passed the little Anderson Gallery, Sheila said, "Look: they're open for business. Let's go in and have a peek."

Though there were a number of very amateur paintings by other local artists inside, most of the display was devoted to the works of Helen and Cyrus Anderson.

A smiling broad-faced woman sat on a canvas-and-metal director's chair under a massive painting of one-half of a cow's skull against a blue-white sky. The single eye socket was painted in violent swirls of red and pink. The painting was signed, "Helen Anderson."

The woman's large hands, unadorned except for a simple gold wedding band, were cupped over the ends of the chair's arms. She smiled at them but said nothing. Paul guessed that she was in her mid- to late forties. Her windblown hair, once red but faded to the color of sand and streaked with gray, rose in a corona around her head. Looking again at the picture of the skull on the wall above her, he suddenly decided the whole composition could be titled, *The Priestess*.

Under her scrutiny, they felt obliged to pretend a greater appreciation than they felt for the paintings around them.

They found little of genuine interest until they discovered, in one corner, half a dozen rather startling paintings of faces. Sheila found, upon closer examination of the primitive portraits, such an essential strangeness of eye and feature that they seemed to roar out of their frames at the onlookers. The visages seemed to be emerging out of fire and wind. What bits of visible landscape could be glimpsed themselves seemed melting and churning. The vitality in these paintings contrasted dramatically with the rather smug and lifeless works that crowded most of the shop.

The proprietress noticed their interest and came over, standing a little behind them as all three faced the paintings. "Those *are* unusual, aren't they?" she said conversationally. "The artist is a local girl—Maria Seloso. She's a full-blooded Tawa Indian. She's only sixteen; she lives with her sister just outside the town. Nobody can walk through this store without stopping to take a long look at these faces."

"I can't say I really *like* them," Sheila said. "I find them, well, *disturbing*."

The woman laughed. "Most people react the same way. They look but they tell me they'd be afraid to have one in their home."

Paul said, "I notice they're all marked 'Not for Sale.' "

The woman nodded. "They're a part of our private collection. We *couldn't* part with them but we feel we can *share* them this way."

Sheila shook her head and turned away, saying, "I get the oddest feeling from them—almost as if they were done by someone disturbed or not quite in her right mind."

The woman nodded emphatically. "You're right, in a way. Those are all trance paintings: every one was done by Maria while under hypnosis during séances. The child is a natural medium. Two of the paintings were done under bright lights; two were done in a darkened room; two were done in the dark after the child was blindfolded. As you can see, the quality of them remains consistent; in her trance state, she exhibits abilities of the most extraordinary nature. We—my husband and I—have been tapping the child's mediumistic talents for almost a year now. We—Cyrus and I—feel that she may be in the class of Eusapia Paladino," and she folded her arms as if the name somehow explained everything.

Paul looked blank; Sheila shook her head. The name meant nothing to either one.

With a sigh and a faint smile, the woman said, "I see you're not students of psychic phenomena. Eusapia Paladino was one of the greatest mediums the world has ever known."

Paul said, "Well, this is all certainly very interesting, but I think, *Sheila*, we should be getting along. I want to see how Jimmy is making out with the car . . . ?"

Sheila refused to take the cue; she said, "We have all day to see about the car, Paul," and she gave him a little smile that seemed to ask, *Indulge me a bit . . .* before turning and asking the woman, "How did you happen to discover this girl Maria?"

"By accident. No, what I mean is, *fate*. We—my husband and I— are convinced that there are no accidents; everything is ordained by fate. We were destined to come to this place at this time and meet Maria and collaborate on The Book."

"You're writing a book, then?" Sheila asked. "A study of trance phenomena? I've always been interested in the religious aspects of things like possession. My grandmother, who was Irish, supposedly had a gift of second sight. She could supposedly tell when someone was going to die because someone already dead would appear to her and she'd know they'd come for whoever was ill. When she died, I thought I saw my uncle—her son—who had died several years earlier. I thought at the time that her gift had been passed on to me." She laughed suddenly. "It scared me. But nothing really ever happened since." She shrugged.

The older woman considered Sheila a moment before saying, "If you had the gift, you still have it. The circumstances just haven't been right—but when you least expect it, you'll become aware of it again."

Paul, sensing an uneasiness in his wife, said, "You were telling us about your book . . ."

"Yes, well, we're less interested in the *how* of Maria's heightened awareness than the message she is transmitting to us from the outside. Actually, neither of us—Cyrus or myself—is really doing much beyond putting down on paper what Maria dictates when she's under the control of other beings. I transcribe in shorthand while Cyrus tapes each sitting. Afterward, we compare the initial transcription with the tape to get an accurate copy. We lose very little except when Maria shouts or mumbles or slips into Spanish or Latin or one of the local Indian dialects. Even then, we can usually piece things together satisfactorily. Both Cyrus and I speak some Spanish; we correspond with several people at the University of New Mexico for the Latin or Native American portions. We send copies of the tape and a phonetic transcription. They've been really helpful, and they keep reassuring us how important our project is."

Sheila asked, "If Maria is only the medium, then who—or what—is dictating the book through her?"

Mrs. Anderson shook her head. "We're not really certain. There appears to be more than one personality involved; they take turns controlling the girl. There seem to be two dominant presences—one masculine and one feminine. When asked their identities, the woman says she speaks for spiritual beings living in a place they call 'Beneath the Ground' or 'Below Place.' The man might be a padre connected with the old mission. He's much weaker; we have a hard time understanding the Latin and Spanish of his communications. Sometimes Maria acts like she's almost choking on the words. What we *can* make out seems to be mostly bits and pieces of history scrambled in with a lot of warnings that make no sense at all, because those are the times when Maria is most unable to force any words out. We've had to terminate several sessions early because of her distress—as if the effort of shaping words was going to strangle her."

Louise Shore, Willie Kavan, and now this woman, Paul thought. El Centro was certainly filled with a fascinating selection of characters. He tried to shoot Sheila a let's-get-a-move-on glance but he was unable to catch her eye. She asked, "What do these—spirits, or whatever—tell you? What is your book about?"

"At the moment, it's something of a jumble. . . . The 'Below Folk' talk about emerging into our world from the 'Below Place' to bring an important message to us. At this point, some sort of barrier prevents their crossing over, but they hope, with our aid, to be able to break through soon. There are a lot of things in what they share that we don't understand: references to kachinas and to the moon and fire and blood. And a sunrise in the west. Cyrus thinks it's all connected with some ancient religious ceremony. If we understand, we might be able to help them cross over."

Struck by a sudden thought, Paul asked, "Mightn't it be dangerous to bring them though? I mean, who's to say their intentions are honorable?"

Mrs. Anderson looked genuinely annoyed. "Our experience with astral beings—with *any* intelligence from outside—has always led us to the certainty that these beings—superior because of their *ethereal* composition—are motivated only by the purest motives. Take my word for it: they are bringing us love and wisdom and nothing more. We're not mistaken; they will bring our world nothing but good."

Sheila said, "It sounds like everything you've discovered about these beings is connected with local Indian religion—I mean, kachinas and so forth."

"Yes," the woman agreed, "but that might just come from Maria's background—some sort of racial memory which is influencing her to express abstract ideas in images already there in her mind. Or there may be some spirit beings called kachinas existing on another plane." She sighed before continuing. "There's so *much* we have to learn. We know there's still a lot of the old Indian religion around, though they keep it pretty well hidden so that most white folk know little or nothing about it."

"Have you lived here long?" Paul asked.

"We—Cyrus and I—moved here just over five years ago. Before that, we owned a chain of Christian bookstores in St. Louis. We sold out—in every sense of the word." She laughed loudly at her own joke. "We'd begun getting interested in the occult, especially in psychic phenomena, through reading about faith healing and glossolalia—speaking in tongues—and so forth. We had enough money, so we decided to devote ourselves to studying these things. At the time we drove West, with an idea of settling in either Arizona or California, because of the climate. But when we stopped here—we thought just for overnight—fate, or a sixth sense, or whatever, said, 'This is where we stop.' And so we did."

"Just like Father Perez," said Paul.

"*Exactly*. We had *our* call as sure as he had *his*. Only our stay here has been less, well, *catastrophic*. We've got a comfortable life. The gallery is more a hobby than a moneymaker. What's most important is that we met Maria. She started out to be our *housekeeper;* now the three of us are working on The Book. We just have bits and pieces of the whole right now, but when we're through, the world is never going to be the same."

She stopped suddenly, shaking her head. "That's enough about me. Where are you folks from?"

Sheila answered, "California. We teach at a private college near Berkeley. I'm in anthropology. My husband is in the English department."

"I known this is a long shot, but by any chance do you know Christabel Winter? She's an old friend of mine. When

I lived in Berkeley with my first husband years ago, I used to work in a bookstore. I got to know Christabel because she was one of the poets who gave regular readings in the store. And she had real psychic talents. I know, because I went to several séances she gave—even though the church I belonged to at the time didn't approve of such 'devil's work.' "

"We've known Christabel for years," said Paul. "She's a good friend who's helped us through some rocky times."

"When you get back to Berkeley, tell her Helen Anderson—I was Helen MacDonald then—was asking after her. I doubt she'll remember me. But you never can tell. Mention it anyway."

"We will. I think," said Paul, making a show of looking at his watch, "we'd better get a move on." He stared emphatically at Shiela.

"All right," she conceded, adding, "I enjoyed talking with you, Helen."

"You know, I don't even know your names. Isn't that crazy?" the other woman said, folding her large hands around Sheila's. "Tell me your names *at once*."

"I'm Sheila Barrett, and this is my husband, Paul."

"I've enjoyed talking with you both. Are you visiting friends in town?"

"Our car broke down yesterday," said Paul. "It's supposed to be fixed by tomorrow, then we're off to Santa Fe."

"Where are you staying?"

"The Four Star," said Sheila.

"Oh, Louise Shore's place," sniffed Helen in a tone that implied she cared very little for Louise or the Four Star. "And I *know* there's not not a decent place to eat anywhere around. Listen! As long as you're staying tonight, why not come over for dinner? We—Cyrus and I—lose touch with the outside world. We'd appreciate your company. And I can guarantee you a meal that will be a change from the deep-fry horrors they call local cuisine."

Her voice took on a different quality. "Maria will be with us tonight. We're going to *collaborate*. You could meet her." She pressed Sheila's hand with sudden intensity. "Don't be difficult now; say yes."

Sheila hesitated, "I don't think we could. I'm—"

"We couldn't impose," Paul added.

But Sheila suddenly capitulated. "No . . . it's a fine idea.

Who could resist a decent meal after all these weeks on the road?" In reality, the woman intrigued her. Sheila's interest in highly personal, esoteric, frequently female-centered religious experiences had been alerted by what Helen Anderson had said. What the woman described seemed, at least in part, religious in nature. But she kept this from Paul, to avoid making the proposed dinner sound like nothing more than an anthropological fact-gathering session.

Paul made no protest but glared at his wife. She met his look and stared right back. In the end, Paul looked away, shaking his head.

"Wonderful," said Helen Anderson as she released Sheila's hand and walked with them toward the door. "Now, run along and do what you have to do. Oh, I almost forgot—"

She gave them directions to her house, which was only a few blocks away. They would be expected around seven.

Outside the shop, Paul snapped, "Why on earth—?"

"She's an original and she's amusing. It might be an interesting evening in an off-the-wall sort of way. I'm bored with the motel and I've still got indigestion from dinner."

The sun seemed to explode in angry waves in his stomach and head. "Jesus Christ! I can't believe you've tied us into an evening of spirit-world nonsense."

Sheila grinned at him, her eyes crinkling beneath her sunglasses. "No one's *forcing* you to do anything, Paul. If you don't want to go, don't go. I'm thinking I may pick up some useful local history, if nothing else."

"This town," he said, staring at the sun-bright storefronts across the deserted street. "What a goddamned *hole*!" He was surprised at the depth of his anger, the suddenness with which it had arisen. He almost felt his anger was a fearful response. But what was he afraid of? The overweight shopkeeper? The empty sunlit street? The fiery-eyed paintings by the Indian girl who had visions? Nonsense—might as well think of Sheila as a threat. Making an effort to control his still-raging anger, he said, "Let's drop the question of tonight—"

She shrugged.

"—and let's see what's happening with the car. Afterward, I want to go for a hike, just to get a change of scenery."

Before setting out, they stopped by the motel to change

to shoes with heavy soles for hiking. They took their hats also: Paul, his blue-and-white striped railroad cap and Sheila, the Stetson she had bought for a joke in Texas but had become quite fond of.

Jimmy Shore's truck was gone; Jimmy was nowhere around. The double doors of the shed were padlocked, so they had no way to see how repairs were progressing.

The afternoon stretched out hotly all around them. They followed a path which ran through the remnants of farm fields behind the repair shop into the desert; their goal was a distant line of cottonwood and willow trees.

The fields they walked through had run to sand and weeds; the fences had mostly fallen down. A rusting tractor with the frayed remains of a yellow-and-black awning over the driver's seat was parked behind the cluster of outbuildings that marked the edge of the property. Past this, they pushed through dried bushes, walking on sand or hard-packed earth. The thread of a path was almost overgrown.

At a distance they could see a little white house, its tin roof gleaming in the sun. Two old horses, swaybacked and as dusty looking as the house's fading paint, were tethered in the front yard. Laundry stirred listlessly on a rope run from the front porch to a withered tree.

The ground underfoot rose and fell, gathering itself into dunes, then opening into shallow depressions. The covering of sagebrush, dried grass, and darker shrubs occasionally gave way to bare patches of sand or sand-colored earth. The sky was an intense blue overhead, flecked with small bits of clouds like fragments of larger cloud-masses.

Once a crow startled them, rising sudden and black from a tangle of dried bushes.

When they turned to look, the town behind them was a tiny scattering of buildings; the highway was marked by a line of diminished telephone and power poles. Everything shrank under the white-hot sun; El Centro seemed nearly lost in the desert sweeping toward the encircling low hills obscured by a bluish early afternoon haze.

They marched on, alert to the dangers of rattlesnakes and thorns and loose rocks.

Sheila spoke first. She had paused to stare at a cluster of lemon-yellow flowers while she rubbed a hand across her forehead and said, "I feel a little dizzy. It must be the sun."

"Do you want to stop and rest? Or should we go back to town?" Paul asked. He felt genuinely concerned about her, though there was enough residual anger in him to derive a certain satisfaction from her discomfort.

After a moment he put out his hand to her but she moved away, shaking her head and saying, "Let's keep walking— at least as far as the creek. I think there must be a creek if all those trees are there. I'll be fine if I can just get into the shade."

She was striding across the sand, pushing aside weeds and sage. She seemed possessed, intent on reaching the ragged line of trees.

His anger flared again. The desert seemed hot enough to burst into flame; his head was throbbing. He ran after her, shouting, "For God's sake, slow down; you're going to step in a hole or something worse!"

She slowed down. He caught up with her, put his hand on her shoulder, and jerked her to a stop, then spun her around to face him. He pulled off her sunglasses so he could look into her eyes. Her expression was unreadable. She seemed oblivious of him. For a moment he thought she had suffered a sunstroke. Then she smiled at him and said, "What are you afraid of, Paul?"

His anger was at full throttle as he shouted, "That you'll break your neck, for openers. What the hell do you mean? You *have* had too much sun!" Again there came to him that fleeting sense of danger, of some menace lurking behind the sunny surface of things. There was a mocking look in her eyes which made him wonder illogically if she saw something he didn't. Did she see a threat she would not tell? "What the *hell* is going on in your *head*?"

She started to respond, then thought better of it. The un-fathomable look faded, leaving only an expression of tired-ness. Finally she said wearily, "I'm not feeling well; I don't know *what* I'm saying."

Then she was walking forward again, this time at a careful pace, toward the cottonwoods and willows, while he stood behind her, staring at her retreating figure. After a few minutes, he followed, but at a distance, feeling his anger drain away as suddenly as it had flooded him, swallowed up by the desert sand as swiftly and as tracelessly as water.

Sheila was surprised by her own behavior. She had felt empty all morning; burned out by the sun. She brushed aside the scrub, was heedless of occasional nettles. She was moving through an empty place filled with sand and dry grass and burning sunlight. She was hardly aware of Paul behind her. The sun was hot on her arms, the dusty, thick air dried her lungs, and she felt hollow as a cistern waiting for long-overdue rain.

She felt a need to cry, but the desert wind sucked her eyes dry of tears. Out of nowhere had come a scorching sense of failure and futility. She longed for evening, for night, for the mystery and coolness moonrise promised. It was the heat, she realized vaguely, making the parched waste around her seem an extension of the landscape of her heart. Paul called out to her but she couldn't understand what he was saying— no longer could bear the sound of his voice.

She ran on past the screen of dry-looking willows and cottonwoods to pause on the bank of a creekbed. The creek itself was nothing but a sad trickle of sluggish, mud-brown water islanded with smooth rounded stones baking in the sun—stones which clearly belonged below the surface of a winter-replenished stream. The flat, sandy stretches of creek bed held patches of mingled red and white flowers; halfway up the bank grew several spindly sunflowers. Near her were silvery trunks and shining leaves of the cottonwoods.

Nothing stirred; nothing made a sound.

She was aware that Paul had come up behind her; she could feel him staring at her. She was trapped in sun-generated confusion; but some hidden truth, some new awareness, she felt, was emerging deep inside her—groping, clawing its way upward into consciousness.

She turned to look at him and discovered just how much they had become strangers to one another.

They stood looking at each other for a long time, then Paul's eyes shifted to someplace just beyond her. He said, "Not much of a creek, is it? Not much of anything out here, is there?"

"No." She was aware of the sun burning her face as she carelessly brushed her hat brim up and away from her eyes. She could feel sweat gathering in her armpits, soaking her blouse, making the cloth stick to her back. She felt as if the whole desert were on fire and that she was burning with it.

His eyes returned to her, studied her. She noticed how his lips were pressed together into a tight line; he rubbed his chin with the fingertips of his right hand.

He started toward her, holding his right hand out to her; she accepted his steadying clasp wordlessly.

She felt that something was about to happen. That sense of something inside of her—some emotion, some consciousness—waiting to be born. Groping toward the light.

She allowed him to lead her down the slope toward the creek bottom. She thought, *to whoever is watching us, we must look like lovers, walking hand in hand*. And found the thought—crazy as it was—disturbing enough to make her glance around as though the flimsy trees, the wind-scorched sand hid some observer.

No one; nothing; no breath of air. When they were nearly at the bottom, he began pulling her along a route parallel to the trickle of muddy water. She could feel his urgency, could sense some growing excitement in him. She had the impression he was searching for something he felt very near to finding.

Though they were utterly alone, Sheila again had the feeling that someone was watching them. She scanned the stream banks for movement and searched the skimpy shadows under the trees for the unseen, merely *felt*, observer. There was no one. Who—or what—did she expect to find?

In the shade of a lone tree which overhung the bank was a shallow depression, filled with brown sand and masses of the tiny red and white flowers.

This was the place Paul was searching for. He dropped to his knees and pulled Sheila down into the sand and shadow with him. She was aware only of the twisted shadow like a maze all around her.

She felt nothing as Paul pulled her face close to his and began kissing her with desperate passion. She was conscious only of the oppressive burden of the heat . . . the disturbing sense of an unseen watcher . . . the certainty of that deep awareness inside of her which was now painfully close to the surface—nearly emergent.

She did not resist or help when he began unzipping her jeans and tugging them down over her hips; but she un-

buttoned her blouse herself, vaguely afraid that, in his eager-
ness, he would tear loose the buttons. With his left hand
against her throat he pushed her back; she could feel his
right hand knotting itself in her bikini briefs, yanking them
down impatiently, then working the zipper of his own pants.

Neither said a word; she was aware of his ragged breathing, of his left hand kneading the flesh on her chest, just
below her neck.

The interlocking shadows of the withered branches seemed
to be twisting all around and over them, though no wind
moved the thick branches above them as she stared past
Paul's shoulder.

Beyond the network of the tree limbs she could see the
empty blue sky; she had the inexplicable idea that the sky
was darkening, as though stained a deep red. But there was
not even the fragment of a cloud visible to mar the hot blue
expanse.

He kissed her again, slamming his mouth against hers,
digging his tongue past her closed lips.

As he thrust himself into her, she could feel stones grinding into the small of her back, into the soft skin of her shoulders, buttocks, calves. She writhed on the sand and prickly
flowers, but her discomfort only excited him more.

She accepted the torment because something inside of her
warned her to be patient, to endure for the sake of the *new-
ness* waiting to be born in her, from her, through her.

Through her heat daze, she felt how little moisture was
between her legs, and there was little moisture from him: he
chafed her mercilessly as he pushed in, pulled back, then
thrust in deeper, urging himself toward climax. Some grains
of sand had become stuck to him; she cried out, but he took
her agony as cries of pleasure.

At the last possible moment, he withdrew and slid himself
into the fold between her stomach and partially raised left
leg so that she felt his semen, hot and sticky, surge across
her thigh and dribble down her left buttock. He gave a grunt
that sounded like surprise. He stared at her as though seeing
her for the first time.

Shaking, he stood up, zipping himself, and walked away
to sit on a large, flat stone, watching the muddy stream. He
would not look at her.

She lay for a moment looking up through the tangled

branches overhead; she still had the impression of shadows massing above her, hiding unseen watchers bent voyeuristically over the sandy hollow which yet held the two of them.

She sat up and found her purse, opened it, and pulled out a handkerchief to begin cleaning herself, noting the little flecks of blood mixed with other fluids.

The blood-moon necklace, tangled in the threads of the handkerchief, fell out and hit the ground with a metallic sound.

She picked it up and stared at it wonderingly, as if it were a talisman of some sort.

Paul stood up and said, "We'd better get back. And you'd better put that thing back in your purse." He continued to look out across the sand, avoiding her eyes.

But when he was not looking, she held it in the sun, fascinated by the way the sunlight transformed the silver moon circle to sun brightness, and deepened the coral red. What was it the old Indian woman had said? "When blood-moon becomes west-born blood-sun . . ." Or had that been something remembered from a dream? She looked up at the sun, just past its zenith, beginning its westward descent. She touched the disk of coral and silver to her lips before she returned it to her purse. When she had reassembled herself as neatly as possible, she said, "I'm ready. Help me up the bank."

As they made their way back to El Centro, neither mentioned what had happened.

Paul was lost in his own thoughts. He seemed to Sheila astonished by what had happened, by the part he had played.

She was aware of the pain between her legs. She felt a sadness because what was reaching agonizingly toward the light had not quite reached the brightness. She had the sense of something inside her shriveling to the size of a marble—not defeated, only momentarily thwarted. She had also the feeling that the watchers had retreated to a great distance—but not so far that they could not see the two of them making their way back to El Centro.

The only thing that remained unchanged was the sense of the desert, burning all around her, longing for the night.

PART TWO

You do advance your cunning more and more.
When truth kills truth, O devilish-holy fray!

A Midsummer Night's Dream: III, ii.

                              Are you sure
That we are awake? It seems to me
That yet we sleep, we dream.

A Midsummer Night's Dream: IV, i.

O monstrous! O strange! We are haunted.

A Midsummer Night's Dream: III, i.

6   The Séance

"I guess you find it hard to believe that anyone would move to El Centro by choice," said Cyrus Anderson, returning with a tray of drinks. "Let me see. . . . Scotch and water for you, Paul. And Sheila: gin and tonic. Club soda for me." He handed the drinks around, then sat down in a battered rocking chair, leaving the tray on the little table between the rocker and the couch on which Sheila and Paul sat.

Helen Anderson could be heard moving around in the kitchen; she had refused Sheila's offer of help, insisting, "Other people in my kitchen make me nervous."

Cyrus Anderson was good-natured, slightly paunchy and graying; he had a easy laugh, but Paul saw how sharply his eyes, behind the thick lenses of his glasses, noted every gesture that Paul or Sheila made and every look that passed between them.

Except for that incisive look, Cyrus struck Paul as more a visiting Rotarian than a man who was a sometime artist and dabbler in the occult. From his first welcome, Cyrus had worked to put the Barretts at their ease. *Apparently,* Paul thought to himself, *the tension we're under is evident even to this stranger*.

Sheila, who was sitting nearer to Cyrus, was having a lively discussion with the older man about the merits of a controversial young artist whose paintings had stirred up a great deal of both critical praise and damnation.

He settled back into the couch, savoring the smoothness of his drink and letting himself become acquainted with the room around him.

It was spacious, with whitewashed walls and a dark-beamed ceiling. The walls were lined with glass-fronted cabinets and open bookshelves crowded with pottery, baskets, pipes, fetishes, kachina dolls, and less-easily-definable items. Above the cabinets were hung samples of Navajo rugs, paintings by both Andersons, a collection of diamond-shaped Mexican "eyes of God," and a painting by the Indian girl Maria, the fire-bright eyes of which seemed to follow Paul's own eyes like those trick paintings in which the eyes appear to follow an observer everywhere.

Directly opposite Paul was a giant skull mask painted black, made from a huge hollow gourd. It had a jagged opening for the mouth; the serated edges were painted white like a demon's teeth. The eyes were two holes, banded with red and white. Paul had the momentary impression of a pair of real eyes watching him from inside the shadowed cavities.

A brick fireplace had been set diagonally into the far corner of the room, with a bright rug on the floor in front of it and two wooden chairs nearby.

The wall above the mantlepiece held a collection of old black-and-white photographs in simple wooden frames showing Pueblo Indian dances.

One picture in particular caught Paul's attention; it was a close-up of a dancer. The figure wore a long skirt of white painted all over with floral and geometric patterns; the shoulders were draped with a long-fringed black shawl of some shiny material which hung down below the waist. The dancer's right hand held a staff topped with a crucifix of unadorned wood; the left hand held a rattle, blurred in the photo because the dancer had moved it faster than the old camera could capture.

The sex of the dancer was indeterminate, due to a black cloth tied over the face, in which eye-slits were visible. The dancer wore a headdress of board, tall and curved at the top, with feathers fastened to either side. The shape of the headdress reminded Paul of something; it was painted white and in the center was a circle containing the design:

He was surprised to recognize the same design that was cut into the coral of Sheila's necklace.

Behind the dancer, less distinct, was a second dancer, similarly costumed.

The wall of a pueblo and a knot of onlookers were little more than a suggestion in the background.

Cyrus and Sheila finished their discussion; Cyrus turned to Paul, then looked to see what had caught the younger man's attention.

"Interesting photo, isn't it?" he asked with pride. "They were all taken around 1900." He got up and walked toward the photographs, still talking. "Those dancers are *matachines*; the dancer in that photo is a *macana*, a dance leader. The skirt is Indian in design but the shawl is Spanish. And the headdress"—Cyrus was in front of the picture now, indicating the various items with his finger "is pretty close to a Catholic bishop's miter. But this symbol"—he jabbed a finger at the design within the circle—"is a traditional symbol of the Earth Mother among many Pueblo people."

Sheila was staring at the design as Cyrus traced it lightly with his fingertip; she said, "I have that same design on my necklace, here," and she drew the blood-moon necklace out of her purse, which had been leaning against the back of the couch.

She held it out to Cyrus, who took it and held it up to the light for a better look. He nodded. "It's identical, all right. This particular version of the symbol is called a *Tapu'at* among the Hopis. The word means 'mother and child.' I don't recall the Tawa term for it at the moment, but it's similar. Anyhow, the main idea is spiritual rebirth from one world into the next. It goes back to the Pueblo idea that the first people came into this world from a lower world inside the earth. . . . Are you familiar with the story?"

Paul and Sheila nodded.

"Good. Well, the straight line running through the opening in the side represents the umbilical cord linking the child and mother and, at the same time, it stands for the line of emergence from the inner world to the outer. If you want to take it a bit further, you can think of the end of the line inside the design as the child within the womb; the other end, just outside the opening, is the child after it's born. There are a lot of other ideas hidden in the symbol, but that's the general idea." He returned the necklace to Sheila, asking, "Why aren't you wearing this? It's such a beautiful piece."

"Oh," she said vaguely, dropping the necklace into her purse, "I didn't feel it was . . . appropriate."

Cyrus shrugged and resumed his seat. "No one is sure of the origins of the dance there. I've heard people say it comes from the Aztecs, and just as many people have told me it derives from Southern Europe—who knows? I bought those photos from Willie Kavan. He charged me an arm and a leg, and to this day, he won't tell me how he got hold of them. He just grins when I ask him. But I think they're worth what I paid, even without a pedigree."

The Barretts were quick to agree.

Cyrus indicated another picture and said, "The women in that circle are priestesses performing a Basket Dance which honors woman as the heart and life-force of the pueblo. Over there—"

Paul tuned out the droning voice. He had finished his drink and hoped that Cyrus would soon offer a refill.

Through the windows he could see the cottonwoods which screened the house from the road. The sky beyond was shading from salmon into blue as night fell. The stillness of the world outside seemed to press against the house. The voices within the room seemed obtrusive.

There was a lull in the conversation. Sheila studied her nearly empty glass. Paul said to Cyrus, "Mrs. Anderson—Helen—explained that it was actually something other than *choice* that brought you here.

Cyrus considered the question a moment before answering, *"Fate.* Yes, I suppose it really was. After all, this is where we began our project; this is where The Book is being completed."

"How long have you been working on The Book?" asked Sheila, looking up from her now-empty glass.

"Ever since we arrived, three years ago. As soon as we drove into town, something assured us that we had work to do here, though we had no idea *what* the work should be— just a gut feeling that we belonged here. We bought this house for a song and redid it ourselves.

"We met Maria almost immediately. We had hired her older sister Rosa to help with the cooking and cleaning. Sometimes Rosa would bring Maria (the child was only thirteen then) along with her. Sometimes Maria would help with the sweeping and washing; sometimes she would just sit on the back porch, staring out across the desert. She'd never answer us—Helen or myself—when we tried to talk to her. And she rarely answered Rosa. Both girls are full-blooded Tawas, by the way.

"When we remarked on Maria's silence, Rosa would just shrug her shoulders and say her sister was *poco loco,* a little crazy. But Rosa is fond of her and always takes good care of her.

"Around noon one day, Rosa discovered that Maria had disappeared from her favorite spot on the back porch. I *still* remember *that day*: it was like a blast furnace. Rosa got hysterical and kept shouting that her sister had wandered into the desert. She told us that Maria frequently sleep-walked or had blank spells; when this happened, Rosa told us, the girl always wandered out into the desert, toward the Sierra Morenas.

"So I took out my jeep and Rosa and I drove around and finally found her collapsed in a heap out near the creekbed. She seemed delirious; she just kept babbling about shadow-people she had seen who had come up through the ground to talk to her—but she was never able to understand the message they gave her.

"We brought her back to the house. She woke up once during the ride back, then fell into a deep sleep. She slept the rest of the day. Rosa sat by the bed awhile, then went back to her chores, looking in on her sister every so often.

"Somehow, when no one was watching her, Maria slipped away again. We searched the desert for two hours or so, but this time we couldn't find her. And it was getting on toward evening. We called the sheriff and he formed a search party. I went out with the men to look; Helen stayed here and tried to calm Rosa, who finally came out and insisted she was going to help us look for her sister.

"As it turned out—Ah! Helen! Just in time! Helen, you tell them about where we found Maria the night we discovered our part in composing The Book."

Helen Anderson had just come into the room. Like her husband, she was drinking only club soda, which she brought with her.

She pulled one of the wooden chairs from beside the fireplace over toward the couch and settled into it comfortably. Then she began, "We were all sure that Maria had wandered off into the desert again. I stayed at home on the chance that she might return; half the town was out combing the desert.

"Well, somewhere around eleven that night, I was trying to read a magazine when I heard this *moaning*. It scared me silly—even though I know a lot about ghosts and the astral world and such. . . . Still, when you're alone in a house on the edge of the desert late at night, a sound like that puts the fear of God in you, I swear.

"But the more I listened, the more it sounded like a child afraid or hurt. The sound seemed to be coming from the basement, so I got out Cyrus's big flashlight and went downstairs.

"It's just packed earth down there. I followed the sound and found Maria curled up—just like a baby in the womb—in the dirt behind some old boxes. Her eyes were open; she was staring at the wall and groaning. I called her name and touched her, but she just shivered and whimpered like a poor lost thing. She didn't really seem to see me at all.

"When I realized she wasn't going to respond, I just picked her up and carried her upstairs and put her in our bed. Then I phoned the sheriff's office to radio the men out searching that the child was all right.

"Then I went back to check on Maria. I had covered her with a blanket, but she just kept making that awful sound and stayed curled up like an infant. And her skin was icy-cold. I thought she was in shock. I called the doctor. When he finally showed up, he examined her and gave her a shot of something. He told me to keep her warm, watch her, and call him immediately if she got worse. I was to call him first thing in the morning to let him know how she was.

"I sat on the bed, stroking her hair and saying, 'There, there, it's all going to be fine,' and wishing Cyrus and Rosa would get back.

"After awhile, even the little whimpering sounds stopped and she seemed to fall into a healthy sleep. I went into the kitchen to get myself a glass of water.

"When I came back, Maria was sitting up in the bed with the blankets pulled around her. She was shivering with cold, even though the house seemed unusually warm that night. Her eyes were wide open; she stared at me with the *funniest* look on her face. Then she said, 'You are the one. The Below People came to me twice today. Once they came to me outside and later I saw them in the house. They said, "These people are to write The Book of the things we will tell them. You will be the eyes to see and the mouth to tell; theirs will be the hands for gathering the message. The appointed time is nearly at hand; we are very close to you.' "

"Of course, it made no sense at all. I thought at first it was a delirium. I didn't mention it when Cyrus and Rosa came in a few minutes later; I told Cyrus about it just before we went to bed that night—after we had put Rosa and Maria in the guest room—and he thought she was just raving.

"But that night we both had a single dream, really. Shadowy figures came to each of us in our sleep and told us to listen to what the child had to say, that she was to be our link with intelligences from outside this world. We were to record the messages they would send through her."

She paused, as if suddenly overwhelmed by the immensity of the job they had undertaken.

Cyrus continued, "Rosa was against our using Maria as a medium. Maria seemed to accept her part in things without question. We've been working on The Book for over two years now, but it's a slow business. We've barely begun to scratch the surface of what those Outside have to tell us.

Sheila said, "Would you show us some of the material?"

Helen smiled. "Later. After dinner—if you're still interested—we can show you a bit." She stood up suddenly. "Speaking of dinner, I'd better see how things are doing." Cyrus, refill everyone's glasses."

She returned to the kitchen; Cyrus dutifully collected the glasses.

While he was out of the room, Paul asked Sheila, who seemed abstracted, "Are you feeling all right?"

"Fine. I'm fine."

"You don't sound very convincing."

"I'm *fine*." She stared at him oddly, then turned to smile at Cyrus, who returned with fresh drinks in hand.

"Well," the older man asked, handing round the glasses, "have you been so taken with El Centro that you're ready to settle down here yourselves?"

"Not quite yet," said Paul, "though, when the quarter begins, with papers to grade and lectures to prepare, I may come running back."

"It's funny," said Sheila, in a serious tone of voice out of keeping with the banter of the two men, "I feel as though I've been here longer than I have. . . . Not in a bad sense: I feel like I've come home." Her voice had a dreamy, distant quality that Paul found obscurely disturbing.

Cyrus responded eagerly, "That sounds something like what we—Helen and I—felt when *we* arrived here. Like we *belonged* here." He leaned toward her with sudden intensity, asking, "Are you at all psychic? Perhaps—"

Sheila dismissed the question gently but firmly. "Not unless you count a bad dream or two."

"Oh," Cyrus said, sounding faintly disappointed. He relaxed back into the rocking chair and sipped his club soda reflectively. After a few moments, he said, "Well, after all, *everyone is,* to some extent. Psychic, I mean. Some have a real talent, while most people only have flashes of ability— and go through their lives never realizing that they've had, just for a moment or two, contact with other dimensions— or a larger consciousness—however you want to characterize the World Outside." He took a large swallow, draining his glass. "Maria has the gift to see and hear things that are hidden from the rest of us. Helen and I, we can sense presences, disturbances of the psychic atmosphere around us— but that's as far as our talents go. For most people, it's like" —he groped for a definition, found it—"seeing an out-of-place shadow in full sunlight or catching a glimpse of something out of the corner of your eye. Blink, turn your head: it's gone. So they shrug it off. It never dawns on them that what they've nearly seen is part of another world. They call it a speck of dust or blame it on eyestrain; they'd call you crazy if you told them they'd had an experience with psychic phenomena."

Paul was just about to ask for a third scotch but Helen Anderson chose that moment to announce that dinner was ready and invited them all into the dining room.

After dinner, they returned to the living room. Sheila and Paul had after-dinner brandies to accompany the cups of strong black coffee Helen brought them; the Andersons drank only coffee.

They had just begun a discussion of local politics when there was a soft knock at the front door. Helen left, then returned shortly, ushering in a heavyset Indian girl about sixteen years old. She did not look at any of them as Helen stroked her hair in a motherly fashion and said, "This is Maria Seloso." The girl kept her eyes resolutely on the floor, midway between the couch and herself.

She wore a simple white blouse and navy-blue skirt too large and gathered in folds. The little toe of each foot had worn through the sides of her grimy tennis shoes. When she overcame her shyness enough to look at the Barretts, Paul saw large almond-shaped eyes of deepest black, a slightly flattened nose, and a lower lip that was being chewed mercilessly. The hair above the broad face was cropped unbecomingly in a ragged Buster-Brown cut; the only touch of finery was a pair of silver squash-blossom earrings and a single turquoise ring on her right index finger.

Helen tried to coax some response from the girl, then gave up with a smile and a shrug; she sat the girl down on one of the wooden fireplace chairs, where Maria remained sitting, uncomfortably rigid, her shoulders never touching the back of the chair.

They finished their coffee quickly; Helen cleared away the dishes with Sheila's help. All the while, Paul was aware of the silent girl in a disturbing way. Something in her face reminded him faintly of Enotea. He glanced over at Cyrus, but the older man was tapping his hand on the rocker arm with impatient nervousness as he watched the women cleaning up.

When the business of cleaning up was finished, Helen called them all back into the dining room. Cyrus escorted Maria to the table and sat her down first. The others all sat down again at the bare round wooden table, from which even the flowery place mats had been removed. Cyrus sat at Maria's right hand; Helen leaned over and whispered something in the girl's ear, then sat down at her left but placed her hands reassuringly over the girl's, which were resting on the table.

Rising, Cyrus said, "I'm going to dim the lights and put Maria in a trance." To the Barretts, he explained, "We've found that if we hypnotize her, she doesn't seem to get as tired—the way she does if we let her enter the trance state unaided."

He extinguished the overhead light and put a small red-shaded kerosene lamp in the center of the table; he drew the curtains against the moon-bright night outside. Paul could feel himself grow tense in the soft red glow.

"Bright lights—electric lights especially—seem to interfere with phenomena," Helen whispered.

He glanced over at Sheila, but in the semidarkness her expression was unreadable. She was staring at Maria, her hands folded in little-girl fashion on the table in front of her. She reminded Paul of a schoolgirl attentive to an important classroom lecture, determined to miss nothing.

He turned his attention to Cyrus, who had taken a pocket-penflash from his shirt pocket. He had angled Maria's chair slightly toward his own. When he spoke, it was evenly, firmly.

"I want you to watch the light, Maria," he said, holding the tiny light in front of her eyes, then moving it slowly downward. "That's it. Concentrate on the light. I want you to relax completely." His voice assumed a quieter, almost monotonous tone. "You are growing sleepy. Your eyelids are becoming heavy. Everything is growing blurry. Look at the light and think about how heavy your arms and legs have become. The only thing you can think about is how tired you're becoming. All your thoughts are drifting away into the dark; follow your thoughts into the dark."

He had gradually lowered the penflash until the girl's eyelids were almost closed. He snapped off the light, telling her, "Now relax completely; let those last thoughts go. Your arms are asleep"—he touched each of her arms in a stroking gesture— "you are asleep but you can hear me. You can still see me. You will answer only the questions I ask you. You will obey only my wishes."

He leaned over and moved her chair back into position at the head of the table. Paul had the curious impression that the thickset girl had grown smaller and thinner while she was being hypnotized. An unexplained nervousness had gripped him; he could feel his forehead and armpits growing moist. He had the sudden urge to giggle like a child at a funeral.

Cyrus turned and said softly, "I think we're ready now." To the entranced girl he asked, "What is your name?"

In a toneless voice the girl responded, "My name is—" She stopped abruptly, then began again. "My name is—"

Again she stopped. She began breathing very rapidly, her frame shaking with ragged breaths. When she spoke again, her voice was hoarse and her breathing, while easier, was still noticeably rapid. Her eyes went wide open, focusing on some vastly distant point. She said, "Someone is coming from the West. Far away now, but coming closer." A pause. "In his hands he holds a medicine rattle and eagle feathers." A pause. "I cannot see his face." A pause. "Around his throat are two necklaces. One is made of bears' claws; one is of silver and red beads." She stopped; for a moment there was only the sound of Maria's breathing in the room.

Cyrus said, "Tell me more about the person you see."

Maria said, her voice still holding a rasping quality, "I cannot see his face. He is wrapped in a medicine blanket painted with magic designs. A corner of the blanket hides his face." A pause . . . her breath came in ragged gasps. "I cannot see the face." A longer pause, then her voice became agitated. "His face! His face! His/his/his—no!—I see now, not *his,* the face, not *h*—" She gave a sudden strangulated cry.

Then she was moaning and writhing in her chair, her hands gripping the arms as though she were afraid of being thrown from the seat by her own motions.

Paul asked what was happening. Helen hissed, "Quiet!

What's happening has happened before. She's not being hurt: she won't even remember that any of this happened."

Paul looked desperately at Sheila, saw her hand stretched partly across the table toward the girl. She was gazing at Maria with horrified intensity. She moved her hand closer but Helen warned, "Don't touch her! You could kill her."

Sheila withdrew her hand part of the way but was clearly agonizing over her inability to help.

Maria's breathing became easier.

Tentatively Cyrus extended a hand to take the girl's wrist. He reported, "Pulse has gone from ninety to one-twenty." Helen jotted this information in the stenographer's notebook open on the table in front of her.

The girl continued to moan, her distress growing in intensity, her head rocking back and forth. She seemed to be fighting off some unseen force.

Paul felt light-headed. The drinks and the tension affected his eyes and made it hard for him to see any of the others in the reddish haze of the room.

Maria's cries stopped abruptly but her body still moved forward and backward, her eyes nearly closed.

"Maria, place your hands on the table in front of you," Cyrus commanded.

When she did this, Cyrus produced a ruler from his pocket and measured the girl's hand. Then he said, in a matter-of-fact tone Paul found grotesque, "Elongation of the hand by one inch."

Helen nodded and noted down this fact.

"Elongation of the face and body above the hips."

This information was duly recorded.

Staring in uncertainty through the red half-light, Paul saw that the girl's hands upon the tabletop now seemed incredibly long-fingered. He touched his own fingers involuntarily to his mouth as he saw that her head was now almost two inches *above* the back of the chair, though a moment before, the top of her head had been just *below* it.

His head was swimming; his mind refused to credit the changes he was apparently seeing in the girl's body. It must be the liquor, the tension, the feeling of dizziness, he reasoned, which made the girl's once-broad features look thin and drawn, as if the flesh of her face had become plastic and then had been drawn upward by some invisible hand.

Now Maria's distorted mouth was moving; she seemed to be struggling to speak.

Paul shivered; a chilling breeze seemed to be flooding the room, though the house a minute earlier had been still warm with the day's leftover heat.

Suddenly the girl slammed herself back in the chair, became quite calm. Her eyes popped open, taking them all in with a nod; the faintest smile touched her lips.

Cyrus, his voice little more than a whisper, asked, "What is your name?"

The voice issuing from the girl was deep, masculine, with a curious accent; it answered simply, "Senecu."

Cyrus explained, "Senecu is Maria's spirit guide—an Indian medicine man of the old Pueblo people. As near as we can determine, he died perhaps two hundred years ago.

Cyrus asked Senecu, "Where is Maria?"

"Her spirit is somewhere else; it will return when I summon it."

"Very good. What messages have you brought us tonight, Senecu?"

Paul noted that Helen was writing everything in her notebook.

In sonorous tones, Senecu began, "Oh, you dwellers above, I will have you know the will of the Below Persons. I will lead you to the path of wisdom, which is the reward of those who do the bidding of the Below Persons. All things are—"

Maria suddenly began twisting about but stayed in place, as though held by invisible bonds to her chair. She began shouting in a loud male voice, "Go away! I order you: leave this place! This is forbidden! *You may not enter here!*"

Cyrus, very much agitated, asked, "Senecu! Senecu! What's wrong? What's happening? Answer me!"

The girl's breathing was very rapid; again there was a tremendous struggle as she forced herself to speak. "Stop.... Do ... nothing ... further." The words seemed spoken at great physical cost, each little more than a painful expulsion of breath.

"Why?" Cyrus asked.

"There is another presence here—an evil presence. There is danger. *Danger.*"

She screamed and screamed again.

Helen's pen had paused in mid-sentence; she looked genuinely frightened.

Maria spoke again. "Hold hands. Close"—her breathing was ragged; her voice seemed to be failing—"Close . . . circle. Prevent them . . . getting in. Close . . . the . . . circle."

Helen ordered, "All of you: *link hands*. We must form a protective circle and use our psychic energy to protect ourselves from this danger, whatever it is."

Maria was rocking violently from side to side. Cyrus took one of Maria's hands; Helen, the other. Paul and Sheila held hands with the Andersons and with each other, closing the circle.

"The circle is closed now. Nothing can enter in. The circle is closed now. Nothing can enter in," Helen repeated in a chantlike whisper.

Maria suddenly tilted back her head. Her eyes were wide open but rolled back into her head; only the whites were visible. She began taking deeper and deeper breaths. Though the rhythm remained the same, the sound grew louder and louder.

"What's happening?" Paul demanded to know.

Helen continued her whispered chant, ignoring him.

Cyrus said, "I think—I'm not *sure*—it's hyperaethesia. She's entering a deeper trance state. This has never happened before."

Sheila said, "Is there a draft in here? I'm freezing." She started to pull her hand out from under Cyrus's, but he said, "Don't let go! For God's sake! I don't know what's going on, but we need the protection of the closed circle. Don't let go!"

Sheila obeyed. Paul sensed that the man was genuinely frightened. He couldn't believe any of this was really happening, but he could feel Helen's and Sheila's hands tightened on his own. The sound of Maria's breathing filled the red-lit room. The sound had become thunderous, pouring out of the walls, until it seemed the room itself was breathing in great, ragged gasps.

"My God! *Look!*" Sheila's voice dropped to a whisper.

"Luminous phenomena," Cyrus murmured, his voice registering amazement.

Hundreds of droplets of light, each tear-shaped and about the size of a matchhead, hovered approximately two inches above the tabletop; they cast enough pale light to reveal the hands and faces of the sitters, swallowing the ruby glow of the little shaded lamp. Paul could see Sheila's head shaking from side to side, as if she were rejecting in her mind what she saw with her eyes. Helen's lips were moving but Paul could no longer hear her chant; Cyrus seemed wonderstruck, staring in astonishment at the lights.

After a moment, the droplets began to melt and flow together into a luminous fog, gossamer-thin. This then gradually compacted itself into a sphere which floated toward Maria to hover in front of her face for a moment. Then the fire-globe suddenly extinguished itself.

Paul started to say something but stopped in mid-sentence.

A spot of light, more intense than the other, had begun to emerge from the region of the girl's solar plexus.

Cyrus said, in the unsteady voice of someone trying to keep his wits against growing odds, "Ectoplasm manifestation."

Paul asked, "What the hell *is* it?"

Cyrus whispered impatiently, "We don't know for sure—a substance drawn out of the body of the medium, made up of body cells, fluids, waste matter, energy. No one *knows*." The man never took his eyes from Maria for a moment.

In jerking movements synchronized with the breathing that roared through the room, a luminous rod of ectoplasm grew toward the center of the table.

A hand began to form at the end of pulplike glowing substance which seemed to Paul unnervingly like a hideous worm erupting from the diminished body of the girl. When the hand had completely taken shape, it hovered over the center of the table, the fist clenching and unclenching in time with the breathing all around them.

A second spot of light appeared on Maria's forehead. This grew rapidly into a disk which covered her face, though her features remained visible behind the veil of light. As Paul watched, the disk attempted to resolve itself into a mask, or head, but it remained grotesquely undefined, amorphous. Ripples ran across the surface; eye-holes and nose-hole and mouth-slit appeared, then were swallowed up in the soft whiteness; no true face appeared.

Suddenly the hand was moving toward Paul, who had the sudden urge to giggle again.

And to scream.

The hand, still attached to the girl by a narrowing thread of luminous matter, was now floating higher above the table on a level with the sitters' eyes. It drifted toward Paul, the fingers grasping empty air, releasing, grasping again. Paul drew his head back, terrified at the thought of those disembodied fingers tangling themselves in his hair, touching his face.

Cyrus shouted, "STOP! THERE!"

The hand hesitated in midair but continued the clenching motion. After a moment it jerked toward Paul, as though breaking through some restraining barrier.

Cyrus, his voice angry now, shouted, "I *commanded* you to stop! Maria is still under my control!"

The ghostly hand moved forward, but only a fraction of an inch this time. The line of light, like an umbilical cord between the girl and the phantom hand, stretched taut, tauter. . . . There was a groan from Maria. The hand turned over, floating palm up now, the fingers in a line with the bridge of Paul's nose.

It began to sweat a reddish substance that looked like blood; the thick droplets dripped onto the tabletop with the sickening sound of heavy raindrops. A red pool began collecting, streaming toward the table edge in half a dozen directions.

"Sweet Jesus!" Cyrus murmured.

The hand dragged itself to within three inches of Paul, then turned palm downward again. Paul could feel Helen's and Sheila's hands gripping his own, could feel their nails digging into his palms and fingers. He was helpless to do anything but watch the gore-dripping, glowing hand in front of his eyes.

Then the hand shot forward, touching his forehead, marking him with blood. He could feel the substance burning his skin with an intense cold, like dry ice; he slammed his head from side to side, but in his terror his voice failed him completely.

Sheila screamed and kept on screaming.

Maria screamed in answer, then suddenly slumped forward onto the tabletop.

All traces of the ectoplasmic hand disappeared; the pool of blood on the table vanished. The burning pain of the blood-mark on his head evaporated, leaving no trace.

Helen turned on the lights; Cyrus helped the unconscious Maria to an upright position in her chair. To Sheila, he said, "That was a very dangerous thing to do, Mrs. Barrett; a medium should never be shocked out of a trance. And ectoplasm should be allowed to withdraw naturally."

Sheila only said, in a dazed fashion, "That thing *touched* Paul. There was blood on him."

"It was still a very foolish thing you did," Cyrus said, massaging Maria's wrists. Helen had gone to help him. Under their ministrations, Maria gradually regained consciousness. She seemed a bit groggy, but otherwise unharmed.

Sheila remained holding onto Paul's hand as tightly as he was holding hers. Each felt terrified of letting go of the other.

After a few minutes, Helen helped Maria to her feet and led the girl out of the room. "I want her to rest for a while," she explained. "It's usual even after . . . routine sessions, which this"—and she laughed a bit too sharply, Paul thought —"was certainly not."

While the woman and girl were out of the room, Cyrus went to the sideboard, which held several liquor bottles and an ice bucket. He picked up a cut-glass decanter and said, "I think a little brandy is in order all around."

Neither of the Barretts objected.

Helen reentered the room to announce that Maria was sleeping, then she wordlessly accepted the snifter of brandy her husband held out to her. She reported that, as far as she could tell, Maria was suffering nothing more than the usual postsession tiredness. "And," she added, "the child doesn't seem to remember anything that happened, just like after any other session."

Cyrus nodded. "That's good. It looks like there are going to be no ill effects from either the ectoplasm production or the *abrupt* termination of the session."

Sheila, having attempted to taste her brandy and failed, said, "I'm afraid this evening has been—" She stood up. "Paul, we've got to leave."

He downed his brandy in two swallows and stood up also. He wanted to get out of the house, which still seemed freezing. The dinner lay like a lump in his stomach; his fear had left a residual nausea in him. He thought if he stayed a minute longer, he would vomit across the Andersons' table.

Cyrus poured himself and his wife a second brandy.

"Yes, well, we understand." He paused. "It has been a most, a most—*amazing* evening."

"I forgot to take notes at the end. Of course, I couldn't break the circle. But we have it all on tape." Helen nodded at the cassette recorder grinding away beside the brandy decanter.

"I'll get your coats," said Cyrus. He seemed relieved at their sudden departure.

The Barretts said their good nights and stepped out into the sudden coolness of the night air.

An immense moon hung over the mountains to the west. The night was incredibly still around them; only the faintest hum of insects was audible.

"Well," said Paul, trying to keep his voice even, "what did you think of all that hocus-pocus?"

Sheila said, "I don't know. I was so frightened. Did we *really* see all that?"

"I don't think so," Paul bluffed. "Not in a real sense. It must have been some sort of group hallucination."

Sheila listened in silence as they walked along. Finally, she said only, "It seemed so real. But I can't believe it. I can't." She took a deep breath and sighed. "I've read too much about religious hysteria. I don't think I want to go through anything like that again."

They walked the rest of the way back in silence.

In spite of the warmth of the evening, she was trembling. Paul could feel some of the chill in the house had crept into his bones to stay.

"Cold?" he asked, and attempted to put his arm around her shoulders, but she shrugged him away, saying, "Don't— I'm just reacting to what happened there. It was . . . pretty gruesome."

"Parlor tricks," Paul said, failing in his attempt at a dismissive tone. "Group hypnosis. Delusions."

"We all saw the same thing. That thing actually *touched* you."

"I'd just as soon forget it."

"How? Something like *that*—"

"In the morning, in the sun, we'll begin forgetting. It won't seem much more than a nightmare. *You're* practical enough to know that. We may have had an exciting taste of telepathy. Whatever the hell went on there wasn't—What are you doing?"

Sheila had taken out the blood-moon necklace. She was turning it over and over in her right hand as if it was a string of worry beads. "Just nerves. Paul, leave me alone, will you? I'll put this away in a minute."

He shrugged. "I still say there was nothing more than a little ESP there. No magic."

"You're probably right," she said, but she continued nervously playing with the silver necklace, which seemed to take on added luster from the starlight and moonlight so that it seemed almost white-hot as she coiled it around her fingers and uncoiled it.

The lights were out in the office of the Four Star. It was after eleven, and the Shores closed their office at ten.

A few different cars were parked in the little court.

Inside their room, Paul fixed them both a nightcap of lukewarm bourbon from the pint bottle he kept in the bottom of his suitcase. Neither of them had the energy to walk to the ice machine outside the office.

When they had finished their drinks, they undressed quickly, both seeking sleep eagerly in their separate beds.

Outside the windows the insects continued to hum, and a moth threw immense shadows across the curtained window.

7 The Second Night

1

Sheila could not sleep. The events of the day churned through her mind, replaying themselves endlessly or suggesting variations and countless new interpretations: Paul's forcing himself on her; the two of them acting out some private dreams; the horrors of the séance . . .

As she lay listening to Paul's breathing and to his frequent tossing in bed, she was aware of how desolate she had become. And how fearful. She felt her life was at one with the chilling, empty desert upon which the little town slept. She felt afraid, of horrors hidden in the seemingly deserted wasteland. Of violence hidden in the one person she thought she knew . . . She felt surrounded by secrets. Threatened by hidden evil.

At some great distance, a train screamed through the silence.

She felt her fear translating into tensed muscles, watchfulness, a pounding heart. She tried to calm herself by calling it the effect of too much coffee and alcohol, of the bizarre events at the Andersons'.

She rose and sat for a moment on the edge of her bed. Then she went and stood over Paul. She leaned down and lightly ran a fingertip from his lips over the curve of his chin and along the line of his throat. She felt a moistness on his skin and wondered if he was being plagued by night sweats and nightmares again, as had happened just before his breakdown. That would explain his restlessness, though he usually muttered and mumbled to himself during a bad dream. Tonight, though he was thrashing about a good deal, he made no sound. He stirred and turned his face away from the touch of her finger but he did not wake up.

She went to the window and stared out into the silent courtyard. She remembered the two of them moaning and twisting on the sand that afternoon. The bloody hand . . . Standing looking out into the night, she was seeing one scene played out at midday in the complex shadows of the overhanging tree, one scene replaying in the red-lit chill of the Anderson dining room.

In confusion, she found herself hating the Paul of the first vision, wanting to strike down and destroy completely the panting, sweating, rutting male who had held her pinned in the shadow of the tree, tormented by the sand, while he had his way with her. Simultaneously, she felt the need to protect the Paul who had been threatened and *marked* by the bloodied hand.

She let the curtain drop back into place, disturbed by the mixed emotions rolling through her with the suddenness of a desert storm. The strength of the emotions within her at this moment seemed stronger than what she had felt in that little hollow in sun and shadow and the heat of the day. Her fears, too, were stronger than when she was seated at the round wooden table. Now her fears were for the *both* of them, though she was uncertain of what was scaring her. After all, *Paul* had been the one touched.

She pushed her fingertips against her temples, massaging them, clearing away the confused thoughts which pursued one another around and around her brain like puppies chasing their own tails.

She shook herself and took a deep breath. She turned on the lamp between the beds, shading it with a hand towel from the bathroom so it wouldn't disturb Paul. She picked up the stack of books he had left on the nightstand, his gift to her earlier that day.

She glanced again through the titles, hesitating at one titled *Legends of the Tawa Indians,* then deciding on a cultural history of the Southwest by Paul Horgan. She had read some of his novels, so she felt she might enjoy this book.

Opening it at random, she began scanning paragraphs,

looking for a passage that would hold her interest until she could relax enough for sleep; she refused to take a sleeping pill if she could avoid it, for it left her feeling logy and useless the next morning.

A chapter of *The Heroic Triad* that dealt with the Rio Grande caught her attention:

Here in sweet dense cottonwood shadows by the water, plausibly a pagan heaven came down to visit Leda on a perishable earth, as all peoples have wanted to unite heaven and earth. Was it here in this grove that Jacob wrestled with his angel, and did Delacroix dream of the scene just as here? The treetops bespeak Saint Francis, and in the flesh his brothers knew this river and still do, in exactly his purpose and purity. What elders today have seen a girl Susanna dreaming awake and naked in the caressing river water? For there is nothing new in the myths of every breast. They only become renewed and real when nature calls them forth. But they never cease flowing through generations of human desire, whether in worship or love, making a river of their own sort.

Why did the passage seem disturbingly significant?

Sheila reread it twice more, but failed to come to any conclusions. The clue seemed to be in the juxtaposing of St. Francis and Susanna. St. Francis made her think of the Franciscan and Casserite padres who had brought Christianity to the Southwest. And Susanna—Jewess, woman of a religion older than Christianity, and very nearly victim of an assault by elders of her own religion. How did they fit together against images of water, of generation, of struggle, of union—the union of heaven and earth and some undefined power? And what was the undefined thing waiting to be summoned forth on the desert, in the shade of cottonwood trees?

She read it again a final time, but could make no sense for herself. The pieces of the verbal jigsaw puzzle stubbornly refused to fit together.

She gave up and closed the book, setting it on the nightstand. Then she got up and quietly dressed in jeans and a jacket. She knew that sleep was hours away for her.

She glanced over at Paul and saw that he had dropped off

into a deeper, apparently less troubled sleep; she snapped off the bedside light and made her way across the darkened room.

Closing the door softly behind her, she stepped out into the luminous night. The sky was a jumble of stars overhead; the distant moon, red-tinted, was dropping toward the horizon.

There was a little cafe on the edge of town which she had noticed earlier boasted, "Open 24 Hours."

She started walking along the edge of the highway which cut through El Centro. She was aware of the night sounds all around her, but she was more intensely alert to the silences, moments when no car swept past and the droning of insects was momentarily stilled. Then she found herself pausing—listening to the darkness, though she had no idea what she was listening for.

A line from *A Midsummer Night's Dream* popped into her mind and replayed over and over: "Night and silence! Who is here?"

She quickened her pace, walking toward the yellow neon sign and lighted windows of the cafe.

The Regal Coffee Shop was nearly empty. The cook, in greasespattered white shirt and trousers, was seated at one end of the counter, reading the sports section of the local newspaper. At the opposite end, the only waitress, a heavy-set, red-eyed girl of around seventeen, was leaning across the counter, drinking coffee and talking with a young, good-looking Indian, who also had a coffee cup in front of him.

Sheila took a seat near the middle. The waitress heaved herself away from her conversation with an audible sigh. She took a glass, scooped it full of ice from a bin, and filled it too full of water. It slopped over and made a puddle when she set it in front of Sheila.

"Menu?" she asked.

Sheila shook her head and said, "Just a pot of tea, thanks."

The chef, who had glanced up to see if his services were going to be needed, returned to his paper.

The girl filled a ceramic teapot with hot water; she set this and a teabag on a saucer in front of Sheila. "Anything else?"

"Lemon?"

"Don't have any. We used them all up."

"Nothing else, then. Thanks."

The girl disappeared through a swinging door into the kitchen. Sheila glanced to her left. The young man (*boy*, actually, she realized) was staring openly at her; then he smiled and touched his lower lip in a gesture that was either merely nervous or deliberately provocative (she couldn't decide which). She quickly returned her attention to the tea, aware that he was still watching her.

She couldn't deny that she was, in some mild degree, flattered by his attention; at the same time, she was dismayed to find herself responding at all. Were things becoming so confused, she wondered, that she would even consider letting herself be picked up in the Regal Coffee Shop in El Centro by someone who might be fifteen years her junior?

She concentrated on drinking her tea and addressed herself to other questions.

Paul had become a stranger to her totally; more disturbing was the feeling that she was becoming a stranger to herself.

As far as she and Paul were concerned, she found that her thoughts did not extend beyond going home and ending something that now had only the look of a genuine relationship. They were no longer in touch; they no longer seemed to interact, except as sources of mutual irritation. Their marriage had all come apart; there could be no putting things back together: too many pieces were missing.

The waitress refilled the teapot and Sheila thanked her absently.

She saw it now, with sudden clarity, as the end of some process that had begun around the time of Paul's breakdown. A time when so many disturbing things had happened.

There had been the horrible death of that girl with the strange-sounding name. The mulatto—so beautiful to have died in such an ugly way. The newspaper accounts had said she was on drugs—Sheila remembered some of the less respectable papers playing up the idea that she was involved in black magic. It must have been one hell of a drug overload to have sent her smashing through solid glass, nearly flaying herself alive, and slamming into the midst of a cocktail party several stories below . . .

Sheila pushed away such thoughts. When news of the girl's death had reached Paul, he had clearly been more upset than the event warranted. At the time Sheila had been uncertain whether the grotesqueness of it all had put additional pressure on Paul's already unbalancing mind, or whether he had been far enough gone to simply latch onto any bizarre occurrence.

Paul's guilt had caused her to speculate—briefly—on the possibility that he had been involved with the girl outside of the classroom. She had never heard him speak of—what *was* her name?—except as a brilliant student with a tremendous potential as a writer if she could discipline her eternally distracting enthusiasms. But he *had* brought her name up an inordinate number of times.

But in the end, she had made up her mind that Paul was punishing himself for having made some criticism of the girl's work, for some failure to respond to an unrecognized call for help, some unwillingness to understand an increasing addiction in his favorite student. Most likely he felt guilty for her death—a familiar reaction pushed to the extreme by Paul's growing inability to cope with mounting stress, a sense of career failure, the impotence which he regarded as the final statement of his inadequacy.

In the end, what had signalled the destruction of their marriage for Sheila had not been suspicions of his unfaithfulness, but the way he had shut her out increasingly from his life. In the final days before his breakdown, during endless hours of desperate sleep interrupted by his rambling monologues in which fact and fantasy ran together, sometimes indistinguishably, Paul had closed her out completely. Even after the doctors had begun the lithium treatments and intensive therapy sessions, he had admitted her back only in a limited fashion.

That was not enough for her. *All or nothing at all,* the song went, she recalled. Paul was giving her too little for her to want to stay married. She would keep up the fiction until their vacation was ended; then, when they were home, she would demand at least a trial separation.

As for herself, these last days she had become so nervous, so forgetful, so self-absorbed that she often felt disconnected from life around her, and afraid. Afraid of something in the heat of the day and the dark of the moon, in the eyes of people she met and in the very desert underfoot.

But more than anything else she was afraid of something inside of her demanding to be set free. She tasted it, sometimes, as an undefined emotion, a sense of rage, a surging power, a cavernous *potential:* a blackness yearning for light, an embryonic blood mass impatient for form, life, birth.

Craziness. Her thoughts were as crazy as Paul's irrational discourses last year on unspecified rodents burrowing in the walls and *mafioso* systematically taking over Oliente College. If she didn't watch herself . . .

She looked down and discovered she had pulled out the blood-moon necklace. Had it displayed out on the counter and was running the tips of her fingers over it—slowly, as if it were a rosary. A part of the chain had fallen into the spillage from her water glass. She did not remember even taking it out: it was a foolish, dangerous thing to do. She picked it up and began wiping it dry with a paper napkin, noting the curious luster of the silver where the moisture had touched it. She felt unsure of herself—realized that nothing had been exactly normal since the start of their enforced stay in El Centro. Her sudden interest in the young man was just a further manifestation of her feeling that something within herself had changed in the past few days. Or was it the world around her that had gone slightly askew, and not merely her?

Nervously she glanced toward the two men on either side of her. The chef was absorbed in a crossword puzzle. The young Indian was staring at the necklace. He was no longer smiling. When their eyes met, he said, "Lady, that's a rare thing you got there. It's called a blood-moon. I only seen one once before. My grandmother showed me one. She wouldn't let me touch it—said it had old magic in it. When she died, no one could find it in her house."

Sheila finished her hasty drying of the necklace. She said quickly, "My husband bought it for me."

The young man shrugged. "Probably worth a lot of money, that thing. They're scarcer than hen's teeth around here—nobody uses that design any more. It's bad luck, they say—unless you're respectful."

"Don't tell my husband that," Sheila said, shoving the

necklace into her purse; "he bought it as an anniversary gift."

When she snapped the purse shut, the Indian returned his attention to his coffee, shaking his head.

She could not rid her fingers of a lingering sense of wet coolness from the touch of the blood-moon. She was simultaneously aware of a faint flushness, a feeble stirring of desire. Covertly she slid her eye over and took in the Indian's bare forearm, the tight curve of his hip, the faded bluejeans stretched tightly over his thigh. Wiping her fingers again uselessly, she was aware of how much she wanted to go over and touch his olive-skinned arm, rest her fingers on his thigh.

What are you doing? she demanded of herself. *What is so attractive about this stranger?*

For the third time she tried to dry her fingers, this time rubbing them so hard that the frictive heat finally eliminated the damp feeling. She dropped the shredded napkin onto the counter and absently began mopping up the last drops of water—letting herself think only of the journey that remained between here and home—estimating how quickly they could return to California once their car was repaired.

"Damn it to double hell, anyhow!" yelled the waitress, who had just burned herself on the coffee urn.

The words startled Sheila out of her reverie. Her tea was undrinkably cold. She got up and left a dollar on the counter.

"Good night," said the girl, who was studying the red welt on her arm.

"Good night," said Sheila. "I hope you didn't hurt yourself too badly."

The girl didn't answer; she was too busy smearing a pat of butter onto the burn.

The night was still fairly mild; the moon was just above the horizon. Two cars sped by as she retraced her path along the edge of the highway toward the motel.

The silence around her was almost absolute. Somewhere a dog barked; she heard faintly the wail of a baby. But these momentary sounds were quickly swallowed up by the imperious silence. The sky overhead seemed to have expanded and grown darker; the stars seemed more scattered, fewer. The lights of the town and the occasional light farther out on the desert seemed tinier than she remembered on her walk over. She felt the blackness around her threatening her in some obscure way.

"Now, now, *now!*" she said aloud, as if the sound of her voice, scolding herself, could exorcise the paranoia her overactive imagination was conjuring up.

The sound of her boots on the gravel seemed abnormally loud and out of place.

"Night and silence! Who is here?" she asked herself.

Another car shot toward her, then went past, its headlights momentarily dazzling her, making the darkness seem more acute when her eyes readjusted.

"Night and silence!" She asked again, "Who is here?"

She had reached the tiny church which marked a point halfway between the cafe and her motel. The wooden walls, sealed in silence, glowed a faint white in the waning moonlight.

Then she stopped, chilled. Had she heard someone whisper her name? She looked rapidly all around her, eyes and ears straining in the darkness. She heard and saw nothing.

Nothing ahead of her except the graveled edge of the road, littered with papers and broken bottles; behind her, only the same desolate stretch of gravel reaching back to the distant lights of the Regal Coffee Shop. The night was empty . . .

She looked again. She could see, or *thought* she could see, a man standing in the darkness behind her. Was it just her imagination, or . . .

Someone whispered her name again. There was a man there, and he had called her by name.

Remaining where she was, she called, "Who are you? What do you want?" Who in this town would know her name? Would be following her along the edge of the road at two o'clock in the morning?

There was no answer, no further sound.

Then the figure took a step toward her.

She wondered if the boy had followed her out of the cafe. But how could he know her name? Or had she really heard her name at all? And if it was the boy, what did he want? *Sex* either given freely or forcibly taken? Or the *blood-moon* which had interested him so?

She turned and began walking rapidly toward the still-distant motel. She would not allow her growing fear to take control of her, but she double-damned herself for being fool enough to go wandering around a godforsaken town in the middle of the night. As she half-walked, half-ran along, she found herself remembering every newspaper story of rape and murder she had ever read.

He called her name again—quite clearly this time. She was not mistaken. Something about the nearly toneless voice frightened her profoundly. She broke into a run. Careless of her footing, she tripped once, nearly losing her balance, but saved herself from falling. She kept on running. The motel, its eaves outlined in lime-green neon, seemed hopelessly distant.

Now her pursuer was running also, but his exertions seemed effortless compared to her own desperate dash for safety. For a few moments he seemed content to pace her; then, as if he had only wanted her to get near enough to the motel to think she was safe before overtaking her, he broke into a spurt. She did not dare look back, but she could hear his feet pounding over the gravel, narrowing the distance between them.

She ran on, feeling she was in a nightmare and helpless to escape whatever horror was following her.

"Oh my God, oh my God!" she was sobbing as she sucked in air and tried to force her legs to an even greater effort. "Oh, God, help me, *please*!"

She was near enough to the motel to see someone standing in the lime-colored light from the neon strips. Even in the dim light, she recognized Paul.

She screamed, "Paul! Paul, help me, please!"

But he remained standing where he was, near the door of the motel office.

Seeing Paul, she felt safe enough to slow down and look behind her. The roadside was empty; no one was behind her any longer. Where had her pursuer gone to? she wondered.

Then she had reached Paul, grabbing thankfully for his extended hand, so cold, so welcome. She began, "Paul, oh *God*, am—"

But she was not looking into Paul's face at all: she was staring into a face that was not really a face at all. A shapeless white mass with two shadowed gaps where the eyes should have been, like holes gouged in uncooked dough. Below the eyeholes, a mouth that was a horizontal slit in the whiteness opened and the voice of someone drowning gurgled her name.

Too terrified even to scream, she felt herself blacking out.

2

Paul was dreaming.

He stood on the rim of a valley which opened in front of him. The floor of the valley was of rust-red sand. He was standing at the point of a rock-defined V, the valley expanding outward, away from him, to encompass blood-tinted mesas and wind-sculpted sandstone pillars. The latter suggested monuments, faces, and figures like the monoliths of Easter Island; he could feel them, frozen, lifeless, yet *aware . . . watching* him.

A gusting wind roared across his face and half-raised hands. But nothing stirred in the persistent wind: no sand, not a leaf on the scattered bushes around him.

Nearby was the twisted and dried trunk of some fallen tree, looking like dried, gray-blue sinew. In his dream he understood that the same wind had blown forever in this place and would continue to blow and disturb nothing. And the monumental wind-carvings had not been shaped by the wind at all, but had existed forever in this place outside of time.

Then he saw something moving in the hazy purple distance.

At first it was nothing more than a series of specks moving across the russet sands. Motion in this place where nothing moved.

The dots drew closer: he could make out hooded men leading half a dozen burros tied one behind the other. The men were singing in Latin. He recognized the phrase, "Te Deum Laudamus," repeated over and over in the manner of Gregorian chant. The wind carried the words to him clearly; he had never before heard the melody which supported the words.

Spatial relationships were distorted: even from his vantage point high above the valley floor, he could clearly see that the men and burros left no print on the sands. In fact, the men, draped in long, dark monkish robes, seemed to glide over the sand as if their feet were not in touch with it at all.

The sun hung at three o'clock in the sky behind them—a veiled purplish-red disk. Everything swam in violent light. No cloud, no bird, nothing marred the violet expanse arching overhead from horizon to horizon.

The little caravan stopped at the foot of the slope upon which he stood.

Inexplicably compelled, he started down the slope, feeling the red hillside underfoot like ashes, feathery-soft and supporting him only when his feet had sunk in as far as his ankles. It was like descending a mountain of feathers.

Halfway down, he turned to look back and saw only the smooth upsweep of the hill unmarked by his descent.

The three robed figures waited patiently, hands buried deep in the sleeves of their robes, heads nodding slightly, faces hidden under high, pointed cowls. The burros, at a short distance, stood with bowed heads—unmoving, not a single tail flicking.

Far away, below the horizon, behind the violet sky, a roaring began, sounding like a cosmic hurricane or waterfall.

He halted a short distance from the spectral monks.

"Benedicite!" the first greeted him, in a voice like wind stirring dried grass.

"Frater!" hailed the second, extending a bone-white hand.

"Liberator!" the third said, moving forward a pace and extending two red-daubed hands.

"Why are we here?" asked Paul.

In answer they merely repeated, *"Benedicite!" "Frater!" "Liberator!"* The sound of their thin voices was nearly lost in the distant roaring, as if some hidden storm was raging nearer.

The wind had become hot and stung him with airborne sand particles now. Veils of sand half hid the dark-robed figures from him. The burros had been swallowed by the sandstorm.

In an instant, the two figures farthest from him were caught by the wind and whirled away like rags into the rust-colored dusk the storm had created. Their twin screams of frustration disappeared after them.

The foremost figure stood its ground, angling its hooded head into the wind. It stood a step closer to Paul, then reached out a hand and caught one of his, holding it tightly. Paul could feel the pressure of the bony hand and the stickiness of the *redness* coating that hand, which he did not dare to look at.

The wind howled ferociously; the monk's cowl blew back and revealed a skull yellowed with age. Paul began to scream, frantically trying to free his hand from the corpse's grasp. The wind snatched the skull off the shoulders and sent it scudding across the sand; the black-shrouded torso collapsed; Paul was left holding only a ragged bit of dark cloth, which was flapping crazily.

He released the scrap and watched it fly off into the brown-violet storm. The winds battered him, shrieked at him, blinded him, clawed him. Somehow he managed to keep his footing as the shrilling violet around him deepened into purple, deepened into black.

Nothing existed except the sun, reduced to a pale ghost-disk, little brighter than the moon.

Nothing existed.

And then the sun returned...

But it was no longer the sun: it had become the moon. It hung immense and insanely red at a midpoint between horizon and zenith.

The wind died away. Though he could still hear it blow, he no longer felt it.

He was in another place—alone, on a mesa top.

The plateau was smooth white sand, painfully bright. A short distance across the sand, a pueblo-city climbed tier upon tier into the sky which held no stars, which was only a smooth expanse of blackest velvet holding the moon which had been a sun.

The smooth facade of the stacked rectangles was unbroken by doors or windows. No ladders offered access to the roofs and walkways above the ground; it was a city in outline only—one never inhabited by men.

He was astonished to find himself wearing dark robes; he rubbed the coarse material wonderingly between his thumb and forefinger.

When he looked toward the pueblo again, he saw a single figure coming toward him, though he had seen no door open, could divine no way for the man to have appeared where he was appearing unless he had sprung from the ground underfoot.

The Indian had the hesitant gait of a very old man; he was swathed completely in a red-and-black blanket, held in place by his right hand. What little Paul could see of his face, beneath a corner of the blanket draped protectively over the man's forehead, was daubed with red and white paint. But Paul could see enough to know that the face was as dry and ancient as the desert itself. The features were withered into lifeless, sexless parody of a human face.

The eyes, like twin black beads amid the creases, glittered with a more-than-human intensity.

He stopped midway between the blind walls of the city and Paul.

Then he smiled and said, *"Benedicite,"* his voice giving the word a strange accent and a mocking quality that frightened Paul.

"Who are you?" Paul asked.

But the old man only shook his head and whispered, *"Frater."* Again, the alien intonation suggested something evil. The old man repeated, *"Frater."* Then he laughed harshly, a series of sharp staccato hisses.

Then the Indian pointed to a smooth white dome like the upper portion of an immense egg, buried deep in the sandy expanse.

The wind died away; the silence around them was total.

The old man pointed at Paul, nodding as if confirming something within his own mind; then he said, *"Liberator,"* in a high, wavering voice.

Then he pointed again at the dome and shouted, this time; *"Liberator!"* He fell to his knees and tossed handsful of something toward the egg shape; then he tossed a handful at Paul, who picked up what seemed to be dried kernels of a grayish-brown corn. He let them slip through his fingers, rubbing them gingerly afterward, as if the alien corn had somehow made them dirty.

He froze suddenly. A thunderous *scratching* sound had started *inside* the dome, as if the monstrous egg was about to hatch.

"What's happening?" Paul shouted.

The old man's laughter hissed through the night-silence.

The scratching was a pounding now, as *something* strove frantically to break free of the curving whiteness that imprisoned it.

"No!" Paul screamed, as fissures appeared on the white surface.

The old man laughed again, louder this time.

Relentless pounding. A piece of the shell flew off, pocking the sand with a tiny spurt of white.

Another piece broke away. Larger pieces were hurled into the air or collapsed into the darkness within the dome.

Something broke free.

An immense hand with long-clawed clutching fingers and red-tipped nails groped its way into the night, reached for him.

More pounding as Paul fell to his knees and buried his face in his hands. . . .

Poundingpoundingpoundingpound—

Hammering on the door of the motel unit.

Paul came awake, sitting up in bed; the back of his neck, his shoulders, his armpits were sweat-drenched.

Someone was about to beat the door of the room off its hinges.

Louise Shore was shouting, "Paul! Mr. Barrett! Wake *up!* Your wife's had an accident!"

Paul scrambled out of bed, grabbing his robe off the foot of his bed and pulling it around him.

Louise and Jimmy Shore were outside. Jimmy was supporting Sheila, who was very pale and holding her right arm with her left hand. Paul could see her arm was badly scraped and oozing blood. She was shaking her head and saying, over and over, dazedly, "I'm all right. Really, now, I'm *all right.*"

The lights had come on in a few other units now. Paul could see several pale faces glancing through the windows or screen doors.

"My God, what did you do to yourself?" he asked. "What *happened?*"

"She fell down, out near the highway," Louise explained, patting Sheila's shoulder. Jimmy helped Sheila to sit on the edge of Paul's bed while Louise closed the door, calling out, "That's the show for tonight, folks. Go on back to beddy-bye."

While Jimmy and Paul hovered around uncertainly, trying not to get in the way, Louise gently pried Sheila's fingers away from the injury, saying, "I just want to get a better look, hon."

To Paul, Sheila explained, "I went out because I couldn't sleep. I walked down the road to that coffee shop that's open twenty-four hours. I was coming back and I—I got . . . dizzy. And I fell down. Or I tripped. I'm not really sure."

Louise said, "Oh, honey, you shouldn't do that, you know? I mean, going to the Regal at this time of night, when it's full of truckers and riffraff."

"Let's see that arm," Paul said to his wife, moving closer.

"It's all right," she said. "I just scraped it when I fell."

Louise said, "I'll get a wet towel." As she stood, she told Paul, "Get her to lie down. She looks a little like she's in shock."

"I'm—" Sheila began.

"I know," Paul cut in; "you're fine. Just do as we say, will you? Lie down. There."

Louise returned from the bathroom with a moist towel and began washing the injured arm, causing Sheila to wince.

Jimmy said abruptly, " 'Course, we got insurance, but it didn't really happen on our property."

"Hush, Jimmy," said Louise. "They're not gonna sue nor nothin'. Especially since it couldn't any way be our fault."

Sheila put her uninjured arm across her eyes as though the light hurt them. She murmured, "I feel like a fool."

"Have you got some peroxide?" Louise asked Paul. When he shook his head, she turned to Jimmy. "Jimmy, go get the bottle from our medicine cabinet." She patted Sheila's good arm gently, saying, "There, there, sweetheart, just relax; everything's all right." To Paul, she added, "I don't think she broke nothin'—probably not even sprained. She'll be as good as new in no time."

When the Shores had finally left, Sheila lay with her arm still shielding her eyes. Her injured arm had been cleaned and the deeper scrapes covered with bandages. She said, "I feel like such an *idiot*." She sounded on the verge of tears.

"It's this town," he said, surprised at the depth of his resentment against El Centro and its inhabitants, as if they were in some way guilty for his dream and his wife's injury. He knew he was being unreasonably harsh in his judgment but he didn't care. He finished with, "God, I'll be glad to get out of here!"

Sheila didn't answer him. A little while later, her regular breathing told him she had fallen asleep.

Paul pulled a cover over her and turned out all lights but the bedside lamp.

Then he sat near the window, chain smoking, until he could find no more cigarettes and the sky had begun lightening into morning. All the time he felt like a sentry on guard against some unguessable, terrible enemy.

8   Ruins and Caves

Jimmy Shore shrugged apologetically and explained, "They didn't send me the parts I need. I've been on the phone twice already this morning, but it's going to be another day or two before we get you fixed up and on the road."

Paul found himself surprisingly calm in the face of this news. Somehow, he had been expecting it. This place was not going to let them go.

Not yet, anyhow.

The thought nagged him, refusing to be dismissed: the idea that the town was somehow controlling circumstances, controlling them.

A ridiculous, paranoid thought, he told himself for the umpteenth time.

A ridiculous, paranoid thought that the facts seemed to support.

"They thought they had all the parts I needed in stock," Jimmy was saying. "Turns out they didn't."

Sheila said, "Well, I'm going to have all my reading caught up, at any rate." She started for the open doors of the repair shed and the hot morning sunlight outside.

Paul followed her. The day was just beginning to heat up. He asked, "Are you going back to read? Isn't that room getting on your nerves?"

"A lot of things are getting on my nerves," she said, not looking at him but across the weed-filled lots toward the motel. "My arm is bothering me. I want to take a couple of aspirin and just sit for a while."

He ignored the first remark and said, "You had no business taking a midnight stroll around this place. You're probably lucky you didn't run into some real trouble."

"Thanks for the advice," she answered; the bitterness in her voice surprised him. He started to say something, then decided it was wiser not to start an argument.

They walked back along the road, almost to the motel; then Paul remembered, "That old man—Willie—the one who runs the curio shop. He said something about taking us to see some Indian ruins and caves. Louise was talking about them, too . . . you remember."

Sheila said offhandedly, "It would be better than a history of Navajo religion and that antique air-conditoner."

"If you're really interested, I'll go talk to Willie."

She hesitated, then said, "Ask him and see if he'll go for it. I'll go back and take my aspirin; I'm sure I'll feel fine later on."

They were near the motel now. Paul said, "You go on inside; I'll go scare up Willie and see if he's still game."

Willie Kavan was interested. Very interested.

"I'm bored as hell today," the old man explained, "and I haven't had a single customer, even though I've been open over an hour and fifteen minutes."

He was seated at his workbench, his green visor shading his eyes, repairing a broken wooden kachina. "Give me forty-five minutes to close up shop and put some gas in the jeep . . . maybe give yourselves a chance to grab a sandwich. I'll pick you up : . . you *did* say you're over at the Four Star, didn't you? Good. Oh, be sure to wear sturdy hiking shoes and take jackets: it's going to be cool down in the caves."

"Are the caves dangerous?" asked Paul. "I mean, is there any chance of getting lost down there?"

"Oh, there's always the *possibility*, but it's sure not *likely*. We'll only look at a few caves near the entrance; I've been through them so many times I could find my way blindfolded."

"Sounds good," said Paul.

"Oh, I promise you, the caves have some beautiful formations. And the ruins of old Agastan are worth a look-see, though there's not much left of the pueblo that time and the wind haven't taken care of. Not many tourists have seen them; it's too far off the beaten path. But a group of archaeologists came out from Miskatonic College in the East and were pretty excited. They did some preliminary digging last year. I went out a couple of times to check on things. I think they're coming back next spring to do a major survey with some big foundation money."

He stood up and rubbed his hands on his jeans-clad thighs. *"So:* you go get your boots and jackets and let me finish up here. See you in forty-five minutes."

Willie drove into the court of the Four Star exactly forty-five minutes later. His "jeep" turned out to be an old Ford Camino which had been red once but now was largely rust-colored.

He didn't get out, just sat in the middle of the yard honking impatiently until Paul and Sheila came out of number twelve. Willie leaned across the seat of the little truck to open the passenger door. The Barretts climbed in, Sheila sitting between the two men.

Willie handled his "jeep" like a teenager let loose after a beer bust. He swung around the court, spewing gravel and squealing his brakes and causing Louise Shore to come to the door of the motel office. She stood silent and pale behind the screen door, looking surprised and annoyed.

Willie took the road out past Shore's Garage. Jimmy was sitting on a crate outside the shop drinking a beer as they roared past. Willie honked; Jimmy waved and shouted something at them they couldn't hear.

Then they were jouncing over a road that quickly declined from asphalt through gravel to a dirt path that was little more than parallel tire ruts cutting through the desert sand and clay. A cloud of dust followed them like exhaust.

After ten minutes, Willie pointed toward the foothills of the Sierra Morenas and indicated a single outcropping of rock, which was their goal.

Willie said, "Father Perez named the mountains for the Sierra Morena range in Spain, near Saragossa, where he was born. Old Agastan is about one-third of the way up that cliff—the one the Spanish called 'Azul' and the Indians named 'Shiwanna'—for the blue color."

The clarity of the desert air was deceptive. The hazy-blue peaks which seemed to be only eight or ten miles distant turned out to be some twenty-five miles away.

All around them, sagebrush and rabbit brush were a dusty-gray sea. As the road grew worse and was interrupted with frequent sandy stretches, Willie slowed the truck to about twenty miles an hour.

He kept up a line of patter to which the Barretts paid only partial attention.

"I used to live up in Taos," he said, "years ago. This area seems pretty tame compared to what shennanigans went on there.

"There was old man Manby found with his head cut off. Funny thing: his head was cut off *after* he was dead. That was in 1929—before my time. My father told me about it. Nobody ever came to trial, though."

"No suspects?" asked Paul.

"No crime! Jury said he died of natural causes, so the beheading, while showing a certain lack of respect for the departed, didn't actually constitute a *crime*." He laughed. "There was another case. A miner named Wilkinson was beheaded after he was dead. Everyone suspected his partner, fellow named Ferguson, who died insane. Story is, he went crazy from remorse and fear. Well, if he killed his partner, there's cause for the remorse. But they don't specify what he was afraid of—apparently it wasn't the law—at least, no law *we* know of."

Willie swerved suddenly to avoid a large rock in the middle of the road, throwing Paul against the door and Sheila against Paul. "Take it easy!" Paul shouted, trying unsuccessfully to mask his fear with a laugh. Sheila said nothing, but her face was unusually pale. Paul began to wonder just how good an idea this adventure really was.

"Sorry 'bout that," Willie said, and continued, "Then there was—Hell! I can't remember her name—this woman who found out another woman had crossed her and stuffed the other gal's stove with dynamite. Pretty messy, that. When they brought her to trial, she told the court she had been bewitched into doing what she'd done. I don't recall that the jury bought that line of defense, but there's always been a pretty strong element of witchcraft hereabouts. Lots of weird goings-on.

"Years and years ago, there were night fires, one after another, which gutted the buildings around the main plaza in Taos. Some folks said they happened because whites had offended Indian spirit-folk. None of the buildings were saved, that's for sure!"

Sheila said, with a thin smile, "Don't you have something a little more cheerful in the story line?"

"Oh, sure; there's been romantic stories. With happy endings, even. One young sheepherder killed a fellow and gave as his defense that he was in love with the other fellow's wife."

"My God!" said Paul. "Now *that's* romantic. I can hardly wait to hear the happy ending."

"The jury let him off," Willie explained. "Said he was too weak-minded to hang."

"Well, I asked for it," Paul said.

They were close now to the sloping mass of rock fragments at the foot of the nearest cliffs, including the peak which Willie had pointed out to them.

He pointed to a ledge several hundred feet up, announcing, "The ruins are up there. Over to the right there used to be irrigated fields, when the pueblo was still operating."

"What did they grow?" Sheila asked.

"Maize, pumpkins, beans. Gourds and cotton. Turkeys too—but they were more interested in using the feathers for decoration than eating them." He pointed out a tangled mass of gold and pink weeds. "There was a creek over there; it's dry now. And the old irrigation ditches have collapsed—there's nothing left of them at all. One of the archaeologists who was here last year said there was a lookout post on the other side of the creek bed, but I couldn't find it. From what I understand, it wasn't much more than a wooden platform two stories high with a brush roof. Whoever was there would keep an eye out for birds or small animals or two-legged thieves like Navajos, Apaches, or Comanches. . . . Well, here we are!"

Willie stopped his truck about a hundred yards from the tumbled mass of boulders which he told the Barretts marked the head of the main trail to the ruins and cave entrance.

They climbed out of the cab. The sun had heated the exterior so that the simple business of locking up was painful.

Willie steered them to the foot of a steep trail zigzagging up the jagged wall of striated brick-red, red-brown, and black rock. Before he started up the path, he picked up a single pebble and tossed it alongside the trail.

"You both might as well do the same," he said.

"Why?" asked Sheila.

"The Indians say it has the power to make the climb less tiring."

"And does it work?" Paul asked with a smile.

"It couldn't hurt."

They dutifully found and tossed pebbles alongside Willie's. Then they began their ascent, with Willie leading the way. Sheila followed and Paul brought up the rear. They made their way slowly, mindful of the loose shale and uneven footing.

After about twenty minutes' climb, the trail suddenly widened and the angle of ascent eased, then leveled off.

They emerged from an outcropping of boulders onto a roughly semicircular ledge protected by the curving cliff face behind and a sudden drop where the eastern edge fell away to the desert floor. Paul estimated the area was about a thousand feet across and perhaps seven hundred and fifty feet deep. The place was empty except for occasional upthrust boulders and a scattering of what appeared to be low mounds of earth or ridges of rock toward the rear of the plateau.

Looking out, Paul could see the little cluster of white and brown buildings composing El Centro; far beyond, so tiny he could hardly see it at all, was a gleaming white speck in the sage-colored immensity of the desert: Mission Nuestra Señora de Agastan. The highway unrolled across the flatlands in a straight line, like unspooled black ribbon. Paul saw it all with such severe clarity that it seemed unreal.

Willie guided them to a point midway between the cliffs and the shelf rim. They found themselves on the lip of an immense, perfectly circular excavation some sixty feet in diameter.

"What is this?" Sheila asked.

"This is the Big Kiva the archaeologists from Miskatonic were so excited about," Willie answered.

Sheila said, "A kiva is a Pueblo holy place, right?"

"Um-hmm," Willie agreed. "But kivas served a lot of purposes. Sometimes the Indians used them for secret ceremonies; a lot of times they just held social gatherings."

For a few moments they just stood looking quietly down into the ruin.

Finally Willie said, "The walls used to stand several feet above ground. The university fellows said it was really something in its heyday."

All that was left now was the below-ground portion and less than a foot of stone-and-adobe wall surrounding the depression.

Inside, a double-bench arrangement ran around the floor of the pit, the walls of which were faced with the same masonry as the coping. The wider bench was about two and a half feet wide and about three feet above the floor and two feet below ground level. A second, smaller bench was set just below the other; this was about a foot wide and perhaps six inches above the flooring of beaten earth and sand.

Paul could make out what were clearly the remains of four masonry pillars made of blocks of stone cemented with adobe mortar. These formed a square within the circling walls; each pillar was set about fifteen feet from the wall. Though the columns had crumbled to within a few inches of the floor, there was enough scattered material of a similar sort to suggest to Paul that they had once extended much higher.

"Did those pillars hold up the roof?" he asked Willie.

"That's right." The old man nodded.

"What did the structure look like when the Tawas used it?" Sheila wondered.

Willie shaded his eyes before he answered, "I heard one scientist figure the pillars at twelve–fourteen feet high and the outside walls a little over eight feet. He figured it sloped from the center down to the walls, so it would have been somewhat dome-shaped, like a half-buried egg."

For some reason, Paul found Willie's description disturbing: it reminded him vaguely of something—like a thing dreamed and long forgotten. He put these thoughts aside and followed Willie and Sheila, who were climbing down into the pit itself.

Willie was telling Sheila, "They cleaned this out and did a lot of digging; it was pretty well filled with debris. A lot of it looked burned, so they figure the place was destroyed by fire. They couldn't decide whether it was an accident or the Indians did it because a kiva no longer in use is supposed to be destroyed. The Spanish might even have burned it during the uprisings, but there's no record of it if they did."

They were standing near the center of the circle now. Paul felt vaguely as though he were trespassing. He had the fleeting impression of a cloud-shadow sweeping across the kiva floor and the surrounding plateau—but the sky overhead was the purest blue, unbroken by a single cloud.

"What was this?" asked Sheila. She was standing over a rectangular depression lined with fire-blackened masonry. About a foot and a half deep, it was filled with stone, ashes, and fragments of burned plaster. It was midway between the two southern pillars.

"That was the fire pit or fire altar," Willie told her. "The community's sacred fire was kept here."

At the exact center of the kiva, Paul discovered an oval hole about two feet by one and a half feet. The upper edges were lined with plaster; the sides sloped down into a round hole about a foot in diameter and perfectly circular, which plunged straight down into the bedrock.

"And this?" Paul asked.

"Most likely a *sipapu,* a symbol of the place where, according to Tawa legends, the ancestors of the tribe climbed from a lower world into this one. It's kind of a symbolic womb." He stared down at it before adding, "Usually *sipapus* aren't as deep as this. Legends about this place say it leads directly to the center of the earth, where certain gods—or devils (it's gotten a bit scrambled over the years) —still live. Indians believe lots of spirit-folk live inside hills or under the earth—like T'yotsaviyo, a child-eating ogre who's supposed to live inside Black Mesa over by San Ildefonso Pueblo. They claim the Black Mesa is honeycombed with tunnels and caves where the monster lives—just like the mountain under us.

"The researchers from the university came up with a lot of local scam on these ruins from pueblos where people are still living. One story has it that when the sorcerer El Brujo was here, he would call up voices out of the earth through this hole. Supposedly, the voices were so loud that the earth shook and the people hid inside their houses. Another story has it that twin gods (or devils—who knows?), one red and one white, climbed up out of the hole to powwow with El Brujo. This was supposed to have been witnessed by men of unimpeachable honesty. 'Course, those stories are beyond being taken with even *two* grains of salt, but they're interesting."

As if compelled, Paul stepped to the edge of the *sipapu* and extended his hand over it. A draft of cool air was blowing steadily upward, accompanied by a faint whistling sound.

He stepped back quickly.

His sense of unease was growing.

Sheila also thrust her hand into the column of cold air, commenting on how icy it felt.

Willie said, "That air is probably blowing up from a cave hundreds of feet down. These hills are riddled with caves. The ones we'll see are just a small part of what's here; there are so many, they may *never* be fully explored."

Sheila asked uneasily, "You're sure there's no danger of getting lost?"

Willie chuckled. "I'm positive. We're not going to go beyond the few I know like the back of my hand. I'm no fool—contrary to appearances," and he laughed again.

They wandered across to the north side of the circle. There the double row of benches was broken by a doorway leading into the remains of a rectangular chamber adjoining the main structure; this little room was also roofless and masonry-lined. The floor of this alcove was on a level with the kiva floor; its dimensions were about twenty feet by ten. At one time the room had been painted red; some reddish coloring still remained in patches of crumbling plaster on the walls.

"This reminds me of something I read," Sheila commented.

"What's that?" Paul asked.

"Cave men would sometimes smear the walls of a small cave with red to make a place for creating magic. The color meant life or blood or fire—or all three. I wonder if this is an extension of the same idea."

"Beats me," said Willie. "You'd have to talk to some of those university types to get a solid answer."

He walked across the alcove and indicated a single circular niche dug into the earth opposite the entrance about three feet above the floor. He explained, "They probably put a kachina here during their ceremonies and set up *pahos*, decorated prayer-sticks, in front of them."

"Were the kachinas they used like the ones for sale in

your shop?" Paul asked, remembering the gaudy wooden figurines in the glass cases in Willie's shop.

Willie nodded. "About the same, I'd guess."

Where patches of red plaster still adhered to the walls, Paul could see fragments of decorative patterns that had been carved into the plaster and filled with white paint. Little of the white remained, making it difficult to decipher some of the designs that wind and rain had nearly scoured away.

Willie pointed out some designs, remarking, "That diamond-inside-diamond pattern signifies the all-seeing eye of the Earth Mother; the little three-pronged trumpets are supposed to be squash blossoms, meaning a lot of things—fertility, mainly. Over here . . ."

But Paul was not paying attention. Just above the chamber floor he found a border made up in part of the design:

He recognized the pattern from Sheila's necklace. He pointed this out to her and she stood staring at it for a long time.

"That's another Earth Mother symbol," said Willie offhandedly. "It's used a lot among the Pueblos."

"I know," said Sheila. "I have it carved on a necklace we bought recently."

"Oh?" said Willie. "I'd like to see it sometime."

"I have it with me now," said Sheila, and handed it over to him.

He turned it over and over admiringly in his hands. "A beautiful piece of work. It's pretty rare now. Only old women of the Tawas ever wore this. How'd you get it?"

Sheila explained.

Willie said, "That old woman *wanted* you to have this; you got a real museum piece for a song. Still," he added handing it back to her, "there's been a lot of stories—good and bad—associated with the blood-moon. I just hope you didn't get more than you bargained for."

Paul, uncomfortable with Willie's stories, said suddenly, in a loud voice, "There don't seem to be any doors or steps. How did people get in and out?"

"You could only enter through a roof hole by using a ceremonial ladder; it's the same with all kivas."

"Oh," Paul said, then added, "Shouldn't we be moving along if we're going to see those caves?"—though he was acutely aware of a sudden unwillingness to enter the dark caves.

They clambered out of the kiva pit and headed toward the northernmost sector of the plateau. There they found the remains of the pueblo proper huddled against the base of the protecting cliffs.

They passed the remains of an outer wall, little more than a ridge of earth now. A series of shallow rectangular depressions were the original foundations of the pueblo; now these were filled with deposits of fine sand. The scattered bones of some rodent littered the floor of one small room; in the corner of another, they discovered a hole about two and one-half feet in diameter dropping into a black pit too deep for them to see the bottom.

A faint *scrabbling* sound arose from the darkness; *something* was moving around in the shadows beneath their feet.

"Jesus!" said Paul, drawing back from the opening. "What the hell is that?"

Willie shrugged. "Rat, maybe. Skunk. Or bat. I'm not about to go down there and find out." He laughed. "Or maybe it's a ghost." His laugh was louder this time.

Paul and Sheila backed away from the hole, repelled by the smell of something dead rising from the darkness into the warmer upper air.

Paul felt the weight of an alien past pressing in on him on all sides. Sheila seemed abstracted herself, and he wondered if she, too, was feeling it.

Willie was staring at him with a curious smile; the old man said, "You feel it too, don't you? That sense of an . . . *energy*, something you can't quite put a finger on?"

Paul nodded, startled by the accuracy of the statement.

Willie went on, "I really believe the Tawa Indians hereabouts were in touch with—oh, call it earth-energy or natural magic or whatever. You'd *think* the power would fade away when the pueblo was abandoned or the clan died out. But in some places—places where it was strongest—I think the power survives. *Here,* for example, I think what we're feeling is a trace of Tawa magic that will last long after even these foundations are gone, because this was a genuine place of power. Or"—he laughed harshly—"maybe I'm just crazy."

Sheila shook her head. "You're not imagining it: whatever it is, I feel it too."

As they followed Willie toward the cliff wall, they passed a number of huge boulders that sheltered a deep, wide cistern cut into the rock. It was dry now, except for a little mirror-smooth pool of water at its very center. It was surrounded by the remains of a low stone wall; several dry-looking bushes grew alongside. Swifts—little gilded lizards—flickered through the sunlight and shadow along the edge.

Behind the cistern was the trail which led from the ledge to a cave mouth several hundred feet above them.

As they mounted this second trail, which was wider and much less steep than the trail up to the ruins, Willie told them, "The other path was designed to be difficult so that the Indians could defend it easily. This trail was off-limits, too—but it had so many taboos and witch warnings that no one, townsfolk *or* invaders, would think of taking a step along it without some pretty strong protective magic. The Tawa always believed caves were places of power and sorcery. Only medicine men and a few hand-picked assistants were allowed up into these caves."

He continued, "Fear of ghosts and witchcraft has always been pretty strong among the Pueblos. This plugged right into what the Spanish believed. I heard somewhere that the Spaniards even claimed the Pueblo Revolts were the result of demonic influences on the heathen Indians."

His explosive snort mixed both humor and derision. "That was probably a convenient way for the padres and governors to explain their mishandling of Indian affairs. The Casserites may actually have believed that story, but I doubt it."

The cave entrance, when they reached it, was low and unimpressive-looking. They had to stoop while they followed a passage that ran perhaps twenty feet; Paul immediately became claustrophobic but fought down his fears, determined not to let the others see his discomfort. At its end, the passage suddenly opened into a large chamber.

The three of them carried powerful flashlights that Willie had provided; in addition, the old man had a canvas pouch full of batteries, matches, and candles. He also carried a Coleman lantern for emergency.

As he led them along the cave floor, which sloped sharply downward, their flashlight beams sliced through the darkness, picking out the trail and outcroppings of interest.

Willie kept up a running commentary all through the initial series of interlocking caverns. "The Tawas believed this was a direct road to the center of the earth, where powerful spirits lived. The first white men to explore these caves were the Casserite padres. I guess the Indians let them in because they were looked on as medicine men themselves. The Spanish priests only went a little ways in. There's one story, though, that says Padre Perez went deep enough into these caves to meet the devil, who was on his way up to the surface. Apparently they had quite a little palaver before Perez ordered old Satan back to Hell. Look!"

The beam of Willie's flashlight picked out a white limestone formation that looked like a giant upthrust hand.

"That's *Maria's Hand*," he said, letting the light play over the curious shape while they paused. "One of the earliest explorers named it that because it reminded him of his dead wife's hand."

The Barretts murmured something appropriate; after a minute, they continued on their way, Willie frequently picking out distinctive formations with the beam of his flashlight. "There's the *Emperor's Pagoda*," he said, indicating a stone shaped like an immense layered cake which towered above them. "And that's *Little Niagara*," he informed them, highlighting a mass of limestone deposit clinging to one wall like a frozen waterfall.

Paul was growing more uncomfortable as the chilly, damp air seeped through his jacket, making it difficult for him to concentrate on the formations. Sheila's initial hesitation at exploring the caves seemed to have departed; she seemed to be honestly enjoying herself—for the first time since they had been stranded in El Centro.

They entered another medium-size cave almost filled by a

perfectly rounded pool of water; only a narrow ledge encircled it. Rust-colored deposits gave the pool a reddish cast.

"This is the *Devil's Mirror*," Willie announced. "The
water is so smooth, it acts like a mirror. Have a look for
yourselves."

Sheila leaned over and studied her reflection, smiling at
the looking-glass effect of the water. Then she turned to
Willie to ask him something about another formation across
the pool from them.

As Willie and Sheila moved further along the path to
study the new formation, Paul lingered over his own reflection. He was startled to see how pale he looked, how weary
—since he didn't really feel especially tired.

He drew back suddenly when, at some slight depth below
the reflective surface of the water, the features of a dark-
faced bearded man appeared momentarily, then blended
with his own mirrored face. His astonishment turned to fear
when, below the melded features, he sensed a dark, monstrous *something* swimming deep within the pool, an inky
blackness upon which the features of the stranger and his
own face seemed to float.

He forced himself to look again, refusing to let his fear
take control of him.

The bearded visage and the shadow within the pool had
vanished. His own anxious features stared back at him. He
decided the whole thing had been a curious optical trick.

Neither Sheila nor Willie seemed to have noticed his
sudden reaction. Willie was starting into the next cave;
Sheila called impatiently to Paul to join them.

He followed after the other two; he found himself in a
passageway which forked to the right and left. He saw
Willie's light bobbing along down the left-hand corridor and
pursued it, trying not to let his nerves get the better of him.
But the darkness around him was oppressive, and his experience beside the *Devil's Mirror* had unnerved him. He kept
telling himself that he had only imagined it. *God knew,*
during his breakdown he had had more than his share of
wild imaginings. Perhaps the light and water had together
played a trick on his eyes. He could rationalize it all, he
realized, and yet he could *not* rationalize away the fear that
had not left him since he had seen—or thought he saw—
that curious double vision in the water.

He peered ahead, saw the disk of Willie's light, and followed it into a passage which branched off from the one he had been following. He glanced at the luminous face of his watch and realized that they had been exploring the caves for over an hour and a half. They should be working their way back soon, he decided. He was thankful that Willie was so sure of the caves, since passages seemed to intersect and run off each other in all directions.

A sudden chill shook him: he realized he could no longer distinguish Willie's flashlight. He stopped and discovered he could no longer hear Willie's chatter or Sheila's voice. He called out to them but they didn't answer. Impatiently, he called again, louder this time. Still they didn't respond.

He snapped off his flashlight for a second to locate their lights.

Suffocating darkness and stillness pressed in on him. He saw no reassuring flicker of light.

Panic took hold of him. He tried to force himself into a calm retracing of his steps but he could discover no sure route back. Passageways opened out all around him. After a few steps he knew he was lost. He looked anxiously for a passage leading up: all the ways seemed to slope down. The tunnel walls around him glistened wetly in the beam of his flashlight.

He became aware of an increasing coldness.

He started along a corridor that at least seemed nearly level, shouting, "Sheila! Willie! I'm *lost*, for God's sake!"

Suddenly he froze in midstep.

A sound like whispering, like a voice speaking from a great distance, issued from a passage opening off to the right. Paul called into the darkness of the entrance, "Sheila!? Willie?!"

The whispering rose again from the darkness. Paul heard a single phrase being repeated over and over, but he could not decipher the exact words. He stepped closer to the mouth of the tunnel, but something kept him from entering it.

The whisperer drew nearer; now he could make out the words, "Here I am. Help me. Here I am. Help me. . . ."

Paul shone his light into the corridor, then yelled as the beam of his flashlight lit up the figure of a man. The face— gleaming pale white in the electric light—was decayed-looking. In a flash he recognized the funerary features of Padre Perez from the statue in Mission Agastan.

The specter's hands were outstretched in a gesture of supplication. The crazy-bright eyes stared straight into his own; the lips were frozen in a shout of horror.

Then the thing glided slowly forward; the hem of the monkish robe hovered an inch above the floor of the passage.

The figure began whispering again, "Help me. Help me. Help me."

In terror, Paul turned and ran along the gallery to his left, only to be confronted, beyond a turn in the passage, wtih the specter again, as the whispers filled the whole corridor with the words, "Help me. Here I am."

As Paul retreated the way he had come, he stumbled over a projection in the floor. Thrown to a half-kneeling position, he discovered the apparition bearing down on him from the very direction in which he had been running.

He scrambled to his feet, backing away, his hands raised protectively.

The horror floated to within a few feet of him, then came to a stop. Frantically it warned, "Too late! Too late! The Old Enemy is here. Not far. Very near now. Nearer."

The image dissolved in the beam of his flashlight. There was nothing but the glimmer of his light on the moist walls in front of which the ghostly figure had stood. Paul felt his knees growing weak under him; he forced himself to take several deep breaths, fighting back the dizziness that threatened to overwhelm him. He dared not lose consciousness now.

A deep breath/a pause to listen/silence/he took another deep breath/paused to listen . . .

Far away, down the passage which stretched arrow-straight in front of him, beyond the limit of his flashlight beam, he heard the terrifying sound of loud bestial breathing approaching him at steamroller speed.

He began to run in the opposite direction.

The sound filled the passage behind him.

Coming closer.

Closer.

He ran in a panic, his flashlight beam bobbing along crazily in front of him, picking out a hasty path, while the sound became a roaring-snarling all around him.

It was almost on top of him now; he was sobbing with terror but he did not dare to look behind to see what had come raging up from the depths of Hell to harry him so.

He felt the flooring underfoot vibrating with monstrous footfalls; a deafening filled his ears. He ran in desperation, sure that it couldn't be more than a pace or two behind him.

Less.

Then Paul gave a sudden shout as the ground fell away from him and he stumbled forward into black nothingness. . . .

Sheila, running ahead of Willie, said, "I'm *sure* I heard something down here."

Willie, in a voice full of worry and irritation said, "If your husband has sense enough to stay put, he won't get very far, and we'll find him quick enough."

Sheila led them a little further down the passage. Around a turn, they spotted a gleam of light. A moment later, they discovered Paul, lying beside his flashlight. He had obviously fallen at a point where a side passageway sloped sharply down into the larger corridor.

Willie knelt beside the unconscious man and did some poking and prodding and listening; then he said to Sheila, "He's all right; just had the wind knocked out of him. Got himself a nice bump on the head, but I doubt there's any concussion."

Even as he was saying this, Paul began to come around. The others were unable to get anything coherent out of him: he was frightened and confused; he only wanted to get out of the caves, away from the darkness into which he stared with unnerving terror.

They helped him to his feet. He murmured a few words of complaint, but neither Sheila nor Willie could understand him. Sheila said, as though soothing a troubled child, "I know. I know. Everything is going to be fine. Let's follow Willie now. I think we've done all the sightseeing we can do today."

Willie, helping Sheila support Paul, led them gradually out of the caves.

When they emerged into daylight, Paul managed a word of thanks, greeting the hot late-afternoon sunlight like a long-lost friend.

Willie insisted that they all sit for a long time in the shelter of a nearby overhang. Paul obeyed, though he wanted to get as far from the caves as he could. Sheila dozed briefly in the sun but awoke suddenly, startled by an unremembered, jarring dream.

Later, as they climbed down to Willie's truck, Paul felt the sunshine burning the cold and fear out of him; he told himself that everything that had happened to him in the darkness was the product of overwrought nerves and an overactive imagination.

He told Sheila and Willie only that he had gotten lost and panicked, and taken a misstep.

They seemed satisfied with this explanation.

When they crossed the plateau with its ruins, Paul insisted, though he could not say why exactly, that they cross as far from the kiva circle as possible. Something about that ancient place of worship seemed connected with the darkness and fear of the caves below; he wanted only to get away from the mountains, the caves, and the ruins.

Beyond that, and more importantly, he now felt a desperate need to leave El Centro. He did not know where the idea had come from that he was in danger as long as he stayed in the town, but he felt, deep inside of him, a frightening certainty that the danger was genuine, even though he could give it no name.

If he lingered, something horrific was going to happen; something terrifying was going to be revealed.

He had to get away from this place before he was forced to learn what that revelation would be.

And its cost to him.

9 Enotea

Paul lay in the sticky heat of late afternoon; he had asked Sheila to turn off the air-conditioner because the clatter annoyed him.

He was alone at the moment. Sheila had gone off somewhere with Louise; the ubiquitous Mrs. Shore had turned up in time to help Willie and Sheila assist a still-dazed Paul out of Willie's truck and into his bed. Sheila had wanted to call a doctor; Paul had refused. Willie had convinced her that there seemed no real need for one, that the worst of Paul's problems would be a sore head in the morning.

Paul felt drained; he had dozed for half an hour. Now, however, in the thick, still warmth of the darkened room, sleep would no longer come. Instead, he found himself pursuing a string of memories which had begun when Louise had leaned over him to fluff up his pillow. There had come to his nostrils a mixture of cloying perfume and sweat which had tantalized him with its familiarity, though he could not remember exactly what it reminded him of.

Until now.

Now he knew what the sweet-sweaty smell was.

It was the same fragrance that had clung about Enotea. Enotea. The name brought a jumble of memories in its wake; he lay in bed, helplessly recalling everything.

He had noticed her from the very first. Her cafe-au-lait skin and copper-colored hair in tight braids decorated with

141

blue and red beads that hung Egyptian-like, framing her face. She had stood out like a sculpture, like a goddess, amid the tiers of pale-faced freshmen in his First Year Survey of English Literature.

She stood out like an exotic, dark oasis in the bleakness of yet another academic year of stale lectures served up to bored or uncomprehending students. At the very moment he felt his career—his life—imploding, Enotea had erupted into his consciousness like a hot perfumed wind, fragrant with spices and dark promises, sweeping him out of his prosaic existence into the excitement of the sensual, the sexual, the forbidden.

And she knew it. She played his beguilement for all it was worth. She sat always in the front row, her sandaled feet with their red-painted nails keeping time to some secret rhythm; her arms, laden with silver and gold circlets, lying along her thighs, on the thin material that clung so provocatively; her tongue tasting endlessly her full red lips.

Paul had no chance—had no desire to resist. He fell in love—in lust—and welcomed the opportunity to escape from all the crushing failures of his life: a marriage gone sour, a career going nowhere, impotence.

Enotea had helped him forget the first two. As for the third . . .

She had come to his office late one afternoon, ostensibly to discuss an upcoming midterm. In fact, they had both abandoned the fiction after a few minutes of carefully sounding out the territory.

She had invited him to go for coffee to exchange ideas in a "more conducive" atmosphere; he had, with a readiness that surprised even him, accepted.

Enotea had selected a small cafe on the Berkeley-Oakland boundary. There, over cappuccinos, she had first insisted he no longer call her "Ms. Smith," but rather, "Taya—the first 'a' is long."

And he had insisted she call him Paul—though he was aware, as he said this, how foolish it sounded: she had been calling him Paul ever since they had backed his car out of the faculty parking lot. She smiled and continued, "I changed the spelling from the . . . Greek, I guess—Tea, because people would pronounce it *tea*—and you know, I like coffee. When they're confronted with the whole name, then

they have to ask for help to get it right. But with a nickname
—well, they're never gonna spell it right or say it right, so I
let them spell it the way it sounds and give them a spelling
they can sound out easy. I talk too much, don't I?" she
added suddenly.

"Not at all. Sometimes—lately especially—I'm not very
good at holding up my end of a conversation. You take up
the slack charmingly."

She tapped her coffee cup against his and smiled. "That's
the nicest, most roundabout way I've ever had anyone agree
with me. What you're saying is, I talk too much but you
don't mind."

"I don't. I'd like to keep you talking. Let's talk about the
midterm or tell me how you got such an unusual name."

"Enotea was a sorceress in classical times. She played a
trick on a wizard once. He got back at her, though. Made
her give birth to fire over and over again. Her suffering was
awful, but I think she got free of it." She paused, then
added, "But the *real* significance is: my mother heard the
name sometime and liked the sound. I have a sister Candida,
named for the sound. That's even more off the wall, to my
way of thinking. Oh-oh—here I go again. Talk, talk, *talk!*"

"Don't apologize. Please. I'm going to get us some refills."

When he returned with fresh cups of the espresso and
steamed milk, they sipped for a moment in silence, staring
at each other appraisingly. She set down her cup and licked
the milk-foam off her upper lip with the tip of her tongue.
A delicate, and delicately suggestive, gesture. Paul felt himself responding and was amazed after the problems Sheila
and he had been having recently.

"About the midterm . . ." he began, making a last effort
to give things at least the appearance of a student-teacher
meeting that was not filled with hidden agendas.

He was disappointed when she said matter-of-factly,
"Yeah, I've been thinking about how you said we could
turn in a paper if we didn't want to take the exam. We'd
just have to clear the topic with you. I've been thinking of
doing a paper on William Butler Yeats and his philosophy
of the phases of the moon."

"Yeats had some pretty complicated ideas," he said cautiously.

"That's why this paper would be *important*!" she said, animatedly. "You *see,* you *see:* I'm in *touch* with what he was saying." She saw his look of confusion and laughed. "Let me slow down a little." She made herself take a deep breath, then continued, speaking slowly, "I'm into psychic phenomena. Auras. Psychokinesis. ESP. The astral world. I've made a study of occult things since I found out my mother had the second sight. It all fits together: the I Ching and the spirit world and the reason people act so crazy when the moon is full. 'The moon in the blood,' some poet said—"

"Not Yeats—"

"No, of course not—don't interrupt, Paul—can't you see I'm trying to give you an *idea?*" Another deep breath, then she continued, "That same poem talks about 'blood-fire,' 'birthblood,' 'the moon and heart on fire'—I'm going to use that poem—"

"You'd better find out the poet's name before you turn your paper in."

"Paul! Please let me finish. I'm going to use that poem as the key to Yeats's philosophy. I'm going to *explicate,* make him clear, because I think his philosophy is what's going to be important. Not his poems—well, they're important because they talk about his philosophy—but it's his *ideas* that are really the center. I want to bring them out, let people see clearly, because he wrote beautifully but he didn't write *clearly enough* for most people to see. And not everyone can have the psychic experiences I've had. If they did, then they'd *know,* in their hearts, what he was saying. You think I'm crazy, don't you?"

Caught off guard, Paul protested that he was intrigued with her ideas.

She finished off her coffee, then set down her empty cup, staring into it, not looking at him.

When she did look him squarely in the eye, she said, "You're not a believer. I'll have to make you into one."

Totally at a loss for a response, he smiled and shrugged, nervously sloshing the remains of his drink around and around the inside of his cup.

She nodded as if it were all decided. "*Got* to get you *believing.*"

"I'm afraid I'm too much of a skeptic."

"I've gotten through to worse than you. Come on, finish

your drink, then we're going to my apartment. I'm just over near the campus."

"I couldn't—" he began.

But in the end, he did. Phoned Sheila, who was at home, and made some excuse about visiting a friend from the department who lived in San Francisco. She was working out the final program for her symposium on "The Role of Women in Native American Religions," and accepted his explanation without question.

So he had driven Taya to her apartment.

It was a recent-vintage student co-op. Fresh beige paint covered walls that had been hastily replastered, covering nicks, gouges, cracks, and what seemed to be a fist-hole. There was a sagging couch, a splitting black beanbag chair that smelled of mildew, a card table with three matching folding chairs, a few cushions to sit on, and a stereo and TV perched on top of orange crates filled with records and books. The records were mostly by soul and blues artists; the books were a fifty-fifty split: half literature, half occult studies—books on the Tarot, divination, kirlian photography, poltergeist, and a tremendous number of books on mediumship and first-person accounts of the lives and careers of famous mediums of the late nineteenth and early twentieth centuries.

Taya brewed them an herbal tea that tasted like boiled broomstraws. She rolled them two joints of potent sinsemilla that sent him into a coughing jag which was followed by a rush that nearly sent his head rolling under the sagging green couch.

While she sat on a purple cushion and he lolled on the beanbag chair, she read his palm. He could never remember what she told him, afterward, but he remembered the sensual friction of her fingertips tracing out the lines of his hand—it seemed to run like a fine line of fire from her elegantly thin fingers through his arm, his body, arousing him to a near agony of wanting her.

She released his hand; he exhaled loudly, breathed deeply, tried to get control of his desire, of the after-affects of the grass.

"I'll be right back," she promised. As he watched her walking to the nearest bookcase, he noticed she was barefoot, noted how silently she moved. Like a priestess. Between a part in the poorly hung, brightly dyed cotton curtains, he could see it was dark out. He tried to read his watch but his arms had fallen asleep and his eyes were not focusing properly. He wondered vaguely if it were late enough for him to worry about Sheila.

But he really only wanted Taya to return, to take his hand in hers again.

When she returned, she pushed a smooth white stone into his hand and folded his fingers around it while she enclosed his fist in both her hands.

"Close your eyes and try to visualize the stone in your mind," she said. "Let's see if you have any talent for psychometry."

To please her, he did as he was told, recreated the smooth circle of white stone in his mind, where it swam like a moon in the blackness of his mind. Cool and round.

Then, unexpectedly, it changed: shading into red, dripping blood; it glowed red-hot, threatened to burn a hole from the center of his mind through the compacted darkness to emerge bubbly, incandescent, from the bone of his skull. He cried out, afraid . . .

She pried open his resisting fingers and pulled away the stone. Darkness swallowed up his vision of the burning disk; he was allowed to open his eyes once more.

Enotea stared at the stone, not at him, saying, "You got some gift. This stone came from the house of a woman I knew who was raped and murdered. She was a poet; the police found this paperweight in the room where she was killed. They think she used it to try and defend herself. What you get first is the violence, the horror her dying mind impressed in the stone. Lately, now, I can get past the *awfulness* and can begin—just *begin*—to see the shape of a man. I think, if I work at this long enough, I'll find the bastard. The police never solved the case, and she was a very good friend of mine."

She replaced the stone on the orange-crate bookshelf.

"You got some kinda seeing," she said, dropping down beside him and lighting another joint.

"It was your grass; more likely I was off on some mini-bummer."

She inhaled, held it, then spoke as she handed him the joint. "Uh-*uh*; you've got the ability."

He shrugged, savoring the marijuana.

As she accepted the half-consumed joint back from him, she said, "You're gonna be a believer, whether you want to or not."

"What time is it?"

"Around eight—you in a hurry to go somewhere?"

"Only eight. That's early." (His mouth was incredibly dry and he was having a hard time shaping his words.)

"There's lots of time. To talk or whatever."

She pulled another joint out of her skirt pocket but returned it unlit, saying, "Maybe I've got a better idea. . . ."

She leaned over and folded her arms around his neck, pulling him toward her. She kissed him quickly, let him savor it for a moment, then kissed him again. This time her tongue slid quickly past his lips and probed his mouth.

Feeling as clumsy as a man in a dream, he embraced her, pulled her toward him onto the beanbag chair. The smell of her perfume and the smell of mildew mixed crazily as they began slipping free of their clothes while never ceasing the increasingly passionate kisses.

Still later, she cooked a mixture of brown rice and tofu and gave him cup after cup of the herbal tea to ease his thirst. Then she let him shower, refusing good-naturedly his insistent demand that she join him in the tiny shower stall that smelled heavily of mildew.

When he was cleaned up and together enough to go home, she pushed him gently out the front door.

Sheila had been asleep when he returned home. She had asked him no questions the next day about his whereabouts.

And so he had embarked on a crazy affair that went against all his best instincts. But he felt so alive with Taya in comparison to the deadliness of his life with Sheila, his faltering career, that he was helpless to do anything but go wherever she led.

Only her insistence on his learning about occult things disturbed him. He was uncomfortable with the seriousness with which she would lecture him—sometimes even while they were making love—on parapsychology or the correct way to interpret tarot cards or the way something Jung had said linked psychology and the astral plane.

At first he tried to be amused, then tolerant; finally he became annoyed. But neither his irritation nor his jokes could dissuade her from her obsession with what she called "the world that's inside us and outside—all at the same time."

Sheila never gave any indication of suspecting anything. Yet, as his involvement with Taya grew, he became more and more convinced that his wife *must know*. He had not the least shred of proof, but he decided that she had discovered the reason behind his lies, his evasions, his increasing absences.

He decided to break off seeing Taya. She was good for him, but she was also leading him—because of the increased pressure on him to keep Sheila in the dark—toward destruction.

That last night, he had made up his mind to tell Taya they had to end it.

When she met him at the door of her apartment, she seemed nervous and preoccupied. He wondered if she already sensed—with that peculiar sixth sense women seemed to possess—what he was going to tell her.

But she took his hand and led him over to the card table and sat him down opposite her, saying, "I have a feeling *tonight* is going to be real important to me." She had put a single candle in a red globe holder in the center of the table between them. She reached up and turned off the overhead light. The room was dark except for the candlelight and some light filtering through the half-closed bedroom door across the room.

"Take my hands," she commanded, and they touched fingertips across the cigarette-scarred tabletop.

Paul went along with it, welcoming anything that would delay the confrontation; he could feel his resolve slipping.

"I want us to become an *opening*," she continued. "I want

us to create a space for that outside energy I feel all around me to come into this world, into our space here."

"What do I do?" he asked.

"Just be there. Where you are. What's gonna happen, will happen."

Her eyes were closed. He sat staring across at her, regretting all that he felt forced to give up. The room, he noticed, was freezing—which was unusual, because she usually kept it at an almost tropical temperature. His teeth began to chatter but he was unsure whether the cold or his increasing nervousness was the cause.

Taya's eyes popped open. She was staring at him with a glassy look that made him doubt she was truly seeing him at all. She smiled a, to him, moronic smile, almost a skeletal smile, filled with teeth, devoid of humor.

She wasn't blinking; her eyelids never flickered. He knew that wasn't right. *What the hell is going on?* he wondered, letting annoyance override the fear which he refused to admit.

"I am the seer," she said.

But the voice wasn't Taya's—not really. It was the sandpapery rasp of a crone. "I see the within that wants to emerge. I see the within striving to become the without."

"Taya," he said.

"I have no one name. And I am all the names you give me. A seer needs no name: she is her ability to see what she sees."

"You're beginning to annoy me, Taya."

"'I am the seer. I see what I see. Thus I look at you and mark the signs I see. Blood sign. Fire sign. Moon sign. Death sign. These four I see. And over your heart, the sign of opening, the sign of the outer dark, the sign of the inward turning outward. Beware of what emerges; beware of the stirring within, of the darkness seeking the light."

"Tay—"

"Not now!" At first he thought this was addressed to him, then he realized that she was speaking not to him but, apparently, to something *behind* him. Instinctively he swiveled his head but saw nothing, only the closed glass doors to the little balcony and the night beyond. From below drifted up the sounds of a poolside party.

"Please, *not yet!*" She was moaning now and shaking her

head, but her eyes remained fixed unblinkingly on him, the smile frozen in place. It felt so cold he was surprised his breath didn't condense in front of him.

Her next words were rasped out with a great effort: "I see whether I wish to or not." Her head snapped futilely from side to side in protest to what she thought she was seeing where he sat.

"Worm, stench, vile maggot-ridden slime!" she cried. "Darkness manifesting. I repudiate the vision. I will not—*Not!*"

Her head was slamming from side to side; spittle flew from her mouth, hitting his face. He was too startled by the violence of her reactions to react himself.

"The gate is open, the way is clear, the dark is manifest!" she screamed. "In you, through you—"

Paul was sure she was on some drug—or an insane mixture of them. She must have popped, shot up, snorted something ungodly. She was on the bad trip to end them all.

"The hand, the claw, the bursting forth. Fire-tempered/ blood-nailed / moon-fleshed / maggot-fingered / groping / reaching—you cannot touch me—I *repudiate* you! I deny you—don't you feel it?—mouth and claw chewing and rending through your flesh from the darkness into light? Don't you feel how you are become open wound and womb disgorging darkness upon the light, moon upon sun, blood upon everything—claw coming for me, groping—"

Suddenly she broke free of his tenuous grasp, stared horrified at him as if he had become monstrous, and, with a final terrified scream, smashed frantically through the sliding glass doors, splattering blood across the little balcony and still-intact door, and then plunged over the railing to her death in the midst of the cocktail party three stories below.

How he kept himself together enough to get away before neighbors and police discovered him, he never fully understood to the present day....

His memories became dreams. Paul slept fitfully.
In the dark, he awoke from a nightmare, soaked in sweat. He could remember nothing about the dream.

Sheila was sleeping in the other bed. He called her name softly but she didn't answer.

The luminous face of the little travel-clock on the nightstand showed it was almost one o'clock in the morning. The back of his head ached dully; he thrashed around awhile until he found a fairly comfortable position.

After a while he fell asleep again and was troubled by no dreams that he could recall.

10   Meetings

The next morning, Sheila and Louise Shore had coffee together in the little kitchen behind the motel office. Louise had come over earlier; after asking how Paul was feeling and finding out that he was still sleeping after a restless night, she had asked Sheila to "com'on over and shoot the breeze awhile."

Louise spent a good five minutes rummaging through several cupboards after she sat her guest down; the object of her search was a milk-glass creamer, companion to the sugar bowl near Sheila's elbow. She assured Sheila, ". . . it's here. I *know* it's here. The set belongs to Mama; I don't wanna lose it." She gave up after a second search turned up no creamer. "Hell! Pardon my French! but I'll bet Jimmy broke it, or he's using it to store nuts and bolts in."

Louise served the half-and-half in a small juice glass, apologizing that it was "more functonal than fancy."

Returning her attention to the coffeepot on the stove, Louise said over her shoulder, "I swear, sometimes Jimmy's just like a kid. He'll use a mixing bowl for paint or a good knife for a screwdriver if he gets impatient. He's worse than a kid, really." She paused, struck by a thought, and turned from the brewing coffee to look at Louise, asking, "You don't have kids, do you?"

Sheila smiled uneasily and said, "We decided we didn't want any. At first we put it off, and then . . . it just didn't seem to be what we wanted."

Louise sighed and said, "We can't have any. I'd like kids; I think Jimmy would too. So, it's hard."

"Why don't you adopt?"

"We talked about it, but we just didn't feel they'd really be ours."

"Maybe you should think some more about it."

"Well, maybe . . ." Louise sounded unconvinced.

Sheila took a minute to look around her. The kitchen had white walls with yellow curtains, a yellow formica countertop, and linoleum with a pattern of yellow flowers. The plastic tablecloth, still sprinkled with toast crumbs from the Shores' breakfast, was decorated with a white-and-yellow daisy design.

Louise brought two cups of coffee to the kitchen table. Sheila accepted hers with thanks and began drinking it black. When Louise had added generous amounts of sugar and cream to her own, she settled back into her chair opposite Sheila and said, "Don't worry—you really *do* look worried, you know?—Paul is going to be *fine*. You *sure* I can't offer you a doughnut or breakfast bar or something?"

"No . . . thanks." Sheila felt tired and disinclined to talk, but their own room had become unbearable. Watching Paul as he slept, long after she was up, she found herself shifting from hatred to pity and back again through a bewildering range of emotions. She felt exhausted because she no longer *knew* how she felt toward him. She could feel motherly one minute and the next resent him bitterly as a stranger inflicting himself on her the next. She felt confused—felt that El Centro was the locus of her confusion. She thought that if they could get the car running again—could get *away* from the town—she would be able to catch her breath and think things through.

As if reading her mind, Louise said, "God, I'll bet you'll be glad to get out of here."

Sheila said offhandedly, "I guess El Centro is no worse a place to be than anywhere else."

"Well, of course, you're *right*. But when things happen here, it's the *exception*, see? And, well, I guess you could say, when things happen here, there's a *difference*."

"What do you mean?" asked Sheila, rising to the bait.

"Things that happen hereabouts are *weirder*. Like the three guys who were killed out by the Agastan ruins. Just drifters, probably. There must have been a woman, too, because I heard they found a silver compact and a bracelet

—both half melted. They probably had some sort of orgy going on out there. They only identified one body; never found a trace of the woman, though they sure tried to bring her in for questioning. But you can't get much of a description from face powder and some jewelry."

"How—how did they die?" Sheila's coffee was sitting uneasily in her stomach suddenly.

"That's the funny thing: the bodies were burned, but the coroner's report printed in the *El Centro Call* said they'd been beaten to death. They figure some crazy person— maybe the woman; who knows?—tried to cover things up by pouring gasoline over the bodies and—"

"Thanks," said Sheila a little weakly; "I get the picture."

Louise apologized, "I'm sorry. I rattle on and forget some people are a little more sensitive about some things like violence and killing."

They drank their coffee silently for a moment.

Then Louise said suddenly, "There's been a lot of odd things happened out here. There was a car found abandoned out by the mission—burned—completely gutted. But there was no sign of the driver—a salesman for plumbing supplies, I recall. He never did turn up. The state police talked of foul play but they had nothing more than a burned car to go on. And they were pretty sure the fire started in the crankcase. When you got a fire like that it can go, you know—" She snapped her fingers to indicate her meaning. "All the way back to the first padres, this place has had funny goings-on."

"I know. I was reading some things in a local history book." She wondered vaguely if she should go and look in on Paul.

But Louise was going on again, talking about the Andersons this time. "They're both a bit dingy, I think. All those séances and stuff. And I don't think their painting amounts to much. They must have some money socked away, because I don't *recall* the last time I heard of anyone buying anything out of their shop. And their being mixed up with that girl Maria—that looks a little, you know, *strange*, don't you think?"

Sheila shrugged and said, "I'm sure her sister would stop any funny business."

"Don't count on *that!* Rosa is the town slut. She'd sell her own soul—or her sister's—if the price was right."

Sheila thought of Maria Seloso's dark eyes: she had seen fear in those eyes, but no taint of corruption. And she firmly believed that the Andersons, though overenthusiastic in their pursuit of occult knowledge, were not dishonest. She protested, "I didn't get that impression of things at all the other night, when we had dinner with the Andersons."

Louise was firm. "You don't know because you haven't been in town long enough. The *stories* I could tell—"

She broke off abruptly, seeing something in Sheila's eye, in the tightening of her mouth.

She fluttered her hand dismissively, saying, "Well, now. Jimmy said your car should be ready to go in another day. Then you're off to Santa Fe, aren't you?"

Sheila shook her head. "I don't think so. I've decided, as soon as the car is running and Paul is feeling well enough, that we're going to head straight home. To put it mildly, this vacation hasn't turned out quite the way I planned."

Louise refilled her own cup; Sheila asked for and received a half-cup only. She was aware of Louise studying her over the rim of her cup, and wondered what had prompted such sudden scrutiny.

After a minute or two, during which she was clearly deciding on which words to use, Louise began, in a too-offhand way, "I just wondered if things between you two were, well, *you know?* You both seem pretty much, you know, on *edge?*"

Sheila, even though she had been expecting something of this sort, found herself resenting it to the point of anger. She forced herself to reply evenly, "We've been traveling for several weeks. That's a lot of driving. Naturally—"

"Oh, naturally. I wasn't saying anything more than maybe that you both need a day or two of resting up before heading back." Louise was, obviously, torn between elation at having hit so close to home and worry over the effect of her accuracy upon Sheila.

Still, she couldn't resist a single last probe. "I have some friends; they always take, *you know, separate* vacations? Jimmy and me talked about it once but we decided we just wouldn't have as much fun alone, both of us. What do you think about a husband and wife taking separate vacations?"

Sheila looked at Louise and said, "To tell you the truth, we've never even *discussed* the possibility."

"Ummm," Louise murmured, and gave full attention to the last of her coffee.

Sheila stood up, thanking Louise for her coffee and her company.

Louise brightened and said, "Any time you want to *talk* —about anything—come on by. I'm usually around. If I'm not, I *will* be, pretty quick."

"Thanks," said Sheila.

Louise walked her as far as the office door, reminding her, "Don't forget what I said. . . ."

Sheila nodded and said, "I'll remember."

Then she walked slowly back across the motel court to number twelve. The late-morning air was still and warm all around her; she felt pleasantly drowsy. Later, in the afternoon, she promised herself, she would take a long nap, when the day was at its hottest.

Paul was still asleep; the bedclothes were tangled around his legs. He was naked; his member half erect. Sheila felt a slight stirring of desire; she buried it in the business of straightening the blankets and drawing a sheet up to his chest.

She touched his forehead with her fingertips; it was cool but moist. His shoulders, the back of his neck, and the pillow were sticky with sweat; she wondered if it were due solely to the warmth gathering in the room. Or had some nightmare followed him into the morning?

He opened his eyes briefly at her touch and stared at her. He did not really seem to see *her;* his eyes seemed focused on nothing. After a moment, he closed them again and fell asleep, muttering a sound of protest. Then he turned on his side, away from her. She reacted to this unconscious gesture as if it were a reproach.

She moved restlessly around the room, picking up, then replacing, the copy of *Shogun* she had determined to complete while on vacation. Nor did any of the other books or magazines hold her interest for more than a few minutes.

She sat on the green vinyl-covered stool beside the dressing table and dug a file out of her purse. She began working on her nails with an attentiveness she hadn't given them in years.

Then she set the file down impatiently and stared into the mirror, studying the reflection of her sleeping husband. When she turned and stared at his bed, she saw that he had rolled onto his back again and was sleeping with an arm across his eyes, as if the light bothered him. His free hand had pushed the sheet down below his waist and now lay cupped protectively over his genitals. Again she felt the unwelcome faint response within her.

She rose up and touched his head again; though cool, it no longer felt damp. She made no effort to adjust the sheet this time, since it seemed to make him uncomfortably warm.

She realized that he might sleep for hours yet. She drew the curtains across the lowered blinds and was annoyed at how little it did to cut down the brightness. After a final quick glance at Paul, Sheila stepped outside. She was careful to bring her hat and sunglasses with her.

The day was warming up rapidly; her watch showed it was nearing noon. She thought of lunch but she did not really feel hungry. The heat and a persistent, growing sense of uneasiness suppressed her appetite.

She began walking, with no real idea of where she was heading. Through the screen door of the motel office, she could hear Louise's television going.

She turned and headed toward the center of town. The sun glinted off the glass and chrome of parked cars, dazzling her eyes even through her sunglasses.

In the shadow of the awning overhanging the grocery store, she met Helen Anderson, who was just emerging with two large shopping bags; the gust of air-conditioned coolness which accompanied the woman out of the store refreshed her for a second before the oppressive heat swallowed it up.

Helen said, "Well, this *is* a coincidence—though I don't believe in *coincidences,* you remember," and the older woman chuckled, adding, "All meetings are preordained, I'm sure."

Sheila smiled politely and said, "I want to thank you for the lovely dinner. And please thank Cyrus—"

"You can thank him yourself, if you want to," said Helen,

and she gestured with an upraised elbow. "He's right over there."

Sheila saw Cyrus climbing out of a dusty gray station wagon parked a short distance away. He came over and helped his wife with the groceries; he and Sheila exchanged pleasantries.

Helen said, "We—Cyrus and I—wanted to talk so much *more* the other night . . ." She asked suddenly, "Have you had lunch yet? Cyrus and I are just on our way home for a bite and we'd love to have you join us. Tell the truth: have you eaten?"

"Well, I—" Sheila began; under the intensity of Helen's gaze, she found herself unable to make a polite lie. "No . . but I *couldn't* impose a second time."

"Nonsense, nonsense, you're not imposing," said Cyrus.

Helen added, as if this decided the matter, "We're just going to have a salad—nothing fancy." She took Sheila by the elbow, gently urging her toward the car. "Come along, now; you just climb in the back seat with me, and Cyrus can play chauffeur."

Sheila had a momentary crazy impression that she was being kidnapped by this middle-aged couple. She protested weakly that she shouldn't leave Paul; but Cyrus quickly extracted enough information from her to decide that "Your husband will probably sleep until late afternoon and wake up feeling fit as a fiddle. Let him sleep; you just give us your company for an hour or so. We feel we hardly got to know you folks at all the other evening."

Sheila surrendered; she was sure the man was right about Paul.

Cyrus drove slowly the short distance to their house. Sheila helped them carry in the groceries from the back of the station wagon.

She refused Cyrus's offer of a drink, settling for a tall glass of iced tea instead.

She sat with Cyrus at the kitchen table while Helen fixed their lunch and firmly turned down all offers of help with the comment, "It's no trouble at all. It won't be fancy—just some cottage cheese and fresh fruit. But on days like this, you don't *want* much more."

Sheila agreed and took a long swallow of her iced tea.

Cyrus said, "We—Helen and myself—were talking after you folks left. We feel sure that one of you—"

"Could be both," Helen interrupted, not looking up from the sink, where she was rinsing a colander full of lettuce, "but that seems unlikely."

"Oh, I agree it's improbable that *both* of you were contributing to what was happening here during the sitting. But it seems a good bet that *one* of you has some psychic talent you may not even be aware of." He fixed Sheila with a firm nod that implied any objection from her would be wasted effort.

Trying to mask her uneasiness, Sheila said, "I've never seen a ghost or someone's aura, and I'm forever losing house keys or sunglasses or books and haven't the *least* talent for finding them again."

"That's not what we're talking about." Cyrus sounded slightly impatient.

Sheila, anxious to put an end to the discussion, said sharply, "I don't want to seem rude, but I'm afraid you're wrong. Paul and I are quite average; I'd venture to say that there's not a single 'psychic talent' between us. Period."

Cyrus turned to his wife with exaggerated enthusiasm, rubbing his hands together. "That salad is going to hit the spot: I'm hungrier than I realized."

Though her appetite had not really returned, Sheila murmured agreement.

"Almost ready . . . here we go," Helen announced, setting a plate of salad in front of each of them. She placed a bowl of dressing in the center of the table along with a plate of Rye Crisps. When she had refilled iced-tea glasses all around and set the pitcher near her plate, she sat down herself.

Sheila spooned a little of the dressing onto her salad and sampled a forkful. It tasted too sweet and rich but she said, "It's delicious."

"It's surely nothing fancy," Helen said, "but it'll have to do." She helped herself to a Rye Crisp and went on, "We're getting excited, the both of us: the most recent messages that have come through to us all indicate that something really important is going to happen soon."

"Really?" said Sheila politely, shaking her head at Helen's offer of additional salad. "What do you think is going to happen?"

"Oh," said Cyrus, with a chuckle, "nothing will *happen*—no fireballs in the sky or dead rising up. It will all be much simpler. A truth will be revealed and the world will be transformed by that truth—just as it was transformed by the message of Christ two thousand years ago.

"It's going to take time, even when we've been given such wisdom, to disseminate it, to reach all the individual minds which make up the great world-mind. Our work will just be beginning. We—Helen and I—will probably have to witness its completion from the other side."

Sheila, her attention focused for no reason on a drop of salad dressing resting on Helen's chin, suppressed a desire to smile at this absurd couple with their talk of great revelations out here in the middle of nowhere. She asked softly, "If everything is goodness and light, how do you explain what happened last night?"

Her host tented his fingers and tapped the tip of his chin reflectively. Finally he said, "All along we've experienced ... *interferences* ... in our work. We feel these disruptions are the effect of malicious *elementals*—on the other side. Semi-intelligent astral beings like imps. Last night was the worst we've seen, but it was just ... playfulness."

In spite of herself, Sheila shuddered. "I don't think I much care for ghostly humor."

Helen chuckled. "It won't happen again, most likely. Our little circle was in touch with less-disciplined forces last night because you and your husband brought"—she stopped suddenly and ended lamely—"changes."

"But how can you be sure that these *imps* won't get really nasty or violent?"

Helen nodded at her for a long time, then said with deliberation, "If we felt the least danger—if we felt we were in error—we would stop immediately. There is a way—" she looked questioningly at her husband; he shrugged and she continued, "a way to seal off the contact point, to close the gateway. We have that power; as long as we are guardians of the gateway, nothing but good can ever come through to this world." She reached out her hand to her husband and he took it reassuringly.

"We're not fools," he added, looking almost accusingly at Sheila, making her wonder guiltily if he had sensed her unspoken criticisms. "We opened the gateway, and as long as we're alive, we can seal it at any time. Forever."

And if you die? Sheila wondered, but she would not give voice to her thoughts. She forced herself, instead, to finish the last of her iced tea in slow, evenly spaced sips. Helen set out a plate of homemade cookies and divided up the remains of the iced-tea pitcher.

For a time, they sat quietly, all caught up in their own thoughts.

Before Sheila left, Helen asked, "Would you sit with us again before you leave?"

Sheila shook her head. "No. I couldn't. What I saw was simply too disturbing." She started for the door, adding, "I have to get back and check on Paul."

"I'll drive you," Cyrus offered.

"No, thank you," said Sheila, "I really prefer walking."

"If you change your mind about sitting with us," Helen said, "we'd be *very* pleased."

"I won't. Thank you again for lunch . . . and all your kindness. We'll see you again before we leave El Centro."

Cyrus handed Sheila her hat and sunglasses and they made their final good-byes.

As she walked along Main Street, Sheila watched Jimmy Shore roar past in his tow truck, the towing rig in back swaying crazily from side to side. She wondered if someone else was stalled on the road to El Centro.

She was not sure exactly when she became aware of someone following her. Twice she turned but saw nothing behind her except the nearly deserted street baking in the bright sunlight.

The third time, however, she caught a flicker of movement near the doorway of the Greyhound Bus Station. After a moment's hesitation, she started back and was surprised to discover the Indian girl, Maria Seloso, half-hidden in the shadow of the doorway.

"Please," the girl began, taking a step back, "Please"—then she paused uncertainly.

Sheila asked, "Were you following me?"

The girl nodded, looking down as if Sheila frightened her.

"Why?"

"I—" she reached forward impulsively and took Sheila's hand. "I was afraid." The girl's hand was ice-cold; the pressure of her fingers was almost painful.

"What are you afraid of?"

The girl raised her head and looked into Sheila's eyes with a kind of desperate longing to be understood. The intensity of the look unnerved Sheila, who said, as gently as she could, "You can tell me; maybe I can help you if I know what's wrong."

But the girl only shook her head, her dark eyes holding fast to Sheila's own. She released Sheila's hand and stood helplessly. Sheila had the impression that Maria might run away, so she put a hand on the girl's shoulder—reassuring her and preventing her from leaving suddenly. "Perhaps, if you want to talk, we could talk more comfortably at the place where I'm staying," Sheila suggested.

The girl stood indecisively. Sheila took Maria's hand, surprised at how tiny and cold it felt in her own; the bones of that hand seemed so delicate that Sheila felt if she was careless, she might snap them like the most fragile porcelain.

She drew the dark-haired girl gently along by the hand.

The girl did not resist; they walked hand-in-hand back to the Four Star. Catching their reflection in a window they were passing, Sheila thought, *We look like a mother and daughter*. The girl seemed much younger than her years, and smaller than Sheila remembered. Sheila pulled her closer to her in a spontaneously protective gesture; for the rest of their walk, she kept her arm across the girl's shoulders, hugging her. In response, the girl put her arm around Sheila's waist and clung tightly to her. But what comfort the girl drew from their being together wasn't enough to keep her from constantly looking around her in a frightened, watchful way that put Sheila also on her guard—though she hadn't the least notion what there was to fear on the sunny main street in the sleepy town.

Back in the motel cabin, Sheila sat the girl down in one of the room's shabby chairs while she perched on the edge of her bed. In the other bed, Paul dozed and stirred and finally dropped off into deeper sleep.

They spoke softly to avoid disturbing him.

"Now," Sheila began, " tell me what scares you so much. What can I do to help?"

The girl gripped the arms of the chair and leaned toward Sheila, her words tumbling out. "Please! Tonight! Come to the Anderson's when they are having the sitting. I'm afraid of the dark. When we began this thing, the dark was friendly, like the night, when I sleep. But this last two times, I have been afraid. Tonight the dark will not be empty, like it was not empty two times now."

"I don't understand," said Sheila uncertainly.

The girl made an effort to slow the outpouring of words and to explain herself as clearly as she could. "When I sit, I am no longer in the room. Not *me*. My soul is no longer with the people who are sitting around me: when Anderson puts me in a trance, my soul leaves my body and goes to a dark place. I stay there until they call my soul back into my body. But before these two times I'm telling you about, I have never been afraid, because I could feel other souls, good souls, all around me. They never spoke to me but I could feel their love; it was always good to go there.

"But last time and the time before that, when I went to that other place, the good souls were gone. I could only feel something bad there in the dark the first time; I was scared because I was alone and the dark was no longer kind. The second time, I saw—"

She stopped, as though the memory of her vision had frightened her. Sheila felt herself shiver in the too-warm room. Her mouth was dry as she asked, "*What* did you see?"

When the girl answered, her eyes seemed to look far into the distance, and she spoke more to herself than to Sheila. "A *lady*. I saw a lady. Her belly was swollen, so I thought to myself, her time is very near; her baby will come very soon.

"Everything was dark around me, but I could *see* the lady. Her skin was black but it was shiny—like black glass or a lump of tar in the sunlight. Her breasts—" the girl faltered, as though embarrassed to talk of such things, but Sheila prompted her to continue, "the breasts were big and full of milk and the same shiny black. Even the"—again a hesitation, but she overcame her shyness herself, this time—"the nipples were black. And I thought to myself, from the look of them, that it wasn't milk in her, but *poison*."

Her voice grew more quietly intense as she continued,

"But this is what scared me most of all: *she had no head and she had no feet.* She was no person at all: just a belly and breasts and big butt and big, fat legs."

Sheila said gently, "You had a dream of some sort, Maria. It was only a dream."

The girl shook her head fiercely. "She was there! I saw her! She had no neck or head, and her legs just went down to nothing, like smoke."

"Did she have hands?" Sheila asked.

"Oh, yes!" the girl affirmed with a vigorous nod of her head. "At first they were folded across her belly. But when she realized I was there in the dark with her, she—she—"

The girl's voice failed her as she remembered; when she was able to speak again, there was a shrill quality to her words which made Sheila fear she was growing hysterical. "She grabbed for me. Her arms were very tiny—thinner than a real person's arms should be. Her hands were like twisted bundles of dried roots. Her nails were *claws.* She was a witch; it was the soul of a witch! I tried to run away but there was nowhere to go in the dark; I had no way to move. She would make me drink her witch milk and I would be her child, her witch-baby; and when I died my soul would burn forever in the fires of hell because not even the blood of our Saviour or the tears of Mother Mary can save a witch from the fires of hell. A witch is damned forever, and I knew I would go to hell if she touched me—oh, I was so scared!"

In Maria's description of the dream figure, Sheila instantly recognized an image of the ancient Mesopotamian Mother Goddess. Devotion to such a female divinity preceded the establishment of religions dominated by male gods like Jehovah that ruthlessly, and perhaps fearfully, suppressed woman-centered worship. In the headless figure—swollen-bellied and full-breasted—was the timeless perception of female power and plentitude that ancient peoples had named Astarte, Istar, Isis.

Sheila could have argued that this was only a manifestation of Jung's well-known theory of archetypes. The idea that everyone drew off a collective pool of images to fill the landscape of a dream made it unextraordinary for an Indian girl in modern-day New Mexico to envision the same figure that might have haunted the dreams of a Chaldean priestess of ancient Ur.

But such an explanation seemed to Sheila entirely too facile. There was something in the image itself that resonated in her mind and heart, mingling fear with a confusing sense of *déjà vu*, as though she had encountered something similar in a recent dream of her own.

Suddenly, Maria threw herself into Sheila's arms and clung tightly to her; Sheila could feel her sobbing. She stroked the thick black hair and murmured comforting words and cursed herself because she felt unable to offer any real comfort.

When the crying had stopped, the girl sat quietly beside Sheila while the latter continued to stroke her hair. Finally Sheila said to her gently, "But she *didn't* hurt you, did she?"

The girl shook her head.

"So you see, you were safe. Someone didn't want you to be hurt. Maybe Jesus and Mary were watching over you. I'm *sure* they were. Jesus wouldn't let you go to hell; and I doubt that Mary would let anyone with her name—remember, *Maria* is *Mary*, after all—be hurt by a witch. They kept you safe—"

But the girl was shaking her head. "No. It wasn't *them;* it was *you*. Just when she was almost touching me, I remembered you were in the room with the Andersons. Oh, I don't understand what was happening there in the dark, but I *knew* that lady without a head couldn't touch me, though she wanted to real bad. She couldn't because you wouldn't let her—because you had power over her."

"But that—it doesn't make any *sense*. I never saw her; I wasn't with you in the dark. How could *I* make a difference?"

Maria shrugged her shoulders and said in a surprisingly matter-of-fact tone, "I told you: I don't understand these things; I just know what I know. You were there and she couldn't touch me. But tonight, when I go to the dark place, I know she will be waiting for me. And if you aren't near me, she *will* touch me and my soul will be damned to hell forever." Then she began to shiver and held Sheila even more tightly.

Sheila said as calmly as possible, "Don't go to the Andersons'; don't sit for them again if it frightens you."

"I have to; I promised. Anyway, it doesn't matter where I am tonight. Since I was a little girl, it happens anyway. I have gone to the dark place many times even before I met the Andersons. When the dark calls me, I have to go. It will call me soon again; I feel it around me. If there is something waiting to hurt me there, then it seems a good thing to me that you and the Andersons will be near to help me."

"Can't you . . . fight it? Can't you say *no* when it calls?"

The girl smiled ruefully. "When the call comes, I have to go into the dark. There is no other way."

"None?"

The girl shook her head. Unable to think of anything to say, Sheila reached for her purse and took out a handkerchief; Maria accepted it with a nod and blew her nose.

Sheila held the girl close to her for a moment; then she promised, "All right, I'll come. Will you see the Andersons this afternoon?"

The girl nodded again.

"Well, you tell them I'll be there at— What time should I come?"

"Seven-thirty. Tonight they will begin at seven-thirty."

"I'll be there."

Maria got to her feet. "Thank you," she said; then she kissed Sheila lightly on the cheek. The woman gave her a final reassuring hug in return.

When the girl had gone, Sheila just stood near the closed door. She felt she could not fail the girl, yet she was confused at how quickly she was becoming involved in things she didn't understand.

Her thoughts were interrupted when Paul woke up and asked sleepily, "Were you talking to someone just now? I thought I heard voices."

"Maria, the Indian girl who sits with the Andersons."

"Oh. What did she want?"

"She asked me to sit with them tonight."

"Of course you said no."

"Actually, I said I would. The child is terrified of something; she seemed to think that if I was there, everything would be all right."

"That doesn't make any sense," he said. "I'll bet the Andersons put her up to it."

"No, I didn't get that feeling at all."

"I can't *believe* you're going back. After what happened last time, you're never gonna get *me* back there."

"As a matter of fact, you weren't invited."

Paul suddenly sounded irritable. "Is there any way to take care of the light? It's so *bright* in here, for God's sake. Jesus! I feel like I've got the world's worst hangover."

Sheila pulled the spread off her bed and draped it across the window, then asked, "That better?"

"Much! Are you having dinner with them, or what?"

"No, no; I'm going over after dinner. We can go out if you feel like it. I'll bring something back if you don't."

"Let's plan on going to that coffee shop down the road. . . . Christ, I feel lousy! Would you get me a glass of water and some aspirin? Thanks!"

As she got out the bottle of aspirin, Sheila realized that her hands were shaking. Paul's mention of the Regal Coffee Shop had brought back her waking nightmare. She had a sudden flash of fear for herself, for Paul.

She tried to rationalize it away as a compound of nerves and the things Maria had said and getting mixed up with such disturbing goings-on as séances. The El Centro area, with its decapitated padres and Indian ruins and town eccentrics, seemed to feed her fears, making her believe that in some ungodly, incomprehensible way, everything was woven together—like a net of events closing in on the two of them. Drawing tighter.

Stop this, now! she warned herself.

If Paul noticed how much her hands were shaking when she handed him the water and two aspirin tablets, he didn't mention it.

11 Past and Present

Later that evening, while Paul was still getting dressed and ready for dinner, Sheila stood on the little concrete porch in front of number twelve. She smoked one of her infrequent cigarettes as she thoughtfully watched the sunset. The sun, a swollen butter-colored disk, was falling through waves of breathtaking gold toward the highest peaks of the Sierra Morenas.

But Sheila was mainly concerned with a memory which had been prompted by her earlier talk with Maria Seloso. She was remembering another evening, many years before. . . .

She was thirteen. She stood near the living-room window of her Aunt Patricia's home and watched the front yard. The late-evening sunlight lent a golden tone to her hand as it rested on the windowsill.

She said, "Aunt Pat, it's there again," in a voice that was little more than a whisper.

Behind her, she heard the rustling of magazine pages turning. Clearly, her aunt hadn't heard her.

"Aunt Pat!" she called, louder this time—the impatient, nervous edge evident in her voice, "Aunt Pat, you're not *listening!*"

The girl's eyes never left the darker blotch swimming in the shadow under the oak tree which grew in the center of the front lawn.

"Mmmmm?" her aunt responded. Sheila turned to look at the heavyset woman in the soft green chair; her aunt finished the paragraph she was reading before she looked across the room at her niece and asked, "What did you say, Sheila?"

"It's there again—out by the oak tree. It's watching us—you, me, the house—but *me* most of all."

Her aunt set the magazine down on a table, still open to the page she was reading, and came over to the window. She slipped off her reading glasses and looked in the direction of the oak tree. After a few moments, she said, "Where? I don't see anything. There's *nothing* there, Sheila." She sounded both annoyed and worried.

"Don't you see? There! There! *There!*" She was jabbing her fingertip against the windowpane, trying to force her aunt to see what she could see so clearly.

"Don't do that, Sheila," her aunt murmured; "it leaves marks on the window."

Sheila ignored her. How could the woman not see it? The formless shadow within the fainter shadow cast by the tree. The thing's very shapelessness seemed somehow threatening. It seemed to float on the warm, heavy air of the evening. Sometimes it swayed slightly, as if stirred by a sudden breeze. But though it moved, it never moved *away*. It remained in one place, as though it had a purpose in being there.

Patricia Hinson sighed and said, "Darling, there's nothing there. Now, I want you to stop imagining these things. I know it's hard for you to adjust to living here with Frank and me after . . . *everything*. But you've got to try." She touched the girl's shoulder and squeezed it gently, reassuringly. "I know how hard it is—really, I *do*. But can't *you* try just a little harder?"

Sheila said nothing.

Her aunt glanced at her watch, saying, "I didn't realize how late it's gotten; your uncle will be home any minute and I haven't even got dinner started." She glanced longingly at her magazine, still open to the unfinished story, and hesitated. Then she shrugged her shoulders and left the room. A few moments later, the girl heard her in the kitchen preparing dinner.

Sheila watched the shadow a little longer; then she turned and started upstairs to her room.

Once, several weeks before, she had run out onto the lawn, trying to touch the mysterious shadow and discover its secret. But it had eluded her. It hovered always just out of reach, drawing closer when she stepped back, moving away if she came too close. In the end, she had given up the pursuit and simply stood watching it; she felt certain that *it* was watching *her* in return. A little later, it had just *evaporated*, the way it always did. It might vanish for a few hours or several days; but it came back, and once again, she would be aware that it was nearby, *watching* her.

From her bedroom window, the girl looked again for the shadow thing, but the jutting first-floor roof hid all but the upper portion of the oak tree, so Sheila could no longer spot the watcher-shadow. She knew it was there, though—invisible to everyone but her, some riddle which only she could solve.

She went and stood in front of the mirror on her closet door. Watching her reflection, she turned slightly sideways. She was losing some of her boniness; she could see the faint softening lines which were the first hints of a figure.

Abruptly she smoothed the front of her blouse and tugged on the side of her skirt, as if to hide the womanliness in her that was just beginning to reveal itself.

She turned from the mirror impatiently. Everything was happening too fast: the accident which had killed her parents, the upheaval of moving in with her aunt and uncle, the confusion of all the changes in her maturing body, and, above all, the *thing* outside. . . .

She imagined it just outside the living-room window now; it dared to come closer as night fell. She envisioned it contracted to a tiny stain in the cold evening air, a dark spot floating against a backdrop of star-points—no bigger itself than the stars. The black spot at the center of an eye; an eye that looked into her life from somewhere outside the world which had changed so drastically for her in a few months.

Every night the girl slept with her window closed, not daring to open it even when the room grew unbearably stuffy. She was afraid of the shadow thing now; she wondered how, that one time, she had gotten up enough nerve to try and touch it. The thought of being so near the mysterious darkness chilled her now. And she left her lamp on all night, taking care to push the edge of the little braided rug against the foot of the door so that her aunt wouldn't see the light and make her shut it off. She knew she was acting like a child afraid of the dark, but there was a difference. A child's boogeyman didn't exist; the shadow creature was *real*. Only *she* knew just how real it was.

That night, Sheila remembered, she had gone to bed early, feeling strangely tired. She had read awhile, but had soon let the book slip onto her blankets; she was vaguely aware of her uncle laughing aloud over the Milton Berle show as she fell asleep.

She awoke with a start in pitch darkness; she knew immediately that someone had come in and turned off the lamp. When she saw that her window was open to the night, she guessed it had been her aunt, who had a prejudice against people sleeping in sealed rooms.

Sudden fear came as she realized that she was not alone in the room.

"Aunt Pat?" she whispered, knowing in her heart that it was not her aunt standing over her in the dark.

The only answer was a chuckle, so faint that she was at first uncertain she had really heard it. Then she heard it again, clearly enough to recognize the note of menace in the sound.

Fear made her too weak to move. She lay watching the space between the foot of her bed and the closed door; it was from here that the sound came. She listened but the sound didn't come again; she felt the house silent all around her. She shifted her eyes just enough to see the luminous clock dial on the bedside nightstand; the hands showed 2:15.

As she stared into the darkness, her eyes became gradually accustomed to it; she was sure she could see a shadowy form the size of a very tall man, standing at the foot of the bed. She could feel unseen eyes watching her.

A wind stirred the curtains; she felt freezing cold.

Then there was a terrifying sound of bedsprings settling on the left side of the bed, as if some body had lain down on the bed beside her. She began to cry out of sheer terror; she was paralyzed with fright.

A smooth, cold, *hard* surface pressed against the side of her head; she felt something disturbing the covers over her arm, as though an unseen hand were playing with the blankets.

"Please" she whispered to her unseen tormentor in an agony of terror. "Please, leave me alone."

The only response was a chuckle which seemed to float into the air several feet above the foot of her bed.

She felt herself growing weak, but she knew she did not dare pass out. She hung onto consciousness only through will power.

The invisible hand slid up and down, massaging her arm through the blankets with sudden intensity. She could feel a heart beating wildly, but did not know if it was hers. . . .

Another stirring. Another protest from the bedsprings. Someone was kissing her on the side of the face; she could feel a face against hers, kissing her with thin, rubbery, ice-cold lips and giggling obscenely into her ear. A faint breathing tickled her ear, but the smell of it was awful, like rotten meat.

The hand moved to grasp her breast through the bedclothes.

"What are you *doing?*" she sobbed, turning her head as far as she could to escape the chilly lips and the stench. She felt weaker still—as if whatever was beside her was sucking out all of her energy. She imagined she was feeling what it was like to bleed to death. She wondered if she were dying, if this *thing* intended to kill her.

"Go away!" she pleaded. "Oh, leave me *alone.*"

But the bodiless mouth nuzzled the nape of her neck; the hand began kneading her breast almost painfully.

Then the covers were snatched off the bed; the unseen hand dragged them to the foot and made them tumble over onto the floor.

Something like the faintest mist—no, *thicker*, like masses of spider webs—hung in the air above the bed. Unseen hands, two of them, began rubbing her arms. She saw the thin material of her pajama tops pushed up past her elbows; she felt the pressure of individual fingertips which seemed to have no nails.

The gauzy-gray cloud over her grew more substantial; it seemed to be taking the material of itself out of the empty air.

She felt the unseen hands begin a gentle tugging at the waist of her pajamas; she felt them beginning to slide down over her hips.

Frantically, she grabbed for the waistband, holding onto it. She heard the chuckle again as the hands tugged more firmly on her pajamas.

Then something slapped her across the face once, with a stinging impact that brought tears of pain to her eyes to mix with the ones arising from fright. Startled, she momentarily loosened her hold on the pajamas, only to feel them yanked down around her ankles.

Sensing, without fully understanding, what was about to happen, Sheila summoned all her will power into refusing to allow whatever it was to carry out its plan. She managed to say aloud, "*You can't do this!*" putting into words what she was thinking with all her energy. She felt, insanely, that she had inside of her some power to resist this final obscenity. She rejected the assault on her with a fierceness of concentration born of desperation.

She sensed, in a way she didn't fully comprehend, some sudden hesitation and uncertainty on the part of her unseen assailant. She understood then that she held some power which could defend her, which might allow her to fight back.

She willed the hovering mass above her away and it shifted position, drifting upward toward the ceiling; she thought she saw it thin a bit to the consistency of exhaled cigarette smoke.

She created a picture in her mind of breezes blowing away that smoke; she imagined invisible hands—hands under her guidance—pulling apart the material of her nightmare.

She sensed a fear other than her own, which was diminishing as she took control of the situation.

The thing was afraid.

It was afraid *of her*.

She stared up into the smoky gray cloud and thought, *I don't see you any more. You're nothing, nothing, nothing!*

And the mist was gone.

She turned her attention to the shadow, still floating near the foot of her bed. She began to imagine it growing smaller and smaller, until it was no bigger than a marble, a bead, a droplet of inky blackness.

Then she willed the droplet out of existence. In the moment before it disappeared utterly, she felt a cry of terror and anguish filling her head, but she did not stop wishing it gone forever.

In her mind she heard a single shout from an impossibly great distance. There was a single tiny snapping sound.

Then she was alone, though the room was filled with the smell of rotten meat, so thick and cloying that it made her choke. She was so weak that she could barely get her head over the side of the bed before she threw up.

When the spasms had subsided, she lay weakly on her bed for almost an hour before she climbed unsteadily to her feet to begin cleaning up the mess. She made no move to close the window; she was confident that the thing would not return.

But when she tried to tell her aunt and uncle what had happened, they only talked of "nerves and nightmares and the flu." She gave up trying to convince them and took comfort in the knowledge that she had been able to protect herself through her own power. She felt that, as long as she could draw on this power, she would never be in danger from the unseen.

In time, the whole thing became nothing more than a memory quickly forgotten in the business of growing up.

. . . Forgotten until now.

It was nearly dark in El Centro. Sheila ground the end of her third cigarette under her boot. It had been years since she had thought about that incident; she was surprised at how vivid her memories of it were. She had the uneasy thought that there was some unguessable connection between recent events in El Centro and that long-ago event.

From inside their room, Paul yelled, "I'm ready if you are. And I really am starving."

"I just want to pull a comb through my hair," she called back, reaching for the screen door handle; "then we can go."

She noted with surprise how rapidly the air had grown chilly around her, cool enough to make her take her heavy jacket with her to dinner, instead of the sweater she had planned to wear earlier.

After dinner, Paul insisted on walking with her as far as the Andersons' gate, but he refused to accompany her to the front door. He restated his opinion that she was being foolish in allowing herself, for whatever reason, to become a party to another séance.

Sheila simply shrugged and said, "I have to go; I gave Maria my word."

Paul sighed, but only asked, "Do you want me to stop by and walk you home later?"

She shook her head. "I'm sure Cyrus will give me a ride. I'll see you later." She started up the path to the house, pausing for a moment to watch her husband move thoughtfully away along the moonlit street. Again she was struck by the idea that he was a stranger to her now.

A breeze rustled the cottonwoods on either side of the path; Sheila hurried toward the porch light.

Helen Anderson greeted her warmly and introduced her to Mr. Corvo and Alicia Hayes, who were also going to sit with them that night.

Mr. Corvo was an elderly mouse of a man with a perpetual look of popeyed surprise. Alicia Hayes, perhaps ten years older than Sheila, was short and red-faced; she punctuated her every sentence with abrupt nods of her head, whether she was agreeing or disagreeing with anyone.

Helen irritated Sheila by telling the others, "We're especially fortunate to have Mrs. Barrett with us tonight. Cyrus and I *suspect* that she has definite mediumistic gifts—though we haven't convinced Mrs. Barrett *herself* of that fact. We're sure her presence will contribute significantly to our session this evening."

Cyrus came out of the kitchen rubbing his hands—eager to begin. He smelled heavily of cologne. He urged everyone to sit at the dining-room table, announcing, "We hope to accomplish a lot tonight, *and* we don't want to waste Mrs. Barrett's time with us."

The others all seemed to know where to sit. Helen indicated Sheila should sit beside her. Maria sat at the head of the table, with the others ranged clockwise: Helen Anderson, Sheila, who held Mr. Corvo's dampish hand, then Ms. Hayes, who held hands with Cyrus. He sat on the other side of Maria, completing the circle.

When everything was ready, Cyrus explained that he had put Maria in a light hypnotic trance earlier; he would use a simple verbal command to bring her into a deeper trance.

Sheila, who had been concerned by the girl's dreamy quality, relaxed a bit when she realized its cause. The girl smiled at her and she smiled back reassuringly. Maria clearly drew comfort from Sheila's presence.

Cyrus gave his verbal signal, and immediately the personality of the spirit-guide Senecu replaced the personality of the Indian girl. Sheila noted subtle changes in the girl's features, a new intensity in her eyes, the hoarseness of the spirit-guide's voice. As before, Sheila felt the changes were genuine, not the product of deliberate fraud. From her studies, she was aware of the long-accepted fact that the mind could produce incredible physical changes in the body. Still, encountering such phenomena first hand was disturbing to her.

Sheila momentarily looked away through an uncurtained window into the night outside.

The sky was red-veined, curiously fleshlike. She felt she was looking at the body of a monstrous, freshly flayed animal that pressed against the window glass. She had the insane idea that the whole house had been swallowed entire by an organism like an amoeba.

She shuddered and returned her attention to the circle of sitters. But now she was aware of an almost-imperceptible shift in her relationship with what was happening in the room. She felt excluded from the circle, as if her awareness was somehow outside the room even though her physical body remained seated at the dining-room table.

She could still see the others clearly; she could feel Helen's dry, cool hand and Mr. Corvo's damp one. She could see their mouths moving, as one or the other made a comment. But she felt like she was in a theatre watching a film with the sound turned down, so that all she could hear were muffled, incomprehensible sounds accompanying the moving lips.

Now one voice seemed more clear than the others. It seemed to come from Maria, but though the girl's mouth opened and closed, the movements of her lips did not coincide with the words Sheila was hearing. It was as if another sound track had been spliced onto the film she was watching, or as if there had been some slippage, so that sound and lip movements were out of synchronization.

The voice commented mockingly, "You can see how they are caught in a spider's web of words."

Sheila heard a little more than a whisper; she had no clue to the sex of the speaker.

Glistening threads appeared everywhere; the room was choked with silvery strands the thickness of heavy twine. They converged on the spot where Maria sat. For a terrifying moment, Sheila could not see the girl; where the girl had been seated, there was only a gaping hole—absolutely black—out of which the webbing emerged and to which it returned. A cold wind issued from the dark opening, which seemed to plunge into another dimension. The sound of the wind among the silvery threads made the whispering sound Sheila heard.

She felt herself growing dizzy, felt the need to say *something,* to hear her own voice and be reassured that she was still a part of the same reality as the others still locked in their circle, oblivious of the silver ropes draping the room, clinging to their very flesh.

She felt her mouth move with a great effort; when she heard her voice, it floated up to her from a vast distance. She said, "I see a black hole in space." Then it was too much of an effort for her to say anything else.

She saw the other sitters turn to look at her. She watched them speak to her, but she had no idea what they said.

"*Daughter,*" said the wind-whisper, the voice of the dark hole.

"Who . . . who are you?" It seemed to take Sheila an eternity to drag out these words; the muscles of her throat resisted her efforts. Her voice was just another whisper hovering in the shadowed stillness.

Her only answer was a single sudden impact against the wall behind her, like an immense fist slammed against the plaster.

Now she could see the others around the table staring at each other in astonishment. Had they heard the sound also? Or were they simply responding to her inexplicable actions?

She saw the Andersons working their mouths simultaneously; probably they were issuing instructions to the other sitters. She connected their unheard directives with changes she saw around her. The webbing filling the room suddenly blazed white-hot, forcing her to shut her eyes. Then, just as suddenly, it cooled to red-hot strands that glowed a dull red, then began to melt away in a rain of blood-red droplets that hissed and sizzled as they hit the floor.

The splatter/hiss became a sound like the voice of fire. In amazement, Sheila heard the voice which was not really a voice at all tell her, "Evil is a name *they* give us because they are too weak to face the changes we will bring. We do what we do because those changes must come, will come. Those who fear us are fools: do you fear the sunrise? Those who deny us might more easily deny the blood that makes them live. Those who oppose us are most foolish: they will perish in the fire of necessity.

"But we count you among the blessed, not among the fools. You do not deny your heart or fear the sun and raise your hands to stop her birthing. We call you now to do what you must do. Because you do these things we call you—"

The voice stopped as the red-drop rain stopped boiling onto the floor. Sheila could see Cyrus shouting something at her, but the only sound in the room was a roaring wind that seemed sucked into, then expelled from, the hole into infinity that existed where Maria had sat.

The blackness grew less intense; it became a vaporous cloud the color of rain-heavy skies. She could see Maria struggling at the center of the thinning substance; the girl was writhing about as if she were suffering the most ex-quisite agonies. Only the restraining hands of Cyrus and Helen kept her from throwing herself out of her chair; they looked shocked and frightened by what was happening. Somehow they were managing to hold Maria back without breaking the circle of which Sheila was and was not a part.

The ghostly gray cloud dwindled and disappeared; Sheila found herself drifting back into a normal relationship with the other people in the room. Things no longer seemed out of joint.

Then the vision was gone, leaving behind only a single whispered syllable that sounded like "*Daugh—*" which was drowned out in the suddenly-audible babble of those around her. Sheila felt herself returned securely to their midst.

Whatever she had briefly been in touch with was gone beyond recalling.

Her first concern was for Maria, who had been such a central part of the whole experience. In her vision, she had seen the girl as the channel through which the webbed darkness had emerged into her awareness, into the world.

Now the girl was thrashing about, foaming at the mouth. There was blood mingled with the spittle dribbling down her chin.

Cyrus yelled, "She's bitten her tongue."

Helen murmured, "What is happening? Nothing like this has happened before."

By common consensus they had dissolved the circle and everyone was standing up. Ms. Hayes and Mr. Corvo were vying with each other as they offered suggestions for the care of Maria, explanations of what had happened, and expressions of their amazement at what had occurred.

Sheila pushed Helen aside but Cyrus continued to hold Maria in place. Sheila put her hand on the girl's forehead. Her skin seemed burning hot—no, she corrected herself, burning *cold*; the girl's flesh burned her fingertips like dry ice.

She stood behind the still-seated girl and reached around, placing both hands on the girl's burning-cold brow. "There," she said in a comforting voice, "there, now."

Her own hands, wrists, forearms seemed to absorb the scalding chill, as if she were drawing a poison out of the girl, who began to grow calm. Though her own hands were suffused with the hot/cold sensation, Sheila could feel that Maria's forehead was merely warm now, and a little damp.

She began stroking Maria's brow, calming, soothing, drawing the damp locks of jet-black hair gently back across the girl's temples. Easing her. Making her easy.

The Andersons and the others were staring at Sheila in open-mouthed surprise.

For a few moments she felt an almost magic healing power informing her ministrations to the Indian girl; Maria's eyes were open but had a strange fixed quality.

Suddenly she relaxed completely. Sheila could sense the last tension in her loosening, seeping away.

Her blank stare was replaced by the confused look of a heavy sleeper dragged suddenly from a deep sleep.

Sheila bent over to kiss the top of the girl's head, making a gesture of benediction and simple sisterly affection.

When the girl was sitting quietly, Cyrus inspected her mouth and announced that she had bitten her lip, not her tongue, as he had initially feared. Then, half-supporting the dazed girl between them, the Andersons led her toward the bathroom to take care of her injury.

Sheila ignored the questions of Ms. Hayes and Mr. Corvo; stopping only to pick up her purse, she went out onto the porch. Outside in the cool night air, she fumbled for a cigarette and lit it. The others, sensing that she didn't want to be disturbed, made no effort to follow her. She could hear their muted voices through the screen door.

For a little while, she had the porch to herself. She stared at the empty road and at the darkened houses. Everything was bounded by a curving wall that was a fusion of night sky and darkened desert.

She tried not to think of anything that had happened, opening herself only to the cool night and the empty air. She concentrated on her cigarette and let no other thought enter.

Then Cyrus stepped onto the porch behind her. She recognized him by something in his step and the faint scent of his cologne. She remained looking out, not turning to face him.

"I can't explain what went on in there," he said after several minutes. "Do you have any idea?"

"You're the experts, not me." Her voice was angry, but she knew herself well enough to realize that it masked her fear of the things she had glimpsed during the séance.

"We've never run into anything *like* this," Cyrus said helplessly.

She turned on him then, demanding, "Did it ever occur to you—to either of you—that you're mucking around where you have no business being? Maybe the stakes are a lot higher than your book!"

"What could possibly be more important?" He made a better effort to conceal his anger than she.

"You tell me," she said, crushing out one cigarette and lighting another.

"Inside," he began, his voice conciliatory now, "it looked as if you were talking to someone the rest of us couldn't see."

"Everyone was yelling—I was just adding my two cents' worth."

He pressed her: "At one point, I distinctly recall you saying something that sounded like *black hole*." He stared at her, waiting for her response.

She looked into his face and said evenly, "I don't remember much of anything that went on until Maria started having convulsions."

He would not let it drop. "*Try* to remember; it might be important to our work. If you withheld information—for *any* reason—you might endanger the project. You might even cause harm to us."

"Cyrus, look: I didn't want to get mixed up in this . . . this *bullshit* in the first place. I came here tonight because Maria seemed scared and seemed to think—God knows why!—that I could help her. For her sake, I'm glad I came. But after what I've seen tonight, I can only think that you and your wife are exploiting that child. I—well, I'll notify the authorities if it doesn't stop. What you're doing looks like a kind of child abuse. I'm sorry, but the whole scene in there turned my stomach."

She stubbed out the last of her cigarette against the porch railing, never taking her eyes off Cyrus for a moment.

When she spoke again, her voice was quieter but there was a knife edge underlining the words. "*I mean what I say, Cyrus.* Don't mistake me. Nothing is as important as the well-being of that girl." She moved toward the three broad steps leading down from the porch, "I'm going back to the motel now. You remember what I said."

She paused suddenly, struck by a new thought. "If you're afraid this—*project* of yours is dangerous, *give it up.* If you can't stand the heat, *get out!*"

Anger rippled across his face, then subsided into an expression of sadness. "You don't understand," he said. "You won't *let* yourself understand."

She walked down the steps, saying nothing.

She heard the screen door slam as he went back inside.

She was almost at the thin strip of concrete that served as a sidewalk when Helen Anderson came running down the path after her as rapidly as the woman's heavy frame would allow.

When she overtook Sheila, she pressed a parcel into Sheila's hands. "Take this," she insisted; "*read* this. It's a copy of the things we've learned so far. You'll see. You'll *see* how important our work is."

Sheila tried to hand the package back but Helen stood

aside, her hands behind her back, shaking her head. She looked, Sheila thought, like an overgrown, grotesque child.

"All right," she conceded, wanting only to get away, "all right."

"It's a loan," said Helen. "You can give it back to me when you've read it."

"Good night," said Sheila, holding the brown paper package in her hand. She continued on her way while the other woman remained watching her until she turned the corner onto Main Street.

Paul wasn't home when she returned. She supposed that he had gone to the Pata Blanca to drink, as he had told her he might.

She looked with distaste at the package Helen had given her; she dropped the unopened bundle carelessly into the middle drawer of the dressing table.

She only wanted to sleep; she felt she could sleep forever. She collapsed onto the bed.

Her last conscious thoughts were, *Where the hell is Paul?* and *To hell with Paul and the Andersons and El Centro!*

Sleep, when it came, was heavy and filled with troubling dreams.

12 Mission and Vision Hill

Paul had indeed gone to the Pata Blanca after leaving Sheila.

This time, however, he entered the little bar which opened off the dining room. The place was deserted except for a young Chicano couple who occupied one of the wall booths. Paul sat at the bar. The bartender, a young Chicano in his early twenties with a thin mustache and a bad complexion, had never heard of an armadillo, a drink Paul had discovered in a bar in San Antonio.

Paul rattled off the correct proportions of Kahlua, cream, and Amaretto and watched the bartender mix his drink to exact specifications.

"Just right," he said, when he had sampled it.

"I never made one of those before," the boy said.

"Well, you did fine for a first time."

"I never heard of those before." The bartender moved to the end of the bar and spoke loudly in Spanish to the couple in the far booth.

Paul quickly finished his drink and signaled the bartender for another. This was served without comment, and the fellow returned to his interrupted conversation.

Paul nursed his second armadillo. He glanced around to see if anyone else had entered the bar. No one had.

There was no reason for him to stay and he had no desire to leave.

He ordered a third drink. While he was waiting for it, he studied the decorations on the walls around him: backlit black metal sculptures of a bull ring, a toreador, a mounted picador, and a bull pawing the ground.

The bartender delivered his drink. The man from the booth walked over to the jukebox beside the rest-room doors and dropped in a coin. The room was filled with a loud salsa beat. The bartender applauded, then went over and dragged the woman out of the booth; she laughed and protested—but not too hard.

They began dancing clumsily; the bartender was showing off and the woman was a little drunk. The seated man was clapping his hands to the music, encouraging the couple. All three of them were laughing loudly. Paul stared at them, resenting their laughter, the way they interacted.

Abruptly he swung around on his barstool and slammed the empty glass on the counter.

The music stopped; Paul glanced around and saw all three people seated in the booth looking at him. The man was talking rapidly and pointing in Paul's direction; the bartender shook his head; the woman just shrugged and whispered something to the two men. All three of them laughed.

Paul got up and left enough money on the counter to cover his drinks. He walked out through the restaurant.

The dining room was closed; a busboy was setting chairs upside down on tables, getting ready to mop the floor. Paul pushed through the double glass doors.

Outside, he looked at his watch; it was only nine-thirty.

The cool air was refreshing, but he still felt flushed. He touched his forehead, wondering if he had a fever. His head felt warm enough for him to think he might.

He began walking slowly in the direction of the Four Star, his hands thrust into his pockets.

As he passed the lobby of the Apacheria House Hotel (Rooms by the Day, Week, Month), he paused to look in through the dusty plate-glass windows.

The lobby was illuminated by the raw light of two overhead fluorescent fixtures, the glare accentuating the grime worked into every surface and corner. A Coke machine and a candy vend-o-mat stood against the far wall, near the deserted registration desk. The floor was covered with disintegrating brown linoleum. On the left, just past the desk, Paul could see the foot of a narrow flight of stairs climbing up into shadow. On the wall above the desk was a lighted clock with an advertisement for a manufacturing firm in Dallas. The plug, thick and black and boasting two repairs in the form of adhesive-tape nodules, trailed across the wall and disappeared behind the edge of a couch covered with an ancient green slipcover.

Two men were sitting on the couch, talking. The speaker at the moment was an old man with thin white hair who sucked his teeth in between phrases, as though his gums hurt him. The man doing the listening was Willie Kavan. He was holding a sand-colored cat on his lap. His head was inclined toward the other man in an attentive posture, but he was staring back at Paul with a little smile, as if he and Paul shared some joke.

Still cradling the cat in his left arm, Willie silenced the older man with a word and a hand placed lightly on the other's knee. Then he beckoned to Paul to come in and join them. Paul smiled and shook his head, but Willie would have none of that. His expression turned to mock anger, and he gestured more emphatically for Paul to come inside.

He shrugged and entered the lobby.

Willie introduced him to the other man, named Edgar, who acknowledged the younger man with a brief "How-do?" He started up his conversation with Willie again, saying, "*Bayley*—*that* was their name. They moved here after he got out of the Army. She'd been born here; said she'd always meant to come back. I remember her folks: they were killed in a car crash out by the mission. She was raised by an aunt in Taos. Brought the aunt with them when they moved here. She seemed normal enough at first—"

Willie rolled his eyes at Paul but said nothing.

Paul waited, regretting that he had bothered to enter, but not ready to face the night or the empty motel room.

Edgar continued, "It all happened pretty fast: the wife gettin' into moods—husband takin' to drinkin'—the old lady off her rocker completely. She claimed she'd hear voices telling her to do this or read that. Her kin tried to keep her from doing mischief; but near the end, she was really out of things. She kept claiming she was an Indian princess or Queen of the May or some such nonsense. She swore she was getting commands straight from Heaven. I guess Heaven forgot to tell her not to play with matches. She set the fire, I'm *sure* of it."

"Which fire?" asked Paul.

Edgar looked surprised to find him still there.

Willie, stroking the cat gently, seemed to speak to the cat when he answered, "People who lived here years ago. Their home burned to the ground with all of them in it. At the time there were a lot of crazy stories about spirit lights and ghosts and voices giving the old lady warnings. Fact of the matter is, the old gal probably *did* set the fire herself. But nothing was ever proved. She was burned to death in the living room; her niece and nephew-in-law died of smoke inhalation in a bedroom at the back of the house. It was officially listed as an *accident*. I don't see"—he stared meaningfully at Edgar—"how anyone could *logically* call it anything else."

Edgar sniffed. "The old woman was crazy—*that's* gospel. *And* there were a lot of strange goings-on. The old woman kept claiming spirits were making her do things she didn't want to do; maybe—and I'm only saying *maybe*—there was something to all that ghost talk."

"Yes," said Willie. "Well, I don't hold much with incendiary spooks. And if the old lady did set the fire, which seems likely, I'm sure it was because she dropped a candle or left something to burn on the stove. *Accidentally*."

Edgar would not concede. "There was another thing happened back in, oh, nineteen-thirty . . . let me see . . ." He paused momentarily to make a mental calculation.

Willie seized the moment, saying, "Yes, well, we'll have to talk about it later. Right now, I promised to open the shop for Mr. Barrett. I'm glad he remembered to meet me here, like I told him; I was afraid he'd forget and be waiting at the shop."

Willie shot a look at Paul, who said quickly, "Yes. We're probably leaving tomorrow, and there's something I want to buy."

"What?" asked Edgar suspiciously.

"A ring," said Willie. "A surprise for his wife. A silver ring with a turquoise inset. Because it's a surprise, we arranged for him to buy it tonight."

"That's right," said Paul.

"And since it's getting so late, we'd better get going. I'll talk to you tomorrow, Edgar," Willie promised. He rose and handed the cat (which never opened an eye during the transfer) to Edgar. "Good night."

Edgar nodded to them both, then turned his attention to the cat, stroking its fur and making soft clucking noises over it.

Outside, Willie said, "When he gets going on local history, there's no stopping him, short of hitting him over the head. You saved me in the nick of time; I feel I owe you a favor. How about a drink at my place, since we're heading in that direction? To tell you the truth, a little bourbon doesn't sound half bad to me." He looked expectantly at Paul.

Paul considered a moment, then agreed. The drink sounded good, and he rather enjoyed the older man's company.

He picked up a handful of dried gray-brown corn kernels out of a shallow pottery dish; he held them up to the light, asking Willie, "What's this stuff?"

"That's called *maíz de brujas*—witch's corn. It's the mark of evildoers; it's bad luck to keep it around."

Paul let the corn slip through his fingers back into the dish. "Why keep it around if it's bad luck?"

"To me, it's good luck. I always walk under ladders or drop mirrors when I get the chance. I have a theory that positive thinking can make any bad-luck charm bring you good luck. So far (knock wood!) it seems to work. And life's a lot less complicated if you don't worry about every crack you step on breakin' someone's back or conjuring up demons every time you spill the salt."

The older man sat on a sagging couch, sipping a bourbon-and-water and watching as Paul circled the room aimlessly, looking at the items scattered across bookcases, old display cases, tables, and one immense sideboard.

The little room was separated by beaded draperies from the main room at the front of the house. At one time, clearly, it had served as the dining room. Willie had furnished it with such a hodge-podge of items that it seemed more storage area than anything else. But the place had a comfortable (if cramped) feel to it; Paul felt himself mellowing out more than he had since his arrival in El Centro.

Beyond the beaded curtains, the front rooms were dark except for moonlight filtering in through the dusty windows.

Paul ran his fingers absently over several dried gourds and a painted medicine rattle. Then he paused in front of an ornate table to stare into the glass case it supported.

The case was about a foot and a half high and perhaps two feet long. Inside were four brightly painted kachina dolls, their features grotesque carved masks; they were dressed in gaudy, finely-detailed costumes. The central figure was a black-robed female; on either side of her stood two black-painted demon dolls. Standing in front of the others was a smaller carving that looked like a hideous child with a blood-red body.

Paul felt himself drawn to and repelled by the exhibit. He stared into the glass case a long time before he asked, "Those are kachinas, aren't they? I'll bet these are rare— I've never seen anything quite like them."

"Right," said Willie. "That's my special pride. Those are Below Person kachinas. They're a rarity. I don't think those kachinas are made at any pueblo any longer. Even the dance is no longer performed."

Paul, his eyes still fixed on the figurines, said, "I'm still a little fuzzy on what a kachina is. Or what it does. I know these dolls are called kachinas . . . but aren't the dancers who dress like them also called kachinas?"

Willie nodded. "It can get a little confusing. I've studied enough Pueblo history to know a bit about them." He took a sip of his drink, then continued, "Mainly, kachinas are supernatural. They can be the spirits of the dead or energies like lightning or rain.

"When a man dresses like a kachina during one of their dances, Indians say he becomes a real kachina and shares in that kachina's power. To further confuse things"—Willie lifted his drink and waved it in the general direction of the display case—"the dolls are also called kachinas, as you pointed out. Indians use them to teach their kids about the spirit-folk. They also remind the adults of the kachinas during the winter, when the spirit-people are supposed to go home under the mountains.

"Kachina dances draw on the power of the true kachinas to control rain and bring good harvests and more or less insure the well-being of the tribe."

"Kachinas are always good powers, then?" Paul asked.

"Not always. There are monster kachinas—but they're used to warn people to be good. Roundaboutly, I guess you'd say they're good too."

"You said something about kachinas being put aside. What does that mean?"

"A kachina is eliminated if people feel its influence is bad. One called the Bloody Hand Kachina was weeded out way back when, because misfortune always followed it when it showed up in a dance. The tribal leaders decided that it had been introduced by people of bad faith—that it was a *brujo,* a witch, and not a true kachina at all."

"Where do all the kachinas come from?"

"In most cases, no one is sure where the original concept came from. Sometimes people dream of a certain kachina and introduce it into the tribe."

Paul ran the palm of his hand across the display case. "And *these?* You say these aren't used anymore. Why? Are they witch dolls?"

Willie finished his drink and contemplated the fragments of melting ice still left, as though reading an answer in them. Finally he said, "That's an interesting question. I don't think there's a cut-and-dried answer. You see, your routine kachina always represents an unchanging quantity. But these . . . changed . . . somewhere along the line. They're a peculiarly Tawan grouping; they never really caught on at other pueblos. For years, though, they were very important to the seven core pueblos of the Tawas . . . the cities the Casserite padres used to call *Cibolita,* Little Cibola."

The old man laughed sharply. "The name was ironic. None of the early Spaniards forgot the stories of Cibola and the cities of gold that lured the first explorers to these parts. What a comedown the pueblos along the Rio Sonoliento were to the Casserites, who dreamed of bringing the word of God into heathen cities with streets and roofs of gold. . . . Well, they found plenty of heathens, at any rate.

"But back to the kachinas: there was, for a long time, an annual dance involving these kachinas. The purpose of the dance isn't too clear (information gets pretty garbled when it's passed along by word of mouth); it was probably first performed to keep these kachina-folk *away*. From the stories I've managed to piece together, the dance was designed to keep these kachinas in the Underworld or in limbo between

the Underworld and this world, which the Tawa call the
Upper World.

"It's a common folklore among the Pueblos that their
ancestors first climbed into this world from another world
below. The Tawa embroidered things a bit: they claimed
that men left the Underworld because certain spirits there
were making trouble; they also believe that ever since, these
creatures have been trying to follow men into the Upper
World. They couldn't follow directly because the Sun Father
helped the Tawas' ancestors by sealing off the road that men
used before the others could get out. But the creatures never
gave up; the Tawas claim they're still trying to find their way
here into the Upper World.

"To keep the troublemaker spirits away, the Tawas came
up with a dance they believed could, in some magical way,
add to the length of the journey the Underworlders would
have to make to get from down there to up here."

Willie was staring at the dolls in the case with a thought-
ful expression now. "It was only much later that someone
suggested maybe they *shouldn't* be kept away. This same
someone said it might be a good thing for the Tawas—for
all Indian people—if the Below Persons actually arrived."

"When did that happen?" Paul asked, turning to look at
the old man.

"About the time the Spanish padres began arriving. I'm
pretty sure it was El Brujo himself who suggested the change.
He seemed to put a lot of faith in the powers of these particular kachinas; he felt their powers could help the Indians
get rid of the whites who were taking away their land and
corrupting the old ways. He convinced a lot of Indians to
change the nature of the annual dance from preventing the
arrival of these kachinas to actually summoning them. His
theory apparently was that the upheavals the padres brought
called for drastic measures.

"Of course, this led to religious fights between the old
school and the reformers. I gather, for a few years, different
kiva-groups managed to stage both versions of the dance.
In the end, the elders of Agastan and most other pueblos
did away with the whole grouping, because they said thinking about them was making too many people crazy.

"The dolls in that case came from a pueblo miles away.
The clans there conducted a traditional form of the dance

and still made the dolls long after their neighbors gave the whole thing up. But even they've forgotten the dance, and the dolls you're looking at are over seventy years old."

Willie stood up and reached for Paul's empty glass, "Here, let me freshen your drink."

While Willie was in the kitchen, Paul discovered a yellowing sheet of paper, neatly typed and taped to the side of the kachina case. It was a transcription of an item from the *Miskatonik University Ethnological Report for 1919*, a description of the figures in the case and the dance which had been built around them.

Paul read:

This dance symbolizes the creation of spider-child by the nameless woman Kachina, who is assisted in her work by her two monstrous sons. They send spider-child to find a way up to the world of men. When spider-child returns and reports he has found a route not sealed by the sun-father, the three full-size kachinas set out, following the child-creature.

The main steps of the dance involve interlocking patterns of parallel lines and circles which symbolize the caves and tunnels the creatures must pass through on their journey to the upper world. The Tawas believe the steps of the dance create a sympathetic magic that brings into being new caves and passages or confuses and routes them back through caves already traversed. This is done to add to the wanderings of these much-feared spirits and prevent them from reaching the surface world.

The main figures of this no-longer-performed dance are:

A. *Nameless Woman Kachina*. This kachina wears a black mask topped with a mass of horsehair dyed red. The mouth is white; the eye-holes are also bordered in white. Her cape, or *manta*, is black and decorated with white and red disks. She wears a plain kilt of buckskin tied with a belt of silver disks. In her left hand she carries a gourd in the form of a skull, dyed red. In her right hand she holds a medicine rattle. Her moccasins are black.

B. *Sons of the Nameless Woman Kachinas* (two). Each of these identical kachinas has a black face mask with protruding snout and prominent globular eyes. There are three parallel bands of white on each cheek; the masks have hair of cedar bark. Each wears a white kilt tied with a black sash. Their buckskin leggings are stained black and red in lateral bands. On each dancer's chest is a red disk bordered in white. Both carry wooden staffs to help them on their climb up to the world of men.

C. *Spider-Child Kachina.* This figure has a mask painted with wide horizontal lines of alternating white and black. It has white eye-disks with black centers located in a black band; the mouth, a black oval with a red center, occupies a white band. The kachina is covered with red body-paint and wears a black loin-cloth. Above his black moccasins and black-painted hands are anklets and wristlets of fur dyed black. On top of his mask are two eagle feathers, one white, one red. In his hand spider-child carries a bell, the sound of which is said to guide the Nameless Woman and her sons as they follow him through the unlighted caves that link the underworld and this world.

When he had finished reading, Paul studied the details of the carvings with added interest. Looking closely, he discovered that inside each red or white circle on the black cape of the female kachina was the blood-moon symbol:

He was tempted to raise the top of the case and lift the figures out for a closer look, but he felt sure Willie wouldn't approve—not if the figures were genuine antiques, as the old man claimed.

Willie returned with two brimming glasses. After a final glance at the display case, Paul dropped down on the end of the couch opposite the old man. He remarked, "It amazes me how much history is crammed into this one little corner of the state. A man could spend his life just finding out about El Centro and maybe a ten-mile radius."

Willie laughed. "That's my life in a nutshell."

While they finished their drinks in silence Paul became very much aware of the sighs and rustlings in the room around him and coming from the rooms beyond the beaded draperies as the house settled in the cool desert night. He was conscious of Willie staring at him with a curious intensity, though he could not guess the reason for Willie's absorbed look. He felt as if the other man's eyes were boring into him. He stood up suddenly and said, "I really should be going; my wife will be worried."

Willie remained sitting as he offered, "One last one for the road? . . . even though you're walking . . ."

Paul shook his head and thanked the older man. He only wanted to be outside, away from the sighs and whispers of the settling house and the fire-bright eyes of the little man. He was beginning to feel the effects of the evening's drinking.

Willie let him find his own way out.

The brisk night air quickly cleared his head and dispelled his momentary uneasiness. He thrust his hands into his pockets and began walking rapidly in the direction of the motel.

When he reached the Four Star, Paul discovered that he had no idea of the time. He looked at his watch, but it had apparently stopped some hours before. Looking across the little courtyard, he saw no lights in number twelve. He decided Sheila was probably asleep.

He peered into the darkened motel office, but he could not make out the time on the little lighted clock face behind the counter.

"A peeping tom, huh?" said a woman's voice behind him. "That's how you teacher types get your jollies?" Then he heard a soft, lightly mocking laugh.

Startled, he turned. He recognized Louise Shore immediately, even though her face was hidden in shadows thrown by the lime-green neon strips along the roof edges overhead. Her hands were the same blue as the neon stars on the motel sign, which had not yet been shut off.

She wore jeans and a denim jacket over a tee shirt; she had sandals on her feet. Her toenails and fingernails were painted silver. He flame-colored hair was subdued in the mingled neon and moonlight; it hung thickly and loosely around her head.

"I was just trying to find out the time," he explained, feeling foolish.

"A likely story," she said. "But if you really want to know, it's later than you think. Later than little boys should be out wandering around in the dark."

She remained where she was, standing half in shadow; he still could not see her face.

"How come *you're* up so late?" he countered. "If it's as late as you say . . ."

"Jimmy's playing cards: that means three–four o'clock in the morning for him—*if* he don't just pass out over at Roger's. And that's *more* than likely."

She pulled a cigarette out of her pocket. Paul fumbled unsuccessfully for a match. She chuckled and lit it herself with a small white plastic lighter while he was still searching.

"I drank too much coffee tonight," she said. "It keeps me wide awake unless I'm *really* wiped out, you know? Sometimes I take a walk. Or go for a ride."

She drew on her cigarette, then exhaled slowly. The rising smoke went from green to blue in the neon light. "I'm glad to see *you* up and about, though. You had us all worried. And your wife is so"—she paused as though searching for the right word, ". . . protective? Anyhow, the poor thing was worried out of her mind over you; that was plain as day. Willie shouldn't have taken you so far into the caves; that was stupid of him. I guess, when you come right down to it, my suggesting the caves wasn't such a hot idea."

Paul shrugged and smiled. "You can't be blamed for my carelessness. *I* was the one who got lost."

But Louise did not seem to be paying attention to what he was saying. She said suddenly, "There's something in the air tonight. It's not so much that it's *warm* as, you know, *close?*"

Curiously, Paul noticed that the air had lost its chill; he felt quite comfortable. *Was the air really warming?* he wondered, then forgot his question as Louise continued, "I can't explain it. I've lived all my life in these parts, and I *still* have a hard time explaining it. It's like the desert has *moods,* you know? Tonight . . . tonight is a downer. I feel it . . . *creepy-*like, sort of pushing in on all sides. When I get feeling like this, I take a spin in my car. I like the feel of the air, the feeling of *moving,* you know? It clears the mind. And talking 'bout that: *you* look like you could use a little ride around too. Com'on . . . it'll do us both a world of good."

"My wife—" Paul began.

"Don't worry; your wife went to sleep hours ago. I saw her come back by herself around ten. Then the lights went out pretty quick and they've stayed out. She's dead to the world; you can bet on it." She tossed her cigarette out onto the gravel, where it continued to glow like a single coal. She said, with a laugh, "Scout's honor, I won't try to make a pass at you, if *that's* what you're worried about," and she raised a hand with the three middle fingers uplifted in a mock salute.

Paul considered a moment, then decided, "All right. I've had too much to drink tonight. A little fresh air will help me sleep later."

"Well, *good!*" said Louise. She reached out and took his hand. "My car is over here. It's a few years old but it's still got *spunk.*"

The touch of her hand was cool in his; he felt a growing excitement. She towed him along like an impatient child.

I wonder what time it really is? Paul thought suddenly, glancing across at the darkened windows of number twelve. And then he thought, *Who the hell cares?*

Louise drove carefully until they reached the edge of town, heading east; once past the city limits, she floored the accelerator, racing out into the desert night. The scattered lights of El Centro rapidly disappeared behind a rise, only to reappear at intervals as the road swept up and then fell away under them. The town's lights seemed to Paul like the lights of a distant fishing fleet rising and falling on the gentle waves of some vast, dark, still sea.

Above them was a sky full of moon and stars, arching

down all around them until it was cut off by the jagged teeth of the horizon.

"If you get cold, let me know," Louise said. "I'll put on the heat."

Paul shook his head, saying, "I'm fine." But he found he was unprepared for the blackness of the desert on either side of the car, for the overwhelming sense of aloneness it gave birth to in him.

As though reading his thoughts, Louise said, "I *like* it out here at night. I like being away from people and just every-day *crap*, you know? It's exciting and scary: you don't know what's out there moving around in the dark and you don't know what's up ahead. Sometimes I really get creeped out when I'm out driving alone. Does that make any *sense* to you?"

"I think so. As a kid, the night would scare me. But I'd love to go out in it anyway. I'd love to wander around when other people were home with all their lights on. They'd be wondering, what's outside the window, what's moving in the shadows? . . . And I'd know, because I'd be standing right outside, staring in at them . . ." He broke off, surprised at how clearly those half-forgotten memories came back to him.

Louise laughed. "So you were a peeping tom even when you were a kid, huh?"

He shook his head. "That isn't what it was about. I felt braver than everyone else in their lighted houses because I was outside and they weren't. But there were times when I'd just stand and listen to all those sounds you never hear during the day and all the special, secret smells that only happen at night." He stopped and said, "Sorry if I'm boring you . . . I haven't thought about things like this in years."

"You're not boring me at all. I *like* hearing you talk. Sometimes, around here, it's hard to find anyone who talks about, well, *anything*—other than how hot it is and what the price of gasoline's going to be."

Paul sensed a warmth in her voice that made him uncomfortable. He did not respond, but she did not seem to mind. He felt a faint increase in the car's speed.

They drove awhile longer in silence. Then Louise turned off onto a side road.

Paul recognized the access road and said, "This is the road to the mission, isn't it?"

Louise nodded. "I've got this crazy urge to look at the place in the moonlight; it can be real pretty on a good night—if that's all right with you?"

"Fine with me," he said, but he felt uncomfortable at leaving the highway. He watched apprehensively as the headlights sliced through the darkness along the unlighted road.

An animal, little more than a white blur, erupted into the headlights and darted back into the night. Louise giggled excitedly as she swerved to miss it.

Paul shouted, "Christ! Watch what you're doing!"

She slowed the car slightly and said, "Don't *worry:* I'm not gonna let some crazy jackrabbit finish us off."

He was regretting this midnight adventure more and more. He suspected Louise had been drinking more than coffee before he met her.

He was relieved when they finally pulled into the deserted parking lot in front of the mission. The facade of the church itself glowed eerily in the moonlight. He noted again the single ruined tower and wondered why it had never been repaired; he asked Louise, but she just shrugged and said, "Lightning, I suppose," as she brought the car to a careless standstill across several parking slots and shut the engine off.

"Let's have a look around," she said.

"Won't the priests mind?"

"They won't even *know* we're here, unless we make a fuss. They're all asleep now, over there." She gestured toward the darkened *convento;* apparently no one was keeping vigil.

Louise slid out of the car and called to him. "Hurry up! I want to climb the hill first."

"Shall I lock my door?" he asked as he climbed out.

"Who the hell's going to bother this heap out here? Come on!" She gestured impatiently, trotting rapidly along the path to Vision Hill. Paul stumbled several times as they began the actual climb; both times Louise steadied him and kept him from pitching forward.

"How can you see so well?" he asked. "You must have cat's eyes."

She laughed. "I'm a witch, didn't you know?"

He laughed back. "So why don't you fly us to the top instead of taking the long way up?"

She giggled and said, "We're almost there; don't give up yet."

When they reached the ledge that circled the top of the hill, she drew him toward the left, to the nearest of the little stone benches which flanked Padre Perez's shrine. The grotto itself was nothing more than a fenced-in mass of shadows; Paul could not distinguish the statues inside.

Louise sat down and beckoned him to sit beside her.

From this vantage point, Paul could see the mission gleaming pale in a vast sweep of moonlight and shadow and infrequent lights—the flickering ones marking the roads; the fixed ones, towns or ranches. To the west, the land was embraced by the dark arms of the Sierra Morenas. He felt tiny in the expanse of his vision; Louise's presence beside him was the one thing that kept it from all becoming frightening.

It was cold on the hilltop; he could feel the ever-present wind through the thin fabric of his jacket.

The cold did not seem to bother his companion; her jacket was still unbuttoned. She had lit another cigarette and was gazing out into the night. Her lipstick, he noticed for the first time, was silver, the frosty kind that always looked wet. The breeze stirred her hair, and she brushed impatiently at a few strands which blew into her face.

Paul had the fleeting impression that everything was waiting for a signal for something to begin.

Louise finished her cigarette in silence. The two of them seemed to have nothing to say to each other. Paul could not decide if it was because they had run out of things to say or because the vastness of the night simply reduced everything —even talk itself—to meaninglessness.

He wanted to go, and he was unable to make a move. Again he felt that he was waiting for a signal of some kind.

Then, with a suddenness and ferocity that were startling, Louise dug her right hand into his crotch and began kneading him painfully/pleasurably. Her left hand cupped the back of his head and pulled his face down toward hers, kissing him, thrusting her tongue past his teeth, deep into his mouth.

Confused, he pulled away, yelling, "Wait a minute! Whoa!"

"Why?" she asked, and began kissing him again, while her hand moved to his zipper. "You want to sit and *talk* yourself into it? No way! Let's get it on now, baby, before it gets too cold to screw. I want you now, out here, in the night. You can talk all you want to *after*. In the car with the heater going. Come *on!*"

Then his hands were on the back of her neck, his tongue was probing her mouth, and he knew this was what they had been waiting for all along. He was straining toward her with his whole body while she slowly worked his zipper down with agonizing, delicious care. "Ease up a little. Hold tight. Don't come in your britches, sweetheart; you gotta *share* the wealth, you know?" She laughed—sharply, sensually.

Her hand was inside his jeans, easing him free of his shorts, drawing him out. He thrust his tongue deeper into her mouth.

Then she broke free of him and ran to the head of the path, leaving him in an agony of need.

He stood up suddenly and leaned against the fence of the grotto, feeling weak. He touched his hand to his forehead and found it warm and moist. He felt feverish all over.

"Bitch!" he shouted, letting some of his frustration and rage spill into the night air and dissipate. "What the *fuck* sort of game are you playing, anyway?" he asked, more to himself than to her.

"Paul!" someone whispered.

"Another game?" he snarled. "Hide-and-seek, this time?"

Someone called his name again. He froze, certain that the sound had come from *inside* the grotto. But that made no sense: the gate was sealed securely; he could clearly see the chain and padlock in the moonlight. And there was no way for anyone to climb over the sharp fence posts high overhead. Was there another way in—a side gate or back path?

"Louise!" he called. "Louise! Where the hell are you? I'm tired of this. Let's get out of here *now!*" He refused to let fear take control of him. He reassured himself that Louise was playing some drunken, foolish prank.

"No more games, Louise," he said, in as reasonable a tone as he could manage. He spoke toward the shadowy shrine. "Let's get the car and get out of here."

His name was called a third time. Louder. In disbelief, he realized that it was a *man's* voice he was hearing.

And it had certainly come from inside the grotto.

As he continued to stare into the shadows beyond the barrier, holding onto two of the railings for support, he suddenly felt dizzy, confused, frightened. He didn't want to look and was afraid not to.

Something moved in the darkness; a bit of the shadow broke away from the larger mass.

He felt he might scream. Or laugh out loud. Or choke in an attempt to do both at once. He could not move; his hands clung to the fence as though it were electrified.

There was a shift in the moonlight; the fragment of darkness resolved itself into the statue of Father Perez. But the statue no longer had its back to the fence and its arm outstretched to the Virgin high up in her niche. Now the arms were outstretched toward *him*.

I have a fever. Paul told himself, *or I'm losing my mind. Maybe someone has simply moved the statue.*

Then he did begin to laugh, because the statue was coming closer. He saw no movement, but with each blink of his eye, the thing inched closer to the fence. To him.

"Help me," Paul heard, but the voice seemed to emerge from the shadows behind the statue. He shook his head frantically, because it was the only response his sudden terror allowed. Still he could not move, could not take his eyes from the grotesque plaster face.

He made a sound that was only a strangulated moan.

The statue was close. Very close. In a moment those chipped plaster fingers would touch his, and he would begin to scream. He stared at those inhuman hands: saw how the flesh-colored paint was flaking away, giving them a diseased look. In one or two places, the fingers had been gouged so deeply that the plaster underneath showed white in the moonlight, like bones sticking through a hideous bloodless wound.

Only inches separated the plaster fingers from those of flesh and blood.

"Help me, Paul," pleaded the unseen whisperer.

Closer. Not quite touching. Closer. Close.

"No!" Paul shouted, and found the strength to wrench himself away. He felt a pain as his hands left the fence, as if metal and flesh had somehow been fused.

Only once did he dare look behind him, and saw the

statue's black-robed arms and leprous white hands thrust through the fence palings.

There was a sound of weeping that quickly became the sobbing of his breath as his footsteps pounded down the path toward the mission shining impassively in the moonlight.

13 Dream and *Campo Santo*

1

There was a singing in the blood; it was a singing *of* the blood, a song rising out of the power she felt coursing through her.

She had come awake suddenly, completely, and was sitting up in bed, was standing beside her bed, was moving around the room in time to the music of her blood and beingness.

She did not turn on the light; there was no need to. Moonlight or sunlight or *some* light was streaming through the red curtains that had been green curtains when she had gone to sleep so long ago, a lifetime ago. The unexpectedly red curtains gave the light the intensity and glow of coals in a fireplace when the fire has gone deep into itself and the coals are the essence of fire, ready to be roused by being blown upon into a steady, hot, *dangerous* radiance. Light like the heart of fire, blood-tinged firelight. Bloodlight.

Around and around the room she moved in wonder at what she was feeling, knowing that there had to be a reason for what she was feeling, but unable to guess at the reason.

The source of light beyond the curtains remained constant, bathing the room in a steady glow. It colored everything pink or crimson.

Paul's bed, she saw, was empty. She wondered what time it was and tried to read the face of the clock on her night stand but could not: there was some distortion in the air or the light or the glass over its face, some rippling effect. It did not matter, so she stopped trying to read it. The time of night and Paul's empty bed mattered not at all.

She continued moving around the room and wondered where the light outside was coming from, but did not dare to move the curtain aside. That would be to die: she would discover the secret she was not ready for yet and she would die because her heart and mind could not contain it. It would mean understanding the truth within the fire and comprehending the song within her blood. And she was not ready . . .

But soon, but soon, but soon, she sang, *I'll know it . . . I'll know it all.*

She stopped in front of the dressing table and pulled open the middle drawer. A manuscript lay in the otherwise empty drawer: several hundred typewritten pages in a blue canvas binder.

She read the larger of two carefully typed white labels.

THE SENECU MATERIALS
(NOTES FROM THE OTHER SIDE)
TRANSCRIPTS, VOLUME I

The smaller label underneath read

PROPERTY OF: CYRUS AND HELEN ANDERSON
#4 ISLETA WAY
EL CENTRO, NEW MEXICO

She remembered carrying it home wrapped in brown paper. Who had removed it from its package? she wondered. She had not touched it after placing it in the drawer.

She lifted up the mass of notes. She opened it randomly and began reading the first bit of typescript that caught her eye:

> . . . then *she* who walks in darkness walks in light at last and sings afresh the ancient songs of power and of truth. All men are merely children who are waiting for the wisdom *she* will bring. And this is the secret *she* will whisper: that meaning is mere dreaming and the earth is absolute. . . .

She flipped through several more pages, then began reading again:

When the world in waiting can wait no longer, *she* will manifest herself. And *she* will bring a new order which in reality is the oldest dominion of all. *She* is ruthless out of necessity, but never evil. Evil is a name men give *her* because they fear her absolute power. They have usurped her for a time, they have fled her power, they have set up a new order in the lands and subverted the old ways. But the circle revolves, the fire burns again, the blood inside beats with renewed vigor. *She* makes ready to reclaim the world that men have corrupted. When the need is greatest, *she* will return from the fathomless dark. *She* is terrible, but never evil. Evil is the name *men* give her. *She* is terrible as Kali, which is another of her countless names. Like Kali she is life source and life's end, birth-giver and devourer of her own children, the Terrible One, the Black Mother, garlanded in the skulls of her offspring, adorned with blood, crowned with fire. Awesome *she* is, but her power is the law of the earth: that all that is born must die, that what comes into being must pass away. *She* is the proof and power of that law, for *she* has passed for a time from this earth, but *she will return again.*

A blank sheet of paper had been inserted between this page and the next typed one. On it Cyrus had scrawled in ballpoint, *More references to a female antichrist. These communications leave Maria distressed for days and hamper our work. Is this a genuine communication or the work of a malicious elemental? These interruptions have nothing to do with the main body of material communicated thus far. My feeling is that they are illegitimate and to be discounted. But we must study this situation carefully. If there is some genuine threat here, we must move rapidly to close off all channels of communication. I'm not worried at the moment, but the situation demands steady monitoring. If the need arises, Helen or I can seal off the threat. But as yet, I do not feel there is any danger to any of us.*

Sheila closed the book and folded it to her breast, cradling it as if it were an infant. She laughed and told herself, *They've been tricked; they've been hoodwinked; they've been led down the garden path. There are secrets here,* she knew, hugging the book more closely to her. *There is truth abounding, but no meaning for* (and here she laughed aloud) *such fools as Cyrus and Helen Anderson of Number Four Isleta Way, El Centro, New Mexico.* They were merely the first point of contact, the first strokes of a painting now rapidly nearing completion.

We have gone beyond them, she realized; we have no need of them anymore. No need, no need, no need, she crooned in whispers to the book she held; no need of them at all. And no patience with the threat they pose to us.

The room seemed to be rippling all around her; the glow from outside intensified so that she had to shut her eyes tightly against the painfulness of it. She hugged the book to her and waited until the hot redness that she could still see even with her eyes closed had cooled somewhat.

Cautiously she opened her eyes.

The light in the room had deepened to the color of old rose. In the red dimness she could see clearly enough to know instantly that she was in another place, another room. But a familiar room: she had been here before.

The book was gone, but she did not feel it mattered.

She looked around and recognized the Anderson's living room. She was standing beside the table around which they had all gathered for a séance—a lifetime ago, it seemed.

The mask carved out of a gourd grinned down at her from the wall; she felt the shadowed eye-holes following her every step; she smiled up at the death's head with a conspiratorial smile.

She thought, *How extraordinary for me to be here. How did I get here?* What, she wondered, would she say to anyone who discovered her? Because there was no reason *she* could give them which *they* could comprehend, she reasoned, she would just have to remain undiscovered. She laughed at the simplicity of the solution, then laughed again because she *knew* there was no danger of her being discovered.

Thick rose light filtered through the crimson curtains which were drawn across every window of the room . . . though there had been white curtains with geometric designs at those windows the last time she had been in this room.

She moved to the dining-room table; she ran her fingers across its wooden surface almost possessively, noting with distaste the gritty feel of bread crumbs and spilled sugar. She lowered herself into the chair at the head of the table— the same chair in which Maria had been sitting. She remained seated, staring into the darkened living room opposite her. No glimmer of roselight touched the absolute darkness of that distant room; it was as black as the bottommost depth of a well or pool, where no light ever reached. And yet, as sure as there were things moving blindly, softly through the weeds and mud of such a pool, there were, she could sense, soft—but *sighted*—presences moving within that core of darkness. She was certain that those *others* saw her sitting at the table, her arms resting on the top of it, palms down, fingers splayed across the sticky, gritty surface. She felt the nearness of those *others* not as a fearsome thing but as an approving—almost a *comforting*—sensation.

She shut her eyes and kept them closed for several minutes, but the quality of the light seeping past her eyelids remained constant.

She opened her eyes.

She felt a warmth around her neck and at her throat. She raised a wondering hand and her fingers discovered the blood-moon necklace. The metal felt unnaturally warm to the touch. The smooth disk of silver and coral almost burned her fingertips, though it felt less hot against the skin at her throat.

She could sense a dark *expectancy* in the far room. The *others* were waiting for something. They were waiting for *her* to do something.

Absently she began moving her hands in twin circles on the tabletop. In her mind she saw again the blue canvas binder with its labels standing out white and sharp. She could clearly read the names of Cyrus and Helen and their address. Over everything was imposed the birth symbol of the necklace etched in firelines.

She was softly humming a tune to which the movements of her hands kept time.

The song was in her voice, her hands, her blood.

The singing went beyond her blood and voice. The very air seemed to vibrate with it. There was a deeper resonance: she felt the very atoms of the house around her singing the song, which grew more intense in her, more feverish with each passing moment.

The tempo increased; the humming grew louder; it was coming from the walls. Surely, she thought, the Andersons would hear, would come downstairs, would discover her and ask her what she was doing. But this song, she reassured herself, was of another order, and so they *couldn't* hear it. Only the *others* in the far room heard it and understood it, because *they* were helping create the song in her, were singing it with her in voices without sound.

A song of redness, of the blood within her, of the fire within her blood. Her hands were moving in frantic patterns independent of each other, free of any conscious control on her part. They traced out a complex design of interlocking straight lines, right angles, curves.

The singing of her blood became a scream that the substance of the house echoed.

And the screaming became a redness/became heat/became fire.

Sheets of flame rippled over the walls, poured up across the ceiling, ignited the drapes at the windows. There was fire everywhere; everything was fire; the world was on fire.

In the center of her mind, the image of the blue canvas binder began to burn.

She threw her arms across her eyes to protect them from the heat and glare, but the image of the burning book lingered in her mind for a short time; then it flickered out and she was alone in the darkness. . . .

Sheila sat up in bed, drenched in sweat. Her heart was pounding. She stared frantically around the room; her eyes took in the soft green glow through the curtains and the lighted dial of the clock, which read 12:37.

She turned on the lamp on the nightstand. Paul's bed was empty; the spread lay smooth and untouched over it.

Where the hell is Paul, anyway? she wondered.

2

The car was where they had left it, still parked in haphazard fashion. Paul ran his eyes across the expanse of the parking lot. Nothing moved in the moonlight; there was no trace of Louise.

Anger was replacing his fear. He wondered where the woman was and what new game she was playing. He had discounted his experience on the hilltop as some kind of alcohol-induced hallucination; he felt almost feverish. Overwrought nerves and too much bourbon had conspired to make him think he saw moving statues and heard disembodied whispers. He had no idea what was going through Louise's mind—whether she was drunk or crazy or simply a flirt not willing to follow through what she had begun.

He no longer cared about her reasons; at the moment he only wanted to get back to the motel and fall asleep.

He went to the car, hoping she had forgotten to take the keys with her. He was almost angry enough to take off and leave her: let the padres arrange a ride for her or let her hitchhike into town with the next day's tourists.

But the car, which Paul clearly remembered leaving unlocked, was now securely locked. Obviously Louise had done this. *Why hadn't she simply driven off?* he wondered.

Then he heard a nearby laugh and Louise called, "Try looking over here!"

He looked across to the church. Some trick of the moonlight made both towers look burned out, like twin clusters of charred skeletal fingers.

Louise called his name; he discovered her, standing in the shadows of the main entrance of the mission building. Her hair burned red and her tee shirt glowed white in the dappled moonlight.

She lingered until he was half the distance toward her, then she ran off to the right. Her path cut across the little patio with its desiccated trees and skirted the expanse of adobe wall, higher than a man's head, that formed the garden's western boundary.

He called to her, "Louise!" no longer caring if the priests asleep in the *convento* heard him. But the windows of the building remained dark; the padres, unheedful.

Louise ran swiftly ahead of him, never glancing back, leaving a thin trail of laughter and perfume in the still air. He followed as though in a dream. He did not understand what the rules were for this insane game of tag. He ran faster, taking care not to stumble on the uneven flagging.

Louise turned a corner at the far end of the patio; when he rounded the same corner a moment later, she had disappeared.

Ahead of him stretched the northern wall of the enclosure that bounded the back of the patio. A narrow path followed the line of the wall to its farthest corner; then the trail extended out into the sandy stretch of cacti and mesquite waste beyond.

Nothing stirred anywhere as far as he could see. He started along the path, running his hand along the wall's uneven adobe surface, as though he needed to reassure himself of its reality. A feverish light-headedness was growing in him; the dreamlike quality of things muddled his thinking.

Midway along the wall, he discovered an opening of massive iron gates, shut and sealed with a heavy chain wound through and around two of the metal stanchions.

He continued on past the gate to the farthest corner but he could see nothing. Louise seemed to have vanished utterly.

He returned to the gate and studied the chain, noticing that there was no padlock on it. On impulse he gave it a yank, and the chain uncoiled and slithered to the ground, hitting the flagstones with a clink.

He pushed open one side of the gate and stepped through. He was in the cemetery, the *campo santo* (he remembered the term from a guidebook he'd read) of the mission, where the founders had been laid to rest. *Somewhere in here,* he thought, *Father Perez is buried. Without a head. They never found his head.* He stifled a nervous giggle and resisted the temptation to locate decapitated figures in every shadow around him.

He concentrated instead on the puzzle of Louise's sudden disappearance. Had she come into the little burial ground to hide? It was unlikely that she could have had time to undo the chain and replace it again, with Paul just a few paces behind her. Still, there seemed no other place she could have gone.

He looked around him. Worn crucifixes, dusty angels, grave markers with their inscriptions worn away, blossomed like insane flowers in the walled and moonlit space. Nothing else seemed to grow here, save a few dried weeds and grasses withered to white straws in the moonlight. The twisted branches of a single dead tree in the corner where the eastern and southern walls met threw crazy-quilt shadows over the ground.

Louise was standing in the shadows under the tree. When she saw that he had seen her, she laughed but made no move.

Paul took a step forward, stretching his arms wide to prevent her eluding him again. "Going to run away this time?" he asked. "Going to *try* to run away?" He made no effort to conceal his anger.

She just laughed again, ignoring his unspoken threat.

Her face was a tangle of ropes and knots of moon-cast shadow; her face was no face at all, just patches of ink and silvery whiteness. He paused for a moment, unnerved by this vision. Then her derisive laughter forced him to act.

He lunged forward and grabbed her arm. She twisted reflexively but made no real effort to escape. She seemed willing to be caught, in fact. He pulled her toward him, out of the shadow. She threw back her head as if she were going to laugh again, but she made no sound. He pressed his face to hers and kissed her, driven more by anger than desire. At first she responded to the kiss, then she began to twist about in his arms. She was stronger than he had expected; she nearly broke free.

Then her writhing stopped as she suddenly sagged in his arms. She moaned softly, helplessly, and he felt himself relax somewhat. He bent over to kiss her once more.

She bit him on the lower lip with a ferocity that made him yell, more with surprise than pain. For a moment he feared she would tear away part of his mouth with her teeth; she made a tremendous effort to break free, but his hand caught the front of her jacket. His blood was on her mouth; he could feel it dribbling down his chin.

Time spun to a halt: they stood and eyed each other like two animals squaring off for a fight to the death. For Paul, there was only pain and anger. He screamed something incomprehensible even to himself and caught his foot behind her ankle, shoving her backward and throwing her off-balance. She fell on her back across a grave mound, narrowly avoiding hitting her head on the stone cross, tilted at a crazy angle, that marked the head of the grave. She thrust out her hand to break her fall; it upset a little pottery vase filled with pink and white plastic flowers, scattering them across the mounded clay.

For a minute she lay as she had fallen: stunned, the breath knocked out of her. She looked startled but not afraid. Her red hair splayed out across the cracked, baked clay.

He straddled her at the waist, panting, almost out of breath himself. Then he leaned forward and grasped the thick red hair in his hands. At the same time, she found breath enough to begin laughing weakly at him.

He yanked her head up toward his chest by her hair, then thrust it backward suddenly, slamming it against the grave. She grunted and stopped laughing, but her eyes still mocked him. He lifted her head again, then slammed it down. He lifted it yet again, then hesitated, feeling her shifting weakly about under him, feeling himself becoming aroused...

The moon passed behind a cloud; shadows filled the little enclosure. The air grew freezing for a moment. He felt disoriented, dizzy, as if the darkness were within him, as in a fainting spell.

The shadow passed. He was alone, kneeling on the grave; his hands no longer held masses of red hair, only bunches of faded pink and white plastic flowers.

Louise laughed somewhere behind him. Whirling around, he saw her as a shadow crowned with hair like fire-lit smoke standing just outside the cemetery gates.

His head was spinning—nothing made sense any longer. He called to her—"Louise"—in the voice of a child calling for help. "Louise, I'm sorry. Please help me."

Her voice was clear and mocking. "Don't you want to play any more games?"

He shook his head wearily. All he wanted was an end to games of every sort. He felt like a tired, discouraged child.

"Then let's get out of here," she said quite matter-of-factly.

He got slowly to his feet and brushed himself off. He had torn the knee of his slacks and blood was seeping through. His lip stung like the devil. When he reached the iron bars of the closed gate, she pulled it open and said to him, "Just follow me."

She led him across the patio toward the front of the church and the parking lot.

In front of the mission building, near the spot where he had first seen her when he came down from the hill, she paused.

"You wait here," she told him. "I left something inside. I'll only be gone a minute."

She pushed through the heavy wooden doors. Paul found it surprising that the doors were not fastened at night. *But,* he reasoned, *everything is crazy in this place.*

Louise did not return. The moon overhead threw a harsh silver-blue light across the cloud patches and lit the front of the church. The opened doorway gaped like a monstrous mouth.

Unable to wait any longer, he started toward the entrance. Was Louise starting another round of tricks? He would take one quick look around, he decided, and if he did not find her right away, he would go and beat on the padres' door until they came and gave him a bed or helped him to get back to town.

He stepped into the darkened church, calling her name. He began moving up the center aisle, searching for her in the uncertain light of a few scattered votive candles and the moon streaming through the windows near the roof.

He halted at the communion railing and looked across at the shadowed altar. Carved and painted, the saints and angels stared back with unseeing eyes. The church was empty; there was no sign of Louise. He returned to the first row of pews and sat down to rest and to try to organize his thoughts. His pulse was racing; he felt sweat soaking his armpits and the back of his jacket.

He closed his eyes for a moment, breathing deeply, trying to calm himself.

Then, behind him, he heard a gentle tinkling sound like tiny wind chimes stirring in a faint breeze. Turning, he saw only the darkened alcove in which the corpse-statue of Padre Perez rested. The sound seemed to come from the shadows massed within the niche.

He was fully alert now, watching that darkness, his hand gripping the back of a pew. The clinking sound came again, louder, accompanied this time by the whisper of rustling silk. He could not face whatever was making that noise.

Swiftly, noiselessly, he hurried to the side door in the wall nearest him.

It was locked; he could not budge it. He looked around frantically. To make a run for the main doors of the church meant passing in full view of whatever *thing* was moving around in the alcove.

He had to risk it; to stay would leave him trapped by whatever was coming to life in the shadows. He began circling toward the far aisle, running along the north wall of the church.

"Paul!" a voice boomed, the sound filling his head, reverberating through the whole church. He froze in mid-step, his eyes riveted on the alcove, which was filled with a sickly blue luminescence.

And he wondered if he was going mad.

The corpse-statue was climbing out of its crypt beneath the statue of the Virgin. The tinkling sound was caused by the metal offerings pinned to the burial robe touching each other as the thing, which had the decayed features of Father Perez, stood upright. Draped in the spangled blue burial cloth, it was taller than a human; Paul had the sickening impression that the top of the peeling painted head almost scraped the alcove ceiling.

The monstrosity took one uncertain step forward, then another.

Paul shouted at the figure, "This isn't happening! This is *insane!*"

He made a break for the main doors. But the moonlight pouring in through the entrance was suddenly cut off by an immense shadow. Something gigantic, misshapen, but walking on two feet, was coming through the door. And whatever it was, was so immense that it nearly bent in half to fit under the archway.

The immense black mass, looking hardly more substantial than the shadows through which it waded, unfolded to full height, blocking his view of the choir loft. The thing's head swiveled from side to side. Two white-hot eyes searched the darkness; the gaping mouth opened to display double rows of jagged gleaming white teeth. From between the grinding teeth came a warning rumble. Moonlight flashed off a belt of gigantic silver disks; beneath the short black cape draped over its shoulders, Paul glimpsed swelling ebony breasts.

He knew that he had seen such a creature once before; it was the original of the Nameless Woman kachina he had seen in miniature in Willie Kavan's collection.

None of this is happening, Paul told himself. *I'm asleep and having a nightmare. Or the DTs. Or Willie spiked my drink with LSD. None of this is real.* He clung weakly to a nearby wall; the rough adobe under his fingers seemed the only reality in a world gone crazy. *This is a dream,* he repeated to himself. But the black shadow-thing, wavering just inside the doors, *persisted;* at the entrance to the alcove, the tall figure of Father Perez *persisted.* Maddeningly, Paul realized that he could deny the existence of the giant figures no more than he could the plaster under his finger nails.

It was freezing in the church. He was shivering now, partly from the cold, partly from sheer terror.

Then, with a roar, the black-caped figure girdled in silver moons advanced toward the giant form of the priest. The ghostly padre, swathed in emblazoned satin like a bizarre suit of armor, moved forward to meet the challenge.

The sound of a vast wind filled the church as the two figures met in mortal combat. Paul, watching terror-stricken and helpless, was sure the monstrosities would devastate the interior of the church as they battled. But the beings seemed to have no substance: intertwined, arms flailing, they passed again and again through pews or vigil-light stands or fonts, but nothing was displaced; the tiny flames in the ruby and yellow glass holders never so much as flickered when a shadowy fist or foot passed through them.

Paul thought of the painted battlefield overhead, but the ceiling was lost in shadow. *Who is triumphant up there?* he wondered, *Lucifer or Michael?* He was sure he heard the clash of armies and cries of the dying above. At the same time he felt he was losing the last shreds of his sanity.

He sank to his knees, burying his head against the cool wood of the pew in front of him. He pressed his hands to his ears, but it had no effect on the roaring, which seemed to come as much from inside his head as from outside.

I will close my eyes to this; I will close my mind to it. This is insanity, and if I refuse to accept it, it will go away.

He kept his face hidden, tried to empty his mind of all awareness. But his fear welled up despite his efforts. And the roars grew until he thought his head would split in two

and he could not contain himself any longer. So he screamed
"Noooo!" so loudly that the sound of it drowned the sounds
of the combatants.

In the wake of his screams, the sounds died away.

When he dared to listen after a moment, the roaring had
subsided. Raising his head, he discovered that the church
was empty of everything except a lingering chill.

"Say a prayer for me, will you?" asked Louise, tapping
him lightly on the shoulder, "or aren't you on your knees to
pray?"

He started at her touch, then quickly scrambled to his
feet. "Where—where *were* you?"

She gestured vaguely toward one of the two darkened
doorways on either side of the main entrance. Paul remembered that one was the door to the baptistry and the other
opened on a steep flight of steps leading to the tiny choir loft
that was nothing but a fan of darkness now. He was sure
that when he had come in looking for Louise, both doorways
had been shut with grillwork gates; now both stood wide
open. Louise, seeing the confusion in his face, said offhandedly, "I was up in the choir loft." In spite of the chill,
she carried her jacket carelessly in one hand, letting a sleeve
drag on the floor.

"Did you see . . . *everything?*" he asked, his voice dried
to a whisper.

"I saw *you,* wanderin' around and then making a run for
the door like something had scared the you-know-what
outta you."

"You didn't see anything else? *At all?*"

"Only you. Like a chicken with his head cut off. Then
kneeling down like you suddenly got it into your mind to
say your prayers." She laughed in a belittling way. "We can
go now—*if* you're through praying."

Drained, he only responded, "You said we can go—
please! Let's go!"

She reached over and patted his cheek. " 'Course we can
go. Mama will take you home right now. Hold my hand . . ."
Too tired to resist, he obediently put his hand in hers.
"Okay, now, here we go." She towed him gently along and
he was content to follow her lead.

She found and opened a door set in the wall; he had not
noticed the narrow wooden panel before. He had overlooked

it in his panic, or he would certainly have tried to escape through it. She said softly, "This will take us where we want to go."

But they did not emerge into the moonlight outside; they had entered a dark passageway lit by a very few smoky tapers. The musty walls were covered with a film deposited by years of candle smoke.

There's something wrong here, Paul thought; *I don't remember any buildings attached to this side of the church.* Had his sense of direction failed him so completely?

Louise turned down a right-hand passage lit in the same inadequate fashion. *Why aren't there any windows here?* he wondered. *Do the padres have a prejudice against electric lights?* He could see a single massive wooden door, closed tightly, at the end of the corridor. A thin line of light was visible underneath the panel; it had the quality of moonlight. *That must be the way out,* he thought with relief.

But Louise took a heavy metal candlestick from a niche and handed it to him. It was unlit; the candle had guttered down to the barest bit of wax and wick. He held onto it in puzzlement, surprised at the object's weight. *Why this?*

She said to him, "*You* have to carry it." And he yielded to the authority in her voice, feeling he no longer had any will of his own. It took all of his energy to think about escaping into the night.

Louise stood to one side while he tried the simple wooden latch. But it was fastened from the other side.

"It's *locked!*" he said with the whining disappointment of a child denied a long-promised reward.

"Knock," said Louise impatiently.

"But who's on the other side? Who's there to unlock it for us?" he demanded, growing petulant.

"Knock!" she said, then laughed, continuing, "Knock and it shall be opened. Ask and you shall receive. Isn't that right, Father?"

He was startled to her her call him Father. But then he realized he was wearing a padre's long-sleeved dark robes, the hem hiding his feet. He could feel his feet were sandal-shod now. A folded-back cowl lay heavily across his shoulders. Dressed in such a manner, it was not surprising at all for her to address him as Father.

"Knock!" the woman whispered in his ear; she was standing directly behind him now.

He raised a hesitant hand and knocked softly on the door. There was no response.

"Harder!" came the faintest whispers at his ear.

He rapped on the panel with greater force. This time he heard a stirring on the other side. There someone fumbled with the latch; then the door was pulled inward with impatience.

He was looking into the face of Father Perez; the priest stood on the threshold of his little cell. Beyond the bearded priest, he could see a simple wooden prie-dieu, the foot of a rude pallet, a statue of the Virgin in an unadorned niche high in the wall. All this he saw in a flash.

"What is it, Brother Tomas?" demanded the priest, clearly annoyed at having been interrupted.

But his answer was to bring the full weight of the candlestick down into that bearded face, crushing the skull and destroying the right eye.

Father Perez collapsed without a cry.

The candlestick dropped from numbed fingers; from the folds of his robes he drew out the knife that was concealed there. He dragged the body into the cell and closed the door gently behind him. Then he set to work, fearful of discovery.

Shortly afterward he left by way of another door from the dead priest's room. He crossed the patio, wandering into the night. He kept his burden hidden in his robes, following the voice inside him, now no more than a rustling in the folds of his brain. Moonlight was everywhere.

Still later, the quality of the moonlight changed to crimson and dusted the desert with russet light. The voice, tiny and insistent within him, forced him on, in spite of the cold night air and his fear of the shadowed desert yawning all around him. He was weary beyond any memory of such exhaustion. But he trudged on because he had to. His robes trailed in the dust, occasionally snagging on growing things, to be tugged free with impatient, numbed fingers.

A lone figure, wrapped in a red-and-black medicine robe, was waiting for him in a circle of sand, salmon-colored in the curious moon-glow. The robe hung loosely, shrouding the thin body, spilling to the ground so that only the tips of a pair of worn moccasins were visible. The face was merely a hooded shadow.

The being nodded at his approach; two brown skeletal arms reached out eagerly to take his burden from him. With a chuckle, the gruesome thing was gathered into the red-and-black medicine robe.

He remembered he had been promised something in payment for the night's work; he held out his hands with their specks of dried redness, cupping them.

The shrouded figure chuckled again and freed one hand long enough to reach into a pouch at its waist; it removed a handful of something. The nut-brown hands, their fingers like withered stalks, wrapped themselves around the priest's hands. The frail-seeming fingers had tremendous strength; they forced the priest's hands into two fists around the contents of the pouch.

He felt a stinging in each palm but did not open either hand.

Then the figure in the medicine robe was gone, slipping away into the surrounding darkness.

He was alone, aware only of the emptiness around him and the pain in his hands. The voice in his head told him to return; he had accomplished what it was he had been commanded to do.

He returned slowly, moving with the gait of a sleepwalker. He held his hands straight out in front of him, still fisted around their secrets like twin talismans.

The mission buildings in front of him were unlit; he heard no hue and cry. His deed had not yet been discovered.

And then a white-clad figure came running toward him from the shadows near the *convento*.

He stopped, startled that anyone should be where he expected no one.

The man in white hesitated a few paces from him; he recognized Old Luis, one of the Indian servants at the mission.

"Padre Tomás?" the Indian asked uncertaintly.

"*Sí.*" He nodded in affirmation.

"Ah!" The Indian took a step closer, then paused, staring at the outstretched fists, very much puzzled.

He beckoned the old man closer, as if inviting him to share in a wonderful secret, saying, "*Venga! Venga!*" His curiosity aroused, the Indian responded to the command. When the fellow was only a step away, he opened the extended fists and held them palm up, so their contents could be viewed. "*Mira!*" he ordered the old man.

His hands held some ashes, pebbles, and cactus needles mingled with a large number of grayish-brownish corn kernels. Some of the cactus spines were imbedded in the soft flesh of his palms, but he paid no attention to the pain.

The Indian stared at the priest's hands, his mouth working silently. Finally the priest said in a whisper, "*Maíz de brujas!*"

For a moment Luis only looked confused, as though trying to decide whether the priest had gone mad or was playing some joke. Then something of the truth dawned on him and fear filled his eyes. He took a step backward, saying only, "*Brujo! Diablo!*"

He turned to run, but the priest was too quick. The knife that flashed in his right hand struck rapidly, one/two/three times. With each blow, Luis cried out, but the desert swallowed his cries. He fell to his knees and then to the ground with only his assailant as witness.

The priest tossed the knife aside into a tangle of bushes and knelt to cradle the dying man's head gently on the dark robe of his lap. The old man tried to say something but he could not make a sound; the man in black bending over him simply shook his head. Then the priest stroked the dying man's brow and repeated over and over, "*No es culpa mía. No es culpa mía,*" until the last fear left those eyes and only a tiny reflection of the moon remained imbedded in each.

The moon had sunk below the horizon before he finished his task. By the time the morning star appeared, he was confident no one would ever find the body of Old Luis.

He did not go directly to his cell, however, but entered the church. Though he no longer felt he had either the right or even the ability to pray, he felt the compulsion to stand inside the sanctuary.

His robes made a soft brushing sound on the stone flooring as he approached the shadowed altar. He felt neither guilt nor comfort, but only vast weariness and emptiness.

To the shadowed cross above the altar and its agonized burden, he whispered, "*Peccado! Peccado!*" And he beat his breast but he sensed the futility of the gesture. He had done the devil's handiwork this night: he could have no hope of forgiveness.

The only response was the sound of ghostly laughter that emerged from the shadows all around him to drift dust-soft in the cool air.

It was the same sound he had heard the night he had first met the figure in the medicine robe during a walk in the night air. Then he had looked into the compelling red-veined aged eyes and had become the devil's pawn.

Again he whispered, "*Peccado!*" The acknowledgment of his crimes was a mere statement of fact, devoid of pride or horror or shame: his soul was in despair—the most heinous of sins in the eyes of God.

He stood staring hopelessly into the shadows above the high altar.

Weariness and emptiness were all he felt. . . .

Weariness and emptiness were all that Paul felt. He stood alone in the semidarkness of the church, unable to decide on a course of action. He guessed that Louise was gone for good; he lacked the energy to go and arouse the sleeping priests. He was worried about what Sheila would think when she discovered he was gone.

Everything was silent around him; nothing lingered in the shadows.

He sat down quietly in the corner of one pew, rubbing his hands back and forth over his thighs and shaking his head. He noted without caring that the cut on his knee had stopped oozing, though the torn material of his pants was drying on the wound. He touched it experimentally and discovered enough fresh blood still seeping though that it stuck to his fingertips.

He reached into the pocket of his jacket for a handkerchief and felt something jammed into it.

He pulled out the thing and stared at it, barely able to see it in the shadows.

It was a kachina doll, the one called the Nameless Woman Kachina.

He had last seen it in the display case at Willie Kavan's house. How did it happen to be there? he wondered.

One more inexplicable thing—would there ever be an end to the insanity he felt closing in on every side, to all the crazy things that had been happening since they first visited the mission and began their forced stay in El Centro?

He propped the doll carefully up in the corner of the pew beside him.

Then he continued massaging his thighs and shaking his head as before.

14   Last Interlude

Louise Shore explained to Willie Kavan, "One of the priests who was going to say Mass found him sitting in the church. They said he was just rocking back and forth, not saying a word. That ugly old thing"—here she gestured at the kachina doll standing on the dressing-table at Willie's elbow —"was on the pew beside him."

Willie made a face at Louise's offhand description of the rare kachina. He said, "The doll is mine. It represents a spirit called the Nameless Woman; it's quite valuable. Mr. Barrett was admiring it last night. He must have a slight touch of what they call kleptomania. I only noticed it missing from the case this morning."

"Ummmm," murmured Louise. From the amount of attention she was giving her cuticles, she was clearly uninterested in Willie's explanation.

Paul, sitting in a chair on the other side of the room, started to say, "I never—" then he shrugged, as if thinking better of it. He said nothing.

Sheila, standing protectively beside him, was the only one in the room who was aware that Paul had said anything, he had spoken so softly.

Her head was splitting. She looked with distaste at the people crowded into the tiny motel room. In addition to Louise and Willie, Jimmy Shore and the town lawman, Sheriff Danvers, were talking together beside the door.

Louise said, "I'd say I was real surprised, but after what happened the other day, I guess it's really not so surprising at all." She glanced over at Paul and seemed to think that her voice wouldn't reach the Barretts. But Sheila heard everything.

Sheriff Danvers was saying to Jimmy, "Tell me again; I want to get it all clear. You got back around midnight . . ."

Jimmy took up the story. "We were visiting friends over in Cottonwood. An anniversary party, their thirteenth—"

"Fourteenth," Louise interrupted.

"Let me finish, will you? The sheriff don't care *what* anniversary it was," Jimmy said. "We left Tom Parkins to cover the desk for us, but he just watched a little TV and fell asleep. Nobody came looking for a room after we left.

"Well, when we got back, Louise spotted right away our car was gone. We'd driven over in the truck 'cause the folks we was visiting live outside of Cottonwood, and the road to their place don't do much for the shocks on a regular car."

Louise said, "I feel it was really my fault, you know? I must've left the key in the car when I got back from shopping in the afternoon. There was a show on TV I didn't want to miss—you understand?"

"I gave her hell about that," said Jimmy, then he shook his head. "Won't do no good, though. I've been after her for *years*, and she *still* goes off and leaves the keys in the ignition."

"Yeah, well, nobody's perfect," said Louise. "I could remind you of a few things you do. Or don't do."

"Louise, no one *cares*." Jimmy sounded exasperated. "We're just trying to sort out the facts here." To the sheriff, Jimmy said, "We sure don't want to press charges or make any trouble. The car's all right; I looked it over myself. And, well"—he lowered his voice, but Sheila could still hear—"you heard from Mrs. Barrett about the Mister not being so well and all . . ." He gave the sheriff a significant look.

The sheriff nodded; he understood completely.

Sheila found herself looking at Willie. What was Willie doing here, anyway? she wondered. Did the fact that Paul had stolen that grotesque piece of carved and painted wood entitle him to share so intimately in this humiliating scene? At least Jimmy and Louise were involved in the theft of a *car*.

But Sheila did not confine her resentment to Willie; for

the umpteenth time she wished them all away—would happily consign them all to nonexistence if she only had the means.

They remained, insensitive to her misery and resentment; they filled the room with their chatter and their inquisitiveness thinly disguised as sympathy.

A stolen car. A stolen figurine. Paul spending half the night in delirium in a church. Sheila turned these things over endlessly in her mind as if, by the right arrangement of these clues, she could make some sense of what it all *meant*. She felt (though she could not say why) that Paul's actions were not merely erratic, but implied some unguessable pattern.

Part of this feeling, she knew, came from Paul's several attempts earlier to explain something to her, only to give up because he could not find the right words or because he himself did not understand what was happening.

And there had been his curious outburst at Louise. In his ramblings, he had implied that she knew something more than she was telling—was in some way responsible for what had happened, over and above the minor matter of leaving the keys in her car.

Sheila had quieted Paul quickly, not wanting the situation further aggravated. For a time she had studied Louise carefully, wondering if there was some truth in what Paul was suggesting.

But the incomprehension in Louise's face seemed genuine enough. And Jimmy had neither the look nor the sound of someone covering up anything. Sheila believed absolutely the story that they had gone together to Cottonwood and had discovered the car missing on their return. There was no way she could *not* believe it, so she rejected Paul's suggestions and her own suspicions.

She looked across at Willie again and was startled to see that he was staring at her with disconcerting frankness. He was smiling slightly, as if *he* knew more than he was telling —or maybe his smile suggested that he thought Sheila knew more than *she* had revealed.

Her headache was growing worse; even with the front door open, the air in the room was intolerably close. She closed her eyes for a moment.

What had happened to Paul last night? A vision? A nightmare? The DTs? Whatever it was, she detected in it something disturbingly akin to last year's breakdown. She only wanted to get Paul back to Berkeley, where she would be on her home turf and could deal better with such a crisis. Uppermost in her mind was the desire to get away from this roomful of magpies, with their questions that never stopped and their eyes that missed nothing.

She opened her eyes and stroked the top of Paul's head. He seemed to draw some small comfort from her touch; she felt him sigh and relax.

"Well," said Jimmy Shore, running his hands down his sides in a characteristic gesture, "anyway, I finished working on their car. They can leave any time." He had the assurance of a man who has discovered the only solution to a highly complex problem.

Sheila was startled by what he said; she had somehow come to feel that, wanting to leave so badly, escape would be denied her. It was the way it seemed to work in her life: her desires always failed her, she felt. What she had wanted out of her marriage to Paul had never really materialized; all their years together had brought them to this sad echo of themselves in a room filled with people she despised. She looked at Paul, sitting so helplessly, his eyes half-closed, and she was angered at his weakness. She felt she had—as always—the strength for both of them.

Sheriff Danvers turned to her and smiled. "I guess you'll want to leave as soon as possible?"

Was there just the hint of a threat in his words? Sheila wondered. She dismissed the thought immediately and said simply, "Yes, of course; we'll be leaving as soon as we can."

Jimmy, who had been looking out through the screen door for several minutes, said, "You may want to hold off leaving a little while—looks like we might have a storm before long."

"It does feel—you know—sultry?" said Louise. "Jimmy may be right."

"Crazy night," said the sheriff, not responding to what Louise said but following some train of thought which had occurred to him, "what with the goings-on here and the fire."

"It's a full moon tonight," said Willie, turning his head to smile impartially over everyone in the room. "All sorts of crazy things happen when the moon is full."

Sheila glanced down at Paul but he was sitting quietly, relaxed into the tranquilizers she had given him when the sheriff had driven him home from the mission over an hour ago.

Then she looked across at Sheriff Danvers, sensing that there was an important piece of information in what he was saying—something to help her make sense out of the as-yet inexplicable. She asked him, "What fire?"

He stared at her for a brief moment, but it was Willie who answered, "Helen and Cyrus Anderson—I think you mentioned you knew them—were killed last night. Fire gutted the house. Seems like the hot water heater may have started it. But it's still under investigation, isn't that right, Sheriff?"

The sheriff sounded somewhat defensive. "We're doing everything we can."

Willie went on, talking to Sheila, "They never had a chance: the place went up like a tinderbox. Not much left but the chimney and the foundations. Fire department was too little, too late."

Sheila's eyes flickered to the closed middle drawer of the dressing table, then back to the sheriff—but not before she saw that Willie's eyes had followed hers. He seemed to be nodding very faintly as he stared at her again with that openly speculative look.

Louise laughed harshly. "Honey, when you sleep through something, you sure do *sleep!* The fire pulled almost the whole town out of bed and your husband was out joy riding in a stolen car—" She stopped suddenly, sensing that maybe she had gone too far.

Sheila lied, "I took some sleeping pills last night because I couldn't sleep." She wondered herself why she had not heard fire engines, but her night had been spent in sleep so deep it had been like drowning. She remembered waking only once and wondering why Paul was not back. And she also remembered not caring enough to rise and try to find out where he was.

Jimmy, still looking out the door, said, "Sure does look like a storm coming. . . ."

"Well," said the sheriff, snapping closed the notebook in which he had been taking down bits of information, "if no one's going to press charges . . ."

He looked questioningly at Jimmy Shore and Willie Kavan.

Jimmy shook his head and said emphatically, "No way!"

Willie merely shook his head, as though impatient at being asked a question long since answered.

"And the padres aren't going to charge Mr. Barrett with trespassing," the sheriff added. "So I guess we'll declare this case closed." He leaned a thick brown hand against the screen door, preparatory to pushing it open, and touched the fingers of his free hand to the brim of his hat in Sheila's direction, saying, "Have a safe trip home, Mrs. Barrett. I hope the Mister gets to feeling better pretty quick." But the expression on his face as he took a last look at Paul was eloquently dubious. "Good-bye, folks—thanks for your help."

The screen door slammed behind him, the sound startling Sheila.

"Good man, Sheriff Danvers," said Jimmy. "Well, Louise, guess we'd better get along and let these folks pack"—and he gave his wife a little nudge for emphasis.

Louise said quickly, "Listen, I've got a fresh pot of coffee brewing—"

Sheila shook her head. "I just want a few minutes to myself to gather my wits—"

"Can't gather your wits better than over a cup of coffee, Mama always says," Louise suggested.

Sheila said, "Thanks; not right now."

"But—"

"*Louise*," said her husband, the edge in his voice underlining the single word; then he added, "These folks want to be *alone*. So let it *drop*. Come on with me. *Now*." He put his hand on Louise's hip, urging her toward the door. As they were leaving, Jimmy said to Sheila, "I'll bring the car by at noon when I come for lunch. We can settle up then."

"Fine," said Sheila; she added with genuine feeling, "Thank you."

Willie watched the Shores leave; then he got to his feet and announced, "I'll be going too. Just let me collect my property." He gathered up the evil-looking doll off the dresser top.

Sheila asked him suddenly, "How did you happen to be here this morning, Mr. Kavan?"

"I noticed the kachina missing this morning when I was opening my shop. Your husband was admiring it last night, and he was the last one in the room. Naturally, I suspected… In any case, I thought we could settle things without a fuss. I never assumed Mr. Barrett had any real intention of keeping the doll. He *had* been drinking last night. *I* had been drinking. I thought he was just playing some kind of game or wasn't really thinking at all."

Sheila said, keeping her voice as expressionless as she could, "Paul hasn't been well for a long time. I thought he was improving; now I see that he hasn't improved at all. I apologize for what happened. Thank you for being so understanding." But she was incapable of putting any feeling into the words; she only wanted to be rid of this little man with his prying eyes.

"Don't give it another thought," said Willie, taking a step toward the door. He was holding the kachina tightly in his hand—for all the world, Sheila thought, as if it were a living thing that might try twisting free.

She said, "Thank you again." The words were his dismissal. She looked directly into his eyes, but she could not read the expression she found there.

He gave her a smile in reply. "Good-bye, Mrs. Barrett. You both take care."

When he was gone, Sheila walked to the door and stood for a time staring out into the sunlit motel court. Somewhere an infant was crying. The sunlight glinted off some bits of gravel. A mangy-looking dog went trotting by, a blood-stained piece of butcher paper locked in its teeth. It saw her and quickened its pace guiltily.

She thought, *Now I can get away. We can go home now.* But the job of packing seemed suddenly overwhelming; she felt her energy draining away as she thought about it. The bright warmth of the morning seemed to slow her down.

She stirred herself into action, recalling her impression that the sheriff had given her a polite "Move along!" and fearing that Louise, no matter *how* firm Jimmy had been, would soon be back, nosing into their business.

But she lingered a moment longer, savoring the calm which followed the confusion caused by the roomful of people.

She remembered a morning in Berkeley the preceding fall. She had been standing by a window in her apartment, daydreaming, smoking a cigarette.

A sudden galelike wind had arisen, then died away just as quickly. Leaves torn off the autumn trees by the sudden gusting, tumbled in its wake into a vast dead space. They were held in suspension, mingling with the dust and dirt hanging like clouds of smoke. Everything was adrift in a curious, fluid quietude. Even the street outside, normally busy at that particular time of day, was deserted, except for one couple on the sidewalk, staring around them at the strangeness in which all of them were immersed.

The uniqueness of that moment was frightening; Sheila had had the wild thought that after this quiet would come a voice from heaven or maybe the single note of an angelic trumpet signaling the end of the world.

Then the wind, fiercer than ever, had returned. The air was blown free of leaves and dust. The moment passed. Across the street, the couple continued on their way, taking up their interrupted conversation.

A cat yowled somewhere outside, drawing Sheila away from the memory of that curious instant. There was an answering hiss; the prelude to a cat fight which exploded, then dissolved into the sound of unseen felines running across the gravel.

She turned to look at Paul. He smiled at her and wet his lips. He said with tranquilized precision, "I will help you in a minute. I just want to sit a little longer. I feel very tired, for some reason." Then he said, "My hand hurts," and he held his right hand out to her, palm up, like a child might.

She investigated and found several cactus spines imbedded in the palm. Some crazy souvenir of whatever adventures Paul had last night? she wondered. She doubted she would ever get the full story; at the moment it mattered not at all.

She removed the spines with a needle from the sewing kit she had for emergency repairs, then daubed it with some rubbing alcohol.

When she had finished, she gently folded his hand shut and said, "Now just sit as long as you want. I can take care of the packing with no problem. I want to leave here as soon as possible."

He closed his eyes and nodded. She could not tell whether he was asleep or merely resting his eyes, since he remained sitting bolt upright in the chair.

She did not begin packing right away; instead, she went to the dresser and opened the middle drawer. The brown shopping bag was still carefully folded around the bundle Helen Anderson had given her.

Unsure of exactly what she expected to find, Sheila undid the stiff brown paper and removed the blue canvas binder it contained. She looked at the neatly-typed white labels. THE SENECU MATERIALS, she read; underneath, the second label had the Andersons' name and address.

It all seemed curiously familiar to her, though she had not touched the package since she had set it in the drawer. She had a sudden vivid memory of Helen Anderson handing the parcel to her, of the woman's near-fanatical look. Odd, Sheila reflected, to know that she was dead. That her husband was dead. That their house was destroyed. A thought came to her: their deaths had freed Maria Seloso from an involvement in their curious experiments. Sheila shook her head to rid herself of the thought that the fire had been, in some way, providential. She refused to allow herself to be that unfeeling; but the truth was, she felt nothing for the Andersons. The fire had released Maria from an obligation to the Andersons; it had released Sheila from an obligation to Maria. She could leave El Centro with a clear conscience now, knowing that the girl would not be involved in the occult experiments which terrified her so much.

Sheila realized that she held in her hand probably the only surviving fragment of the Andersons' long years of research. She lifted the cover of the binder and stared at the mass of typescript it contained.

On the first page, obscuring most of what was typed there, was the scorched imprint of a right hand. It looked at though a human hand, heated white hot, had impressed itself on the paper.

Sheila's hands were trembling as she turned to the next page. Again there was the same charred impression of a hand. Rapidly she began turning the pages, not reading what she saw typed there, but racing through to see the impression of the hand, which showed fainter and fainter until it disappeared altogether on page 93.

She returned to the first page and the clearest imprint of the hand. She closed her eyes for a moment, feeling a sudden dizziness. Then she set her own hand down over the mark of the burning hand.

They matched perfectly. She jerked her hand away, almost choking with fear. She was terrified that this tangible bit of nightmare had followed her into her waking life.

She hastily shoved the book into its paper-bag wrapping, which she folded shut.

"I'll be right back," she told Paul; "I've got an errand to run."

He nodded without opening his eyes.

She carried the package around to the row of garbage cans she had noticed behind the motel. One of the cans had been overturned by some animal and its contents pawed through and scattered. The exposed garbage was ripening in the sun, giving off an overpowering smell. Flies buzzed thickly around, crawling in blue-black masses over everything.

Trying not to inhale, Sheila pulled the lid off an upright can and jammed the parcel as deeply as she could among its contents. She replaced the lid securely.

She kept holding her breath as long as she could, only pausing to take several rapid deep breaths when she could stand it no longer.

Back in number twelve, she rapidly began packing the suitcases. Somehow the stink of the warming garbage had followed her back. The heat in the room (she had been unable to start the air-conditioner, which had given up the ghost early in the morning) and the faint but persistent stench made her nauseous. She forced herself to concentrate on the packing; she refused to allow herself to become ill.

Paul continued to sit quietly. Sometimes he sat with his eyes closed; sometimes he watched her efforts. He said nothing. She could not remember him ever being so susceptible to sedatives before. Whatever he had gone through last night, she realized, had robbed him of his last reserves of energy.

Some things would no longer fit into the suitcases out of which they had been taken. Sheila rolled these into two clean bath towels taken from the bathroom rack and thought, *Well I can't be the first to rip off a towel or two from the Four Star—and I certainly won't be the last.* She hoped that she could toss the towel-wrapped bundles into the trunk without Louise, who seemed to miss very little, noticing. She smiled a little ruefully to herself, thinking. *We're a class act all the way. First Paul takes their car and now I'm doing a number on their towels.*

She decided that if anything was said, she could simply pay for the towels, throw the stuff loose into the back seat, or leave it behind. All that mattered to her was getting away from this place where everything had gone wrong—before, she thought uneasily, something else goes wrong.

Jimmy Shore delivered the car just after noon. Sheila arranged to pay for the repairs when she stopped by the office to settle their bill. Jimmy offered to take her for a test drive, but she told him that if he was confident the car would get them home, she was satisfied.

He offered to help her pack the last suitcases into the car; she accepted thankfully and then regretted it when she remembered the towel-wrapped bundles on the floor of the back seat. But if Jimmy noticed them, he never mentioned it.

While the two of them shifted the suitcases around in the trunk and back seat to make the best use of the available space, Sheila glanced uneasily at the sky. Clouds were massing over the blue and purple slopes of the Sierra Morenas; some actually seemed caught on the jagged uppermost peaks. Even as she watched, the cloud bank grew thicker and blacker and began spreading across the sky.

Jimmy looked too and said, "It's a thunderstorm, all right. But it'll probably blow over pretty quick. I wouldn't worry. You should still be able to leave later today if you want."

She thanked him for his help and watched him walk across the courtyard toward the motel office. Only Jimmy, of all the people she had met in El Centro, was someone she would miss; his refreshing candor and innate kindness had always seemed to Sheila like a breath of fresh air in the stifling atmosphere of El Centro.

For a while she continued watching the sky, praying that the threatening storm would cease threatening. She did not want to drive through a storm if she could avoid it.

Inside she found Paul had moved from the chair to her bed and had fallen asleep. She decided not to wake him until the moment they were ready to leave.

She pulled back the curtains and sat down on the side of the second bed to watch the massing clouds drown the Sierra Morenas in shadow. They roiled about, changing from blue-gray to gray to gray-black. Thunder erupted from the direction of the now barely-visible mountains; lightning crackled into life. She watched with a child's awe as the jagged white-hot fibrillations threaded the sky suddenly, each time giving the air an intense violet glow that deepened to purple as the light died.

She had the impression of the rain-heavy sky as a kind of flesh veined with arteries of purple-white fire. She felt that she—the whole town—was somehow enclosed in a cave of dark, wet warm air, as if it was inside some gigantic alien womb.

More lightning flashes, nearer this time: they forked down into the desert midway between the mountains and the town. She grew fearful, wondering how close to the town the lightning would strike; she wondered about danger to herself and Paul.

She turned uneasily from the window and pulled the curtains back into place. She snapped on the overhead light and the lamp on the nightstand between the beds. Paul slept on, unmindful of the light or the sounds of the storm.

She looked around for something to read, something to take her mind off the storm outside the growing tension in herself. She thumbed through a novel or two and then through several magazines, but nothing captured her interest. Finally she picked up one of the books Paul had bought for her; it was still on the nightstand, waiting for her last hasty sweep through the motel room before they left.

The thin volume was titled simply, *Legends of the Tawa*; the stories had been gathered by someone named Mavis E. Martin, Ph.D. Ignoring the roaring thunder as best she could, Sheila sat down in the chair Paul had abandoned and she began to read.

The Tawa people originally lived in another place underground. They lived there for a long time in peace. Then there came into the Lower World some others who were not men but who sought to make men do their bidding. When the elders of the tribe would not let this happen, those others caused confusion in that place.

Then the elders besought the medicine men to seek aid from the Sun Father. The medicine men beat their drums and used the magic of their medicine to call the Sun Father. The Sun Father sent an eagle as messenger to the medicine men and told them that he would make them a ladder of his rays, by which they would climb to the Upper World. The eagle warned them that the people were to carry nothing in their hands because both would be needed for climbing. And he told them that only persons of good faith should mount the ladder, because it would not bear the weight of one whose heart held bad faith.

So the medicine men told the elders what the eagle had told them. The elders gathered the people and warned them that they must be of good faith and carry nothing in their hands if they hoped to reach the world above. Then the Sun created a hole in the roof of the world like the hole in the roof of a kiva. And he sent down a ladder of his rays.

The Tawa people began to climb; soon the sun-ladder was filled with people.

But when those others saw what was happening, they hurried to the foot of the sun-ladder. The first to reach it were the most powerful of those others: the Nameless Woman and her two sons. They tried to climb the ladder but the elders called down "You cannot climb: your hearts have bad faith in them."

At this, the sons of the Nameless Woman roared in anger and attempted to climb anyhow, but the Sun Father dissolved the ladder and they tumbled back down to the Lower World.

That is how the Tawa People came to this world.

Sheila looked up from her reading as Paul stirred and mumbled to himself. She wondered if he was going to wake up, but he simply shifted around until he found a more comfortable position and continued sleeping.

Sheila turned a page and began another segment of the book.

Now, when the sons of the Nameless Woman saw that they could not follow the Tawa Folk into the Upper World, they howled in a great rage.

But the Nameless Woman drew apart and considered for a time. Then she called her sons to her and with their aid, she created the Spider-Child and sent him to search the Lower and Middle Worlds for another way to the Place Above.

After a long time, Spider-Child returned to the place from which he had been sent. He summoned the Nameless Woman and her two sons and told them that he had discovered another way to that place where the Tawa Folk had gone. When the Nameless Woman questioned him about the path, Spider-Child answered, "The way is difficult and the journey a long one, for there are many places between this world and that, which must be crossed. The way I will show you is called Moon Path, and those who set out upon it must mark themselves with the sign of blood.

Thereupon the Nameless Woman nodded and scratched her palm with a sharpened stick. When she had drawn blood, she daubed it on each of her monstrous sons and on the Spider-Child. But for herself, she said, "The bloodmark on my hand will be my protection against the dangers of the way. Now let us seek the way to the Above World.

So they set out, Spider-Child leading and carrying a bell which the Nameless Woman gave him, so that they would always know where he was as he led them along the shadowy Moon Path.

And they are on that path even now, making their way toward the world of men. So men must be ever-vigilant and faithful to the old ways and seek the protection of the Sun Father. With his blessing, Nameless Woman and her monstrous sons will not be able to find their way to this place, nor come again to trouble the peace of men.

Sheila closed the book gently and left it in her lap with her hands folded upon it.

She leaned back in her chair and closed her eyes. She could hear the first heavy drops of rain clicking against the windows. The closeness of the room lay against her skin like a warm quilt; she was aware of a desperate need to sleep, if only for a few minutes. She decided a nap would leave her refreshed for setting out later—*if* the storm followed Jimmy's prediction that it would not last very long. Her last conscious thought was a fervent prayer that Jimmy was right.

Then she gave herself over to the warm room and the soothing sound of the rain and the dark infinities behind her closed eyelids.

There was no rain or room or darkness in the place she went to in her dream.

She stood with a group of Indians dressed in white on an expanse of blindingly white sand. There was no horizon, only curtains of heat-shimmers so thick that they hid everything in the distance. There was no sun overhead, just an overarching brightness that was too painful to look into. No one threw any shadows in this place.

The only break in the smooth sand was a shallow pit perhaps six feet across and two feet deep at the center. The excavated sand had been piled up on the far side of the bowl-like depression. Sheila and the others were ranged in a rough semicircle around the edge of the grave, in which she saw the body of a man outstretched on its sandy floor.

With a start she recognized the body of her husband. How had he died? she wondered; she could see no wound, no blood. There was no sign of breathing, not the faintest flicker of the closed eyelids: he was dead beyond denial.

Two elderly women, barefooted, wearing undecorated white cotton skirts, and with heavy, white *mantas* drawn over their heads, knelt beside the body and pulled off the cotton tunic and kilt he was wearing. Sheila wondered to herself why Paul was dressed in Indian fashion. She knew that she was standing in jeans and a blouse. No one questioned her presence or dress with a word or look.

When the crones had freed the corpse of all garments except a linen loincloth, the one kneeling nearest Sheila called out sharply, repeating a single incomprehensible word twice. In response, two old men wearing similar white tunics and kilts came forward. They were barefoot like the old women, but each man wore a single necklace of blood-coral. They knelt on the side of the body opposite the women and began systematically tearing little holes in the dead man's clothes.

Some younger women joined the onlookers, appearing from out of the shimmering heat-veils. They carried bundles of clothing and other items, including moccasins, turquoises, weapons, tools, a rattle, a red coral necklace, and a bundle of eagle feathers. The old men accepted the garments and tore little holes in them. The other items were piled to the side.

When they had finished their task, the old men set the torn clothing aside, crossed the dead man's arms on his breast, and tied his wrists together with a length of fibrous rope. Then, with the assistance of the women, they folded Paul's legs up against his body and tied them in place also. Sheila felt vaguely that she should offer them help because Paul was her husband, but she was unable to do more than look on.

When the body was secured in a fetal position, other women of all ages, moving in a slow procession through the white glare, came bearing crude gray-white cotton blankets. The four kneeling attendants used these to swathe the body. When they were done, a heavy robe decorated with turkey feathers was produced and gently wrapped around the corpse. Lastly, a covering of dark woven vegetable matter was folded over all and secured with a red sash.

The four oldsters stood up. Sheila shifted position slightly to have a better view of what was happening.

A young girl handed the four elderly Indians two pottery

bowls decorated with a black-and-white pattern that Sheila recognized immediately:

The bowls were passed around by the four. From one they took a mouthful of water, rinsed their mouths, and turned away to spit. They washed their hands in the second, slightly larger, bowl.

When the same girl had taken the cleansing bowls away, one of the old men muttered something Sheila could not understand.

One of the crones responded with a brief sentence; Sheila recognized only the word *sipapu*.

The old man nodded and answered briefly in unison.

The old women repeated the phrase, in which Sheila again caught the word *sipapu*.

In a final gesture, several undecorated pots holding water or corn, and several dried gourds were placed in the grave pit beside the shrouded figure; those placing the objects there took great care not to touch the mat covering the body.

Then everyone began silently pushing sand and stones into the depression. Some of the youngest women set a layer of heavy stones directly over the body. More sand was poured in, so that even the layer of stones was totally hidden.

When the pit was completely filled, the two old women who had prepared the dead man for burial took brushes of plant fibers and smoothed the surface of the grave. Then the two old men repeated the brushing strokes with bunches of eagle feathers.

Without another word, the Indians began drifting away into the surrounding heat-shimmer. In a short time, Sheila was left alone, standing beside an unbroken expanse of white sand.

It was done; it was over. She felt a peculiar sense of relief as though an unpleasant but necessary task had finally been taken care of.

She was aware of a hand on her shoulder.

Someone was shaking her gently, calling her name.

She recognized the voice: it was Paul's. But that made no sense, because she had just seen him buried. Paul was *there*, underneath the sand and stone in front of her; Paul was *dead*.

She turned her head and blinked her eyes; she had to *explain* to Paul that he was dead, *there*—not standing *here*, behind her, with his hand on her shoulder. She tried to say something as the quality of light shifted from blinding white through black to the lamplit interior of their room. The curtains were still drawn across the windows, but someone had left the door ajar. She could see that the day was brightening outside.

"Paul," she said, "you can't—" then she stopped, no longer remembering what she wanted to tell him.

"Can't what?" he asked, his voice as sleepy-sounding as his half-opened eyes looked.

She shrugged as she took in the motel room and the last dream fragments melted away and vanished. She explained, "I had a dream. I don't remember what it was about. I only remember we were both in it."

He said, "I woke you because the rain has stopped and the sun is coming out. I think we can leave, if you're ready."

"How do you feel?" she asked cautiously, watching his face intently.

"Oh, I'm fine. Just very tired. I'll probably sleep in the car—if you don't mind driving?" He smiled an agreeable smile; Sheila felt it gave him a foolish, almost idiotic look.

"No, I don't mind," she said gently, prompted by a recollected sadness left behind by her dream.

She opened the door a little wider and looked out. Overhead, winds were tearing the gray cloud banks apart to let the late-afternoon sun stream through.

She looked at the little travel-clock. It was almost three o'clock.

"Do you want to stay another day, get a fresh start in the morning?" Paul asked her.

"No way," she said. "I want to get at least a few miles between me and here before we have to stop again." But she continued to watch the thinning, churning clouds for a few minutes. She remembered reading about ancient Chinese soothsayers who could foresee the future in the movement of clouds. Did the gray-white cloud cover overhead hold some clue to their future, she wondered, if she only knew how to read it? She put the foolish thought aside and turned her attention to final preparations for leaving.

Paul wandered around, trying to help but more often getting in her way. She struggled to keep from losing her temper, and finally put him to work washing the car windows.

When they were ready to leave, she sat Paul in the passenger seat of their little car; he seemed incapable of fastening his safety belt and shoulder harness, so Sheila finally had to do it for him. He sat silently while she adjusted the straps for his comfort and double-checked to be sure the hooks were all secure.

She gave a half-hearted once-over to number twelve to satisfy herself that they were leaving nothing behind.

She let the car idle for a few minutes, surprised at the engine's smoothness—proof of Jimmy Shore's mechanical skills. A steady wind was blowing from the west, the last reminder of the storm. Most of the moisture was drying up already. The air seemed cleaner than she could remember it being since their arrival in El Centro.

Sheila felt exhilarated, suddenly. *At last,* she whispered to herself, *we're going home.*

She drove around to the motel office to settle up. Inside, she transacted her business with the Shores as quickly as possible.

Jimmy Shore handled the details. Louise leaned across the counter, her arms folded in front of her breasts. She said, "I'm sure your car won't give you no trouble going home. Jimmy does first-rate work."

"I'm sure of that," said Sheila, not looking up from the

task of signing traveler's checks to pay for the car repairs and the room rental.

"Your husband is gonna be just fine," Louise said; "I *know* it."

"Thank you."

"Louise," Jimmy snapped, "will you let us finish our business, for God's sake?"

"Hmmmpf!" Louise sniffed. "Don't let *me* interrupt nothing." But she continued to watch Sheila in a way the latter found more annoying than the woman's chatter. Sheila signed the last check thankfully and handed it with the others to Jimmy. He counted them twice, punched some keys on the cash register, and carefully counted out her change to her.

Then he pointed to a local map under a sheet of clear plastic taped to the counter. "You know your way back all right?" he asked, tracing the Barretts' route with his finger.

Sheila nodded. "Yes, I've got it memorized. And I have lots of maps in the glove compartment."

Then something under his moving finger caught her eye. "What's that?" she asked, indicating a red-pencil line that ran from a point on the road some miles outside the town and ended near the foothills of the Sierra Morena range.

Jimmy said, "I drew that in last year. The university people out at the ruins ran a road in to bring trucks and equipment there. It saved 'em a few miles and lots of wear and tear on the equipment. Some of them stayed in town here at the Four Star; I drew that to show newcomers how to find the access road."

Sheila stared at the crimson line a moment longer. Some memory stirred and, not really sure what compelled her, she asked Jimmy suddenly, "Have you ever heard of an Indian custom of tearing little holes in the clothes of a person who's died and being readied for burial?"

Jimmy looked totally puzzled at the question. He shook his head and said, "That's news to me. Why'd you want to know?"

"I read . . . somewhere . . . something about it. I wanted to know why they'd do that—put holes in the things."

"Well, *I* know," said Louise with a smile.

"How the hell would you know?" asked Jimmy. Sheila had been aware from the moment she walked into the office that there was tension between the Shores; she had assumed it was one of those marital squabbles which blow up from nowhere and subside just as suddenly, but never without some blood being drawn on both sides.

She answered her husband smugly, "Willie Kavan told me. He cornered me one time with a lotta historical crap. You remember how he used to hang around here last year, always trying to talk with some of those professors digging out at the ruins. They never had much time for him, so he had to settle for me. Seems people are *always* getting *me* 'cause they can't get nothing better." Jimmy ignored the barb; Louise turned to Sheila and said, "They tore those holes so's the dead fella's spirits could escape. They thought some part of a man's ghost would hang around in his clothes if it didn't have those holes to slip out of. They didn't want no ghosts hanging around. Have to admit, they were neater than the Spanish: *they* left old Father Perez hanging around looking for his head." She laughed. "Maybe they should have poked a few holes in his clothes after they cut his head off—so's he wouldn't have to moon around these parts all the time." She lowered her voice slightly. She kept on talking to Sheila but her eyes were on Jimmy as she said, "It's a pretty depressing proposition, sticking around this place all of your life. Or death. Sometimes this whole town is so dead it's hard as hell to decide if you're alive or dead."

"Yes, well," said Sheila, embarrassed for Jimmy and annoyed at the way the other woman was trying to use her to get back at her husband, "I guess we'd better be on our way. Thank you both for everything."

She started for the door but Jimmy called her back, saying, "I didn't give you your receipt for the car repairs." Though she didn't care in the least, Sheila was forced to wait politely while he carefully wrote out the receipt and handed her a copy.

Jimmy walked her out to the car and closed the door for her when she was safely inside. She rolled down her window.

"You be careful," he said. "You'll be home in a day or two and all of this will seem like a bad dream. You'll see. Everything will turn out fine."

On impulse, Sheila took his hand and squeezed it. "Thank you. Thank you *very much*, Jimmy."

He smiled back at her.

Louise, holding open the screen door of the motel, but staying in the shadows out of the sunlight, laughed and called out something which Sheila did not understand. Sheila just smiled and nodded and waved. This seemed to satisfy Louise.

Paul smiled at the Shores and nodded as though he understood everything that was being said around him.

Jimmy stood back from the car. Sheila started the engine.

Then they were on their way. She waved again to Jimmy, saw Louise waving vigorously from the office doorway.

We're on our way, Sheila told herself with something like surprise. *We're really leaving El Centro.*

Going home.

PART THREE

If you will patiently dance in our round,
And see our moonlight revels, go with us.

A Midsummer Night's Dream: II, i.

I have had a most rare vision. I have had a dream,
past the wit of man to say what dream it was.

A Midsummer Night's Dream: IV, i.

15   Ghost Dance and Blood-Moon

It's so easy, Sheila thought, as the town dwindled behind them. *Leaving is the simplest thing in the world*. El Centro was compressed into her rearview mirror; then it disappeared completely, swallowed by brown-gray waves of sand dunes and sagebrush.

Paul dozed, held upright by his shoulder harness, with a small pillow wedged behind his head. She had given him another tranquilizer just before they left the motel.

She drove slowly, keeping a careful watch on the right-hand side of the road.

The road ahead, filled with dancing heat-shimmers, ran directly toward the foothills of the Morenas; from the maps she had studied, Sheila knew that soon it would begin curving south, heading toward the main artery that would carry them back to California.

She let her mind wander over the events of the past three days, but none of the pieces fit together into a coherent pattern. Still she kept her eyes on the road, paying special attention to the strip of sand and gravel along its right edge.

She slowed to twenty-five miles an hour. A camper roared up behind the Volkswagen and honked angrily. She pulled as far to the right as she could, letting her tires thump along the shoulder of the road. She slowed even more as the car began to bounce dangerously when it left the paved road. The camper raced past; Sheila saw a teenage boy yelling at her and making a rude sign with his hand. She paid no attention—simply waited until the camper was far enough ahead and then pulled back onto the road. She continued to follow the road west.

Bars of sunlight slanted down through the dispersing clouds. Or were they dispersing? Sheila wondered; it certainly seemed to her cloudier than half an hour ago. The sun's rays occasionally highlighted masses of yellow flowers growing near the road. The westering sun gave things a soft russet ambience as it dropped nearer the highest peaks of the Sierra Morenas. Sage, shrubs, cacti, and outcroppings of barren rock were tinged salmon, rose, rust, vermillion, heliotrope, and a hundred other shades of red.

The Sierras seemed very near now, the eastern slopes turning to shadowy indigo as the evening advanced. She thought again of the red-pencil line on Jimmy Shore's map. Had she missed it? The road would begin curving south in a little while and then she would know she had driven past the access road. *Or maybe,* she thought, *the road doesn't exist anymore. The wind and rain might have dissolved the road the way my dream dissolved this afternoon when I woke from my nap.*

She was just deciding to turn around and retrace her route when she discovered the simple wooden marker that indicated the access road she wanted. She saw with dismay that the road was little more than parallel ruts and some gravel cutting away at a right angle to the highway. *Well,* she decided, *since I have no choice in the matter, I'll just have to brave the potholes and all and hope that the car's suspension hangs together.*

She slowed almost to a full stop before she turned cautiously onto the road. She kept the car at a crawl as she moved along the rocky, rutted surface, her ears straining for the sound of a blowout or engine trouble that could leave them stranded in the middle of nowhere.

Cloud fragments swept across the setting sun; shadows washed over the landscape. Other shadows, their origins unguessable, danced on the edges of her vision. She sensed them only as faint ripples of darkness in the red desert air.

But though the car jounced terribly and the undercarriage groaned and rattled a good deal, they continued on at a steady pace. When Sheila rolled down the window, the air blowing into her face felt hot and clean and vital. She had the impression that powerful, unseen energies, which had come to life in the storm earlier, were transforming the very air and land around her in some mysterious fashion.

The fast-falling night, she sensed, could be no ordinary one.

For Sheila, El Centro and Tucson and Berkeley all seemed light-years distant. Her world had contracted to nothing more than this almost-road, the surrounding desert, and the blue-purple foothills ahead.

Panic swept over her. She slammed on the brakes. The car swerved and came to a standstill broadside across the road. She began to cough as dust from the sudden stop boiled in through the open window. Beside her, Paul stirred and wiped at his face as though insects were plaguing him, but he did not wake up.

She lay her forehead against the steering wheel, fighting back the nausea which was following her initial panicky reaction. *My God!* she thought. *Am I losing my mind? What am I doing here? Why did I leave the highway?* She raised her head and looked toward the Sierras as if their steadfastness held an answer . . . but they remained vastly mysterious and indifferent to her.

When the dust settled, the air was again still and clear—but now its warmth seemed stifling. Everything outside the car wavered in the shimmering heat. Sheila could see shadows lengthening across the desert.

It would be evening soon.

Then night.

She was afraid of being out here at night. But still she sat, her hands on the steering wheel, making no move to start the car, to turn around, to escape.

She tried to think things through; but though there were clues in abundance, she could discover no solution to the mystery they suggested. Did it all tie together somehow? she wondered. A centuries-old murder of a Spanish padre. Stories of Indian witchcraft. The talk of lingering ghosts. Paul's breakdown. The fire that killed the Andersons. Her own disturbing half-remembered dreams. The hideous kachina doll Paul had stolen from Willie Kavan. Where was the secret tying all these elements together? She felt that if she could understand that, she might comprehend the force within herself that had compelled her to leave the highway and plunge into the middle of this godforsaken desert.

Try as she might, she could make no sense out of anything. She looked at Paul sleeping beside her. She studied him as though seeing him for the first time, noting his unshaven face, the troubled look not even sleep could ease, the twin lines of sweat running from his left temple down the side of his face to drip onto his shirt.

She tried to remember him as he had been when she had first met and loved him; and she tried to think of him as he was in the aftermath of his breakdown, when she pitied him and took responsibility for him as she might a helpless child.

There were no feelings of love or even pity in her now. She could remember only her feelings of three days before, when he had taken her with the urgency of an animal in rut. She remembered only how much she had hated him then. How much she continued to hate him. She had guessed then that he had done what he had out of rage, because she no longer loved him, and out of disgust for the pity, so often bordering (she admitted it) on contempt, which had replaced her love. In some insane way, she suspected, he had hoped to either win back her love (impossible: that was gone forever) or gain the dominant role in their relationship (also impossible: he would always remain the weaker of the two). He had tried to win love, or at least respect, from her. It never occurred to him, she thought with sudden surprise, that the only thing he could possibly gain was her hatred.

Her hatred was a pure one now, no longer tempered with memories of an earlier love or the softening tendencies of pity.

Strange how clearly she saw what had happened to them both. Even three days ago, she would still have said that there would never be a crucial turning point for them, only a drifting apart not localized in time. Now she knew that the turning point had arrived that moment in the arroyo, amid the massed pink and white flowers, with the feel of sand against her face—sand which had swallowed her tears of loss and pain and rage. She had let him—*let* him—have his way because she despised him so much. The sweat/stink/hot breath/rut-fever of him she had suffered willingly because it freed her of any lingering feeling of obligation to him. If, as Helen Anderson had so often repeated, everything was fated, then that moment in the twisted shadows of the creekside tree was necessary for some as yet unfathomable reason. There had been a transformation that afternoon: she had sensed, without admitting it, the deeper shadows hovering over the two of them—shadows which had entered her.

Now she began to understand. It was the voice of those shadows within her which had guided her to this place; it was a pair of shadowy inner eyes looking out through her own which sensed and strove to comprehend secrets within the clouds overhead or in the darkening fastnesses of the Sierra Morenas.

These thoughts were emerging into her consciousness from a source deep within her. *Have I been taken possession of?* she asked herself, *or have I simply taken possession of hidden powers that were always here inside me?*

She would resolve that problem later, she decided. Right now her uncertainty seemed to be the result of the willingness of her conscious mind to explore these newly perceived changes within herself.

She closed her eyes and emptied her mind. She listened with an inner ear for the truths she knew resided in her. And, summoned by her, they emerged into her eager mind. The voice within her mind would become her own thoughts if she let it; those other, secret-discerning eyes would meld with hers if she permitted it. From that moment in the dry creek-bed, she had been offered a chance to become *whole,* if she accepted such awesome gifts—*and* the *obligations* those gifts entailed.

Yes, she agreed, willingness and desire resonating through her whole being, *I accept everything. Freely. Joyfully.*

When she opened her eyes again, she saw with a unity of vision and an undreamed-of clarity of thought.

She started up the car and straightened it out. When

she had eased it completely back onto the road, she touched the accelerator slightly.

She drove on toward the foothills, which were now deepening to purple-gray as the sun slid further west. She restrained her desire to slam her foot all the way down on the gas pedal. Such impulsiveness, she knew, might leave her with a flat tire and keep her from reaching her now clearly-recognized destination before nightfall.

Forty-five minutes later, she stopped the car long enough to give Paul, who had grown restless, another pill and a swallow of lukewarm bottled water to wash it down. He tried to say something to her, but she did not understand. She murmured something soothing and smoothed his forehead, feeling as detached as a nurse calming a restive patient. When he was asleep again, she continued on her way.

On and on they drove, while the sun declined and finally slipped behind the upper reaches of the Sierra Morenas, backlighting the mountain range with a russet glow so the jagged heights stood out in impressive silhouette. The sky immediately overhead went butter-and-egg yellow; what clouds there were, were banded orange, scarlet, rose, and violet.

She realized she was singing softly as she drove, a song from a production of *A Midsummer Night's Dream* which their college had presented two years ago. She had worked as assistant director on the play. One of the seniors had composed some quite good incidental music for the play, including the tune she was now singing. Oddly, she could not remember the woman's name, but the melody she composed to accompany Shakespeare's lines came unfailingly back to Sheila as she sang:

> O Sisters Three,
> Come, come to me,
> With hands as pale as milk;
> Lay them in gore,
> Since you have shore
> With shears his thread of silk.

On either side of the road, the outlines of cacti seemed like skeletal hands, clustered and upthrust as though waiting for some offering to drop from the skies, which they would catch and cherish. All around her, Sheila sensed the world was waiting for something.

She had the curious impression that someone else was guiding her. It was as if another woman were inside of her, had slipped into her skin with the smooth fit of a hand in a perfectly molded glove. This woman inside was strong, was energizing her, was making her feel as alive as she had felt during the séance, when the room around her had roared and crackled and chilled her with a powerful sense of another's *presence*. Or like the feeling in her dream when a force had filled her, erupting in waves from inside her, surging through every nerve in her body, manifesting itself as light and heat and blood-power.

She *was* that interior woman now; and in their melding she felt transformed—became a matrix of energies of earth, sky, and self. Goddesslike. That was it: she had the sensual, frightening, liberating impression that she had become one with Ishtar, Astarte, Isis, Kali, and the thousand other named and nameless (because their names were forgotten or because no one dared utter such words of power) incarnations of the power that was all around her, pouring through her, roiling within her.

The power was hers.

The Volkswagen hit a stone in the road, swerving dangerously; she fought to keep control of the car. Twisting the steering wheel frantically, she lost a part of her vision. But the feeling of transcendence, of *power*, resonated in her being more dramatically than the jolts from the car's protesting springs.

The wind shifted, blowing sharply from the east. It sent tumbleweed scudding across the road in front of the car. She laughed at the bulbous scurrying shapes because they seemed to her like little creatures scattering before a person of importance, a person gifted with a secret and wonderful power, which was her wholeness of vision and wholeness of spirit. This power made her important.

The foothills, night-wrapped and mysterious, were only a short distance away now.

The yellow faded from the sky; the heavens were striated red-gold, red-orange, red-violet. The colors suggested

a fire within the sky or behind the Sierras. Sheila felt
herself responding to more than just the simple beauty of
the evening sky: she felt the fiery colors igniting a fire
of *beingness* within her mind and heart.

Now the last light of day was a crimson haze all
around; she felt as though she were moving in the depths
of a red sea. Rapidly the fiery light became blood-red,
then red-purple, then purple, and finally darkened into
a moon-tinted night.

The road had disappeared, but in the moonlight she
saw a familiar sandy open space ahead. She brought the
car to a careful halt almost on the same spot where Willie
Kavan had parked his jeep two days before, when the
three of them had gone to visit the ruins of the Agastan
pueblo.

She sat in the car, listening to the night through the
open window. Somewhere a mountain lion shrieked; a
coyote howled; an owl's wings beat the warm night air.
The night was alive around her. The night was singing
a muted song of power, and the energies gathering within
her surged joyfully in response.

The stars were diamond-clear and intense overhead.
The uppermost peaks of the Sierra Morenas were highlighted by the bluish afterglow of the departed sun.

From her purse, jammed into the crevice between her
seat and Paul's, Sheila gently lifted out the blood-moon
necklace. The metal lay warmly in her hand; it felt like
some living thing coiled in her protecting fingers. She
raised it up so that the disk of red and silver dangled at
eye level. The coral insert blazed like a perfect ruby,
while the circle of silver which framed it flashed white-
hot—seemed to draw an energy from the moonlight suf-
fusing the night air with enough light for a dozen moons.

She began unbuttoning her blouse, leaving only a single
button above her belt fastened. Then, with the care of a
priestess donning a ceremonial ornament, she put on the
necklace. She was wearing no bra; the necklace settled
into the cleft between her breasts, with the blood-moon
itself dangling just below them. The metal lay warm and
alive against her bare skin; she felt an almost erotic energy
from the contact of her flesh with the ancient silver.

She climbed out of the car. From the trunk she dug

out the heavy metal flashlight Paul kept for emergencies; its handle was almost a foot and a half long and held extra batteries. She snapped it on and a powerful shaft of light bored through the night. Satisfied that it would serve her purposes when she needed it, she turned it off. She also pulled out the tire iron from their tire-repair kit.

She opened the door on Paul's side of the car and shook him awake; he returned to consciousness protestingly. But he obeyed her when she told him to climb out. She had to help him to stand. He was groggy and clumsy; she had to lean him across her shoulder. Then they began their slow journey to the foot of the trail which wound up to the plateau and the ruins above. It was the ruins, that place of ancient-most power, which was her goal. She sensed, with her newfound inner surety, that all the promises the night whispered in her heart would somehow come to fruition there. The desire surging in her blood would find its consummation.

She made her way to the foot of the pueblo trail unerringly. Supporting Paul with her left arm and holding the flashlight with her right, she began the ascent. Floating serenely overhead, the full moon had turned the sky to cloth of silver; it flooded much of the path with light, but the shadows cast by overhanging rocks made the couple's upward climb slow and hazardous in the extreme.

Several times Paul protested fuzzily, demanding to know where they were and where they were going. Each time she would answer, "Only a little way to go . . . only a little further."

That seemed to satisfy him, for he would keep on, though he stumbled frequently, in his somnambulistic state. Twice he managed to bring them both to their knees, with consequent jarring pain for Sheila.

But the power surging through her sustained her; the moon, in its constancy, encouraged her as they made their tortuous ascent up the ages-old trail.

And then they reached the plateau, which was gleaming with hot silver moonlight.

Paul wrenched free of her grasp and tried to take a few steps on his own, then he stumbled and fell full length. For a moment she was afraid that she would not be able to arouse him: he seemed almost comatose. But she slapped and cajoled him into half-wakefulness and managed to pull him to his feet once more.

They shambled across the sandy expanse until the circle of the great kiva floor yawned in front of them. She led Paul carefully down into the excavation and sat him on the lower row of benches, in the shadow of the wall. He leaned back against the base of the upper row of seats; from a distance, his eyes looked heavy-lidded enough for him to be sleeping. But Sheila knew they were sufficiently open to be watching her every move. *Does he have some understanding of what is happening?* she wondered; then she dismissed the thought. *How could he guess what I'm only beginning to understand in myself?*

For a moment she stood near the center of the kiva floor. With her arms outstretched at shoulder height, she slowly turned round and round. She could feel the power in this place resonating in her; she partook of the vast powers so long dormant on this spot, now beginning to stir after dim centuries. Spinning slowly, she imagined she was drawing into herself all the magic of this moon-blessed, enchanted place. She did not give in completely to the urge to whirl with the speed and abandon of a dervish; she sensed that if she gave herself over wholly and without restraint, she would spin faster and faster until the friction of the air would ignite her clothing and hair and flesh, and her body and spirit would blaze like a torch erupting blindingly into the night.

She came to a dizzy halt and rested a moment to catch her breath. If she was not careful, she realized, the powers she was drawing on might overwhelm her and destroy her. *Caution,* she warned herself, *you have so very much to learn.*

When her head had cleared sufficiently, she heard again that voiceless whisper in her mind which was formulating her plan of action.

She went into the remains of the red-walled alcove that opened off the main circle. There she began gouging at the wall with the tire iron she had carried up with her. The chisel end of the tool bit deeply into the wall, at a spot approximately a foot and a half above the floor, near the left-hand corner of the chamber. Her labors effaced one of the white-etched familiar emergence designs as she dug deeply into the clay behind it. After several minutes of teethjarring effort, she exposed what at first glance seemed a bit of yellowish stone. Working more cautiously, she uncovered what was in actuality part of the cranium of a skull.

Sheila put the tire iron down and used her fingers, careless of the way the dry clay broke away her fingernails and shredded the skin of her fingertips.

At last she managed to work it free of the impacting earth: a skull, with its forehead and right eye crushed. Several bone fragments were missing; they remained mixed with the red-brown clay like bits of yellowed eggshell.

She carried the skull out into the center of the ceremonial circle, where she turned it over in her hands several times, studying the grotesque relic in the moonlight, a few times holding it up briefly to the moon as a kind of offering. Then she walked over and handed it to Paul, folding it securely into his hands. He accepted it dumbly and sat quietly with the thing cradled in his lap.

Guided entirely by the voice within her mind now, she went and dragged the heavy broken slate covering to the nearest of the two pit mouths flanking the *sipapu*. She covered the opening as completely as she could, leaving about one-third of the pit opening uncovered. She rapped sharply on the slate with the tire iron, but the sound that resulted was thin and metallic and not at all satisfactory. She flung the metal tool aside impatiently and climbed out of the kiva circle. She began a systematic search of the plateau until she found a branch which, in spite of being charred at one end as if it had been part of a campfire, was still long enough and sturdy enough to serve her purpose.

She carried this back to the kiva, and, kneeling down, began to beat upon the slate lid. The pit acted exactly like a sounding box or oversized drum: a deep booming sound welled up from deep inside the earth.

High above, the moon seemed to have been stained deep red by some magic—the same magic she felt coursing through the whole of her being. She continued her drumming, summoning the ones she sensed were awaiting the call to come forth into the bloodlight from the darkness she felt yawning beneath her feet. She had a dizzying perception of the rock below her as hollow as a drum, yet as filled with yearning life as an egg or a womb. All around her she felt a matrix of earth- and sky-magics.

The night sky was underlit with red; a line of fire limned the mountains circling her, as though dawn was breaking at the four corners of the world.

Now, as she listened—hardly daring to breathe—she heard all nature of sounds issuing from the nearby *sipapu*: whispers, murmurs, laughter, and the ghostly tinkling of a bell. The voices she heard, amid the mindless other sounds, seemed laden with meaning, but the words were distorted or in a language unlike any she was familiar with; they made no sense to her.

She continued pounding on the makeshift drum, following a rhythm established in the beating of her heart and the blood pounding at her temples.

Then she stopped, staring at the *sipapu*, unsure for a moment whether her eyes were playing tricks on her. The opening in the bedrock had begun dilating, then contracting, like a birth passage in the first stage of labor.

Sheila gasped suddenly as her own uterus contracted in a sympathetic convulsion. She cried out, the pain was so intense; she looked across the moonlit arena to Paul for help.

He sat where she had left him, holding the skull. He was using his fingers gently to touch and explore the wound in the forehead and the ruined eye socket. As she watched, he hugged it to his chest the way one might hold an infant. He paid no attention to Sheila; he seemed unaware of her, kneeling in the sand and breathing deeply in a manner that eased her pain slightly.

The birth pang caught her again; she folded her arms across her womb and doubled over, so that her forehead nearly touched the sandy floor of the kiva. Her pain was too great; she felt too weak. She could no longer continue the summoning.

But it was no longer necessary for her to summon up magic: the opening continued its spasms. When the pain subsided momentarily, she raised her head and looked around her. All along the rim of the kiva pit was a circle of silent shadowy figures, the forms of ghostly Indian men and women.

Paul did not look up from fondling the skull; he remained unaware of the shadowy onlookers.

The men upon the pit edge, Sheila saw, were bare-chested and wore white kilts. The women wore black mantas, fastened at the waist with red-and-white sashes; their mantas were arranged to leave their left shoulders bare. The men were bareheaded; the women wore circular headdresses painted with squash-blossom designs painted around the familiar emergency symbol.

Another set of contractions made her convulse in agony; Sheila watched the *sipapu* straining, relaxing, straining wider. She felt all this within her own body—felt her body was tearing in two.

The spectral figures surrounding her began to chant, their voices growing to the sound of a roaring wind. "Hu-hu-hu-*hu!*" they cried, "hu-hu-hu-*hu!*" The chant had a monotonous, unemotional sound to it, but Sheila felt the powerful undercurrent of excitement in the rigidly modulated sounds. She felt the ritual sounds arousing new energies within the night, within the kiva, within her.

"Hu-hu-hu-*hu!*" Now the chant was an echo of her own cries. She realized with a shock that she was giving voice to the mind-filling cries of the earth upon which she sprawled. The sandy floor was a birth medium that had no voice save hers to agonize over its own birth pangs—as though the plateau, the Sierras, the very world itself were bursting with inarticulate near birth, like the headless very pregnant torso Maria had seen in her vision.

"Hu-hu-hu-*hu!*" The men and women chanted in unison, but the women sang an octave higher.

She was forcing herself to breathe deeply, since this seemed to ease her pain somewhat. She was amazed at the number of ghostly dancers assembled; she wondered if some long-departed tribe had been reassembled entirely to participate in this great medicine dance beneath the blood-tinged moon.

In their right hands the men carried medicine rattles, like those Sheila had seen in Willie Kavan's shop. Made of dried gourds filled with pebbles or seed pods, decorated with turkey feathers, they made a sound like angry snakes or hail boiling down from the sky. The rattles moved steadily up and down in cadence with a rising and falling motion of the right foot.

The women carried pine boughs in their right hands; the men had pine boughs tied to their arms. Both men and women carried bunches of eagle feathers in their left hands.

Now the circling figures began a slow dance while their chanting grew louder.

STEP-step-step to the left; STEP-step to the right; STEP-step-step again to the left. The line of dancers began a slow progress counterclockwise. Sheila felt that she lay at the hub of a slowly revolving wheel.

The dancers kept their bodies rigidly erect; their knees, bent slightly. When she looked into their eyes she saw they were black as obsidian chips—a glittering hard darkness. They did not look at her; rather, she felt they gazed into a secret place inside their hearts or outward toward something hidden beyond the horizon. To Sheila, the steady motion, the increasing volume of the chant, the total melding of the dancers with their dance—all this was the visible expression of the tremendous ingathering of energy she felt in every fiber of her being. She was carried along almost beyond her pain by the *ecstasy* flooding her as the dancers channeled their energies into her, and her whole being resonated with the power they gave her. She felt this power as a mixture of spiritual and erotic feelings, each complementing the other and transforming it. Sheila wanted to cry along with the ghostly dancers to the blood-colored moon but felt too weak, overwhelmed by alternating currents of power and pain. She felt the night embrace her as a lover might and transform her as a god might. And she did, finally, manage a single cry at the sheer joy she felt within the fullness of her being. She felt a completeness in herself unlike anything she had ever experienced before; she felt totally at one with the moon/mountains/night/dancers/straining earth.

Magics were swirling around her in a vortex, unseen but intensely felt, while she knelt doubled over in the calm eye of this raging cyclone of power. She was adrift in an exquisite sense of completeness. Paul, sitting across from her, was little more than a ghost himself. She felt vast creative energies churning within her—in her womb, especially, but charging every cell of her being. Realities were altering around and within her. She was herself/she was the totality of this moment and all its participants/she was wholly *herself*.

Again came the stabbing pain between her legs. She forced herself to maintain deep breathing, not daring to look at the *sipapu* now. But the sensations of constriction and relaxation continued unabated.

She ran her eyes over the ranks of dancers; among the Indians she saw (or *thought* she saw, for, when she stared too long, faces and forms became fluid and seemed to waver uncertainly) the figures of Cyrus and Helen Anderson. But their faces were charred nightmares now, and no fanatical light shone in the empty eye sockets. Their scorched clothing flapped in the light breeze; their ruined mouths kept up the cry, "Hu-hu-hu-*hu*!" Sheila's stomach churned at the sight of them and she looked wildly around, sudden fear replacing the good feelings of the moment before. Now, scattered among the dancers, she recognized several who were dressed like mission padres, draped in dark robes, hoods raised to hide their faces in shadow, white cinctures swaying as they danced and chanted, "Hu-hu-hu-*hu*!"

And Maria Seloso was there. *No!* Sheila cried to herself, *she doesn't belong here.* There was this difference about Maria: her eyes were neither impassive nor destroyed nor hidden; they were fixed on Sheila in a look of purest terror. She seemed to struggle to shape a sentence or a cry for help, but she was locked into the dance and the only sound she made was "Hu-hu-hu-*hu*!"

It's not fair that Maria is here, thought Sheila; and in the space of that thought, Maria's form wavered and became the figure of the aged Indian woman Sheila had seen at the trading post. Sheila looked quickly around for the girl, but she had vanished completely. The old woman touched her throat and Sheila saw she was wearing a blood-moon necklace. Instinctively Sheila touched the necklace she wore around her own neck; the crone nodded and smiled and touched her own necklace again. Then the old woman was transformed into the bloodied corpse of the girl, Enotea, who had died in Berkeley. Blood oozed from a hundred gaping cuts and the side of her head was grotesquely flattened; but her face was locked in a hideous smile that looked to Sheila more like a rictus. Then this ghastly shape was replaced by the form of a squat Indian woman. Maria, the old woman, Enotea had disappeared. So had the gruesome forms of the Andersons. Even the priests had vanished. Had she really seen any of them? There were only the ghosts of the Indian dancers and the unchanging pattern of the dance itself left now.

A burbling sound emerged from the *sipapu;* Sheila felt the most severe pain yet. She cried out for help. But who, she wondered desperately, could help her in this circle of moonlight and bloodlight? Paul never looked up from the skull he was holding; the dancers danced on implacably.

She turned to face the niche in the kiva wall. From its half shadow emerged a figure swaddled from head to foot in a red-and-black ceremonial robe. Two fists were outstretched; to Sheila the hands looked as though they were composed of bone and parchment. The emaciated form, only as high as Sheila's shoulder, came over and stood in front of her. Two eyes burned at her, enigmatic, holding neither compassion nor threat; the fire-brightness blazed with an intensity of vision that spanned infinities. The rest of the face was buried in the folded shadows of the robe.

Sheila turned her eyes away, not daring to gaze directly into those alien eyes which, she felt, held a power in them capable of drawing the very soul out of her if she looked into them too long.

Out of the figure's slowly-opening left hand trickled an offering of grayish-brown corn; out of the right, a mixture of pebbles, cactus needles, and ashes.

"Who are you?" asked Sheila, still averting her eyes.

From behind the fold of the robe hiding the lower portion of the newcomer's face came a single harsh chuckle.

"El Brujo!" the creature said and laughed again. "El Brujo!" The voice that spoke to Sheila sounded like sand tumbling onto parchment.

The laughter was nothing more than a series of sharp staccato hisses. It broke off abruptly. The dancers continued their endless chanting, "Hu-hu-hu-*hu*!" But the sound was subdued now. Sheila felt frightened and alone, thankful only that the pain had subsided somewhat with the appearance of the robed figure.

A hand, little more than a dried claw, reached down and cupped Sheila's chin, drawing her face upward. The touch of those ancient fingers burned like dry ice. The eyes and folded bit of robe that made up the face leaned down close to hers as if to impart a secret. "Brujo, Brujo, Brujo!" Again she heard the laughing hiss.

There was a pause, a silence that seemed to expand forever. Even the dancers were silent.

The silence was exploded with a single word, uttered with all the impact of a challenge: "Bruja!"

The cloth covering over the figure's face fell away, but the face that was revealed was so aged that it was sexless. Sheila's look must have registered her incomprehension, for the medicine robe was parted down the front to display a withered, naked body. One ancient hand took hold of Sheila's and touched it to the dried dugs and pushed it against the pudenda. Sheila submitted to this all without protest, but she kept her eyes fixed on the neck of the ancient woman. There she saw two necklaces; one of bear claws, the other, a chain of silver supporting a silver-rimmed disk of blood-coral, in the center of which was the design:

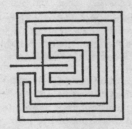

When Sheila pulled her hand away, comprehending the femaleness that was the other woman's secret, the figure rearranged its robe and laughed her hissing laugh, as though she had shared the greatest joke in the world.

The dancers took up their chant again; the stamping feet began their incessant rhythm. The slow circling around the kiva floor continued. The inverted bowl of the night sky echoed with the pounding feet and the monotonous chant until it seemed to Sheila that she was inside a vast world drum, summoning unthinkable magics from across unimaginable distances.

STEP-step-step, left, the measures of the dance went; STEP-step right. Then left again, STEP-step-step.

Sheila gasped again, feeling another spasm which was the earth's, hers, *theirs*. Another. The contractions were coming faster now; some sort of birth was drawing near.

The eyes of the witch figure above her watched eagerly. Suddenly the old woman extended her thin arms upward to the sky in a gesture of supplication—no, Sheila corrected herself, rather as a calling down of power. She spoke the words of an incomprehensible spell with the confidence of one who has the right to command such power.

Between the witch's upraised hands, a circle of light began to gather. It rapidly resolved itself into a sphere of absolute darkness about a foot in diameter, over which sheets of flame rippled—but the fire-veils never obscured completely the infinite depth and emptiness of the black globe. *It's like a dark star,* thought Shelia wonderingly, *like a black hole.* Sheila sensed the globed darkness simultaneously as a door, an eye, a power source from beyond this earth. It terrified her to look at the fire-sheathed darkness. With an effort, she looked away, toward the moon overhead. It shone redly amid the clouds, seemingly circled with fire itself. The after-glow of sunset beyond the mountains had grown more intense, had taken on the intensity of firelight. It almost looked as if the earth were consuming itself in apocalyptic fire just beyond the horizon.

"Heheya!" cried the witch-woman, "Heheya!"

Then she whispered, "Hineneya!"

She lowered her arms but kept them outstretched in a kind of embrace; within the circle of her arms, the sphere of fire and darkness descended to hang suspended just in front of the woman's chest, a little above Sheila's head. She could feel the thing radiating intense cold rather than heat.

The clear night sky above was split with frequent, unexpected flashes of summer lightning. But no thunder accompanied them.

The old woman brought her arms a little closer together, as though she would gather the power source to her, but she stopped short of that. The globe remained floating within her loose embrace, equidistant from either arm.

STEP-step-step; STEP-step: the dancers continued their midnight round.

The witch-woman walked across and stood on the far side of the *sipapu*. She leaned forward so that the fire sphere hung directly over the dilating/contracting opening in the ground. Then she dropped her hands to her side and stood back, while the fireball remained in place, casting a roseate glow over the now-writhing earth-lips.

La Bruja chanted in a loud voice, "Hineneya neya ha-aha he-ha ah!"

The ghostly dancers stopped their motion and took up the same cry.

The witch-woman leaned eagerly toward the *sipapu,* but a moan was all that issued from the opening. She made frantic motions with her hands; the fireball blazed suddenly, then died away to a softer glow. Still there came forth nothing but moans: the cries of a woman in anguish; the grief of a woman who could not give birth when her time had come. The sounds expressed simultaneously the anguish of Sheila and the groaning earth. She could feel within her own body the denial of the long-awaited birth.

The sorceress traced the design etched into the necklaces in the air. The lines appeared as strokes of blinding silver fire in the air and lingered long after the witch's hands had dropped back to her sides.

"Hineneya ney ha-aha he-ha ah!" the witch-woman shrieked in desperation; the circle of onlookers cried out all the louder. Sheila looked and saw once again the Andersons, Maria, Enotea, the priests, woven into the ceremonial circle; now they were adding their voices to the witch's cry of despair. They begged for a new birth, for an end to waiting —even as they saw that birth denied them.

There will be no birth, thought Sheila. The *sipapu*— mouth and uterus at once—writhed and wailed in the anguished voice of a woman whose labor will have no issue.

Why must it fail? Sheila wondered. She felt clear-headed as her own pain grew less. She was convinced that the clues to the failure of this birthing lay all around her. If she had time to sort it out, she was confident she could discover the answer. But she was aware that time was running out.

The voice of the witch-woman/midwife was fading; the voices of the ring of spectators/dancers were growing as faint as the rising wind that blew across the plateau. Sand sifted over the edge of the kiva, trickled onto the benches.

The gathered power was fading; the moment, passing; the magic, departing. Centuries of waiting and longing, a desire that went beyond time, a complex web of people and events—everything was dissolving in the rising wind; the fires beyond the horizon were dying away.

The magic must not fail! she cried within herself.

She looked around, searching for an answer, horrified at the way the pain within her was diminishing unfulfilled.

Where is the answer?

She stared at the dried particles of grayish-brown corn. The pebbles, ashes, and cactus needles spilled on the ground were being scattered by the increasing force of the wind. Sand and dried earth and stone: what was the secret they contained? She saw the withered arms of the witch-woman and remembered her voice like spilled sand and the touch of breasts and pudenda dried like the husks of ancient fruit. She looked at the pale, bloodless faces of the dancers surrounding her and at the dried and burned stick she had used to summon them here.

All around her were the trappings of an age-old magic, but it was a magic now dried and lifeless. It was withered and dead and without the life force that could bring about the longed-for birthing. Sheila felt that only within her was the true power, the singing within the blood, the singing of her blood. The power men had named in awe or terror Kali. Ishtar. Isis. Astarte.

The circling horizon fires were gone; thickening clouds obscured the moon. Darkness was cooling away the red intensity.

Her pain was gone now. But the singing within her blood remained; the blood coursing through her living body was the secret power within her; the blood pounding in her heart and temples was the voice of the magic still rolling inside her.

The dancers, little more than shadows now, their voices reduced to the faintest whispers, took up another song. This time the words were not strange to her; she understood them all:

> The Moon shines, It is finished
> The Fire blazes, It is finished
> The Blood flows, It is finished

The song grew in them, in her; it was a song of desperate unconquered need.

With a sound like a forest blaze, One approaches
Amid roaring thunder and zigzagging lightning, One
    approaches
With a sound like a mountain splitting asunder, One
    approaches
Let your heart soar and welcome the One who
    approaches

The words yielded understanding. She touched trembling fingertips to the blood-coral disk under her breasts; it was alive, electric. A burning energy surged from it through her, bringing her a new clarity of thought, a new comprehension.

She knew now what she had only guessed before: *a blood welcome is demanded for the ones we have summoned this night.*

She climbed unsteadily to her feet. The witch-woman and dancers and all outward signs of magic had faded away and been scattered by the wind. They were nothing more than memories within her now.

The *sipapu* was simply a still, dark hole in the earth at her feet; the pain had left her body completely.

She went over and took Paul gently by the hand. He set the skull regretfully on the higher tier and obediently took her hand as she led him to the center of the kiva floor.

"Wait one second while I get the flashlight," she said, leaving him standing beside the *sipapu.*

Like a man floating upward from near drowning in a sea of dreams, he asked, "Where are we?" Then he looked around and asked, "Is it over?"

"Yes," she said, returning to stand just behind him, "it's finished."

She swung the heavy flashlight once, catching him at the base of the skull so that he dropped with a single cry that was little more than an astonished gasp. He lay sprawled, breathing in ragged, liquid gasps.

From his pocket she fished out the little pocket knife he always carried. His outflung right hand had fallen on the very edge of the sipapu. With the knife she made deep gouges in his wrists and started a little torrent of blood trickling over the edge of the opening, dribbling down the side toward the darkness below.

From far down in that darkness rose a bubble of laughter. Of hope. Of triumph.

Sheila heard the sounds of something climbing upward from unguessable depths.

Out of the night came a cry like the cry of an immense owl, splitting the sky from horizon to horizon.

The skies blazed crimson as if they had caught fire from horizon to horizon—as if a midnight sun were rising in blood-colored splendor.

She sang softly, soothingly, as one might a lullaby.

> We we lo lo,
> We we lo lo.

The sounds she found buried within her mind; she sang them to the music of her own heart's composing.

Overhead, the red intensity burned away the stars and faded the moon to the faintest luster of pearl as it hung like a silver pendant in the red-colored sky—the sister jewel of the circle of silver and blood-coral Sheila wore. She could feel the jewel burning into her skin with a cold fire, branding her forever as mediatrix of the powers above, upon, and —most importantly—*within* the earth. Within *herself* she felt all the creative powers so long denied, so long held back, surging upward, outward, filling the air, sky, carried joyfully on the winds.

The pain returned and she accepted it willingly, gratefully. The *sipapu* yawned wide, remained like a frozen victory cry.

The earth underfoot rumbled as if it might split apart; magic filled the night with silver-and-red wonder.

Sheila felt delirious with agony and profoundest joy.

"Hineneya ney ha-aha he-ha ah!" sang the voice of the witch-woman somewhere behind her.

"Hineneya ney ha-aha he-ha ah!" echoed the unseen dancers triumphantly.

"Hineneya ney ha-aha he-ha ah!" Sheila took up the cry. But she did not look away from the *sipapu*, grown immense now. It was so large there must have been a tearing of the very substance of the earth.

Distantly she heard the sound of a single tiny bell—small and clear in the night air, vast in its implications.

Out of the earth-womb crawled a single huge spider, its ebony fur dusted red by the blood-red moon overhead; its multifaceted obsidian eyes glowed like twin black crystals.

"Ah-ah-hah-hi-ah-hi!" cried the witch-woman, her voice filled with victory and vengeance. "Ah-ah-hah-hi-ah-hi!"

"Ah-ah-hah-hi-ah-hi!" echoed Sheila, as first one, and then a second, monstrous, shining black hand sought purchase on the sides of the earth-womb-opening. The most powerful of the Awaited Ones began raising herself into the Upper World.

EPILOGUE:
The Morning After

The howling of the cat somewhere awoke Willie Kavan, who had been asleep in the little bedroom at the back of his house. The clock showed just past midnight, but Willie decided the clock must have stopped, because his room was suffused with the red glow of sunrise filtering through his dusty, uncurtained windows. "Red sky at morning: Sailor take warning," Willie muttered; then he added a curse for the cat which continued its nerve-wracking yowls.

Willie sat up in bed; he was so tired, he could well believe it was only midnight. But the red morning light was stronger now.

"Shut up, goddam cat!" he yelled as the feline's terrified wailing intensified.

He yanked aside the window curtains, searching for the cat outside, and then he gasped in astonishment, his fingers frozen in the drapery fabric. He could only stare in terror, unable to make a single sound.

The sun—or whatever was the source of the red sky-glow —was breaking over the Sierra Morenas. The sun—if sun it was—was rising in the west.

Willie stood helplessly staring through the grime-streaked window, waiting in dismay for the day such an unholy sunrise would bring.